Praise for

UNLACED

"...eated romances." —*Genre Go Round*

"Together [the stories] make one heart-melting read."
—*Wild on Books*

"Sexual encounters that will make your toes curl."
—*TwoLips Reviews*

Praise for the Authors

JACI BURTON

"Spicy bedroom scenes . . . make this one to pick up and savor."
—*Publishers Weekly*

"Burton's book packs a wallop." —*Romantic Times*

JASMINE HAYNES

"Intense, hot, and purely erotic." —*The Road to Romance*

"Try this one—you won't be sorry." —*The Best Reviews*

JOEY W. HILL

"One of the finest, most erotic stories I've ever read."
—Shelby Reed, author of *Seraphim*

"A must-read." —*Romance Junkies*

DENISE ROSSETTI

"Darkly intense, warmly romantic, and blazingly erotic."
—*Beyond Her Book* (*Publishers Weekly*)

"Swirls in magic, romance, betrayal, passion, and heated desire."
—*The Romance Studio*

Laced with Desire

JACI BURTON

JASMINE HAYNES

JOEY W. HILL

DENISE ROSSETTI

Heat | New York

THE BERKLEY PUBLISHING GROUP
Published by the Penguin Group
Penguin Group (USA) Inc.
375 Hudson Street, New York, New York 10014, USA
Penguin Group (Canada), 90 Eglinton Avenue East, Suite 700, Toronto, Ontario M4P 2Y3, Canada
(a division of Pearson Penguin Canada Inc.)
Penguin Books Ltd., 80 Strand, London WC2R 0RL, England
Penguin Group Ireland, 25 St. Stephen's Green, Dublin 2, Ireland (a division of Penguin Books Ltd.)
Penguin Group (Australia), 250 Camberwell Road, Camberwell, Victoria 3124, Australia
(a division of Pearson Australia Group Pty. Ltd.)
Penguin Books India Pvt. Ltd., 11 Community Centre, Panchsheel Park, New Delhi—110 017, India
Penguin Group (NZ), 67 Apollo Drive, Rosedale, North Shore 0632, New Zealand
(a division of Pearson New Zealand Ltd.)
Penguin Books (South Africa) (Pty.) Ltd., 24 Sturdee Avenue, Rosebank, Johannesburg 2196,
South Africa

Penguin Books Ltd., Registered Offices: 80 Strand, London WC2R 0RL, England

This book is an original publication of The Berkley Publishing Group.

PRINTING HISTORY
Heat trade paperback edition / February 2010

Library of Congress Cataloging-in-Publication Data

    Laced with desire / Jaci Burton . . . [et al.]. — Heat trade pbk. ed.
      p.   cm.
    ISBN 978-0-425-23229-3
    1. Erotic stories, American.   I. Burton, Jaci.
    PS648.E7.L33   2010
    813'.60803538—dc22
                     2009037786

PRINTED IN THE UNITED STATES OF AMERICA

10 9 8 7 6 5 4 3 2 1

CONTENTS

No Strings Attached

JACI BURTON

For Charlie, the man I love being tied to. Forever.

One

Budgets and bids and the upcoming contract next year all torna-doed around Ella Hicks's head. She tapped her pencil and tuned out the Tulsa Building Industry president's speech. Business as usual at the monthly meeting, as it had been for the past five years since her husband, James, had died suddenly, leaving her the CEO and chief of everything involving Hicks Construction.

Thank God for work, for the unending seven-day-a-week sched-ule that had saved her sanity after those shocking, bleak days fol-lowing James's death, when she couldn't wrap her mind around how a healthy, robust thirty-year-old man could simply fall to the ground and die. Just like that. One second he'd been alive and laughing with her, and then, just like that, he was gone.

She'd spent the last five years reliving that day, remembering the shock, the crushing pain, the thought that her life, too, was over.

But she hadn't died with James. Because they still had a business to run, and it had fallen on her to do it. She couldn't let James down, refused to fall apart. He'd have hated that, would have wanted her to pick up and get the job done. So she had. For five years she'd worked sunup to sundown on Hicks Construction. She'd fought with the foreman and the business manager, had gone head-to-head with the workers and other owners, and had stood her ground, letting her grief out only when she came home at the end of the day, dusty, dirty and too tired to even think. Then she'd strip and turn the shower on, letting the steamy water pour over her. Only then would she allow herself to cry.

She tapped her pencil on the paper, not even able to remember how many nights she'd sobbed uncontrollably for hours, until the water had gone cold, until she'd dried off and climbed into bed, falling into a—thankfully—dreamless slumber. And so it had gone, every day like that.

For too damn long. She'd eventually stopped crying at night, but she still worked herself hard, just like she worked everyone at the company. There was nothing she asked them to do that she wasn't willing to do herself. Staying busy had been her lifeline, and she was grateful to have it, to have this tiny piece of James to tuck away in her heart. His name, his company.

No. *Her* company now. And she'd succeeded. She'd made it work. James would be proud of her. But James was gone and it was time she found a life again.

Though it wasn't a whole new life she was searching for. Not right now anyway. There was only one thing she needed, and she intended to get it—soon.

"The bids for three upcoming projects should be posted at the beginning of next month."

Ella pulled her focus to the business at hand, jotting down a few notes.

"You aren't paying attention."

She shifted her gaze to the man who'd whispered to her. Clayton Mansfield—Clay—owner of Mansfield Builders, one of her biggest competitors. Same age as her late husband, Clay and James had been good friends as well as rivals. They'd gone hunting and fishing together, and Clay had been nearly as devastated as she had been over James's death.

He'd also been a very good friend to her over the past five years, had helped her with the business when she'd needed it, despite it not being in his best interest to do so. But he'd been James's friend, and she knew that was why he'd been there for her. She was grateful to have a strong shoulder to lean on, someone who knew the business end of things inside and out, because while she and James had worked side by side to build Hicks Construction, she'd focused more on the office side of things. Getting out there and getting dirty had been James's job. After his death, it had become hers. That was where Clay had helped her.

He nudged her with his elbow. "Late night?"

She smothered a snort. "Hardly. Just trying to stay awake through the droning."

Clay nodded, stretching out his jean-clad legs under the table. "Next time we vote on a president for our council, we need to make sure they can talk, and talk fast."

"Agreed."

He shifted again, folded his arms over his middle. He'd rolled up his shirtsleeves, and she glimpsed dark hair over tanned skin. And muscle. A lot of muscle.

Stop. Do not look. She never looked. Okay, she did. What breathing woman wouldn't? At six-five or so, Clay was imposing. And he was model gorgeous, with sea blue eyes, coal black hair and a body that spoke of a man who really worked for a living. And his mouth—she'd always been drawn to his mouth. Full bottom lip that she'd thought of often lately . . . though she shouldn't. Wouldn't. Not with Clay.

Which was why this new . . . project . . . was so imperative. She'd been thinking of Clay . . . of *that* . . . a lot.

"That should wrap things up, unless there's any new business?"

Ella held her breath, praying no one would speak up. They'd been in this meeting for two hours and her ass was numb. She had things to do, plans to make.

Fortunately, they adjourned. Ella pushed back her chair and resisted the urge to rub her butt.

"Finally."

Ella nodded. "Thanks for letting us use your conference room."

He shrugged. "No big deal. Easier on me. Now I can get back to work." He winked, and she felt butterflies in her stomach. Ugh. Things between her and Clay had always been easy. She'd never felt anything for him. Ever. Of course there'd always been James, and then there'd been mind-numbing grief. She hadn't felt anything . . . for anyone.

But now she was starting to feel again, the grief for her husband diminished to one of aching loss. She'd reconciled it, come to grips with the realization that James had died, not her. It was time to start living again. With that in mind . . .

"Is Tish in today?"

Clay arched a brow. "Yeah. Should be at her desk. Why?"

"She has a condo in Hawaii she told me about."

"You going on vacation? Finally?"

She offered up a bright smile. "Yes. Finally. And I'm going to take Tish up on her offer to let me use her condo. She said it's right on the beach."

"It's a nice condo complex. I've got a place there myself."

"Do you? So it's worth the trip?"

He nodded. "Definitely worth the trip. When are you going?"

"Next week. We're on the tail end of a few projects, and since it's not quite spring here yet, I have a month or so before the new ones start up."

"Perfect timing. Hawaii is great this time of year."

"So I've heard."

"Taking anyone with you?"

She shook her head. "No. Going alone."

He leaned against the conference table. "That's no fun."

"Oh, believe me. I intend to have a lot of fun once I get there."

"Yeah? How so?"

Her body heated at the thought. Or maybe it was just standing so close to Clay. She took a step back and grinned. "Can't tell you everything, you know. I'm off to find Tish. See you soon." She waved to him and hurried down the hall toward his offices.

She intended to make these plans and make them fast, before she changed her mind.

Tish smiled at her as she approached. "How was the meeting?"

"Mind-numbingly dull. So do you have the reservations?"

Tish nodded. "All set. You sure you want to do this alone?"

"Yes. Of course. I'm ready."

"Are you? Are you sure?"

Tish had been one of her closest friends in the industry. She'd actually started working as a clerk for Ella and James, until Clay had recognized her talents and lured her away to work as his assistant.

Ella remembered how pissed James had been over that. He and Clay had had words. Serious words. But Clay had told him it was business.

She'd hated losing Tish, mainly because they'd worked together in the office and gotten close. That hadn't changed after Tish went to work for Clay. They got together for lunch once a week, and hung out whenever Ella wasn't busy with James.

After James's death, Tish had been her rock. Ten years older than Ella, Tish had lost her husband, John, to cancer. She knew how it felt to lose the man of your dreams, the other half of yourself. And Ella had leaned on Tish—hard. Tish had strong shoulders and had weathered a lot of crying on Ella's part. She hadn't said a word, either—until Ella had been ready to talk about it.

She loved Tish like a sister.

So she expected Tish to look out for her, even now, five years later. "I'm sure. I think."

Tish laughed. "That's what I thought. Hey, if nothing else, you'll get some rest, a great tan and you'll come back relaxed. You work too hard."

"I need to work hard."

"No, you don't. Not anymore. It's okay to let your guard down. It's been five years, Ella. Let go."

"I'm trying. That's what this trip is all about."

Tish shook her head. "I don't know why you need to go all the way to Hawaii to get laid, but whatever."

Ella pulled up a chair in front of Tish's desk and leaned forward. "You know exactly why I have to go all the way to Hawaii. Who do I know here? Who do I associate with? All the men in the industry. Do you think I'm going to . . ." She cast a quick glance around the room. "Do you think I'm going to have sex with any of them?"

Tish leaned back in her chair. "I think there's some mighty fine men in this business. Open your eyes. Take your pick. Don't you see how they look at you?"

She shook her head. "No. I don't pay any attention. These men all knew James. I want a stranger."

"Bleh. That's not good. You don't know what you'll get."

"Laid, Tish. I'll get laid. I'll have phenomenal sex, get it out of my system, and I'll come home relaxed and ready to go back to work without the added distraction of . . ."

"Being horny?"

Ella laughed. "Yes."

"I think it would be a lot easier to scratch that itch with some-one you know."

"Oh, hell no. That's the last thing I want. Trust me, this is the best way."

Tish sighed. "If you say so. The condo is booked for you. Have a good time. And for God's sake, be careful."

"I will." She stood and walked around the desk and threw her arms around Tish. "I love you."

"I love you, too." Tish waved her off. "Now, get out of here before I get all mushy and ruin my makeup."

Ella laughed, excitement pouring through her. "Okay."

She turned to walk away, but Tish stopped her with a, "Hey."

Ella pivoted. "What?"

"We need to go shopping. You can't wear dusty blue jeans, work shirts and boots on Waikiki beach."

⊱∞⊰

Clay waited until Ella had left the offices. Then he came out of one of the workrooms and stopped at Tish's desk.

"She taking the condo?"

His assistant shifted her gaze away from her computer and over to him. "How do you know about that?"

"She told me."

"Oh. Well, then, yes."

"When is she going?"

Tish regarded him with a suspicious glare.

"I'm concerned about her, Tish. You know how it is. How we all are."

Tish nodded. "I know. Me, too. She leaves Sunday. She'll be there a week."

"She's really going alone?"

"So she says."

"I'm not sure I like that."

Tish laughed. "I'm pretty sure it's none of your business."

He smirked. "Probably not. But when has that ever stopped me?"

"Never."

His smile widened. "What does my calendar look like for the next week and a half?"

She brought up the calendar on the computer. "A couple meetings. Nothing major."

"Move them. And book my condo for Sunday."

Tish shook her head. "For a week, I suppose?"

"Yeah."

"Ella isn't going to like this."

"Ella has nothing to do with it. I'm going deep-sea fishing."

Tish snorted. "Sure you are."

"And if I happen to run into Ella while I'm there, I can make sure she's okay."

"Ella does a fine job taking care of herself."

"I know she does. But just in case . . ."

Tish's fingers flew over the keyboard. "I sure hope you know what you're doing."

So did he. He didn't do impulsive things like this. Ever. And he'd been hands off Ella . . . always. But after James's sudden death, and the way it had taken its toll on her, he'd stepped in as James's best friend and found himself . . . looking after her. In an unofficial capacity, of course. Strictly business related. He didn't go to her house. He didn't see to her personal welfare. He never saw her at all other than at business functions. On the job. Nothing personal between them at all. Ella had family and friends for that. She had them to lean on during the bad times. He'd just been there to help her out with the business.

This wasn't business.

So why the hell was he going to Hawaii?

Two

The condo was amazing. The oceanfront room was open and airy with white tile floors, pale bamboo and wicker furniture with glass tabletops. And the view took her breath away. Miniature palms waved to her in greeting as she stepped out on the balcony and got her first clear look at the ocean.

Wow. Just . . . wow. She took a deep breath and inhaled the tangy ocean air.

She'd been in Hawaii for all of an hour and she was already madly in love with the place. How did people ever leave? She wanted to plop down on the chaise, put her feet up, stare at the never-ending miles of clear blue water and just do . . . nothing. Quite possibly for the rest of her life. Okay, maybe she'd add a piña colada. Other than that, she couldn't think of one other thing she'd need to be happy.

Sex.

Oh, right. That was why she was here, wasn't it? Though she could get used to a life without sex if she could live in a place this nice. It was so peaceful watching the waves as they raced to the shore, listening to the sounds of people below, and yet she remained detached from it all, an observer.

And that was her problem, had been her problem for too long now. She'd been detached, observing. Not participating. Which meant no more sitting around watching the world go by. It was time to join the party.

She grabbed the suitcase she'd dropped at the front door and headed to the bedroom, her jaw dropping.

Clay had been very good to Tish when he'd given her this condo. The bedroom was lush, with a king-sized bed and a lazily twirling ceiling fan overhead. There was no television—really, who needs TV in paradise? The double doors gave way to another stunning view of the beach and the ocean.

The bathroom had a double vanity, a shower built for two and a Jacuzzi tub. It was huge and every woman's dream. Ella could use one of those at home after a muscle-bruising day. There was even a small kitchen in case she wanted to cook instead of eat out every night.

She'd be content to never leave her room. Except she had to get out. It was unlikely some hot stud had heard about her arrival and was about to knock on her door to offer up his services.

She laughed at that, tossed her suitcase on the bed and opened it up, still awed by all the color she saw in there.

Tish had pushed her into going shopping. Okay, Tish had grabbed her and taken her shopping. So she owned only ragged cut-off shorts, or the ones she wore during her occasional trips to the gym. And she couldn't remember how long it had been since she'd last put on a swimsuit. Plus, she'd lost a lot of weight and most of her clothes didn't fit anymore.

But what reason did she have to go shopping? She wore jeans and work shirts all the time.

Which meant her wardrobe was in serious need of some updating. And she had to admit she'd enjoyed the hell out of picking out new clothes. She went hog wild, too, buying some things for Hawaii she knew she'd never, ever wear again.

But what the hell. She of all people knew life was short—sometimes too short—and she wanted to have the fling of a lifetime in Hawaii. What better way to start than by purchasing scandalous clothes?

She unpacked, then put on her swimsuit, surprised at what she saw in the mirror. She'd lost a lot of weight and gained a ton of muscle. Running from one jobsite to another kept her fit. Grief and focusing more on work than on eating had taken away those extra twenty pounds she'd always hated. For thirty years old, she looked pretty damn good. Maybe she could pick up a hot lifeguard or surfer, someone young and sexy—with stamina. She'd definitely want someone with stamina. She needed lots and lots of sex.

Even a little sex would be good. Any sex at all. She wasn't going home without it. She hoped she wouldn't have to assault some poor guy to get it.

Yeah, right. As if she was that forward. She'd had one—exactly one—sexual partner in her lifetime, and that had been James. She'd been seventeen when she'd met him, eighteen when she'd married him.

And a widow at twenty-five.

She shook off the shroud of melancholy that threatened to put a damper on this beautifully sunny day. Which was exactly where she belonged—out in the sun. It was time to shake off Oklahoma's winter and dig her toes in the sand.

She went downstairs to the pool, tossed her things under the chair and spread out her towel, lathered up with some sunscreen, giddy with excitement when a cocktail waitress came by to take her order. It was one in the afternoon. And she'd just ordered a Bloody Mary. Normally her day wouldn't be even half over yet.

So far, this vacation was pretty damn good. She sipped her drink and surveyed the pool area, an expansive, winding behemoth so large she couldn't even see the other side of it. It was crowded already, too. But not wholly by single men, unfortunately. Lots of couples as well as families with their children in tow. She decided to ignore them and scan the area for men traveling alone. Surely there were conferences here. Then again, men attending conferences might be busy during the day, and available only at night. Which meant she'd have to hit the clubs and bars. She could do that.

Right, because she was so worldly. She snickered and took a sip of her drink, put it on the table next to her and adjusted the chaise flat.

Time for some sun worshipping. She'd go man hunting later.

⋙⋘

Clay surveyed the pool and ocean from his spot on the upper bar deck. He'd gotten in late—really late—last night, had done some work on his laptop and promptly passed out. This morning he'd gone for a workout in the gym, taken a walk on the beach and had breakfast, then gone to his room to make a few calls.

Yeah, so far, some vacation. But Tish told him Ella's plane got in late this morning, so he figured he'd run into her sometime today. In the meantime, he decided to soak up some sun.

This condo complex was packed. A lot of couples—on their honeymoons, probably—and families with kids running around screaming.

He liked kids. A lot. Someday he might want to have some. Maybe. If he had time. His father was a career-driven workaholic, and Clay couldn't remember spending much time with his dad. Nothing worse than an absent parent to make a child feel worthless. He didn't want to do that to his own kids. Better not to have any.

Of course since he never delved into a relationship past three or four dates, the chances of actually marrying and having children with someone seemed pretty damned remote right now.

Because he'd also seen how lonely his mother was, how his father's frequent absences and preoccupation with his career had affected her. And he'd never do that to a woman, either. It was best to keep them at arm's length, not get too involved. Then he wouldn't have to hurt them.

Damn. Too much downtime equaled too much time for reflection on how fucked-up his personal life was. No wonder he liked working nonstop. He flagged down the waitress and ordered a beer, then flipped his sunglasses over his eyes and surveyed the pool.

One woman caught his eye. A flash of red swimsuit, long brown hair, and just something about her—

He straightened, leaned forward, then stood and walked to the railing of the deck to get a better look. She was lying on the chaise, one knee bent, sunglasses on and a hat shielding the upper part of her face from the sun, so he couldn't really tell.

And damn, he'd never seen Ella . . . uncovered, but this woman's body was a knockout. A light sheen of sweat glistened on her skin, looking as though drops of gold had been sprinkled all over her.

She stood, and Clay sucked in a breath. Her breasts were full, but not overly large. Just perfect for her frame. Her hips flared out below her small waist, her belly was flat and she had beautiful, shapely legs. Toned arms, rockin' shoulders . . . This woman either worked out like a demon, or worked for a living.

She pulled off the hat and dragged her fingers through her hair, pulled off her sunglasses, then headed to the pool and dove in. She swam a few laps, then came up the stairs, water sluicing off her body.

Clay finally exhaled. It was Ella. Holy shit. She sure looked a lot different in a bikini than she did in boots, jeans and a work shirt. He almost felt guilty over the tightening of his cock.

Almost.

She smiled when the waitress brought her a fresh drink. He loved her smile. She didn't do it often enough.

Clay took his seat again, peering at her through the slats on the deck. No one approached or sat next to her. She seemed to be alone, at least here at the pool.

But was she meeting someone?

He still had no idea what he was doing here. He had yet to book the deep-sea fishing excursion he'd used as an excuse for coming to Hawaii. It sure as hell wasn't entirely for Ella. Just partly. He felt responsible for her.

So he wanted to make sure Ella was okay.

Then he'd go fishing.

Or so he kept telling himself as he spent the better part of the afternoon ogling Ella while she sunbathed and took a few dips in the pool. He felt like a stalker. Or a private investigator. Only no one had hired him to watch her. That one he'd decided on his own.

She finally left the pool about five, and he did the same, feeling ridiculous for spying on her. What was he going to do if she met a man? Lurk behind the nearest tree and watch them? And then what? Get a telephoto lens so he could see in her room and watch them get it on? Which would be physically impossible since she was on the tenth floor.

Hell. He didn't know what he was doing here, other than acting like a dumbass.

He took a shower, made a few calls, then worked on his laptop for a couple hours. Sitting in his room made him stir-crazy and he was getting hungry. He got dressed and decided to see what was going on downstairs.

If he was smart, he'd just call Ella's room and let her know he was here.

But he wanted to lie low, at least for a bit, to see what she was up to. If she was, in fact, meeting up with some guy, he'd be embarrassed as hell. This way, he could sneak a peek at her, make sure she was okay, then go fishing.

He had a bite to eat at the restaurant—no sign of Ella in there. After, he followed the sounds of loud music to the club across the walkway from the condo. Neon lights and blaring bass signaled he'd reached the hot spot.

The club was packed when he shoved through the front door. Definitely no kids here. All adults, some couples, a few singles, a lot of them crowded together on a giant dance floor swirling with colored lights overhead. Clay made a beeline for the bar and grabbed a beer, then leaned against the padded leather edge and surveyed the crowd.

How the hell was he going to tell if Ella was even in here? There had to be more than a hundred people in the place, all packed together like sardines. He supposed he'd have to just make the rounds.

He pushed off the bar and strolled around the tables. It was so damn dark in there he couldn't see a foot in front of him. He guessed the club considered this trendy or even romantic, but he found it damned irritating, mainly because he couldn't make out any faces until he was inches away. How was he supposed to find Ella—if she was even in here? And keeping the fact he was here a secret was going to be impossible if he had to get in everyone's face.

He finally gave up after about ten minutes and moved back to the bar, ordered another beer and stayed there. But then a miracle occurred. The band took a break, the lights came up and he could actually freakin' see. The sardines from the dance floor took their places at tables or at least disbanded enough that he could take quick glances at who was in the club.

That was when he saw a brunette wearing a white dress flash by not more than ten feet in front of him. He skirted his gaze in that direction. It was Ella, wearing some skintight dress that looked as if it had been painted on her. She had her hair down, loose waves curling over her shoulders. She wore red shoes—high heels—and matching red lipstick. Not that he was noticing every fucking thing she had on or anything.

Goddamn, she looked sexy as hell. And she made his dick hard.

And worse than that, she wasn't alone.

Shit.

Three

Her first night, and Ella had already scored a major hot guy. Single, in Waikiki on business, Shawn was from Los Angeles and came to the island four times a year as a tech for his software company.

He was talkative, tall, well built and easy to look at with curly, sandy brown hair and green eyes. He liked to surf and promised to teach her tomorrow.

After she'd left the pool this afternoon, she'd taken a nap, then showered and come downstairs to the restaurant for dinner. That was where she'd run into Shawn, who'd been seated next to her table. He saw her dining alone and came over, cocktail in hand, asking if he could join her.

She couldn't have planned it better than if she'd—well, if she'd planned it herself. They'd had dinner together and hit it off right away. He kept the conversation going since he seemed to like to talk about himself and his career—and okay, maybe he liked to talk about those two topics an awful lot, but it was better than awkward silences.

And she didn't mind listening. It gave her time to look at him, and he was nice to look at. Plus, it gave her an opportunity to ponder all the what-ifs for tonight, the possibilities of what might happen between them.

She could definitely have sex with Shawn. He was nice-looking, clean, professional, had introduced her to a couple of his business associates who'd passed by their table, which meant he was on the up-and-up about being here on business and really wasn't a lone serial killer. And he'd paid for dinner and invited her to the club across from the condo. There, he'd bought her a few drinks. He even danced well.

So far, he'd passed the test. She was enjoying the club, having a great time getting out on the dance floor. For the love of God, she was with a man for the first time since . . .

James.

No. She wasn't going to think about James tonight, wasn't going to think about the last time they'd gone out, the last time they'd had a moment together, the last time he'd held her, kissed her, touched her—

Tonight was all about new beginnings.

"You went quiet on me, Ella."

Shawn slid his fingers under her chin and focused her attention back on him.

"Oh. Sorry. Was just catching my breath. You do like to dance."

The cocktail waitress brought them fresh drinks. "Okay, then. Quench your thirst so you're ready to go when the band starts up again."

She took a couple deep swallows from the wine the waitress had placed in front of her, then exhaled. The dress she'd bought was sinful—it was white and it hugged her curves in all the right places. And the red stiletto heels were just the perfect added touch.

"You are so beautiful."

She smiled at Shawn. He'd said that about ten times in the past hour. "Thanks. Again. You don't have to keep saying it." She stopped just short of telling him that she was pretty much a sure thing and he could stop trying so hard. Then again, what would she know? Maybe this was dating and how men acted. It wasn't as though she had a ton of experience. She'd had James, who'd fumbled around with half-assed compliments when they were younger and she'd fallen madly in love with him. There'd been no looking back after that.

And no one else since.

So maybe Shawn's slick presentation was the norm. He was clearly the expert here and she was the novice.

She finished her glass of wine just as the houselights went off.

"You ready to hit the dance floor again?"

She took a glance at the dance floor and palmed her stomach. Between the tight corset and the three glasses of wine, not to mention the packed-in dance floor, she shook her head. "Too crowded. I need some air."

Shawn nodded and stood. "How about a walk outside to clear your head?"

"Perfect." With great relief she took his hand and he led her down the stairs and onto the outside deck. The night was warm, but there was a breeze, and she could breathe infinitely better out here.

He walked her to a corner area out of sight from the doorway. Low-hanging palm trees waved in the breeze. It was dark, private, very romantic.

He led her to the railing, where the sounds of the ocean crashed against the shore. They were alone. Maybe she didn't have butter-flies fluttering in her stomach, but she'd get there . . . eventually.

She leaned against the rail and turned to him. "This is nice."

He moved in, slid his arm around her waist. "You are so beautiful."

Okay, that line was starting to get old.

"Thanks. You look nice, too."

"I want to kiss you."

Then do it. Don't tell me about it.

His face was inches from hers. He stared at her . . . and kept staring at her. Ella noticed his eyes were a little glassy. They'd been at the club for a few hours now. How much had Shawn had to drink? She'd had three glasses of wine, but she'd danced off the effects and hadn't paid much attention at all to the shots he'd been slamming. He'd seemed okay. Plus, he was really tall. And she was used to hanging out with men who could drink her under the table and still be stone-cold sober at the end of the night. Surely he was okay.

"Can I kiss you?"

Oh, for God's sake. "Sure."

After his tentative request, she expected light, an easy brush of his lips across hers. He shocked the hell out of her by jerking her into his arms and jamming his lips on hers. His tongue thrust inside, jabbing in and out, in and out. He tasted like whiskey, and his hands roamed down her back to grab her ass. He drew her against his cock, which was already hard.

She was *not* turned on. This was not pleasant. It wasn't romantic. It wasn't sexy. She palmed his chest and pushed away, resisting the urge to wipe her lips with the back of her hand. "Whoa, tiger. That was a little sudden."

He looked perplexed. "You said yes."

She blew out a breath. "Yes, I did, didn't I." She started to explain, but he grabbed her again, kissed her, turned her around so her back was against the railing. He held tight to her while he plundered her mouth. This time, when she tried to push him away, he didn't stop.

He didn't stop.

She didn't like this. She tried to wrench her mouth away but he lifted one hand to the back of her head and held her there, made moaning noises and ground his cock against her hip.

She felt sick, violated, wanted out of this. She wasn't ready—not for this.

Couldn't he tell she wanted to stop? She finally wedged her arm from his tight hold and scratched his neck. He jerked back.

"Ow. What the hell was that for?"

"I was trying to get you to stop. Are you oblivious?"

"You wanted this. You want this."

She shook her head, wrapped her arms around herself. "No. I don't want this. I don't want you. You need to go." How could this night have turned so bad?

"You started it. You agreed. You said yes."

Oh, no. She might be inexperienced, but she wasn't stupid. This guy was history. She narrowed her gaze. "And then I said stop. I said no. What part of me desperately trying to push you away did you not understand?"

"And when a lady says no, she means it, asshole."

Ella's gaze whipped to the sound of a very familiar male voice behind Shawn.

Clay?

Clay was here? What the hell was he doing here?

And he was pissed. His brows were knit in a furious frown as he advanced on Shawn and fisted his hand into Shawn's Hawaiian shirt.

"You look like a smart guy. Smart enough to read a woman's signals. When she says no, when her body language says no, you'd better be smart enough to start listening."

Shawn was no short, lightweight guy, but he was dwarfed by Clay. He cast a decidedly uncomfortable look up at Clay and nodded. "Yeah. I got it."

Clay pushed him aside. "Take a hike."

Shawn stumbled over himself in his eagerness to get the hell out of there.

Ella slid onto the nearest bench, stupefied.

Clay came over and squatted down in front of her. "You okay?"

She nodded. "I'm fine."

He drew her hands in between his. "Your hands are shaking."

"He scared the shit out of me."

"He was a dick. Want me to go kick his ass?"

She laughed. Clay would do that, too. "No. I think you got your message across. He probably peed himself."

Clay's lips lifted. "Good. He deserved it."

"Clay, what are you doing here?"

"Fishing."

She arched a brow. "Fishing?"

"Deep sea. There are a couple great excursions this time of year. And you know it's a good time of year in our business to take a few days off."

She nodded. "True. I can't believe we're at the same place." But then it hit her. Of course. Clay had gifted the condo to Tish and her husband. "You mentioned at the meeting the other day that you have a condo at the same place as Tish."

"Yeah."

"And you knew I was coming here."

"Yes, I did."

"You followed me?"

"No. I came here to go fishing."

She didn't believe him. Then again, what kind of ego did she have that she thought he was here for her? That was ridiculous. "So this is all coincidence."

"I came over here for a few drinks and to check out the action at the club. Noisy as hell in there. So I came outside for some fresh air. That's when I spotted you tusslin' with that asshole."

She lifted her gaze to his. "I'm glad you showed up when you did. And thank you."

He laughed. "I didn't do anything. Looks like you had him under control when I got here."

She pulled on his hands and he sat on the bench next to her. God, he looked fine. So different from his jeans and long-sleeved shirt. Tonight he wore black linen pants and a black silk short-sleeved shirt. His face was always tan from working outdoors, and his blue eyes mesmerized her.

"I think your intimidation helped get rid of him. I'm not sure he was ever going to get the hint."

"Well, he's gone now."

"Yes, he is."

He studied her without saying a word. Ella found herself not minding that at all.

"You look different."

Leave it to Clay to say something like that. "Is that good or bad?"

"It's good. You always look beautiful. You just don't look like you usually do. I like you just fine in jeans and a T-shirt. But this dress . . . Goddamn, Ella. You look hot."

Her heart stopped. Shawn had told her at least thirty-eight times that she was beautiful. It had meant nothing to her. One compliment from Clay and she had melted to the bench. "Thank you. I wasn't sure you even knew I was a woman."

He arched a brow. "I've always known you were a woman. I just try not to treat you like one."

She laughed. "I'll take that as a compliment."

"Good."

Being with Clay was so . . . easy. She knew him, had known him since she and James had started in the construction business all those years ago. With Clay she could be herself, didn't have to pretend. He'd seen her at her very worst. There was nothing to hide from him.

"Ella, why are you here?"

Well, maybe she had one thing to hide from him.

"I'm on vacation."

"And that's it. You came all the way to Hawaii—by yourself—to rest."

"Yes."

"Bullshit. Tell me why you're really here."

She arched away from him. "I don't think that's any of your business."

"I'm making it my business."

"Now you're being a pushy bastard."

"Yeah? And?"

She couldn't help herself. She laughed. "Why can't I stay mad at you?"

"Because I'm irresistible."

She rolled her eyes. "You probably use that line on the ladies. And it probably works."

"It does."

"God. You're unbelievable."

"They all say that, too."

She liked that he was here. Despite wanting to do this vacation on her own, she was happy Clay had shown up. Though it did put a major crimp on the sex thing. How was she going to pick up a guy with Clay around? And she still had a niggling suspicion . . .

"So I'll tell you what, Clay. You come clean with me and I'll do the same. Tish told you why I was coming here, didn't she?"

"No. She didn't. But I was kind of hoping you would."

He was telling the truth. Damn. She and Clay had gotten close after James's death. But not that close. Not close enough to divulge her desperate need for sex.

"Um . . ."

"You didn't know that guy, did you?"

"No."

"Okay." He looked away.

"What?"

"I thought you had come here to meet someone."

She blew out a breath. Explanation time. She hated this. "I did."

He shifted his gaze back on her. "But not him."

"No."

"Then who?"

She shrugged. "I have no idea."

"That doesn't make sense."

"I know. This is difficult for me to explain to you. You and I . . . we don't have the kind of relationship where I can talk about . . . intimate things."

"Oh. Well, sure we do. Okay, we don't. Not yet, anyway. But we can." He leaned back and slung his arm across the back of the bench. "You can tell me anything, Ella."

She probably could. And Clay got around . . . a lot. He knew things . . . about sex. About relationships. Maybe he could help her figure this out. If she could survive the embarrassment.

She took a deep breath, then let it out. "I'm here for sex."

Four

Ella tried not to grimace when Clay's jaw dropped.

"Um . . . what?"

"Sex. S-E-X. I need sex. That's what I came to Hawaii to get."

"You mean you haven't . . . ?"

"Since James died? No, I haven't."

"Oh. Well. Really? No one? It's been five years, Ella."

"I know. I wasn't ready."

"And you are now."

"Yes."

"Then why can't you get that back home? I mean, honey, I'm sure there's plenty of guys in Tulsa who'd love to fuck you."

She laughed. "That's nice of you to say. But that's not what I want."

Clay rubbed the spot above his brow. "I'm confused. You can't have sex with any man you know in your own hometown. Why not?"

She shifted to face him. "Because I know all those guys. They're all friends and coworkers of James. I don't want to have sex with someone who knew James. Someone who knows me, who knows my story. I want a clean slate. I don't want a relationship."

"And you think no one will have sex with you—without strings?"

She shrugged. "I don't know. I just didn't want to go there. Not with guys I know."

"And not with men who knew James."

"Yes."

"Not every man in that city knows you or knew James."

"I know that, too. I just wanted to get away." Away from the familiar, away from memories of the man she'd loved, from the place where the two of them had built their lives together, where every building, every street, didn't remind her of James.

"So you came to Hawaii, intending to pick up some random guy and fuck him?"

"Yes." But now that he said it out loud it sounded like a really stupid idea. "I guess I hadn't really thought that one through."

"It's not safe, Ella."

She rolled her eyes. "Guys do it all the time."

"Guys can take care of themselves."

"And women can't? You know I can."

"Yes, I know you can. I just wish you wouldn't. Not here. Not by yourself."

"Not where you can't keep an eye on me? Come on, Clay. What are you going to do? Stand in the bedroom and watch over the guy I'm having sex with to be sure no harm comes to me?"

He looked horrified. "Uh, no."

She laid a hand on his arm. "I'm a grown woman. And I'm not stupid. I can handle this."

He shook his head. "I know you think this is a great idea. But there has to be a better way to jump back on the horse again."

"If I knew a better way, I'd do it. I'd have already done it."

"Need it that bad?"

She laughed, and at the same time heat pooled low in her belly.

Talking sex with Clay made her body heat up. They'd never had a conversation this . . . personal, this intimate before. He wasn't a "best friend" kind of man. He was a man. All man. Hot, sexy, but their conversations were usually all business. She'd never thought of him in that way other than the occasional admiration for his body, his looks, the way he commanded a room and the men who worked for him. She'd learned a lot watching him, and maybe while watching him she'd had a feminine appreciation for him as a man.

But in her life there'd always been James. And she'd loved James with her whole heart. So no other man had attracted her.

But James had been gone for five years now. And in the last year or so, she might have started noticing Clay as more than a business associate. Still, she'd never once thought . . .

Yet here she was in Hawaii, talking about sex with him. Not just sex in general, but her sex life. Or rather, her not-quite-but-impending sex life. The whole thing was surreal.

"I might be able to help you."

Finally. "Great. What do you suggest?"

"What about me?"

Her heart dropped to her stomach. "What?"

"You can have sex with me."

Her throat had gone dry. Where was that glass of wine now? "Are you kidding me?"

His smile died. "I never joke about sex."

She'd just bet he didn't. He probably took it very seriously. She could already imagine . . .

No. No way. Oh, definitely no way. "I . . . We . . . Oh, hell, no."

She clamped her mouth shut. *Way to insult a man's ego, Ella.*

But instead he tilted his head back and laughed. "So, you think I'm repulsive."

"Oh, God. No. I didn't mean that at all. I think you're hot, Clay. Any woman would want to have sex with you. I mean, you probably have women falling all over themselves wanting to . . ."

Again . . . she clamped her lips shut when she saw the grin on his face. "I think I should just shut up now."

He walked his fingers along the flesh of her back. "No, you're doing great. Keep going."

She shivered at his touch. Shawn hadn't elicited one-tenth of the response in her that Clay did. This was bad. Really bad. "Don't you see how this couldn't work?"

"No."

"We work together. We own competing businesses."

"So?"

"We'd have to face each other . . . afterward."

"So?"

She blew out a frustrated breath. "It would be awkward. Plus, what would everyone think?"

"Are you going to tell them?"

"Oh, my God, no."

"Neither will I. What goes on between you and me is just that . . . between you and me. And why would you feel awkward about having some fun?"

Dammit. He made it sound so logical. "Clay, you're too . . . familiar."

"Huh?"

"I know you. You're too close. The last thing I need for this is someone I know."

"I disagree. That's exactly what you need right now."

Clay watched the mix of emotions on Ella's face, and still couldn't believe he'd offered himself up as . . . what? Stud? Sex partner? Hell, even he didn't know. He just knew he'd seen red when that guy had pushed her too hard. And he'd be damned if he was going to let some other guy touch her.

Unfamiliar territory. He'd come here to make sure she was okay. And she had been handling the situation okay, but he'd wanted to knock that guy hard—like onto the next island. The only thing that had stopped him was Ella standing there.

And then listening to her talk about wanting to have sex with some random guy?

Oh, hell, no. But he hadn't known he wanted the guy to be himself until tonight, until he'd seen another man kiss her, put his hands on her. He knew then that the only man he wanted touching her was . . . him.

"You need someone you know, someone you trust, someone who can lead you back into sex and expect nothing in return."

She tilted her head to the side, exposing her neck. He wanted to kiss her neck. Okay, he wanted to start there, then put his mouth all over her.

"Yes. But that's my whole point. Someone who expects nothing in return. That's the great thing about anonymity."

"Anonymity can also be dangerous. That's where the trust is lacking. You can't trust a stranger. A stranger doesn't know you."

"And you do."

"You know I do. I'll also keep you safe."

She sighed. "Okay, I hadn't thought about that part. I was just so excited about this trip I hadn't thought about the danger aspects. Stupid, I know." She looked down at her hands. "It's just that I've finally started to feel whole again. And that took a long time after James died. I never thought I'd ever want to be with another man after him."

"But now you do."

"Yes and no. I don't want to fall in love again." She lifted her gaze to his, and his gut clenched at the sincerity in her big brown eyes. "I can't ever love anyone like I loved James."

"But it's not love you're after. It's sex."

"Yes. Lately it's all I've been able to think about. And all I want is meaningless sex."

He slid his fingers under her hair and teased the nape of her neck. Her hair was soft, her skin even softer. "Sex is never meaningless, Ella. Or it shouldn't be. And I'd be really disappointed if that's what you're going for."

She snorted. "Oh, right. I'm sure all your sexual escapades are filled with meaning."

"If you're implying that I have fulfilling, long-lasting emotional relationships, then no, I don't. My life isn't conducive to long-term relationships, and you know that. But I never have meaningless sex. I don't fuck someone and drop them the next day. Sex means something. You should never take it lightly."

She looked down at her hands again. "Damn you. I wanted it to be meaningless."

"Did you?"

"Yes."

"Why? If your objective is just to get off, you can do that yourself."

Her gaze shot to his, her mouth dangling open. Her lips were full, soft, and it took every bit of willpower he possessed not to kiss her.

"I can't believe you just said that."

"I think we're past dancing around each other. If you just want a release, you can do it yourself. That's not what you want."

She stared at him for a few seconds, then said, "You're right. It's not what I want. But I also don't want a relationship. I don't want any strings. I don't want to get involved with someone."

"Neither do I. That's why you and me are perfect for this."

He didn't know why he hadn't suggested it before, other than he figured she'd already been having sex.

Five years? That's a long damn time to go without. Then again, he knew nothing about love, or grieving for someone you'd lost. He'd never loved anyone, or lost anyone he cared about. Maybe it did take that long. He knew Ella had loved James. And it just wasn't right when someone that young died. But it happened. He'd seen it happen all the time, especially in their business. There were no guarantees.

"I do trust you."

It meant a lot to him that she did. And okay, maybe he wanted to get in her pants—had wanted to for a couple years now. He wasn't bothered by James's memory. He and James had been friends. But James was long gone now. And Ella had a right to a life. She hadn't died.

"I'm glad you do. And you know I won't try to tie you down with any relationship when it's over. You go back to your job and I'll go back to mine. And we'll never talk about it again."

"Yes." She blew out a breath. "That would be perfect."

"But while we're here, we can have one hell of a good time, Ella."

"You're right. We could." She took a deep breath. "Okay, then. Let's do it."

Ella wasn't sure how this was going to play out, but now that Clay had offered, the thought of getting him naked was first on her list of things to do.

"Come on." He stood, held out his hand for her. She slipped her hand in his and followed him. He walked back inside the club and Ella bit back the disappointment, which turned out to be only momentary as he walked through the double doors and outside.

"Thank God," she said. "I thought you were going to drag me on the dance floor."

Clay laughed. "Not a chance. I can't dance for shit."

She arched a brow as they strolled along the walkway between the club and the condo. "I'm going to have to see that."

"No, you really aren't."

"That bad, huh?"

"That bad."

"You've shattered my illusions. I thought you were perfect." She liked that he didn't stride fast, instead strolled along at a slow pace so she could keep up with him. In her work boots, she'd have no problem. In these heels? She'd have to run.

Once back at the condo complex, he took her up in the elevator to the top floor, then used his key to enter his suite.

"Suite, huh? Well, aren't you special?"

He tilted toward her as he pushed the door open and flipped on the light. "I like Hawaii. And as we know, property is a good investment."

Investment. Hell. It was a palace. Twice the size, at least, of her condo. Spacious and open, with lots of windows and doors overlooking the ocean. "Just leave me here. Don't tell anyone you saw me. They'll never notice I'm missing."

He laughed and opened the sliding-glass door. A breeze blew the curtains inward. "Bullshit. You run that company with an iron fist. Your lazy crew would revolt if they thought their leader was gone."

"My lazy crew?" She arched a brow and put her hands on her hips. "My crew can work circles around yours."

He moved toward her. "You field a bunch of pussies and you know it."

He was teasing her. She liked it. He'd never once treated her with kid gloves—not even right after James had died. And that was exactly what she'd needed—someone to drive her to get in there and do the job. That was what James would have expected from her. That was what Clay expected from her. She'd adored him for that, for not coddling her and holding her hand other than showing her the ropes of the business.

She glared at him. "When we get back to work next week I'll pony up my guys against yours, and we'll see who can put in an honest day's work without lying down on the job."

"You're on, cupcake."

He was right in front of her now, all six foot five or so of him. Imposing, sexy, an expanse of tanned skin visible over the top button of his shirt. She wanted to reach in there and touch it—touch him. That she could now—where before she supposed it had been either forbidden, at least in her mind, or something that would never have occurred to her. It was unnerving. She swallowed and tilted her head back to look at his face.

His smile was devastating. How did women resist him?

Oh, yeah. They didn't.

The dynamics had changed. They were no longer coworkers. They were friends, always had been, always would be. But tonight they were going to become lovers. This whole thing was surreal.

His smile shifted, became a little less wide. "You're thinking about something."

"Yes."

"James?"

Funny he would think that. "No. Actually, I was thinking about you and me."

"Yeah? How so?"

"About how our relationship will be changing."

He slid his knuckles over her cheek. "Just for this week. Only while we're here. After that, it goes back to the way it was."

She reached up and wrapped her fingers around his wrist, needing the solid, warm touch of male flesh. It had been so long. "You make it sound so easy."

"It can be, if we let it."

"You've done this before."

"If you're asking if I've had sex with women in the business, you know as well as I do that there aren't that many women in the construction business."

She smiled. "Yes, but leave it to you to find them. Plus, you travel a lot. You have contracts out of state."

"True."

"You have done this before."

"Not with someone like you. Not with someone I've known so long. Not with someone I—"

She cocked her head to the side. "What?"

"Nothing. I just know you better than any woman. I don't work with the women I date. So this is new territory for me, too."

"But we're not exactly going to be dating, Clay."

"Oh, I think we are." He slid one arm around her waist and pulled her against him. Her breath caught at being so close to him, at feeling his chest against her, the muscles of his thighs. "Did you think I'd strip you naked, chain you to my bed and fuck you non-stop for the entire time we're here?"

Her stomach quivered, her mind filled with thoughts of the two of them naked. Of her tied, spread-eagled, to his bed. Of Clay doing . . . everything . . . to her. "Now, there's a visual."

"Well, if that's what you really want, I'll be happy to oblige. . . ."

She laughed, startling herself at the husky quality of her voice. She didn't sound like herself, knew it was because she was nervous. She had no experience here; she wasn't a flirt, nor was she trying to come across that way.

What was going to happen next? She had no idea what to do. With James, it had been easy. Familiar. She couldn't even remember when they'd first met. It had been so long ago. How did two people . . . start?

Clay took her hand and led her to the leather love seat situated in front of the door. "It's nice out. Let's sit down. You want something to drink?"

"Water would be nice. I think I had enough wine at the club."

She took a seat and Clay brought water for her, then filled a short glass with amber liquid for himself.

"Whiskey," he said, taking it down in one shot.

She half turned to face him. "Courage?"

His lips lifted as he set the glass down on the table. "I'm not a virgin, if that's what you're asking. And no, I'm not nervous."

She nearly dropped her glass of water. She laid it carefully on the table. "Uh, I definitely didn't think you were a virgin." And she still couldn't believe she was having this conversation with Clay.

He picked up a strand of her hair, sifted it through his fingers. "Yeah? And how would you know?"

"I don't. I just . . . Come on, Clay. You've been around. You bring a different woman to every event. I don't think I've ever seen you with the same woman twice."

He studied her. "Really."

"Yes."

"I didn't think you were paying attention."

"I wasn't. I mean, I do. I mean . . . hell. For God's sake, Clay. I don't know what I'm talking about."

"I think we've done enough talking."

Five

Ella held her breath as Clay leaned in. He didn't pause like Shawn had done, didn't ask for permission. But he didn't pin her, crowd her or take what she wasn't offering. He simply pressed his lips against hers. A soft, light brush of his mouth on hers, enough for her to taste, to feel the warmth of his breath, the tangy flavor of whiskey.

Enough for her to want more. She leaned into him, laid her hand on his chest. So solid, so male. He snaked his arm around her waist, once again, not too much that she backed away, but enough that she knew he was there, that he was touching her. His fingers splayed across her waist, and he increased the pressure of his mouth against hers. The tip of his tongue teased hers, and she opened, laid her head back against his forearm and invited him in.

He cupped her cheek with his other hand, scooted over so his thigh touched hers, and deepened the kiss, his tongue fully involved with hers now. She had forgotten what it felt like to have so much powerful male around her. Heat swelled inside her, the butterflies she hadn't felt with Shawn, the awakenings of arousal—what she'd come here for.

This . . . this was what she'd needed—what Shawn hadn't given her. Maybe he never could, because despite wanting impersonal, with Clay it *was* personal. She knew him, knew his looks, his mannerisms, his moods. She'd known him nearly as long as she'd known James, and she felt safe in Clay's arms. This was a giant first step for her. Clay had been right—she needed to feel safe.

And yet she didn't love Clay; she could get what she needed and walk away when it was over. But for now, she wanted to relish every moment, to think of nothing and no one but this man. The way he smelled, the way he tasted, the way he touched her. It was a brand-new experience and she was giddy with it.

Clay didn't seem to be in any hurry, just held her against him, his mouth doing delicious things to her senses. And oh, man, could he kiss. Devouring her mouth one second, his tongue diving deep inside to meld with hers. Then switching things up to take small nips of her lips. Then he'd start the whole process over with deep, tongue-swirling kisses that made her toes curl.

Other than touching herself, bringing herself to orgasm, which was more of a perfunctory thirty seconds to a few minutes of physical release, she hadn't spent much time on pleasure in the past five years. This was overload. This was like going from the desert to an oasis.

He moved his hand from her waist to her rib cage. Her heart pounded against his hand. Could he feel it?

He lifted his head. "You scared?"

She laughed. "No. Yes. Maybe. I haven't done this in a while."

"Are you sure you're ready?"

"Yes." She reached up and covered his hand with hers, brought it up over her breast. And nearly died when he rubbed his thumb over her nipple. Hot, tingling, her breast swelled, her nipple tightened.

"You'd better be, because I want you. I want you naked. I want to put my mouth all over you. I want to make you come, to hear you scream when you do. And I want to fuck you all night long, over and over again. So tell me now if you're not ready."

Good God Almighty. His words evoked images that made her

melt all over, things she'd only dreamed about. Things only James
had done to her.

For so long she'd been faithful to James. Faithful to the memory
of their marriage, their life together, their love. She thought there
was only going to be James. Forever.

But it was time. Time to let go, to give herself a chance to experience, if nothing else, sex again. It was time to push James aside,
at least for a while.

"I'm ready for it, Clay. I need to be with you."

He swooped her up into his arms—she felt weightless and so
small next to him—and carried her down the hall and into the bedroom. He set her down on the soft carpet between the bed and the
doorway. Tangy warm air billowed through the open doorway, waft-
ing over her hot skin. Clay turned her toward the door and placed
her back against his chest, then leaned down and brushed her hair
to the side. He kissed the nape of her neck and drew the straps of
her dress down her shoulders.

She shivered.

"You cold?"

She leaned against him and raised her arm to twine it around his
neck. "No."

His hands followed her straps, skimming along her skin. He
stopped midway down her arms. "My hands are rough on your soft
skin."

"I like rough."

"Do you?"

"Yes. I think so. I don't know, really. I just know I like the way
your hands feel on me."

He moved closer to her, wrapped his arms around her, his forearms resting just under her breasts. Her breath caught.

"I guess we'll have to explore that together, then."

She found it hard to breathe having him wrapped around her
like this. "I guess we will." The thought of it thrilled her. James had
always been tender, sweet in his lovemaking. He'd never been rough
with her. Not that it was a bad thing. But she would dishonor his

memory because it would sound like a complaint. And she had no complaints. She'd loved her husband. Making love with James had been ten slices of heaven. He'd treated her like an angel every time he touched her.

She swore she'd no longer dwell on the past or on James.

Now she was ready for something a little different. She didn't know why. Maybe because she could? She'd spent a long time deciding to go for this. This was her chance to explore. And oh, she wanted everything. Having Clay here with her, his body intimately pressed against her, his warm breath against her neck, was more than she had ever fantasized about.

She settled against him, felt the hard ridge of his erection against her butt, and shuddered, expectation ratcheting up both her nervousness and excitement.

"Are you sure you're not cold? I can shut the door."

She turned in his arms so she faced him. "Don't. I like the breeze coming in. Everything is perfect." She was almost afraid it was too perfect. Something was bound to go wrong and she didn't want it to. She had thought about this moment for so long.

But then Clay kissed her, and all her worries melted away with the touch of his lips, the slide of his tongue, the masterful way he stroked her libido to fever pitch with his mouth. He knocked her senses sideways and she was lost in him.

When he reached for the zipper on her dress, she began to tremble. But this time, he didn't pause, didn't question whether she was ready or not. This time, he wasn't going to stop. Thankfully.

He drew the zipper partway down, then stepped back. She looked up at him, at the smoldering look of desire on his face—a look she'd never seen in a face that had grown so familiar to her over the years.

He reached again for the straps on her dress. This time, when he pulled the straps down her arms, the top of her dress went with them.

She should be nervous. She wasn't. Not even when he bared her to the waist. She hadn't worn a bra, didn't need one, really, since the dress was so tight. She reached behind her and finished unzipping the dress. It fell to the floor and she stepped out of it, then kicked off her shoes.

Clay removed his shoes, then undid the button on his pants and drew the zipper down. Only then did she start to feel those nervous butterflies fluttering in her stomach. She'd been with only one man her entire life. What if she really didn't know how to . . . do this? What if she was lousy at it? What if after they had sex Clay found her lacking? She'd be mortified.

But all thoughts of uncertainty fled when Clay began to unbutton his shirt, revealing a wide expanse of beautiful chest and flat, ridged stomach. He shrugged off the shirt and let his pants fall to the floor. He was so different from James—muscular where James had been lean and wiry. She hated that James kept entering her mind, but he'd been the only man in her life. Visions of him still swam in her head.

Until Clay tugged his boxers down his hips. His erection bobbed, thick and rigid, impossible for her to ignore. She felt heat and moisture between her legs, as well as the urge to rub the swelling throb of her clit.

But tonight she wouldn't have to touch herself, wouldn't have to imagine a man between her legs satisfying all her desires. Tonight there'd be reality instead of fantasy.

Tonight there was Clay.

She drank in the sight of him, so incredibly beautiful from his dark hair to his muscular legs to his erect cock that made her mouth water. He bore scars on his arms, some she remembered him getting on the job because they often worked side by side on shared projects. He'd blow off most cuts and gouges and scrapes no matter how deep. He was tough.

He sat on the bed. "Come here, Ella."

She moved forward on shaky legs and stopped in front of him, her breasts level with his face. Her nipples puckered and he apparently noticed that, because his lips curled up.

He reached out and traced his finger around each nipple. Her breath caught, her body shuddering all over at the contact. It had been so long. So damn long. Tears rushed to her eyes and she blinked them back.

This is just sex. Quit making such a big damn deal out of it. It doesn't mean anything.

He slid his thumb over her nipple, a soft back-and-forth action. Her sex quivered with delicious sensation. For the first time in years, she felt her body swelling, coming to life, arching toward a man's touch. It felt achingly familiar and yet oh, so different.

He widened his legs and pulled her between them. His thighs were warm pressed against hers. He moved his hands from her thighs to her hips, ignoring the panties she still wore, sweeping his touch over her waist as if he were memorizing every inch of her skin. This slow exploration made her pulse skitter, her body temperature rise.

"You have a beautiful body, Ella. It's a shame no one's touched it in so long."

He swept his hands around her back and drew her toward him. She braced her hands on his shoulders as he fit one nipple into his mouth. Slow, easy, teasing her as his tongue snaked out to lick around the areola, tantalizing her with his warm, wet tongue until she couldn't take it any longer. She dipped farther in, sliding her breast against his tongue. His low hum of approval melted inside her, made her tingle in anticipation.

He fit his mouth over the bud, sucked gently and rolled his tongue over her nipple. She tilted her head back and moaned at the nearly unbearable pleasure of it. With each tender suck her pussy quaked. She had no idea that connection could be made. Had it just been so long that she didn't remember?

That had to be it. She'd felt pleasure with James. Sex had been good with him. Really good.

Stop. Thinking. About. James.

Not now, not when the pleasure was so great, when it was only Clay she wanted to think about. She wouldn't compare one man to the other, wouldn't think about being in bed with Clay and what it meant. It meant nothing.

It meant everything. It would be the first time she was going to be with another man besides James.

Clay leaned back. "Something on your mind?"

She was panting, her body on fire from his mouth on her breast. "No. Yes. I'm sorry."

He released her and she sat next to him.

"It's James," he said.

"Yes."

"It's okay to think about him, Ella. You can't try to pretend he didn't exist. You loved him."

She looked down at her hands. "It doesn't seem right."

He tipped her chin with his finger, forcing her to look at him. "Was he the only man you were with?"

She nodded.

"Then it's natural you'd feel strange about this. I don't expect you to erase James from your memories. You shouldn't feel that way, either."

She loved that they could talk about James. Sitting naked on the bed together, they were having a conversation about her dead husband. She'd never be able to do this with anyone but Clay.

"Just let it come naturally and quit putting so much pressure on yourself to be perfect. If he occasionally pops into your thoughts, there's nothing wrong with that."

"Most guys would hate that."

He leaned in, kissed her. "I'm not most guys."

She was beginning to see that. "Thank you."

"I'd like to think he'd be okay with this. That he'd trust me."

She smiled. "I know he would."

"Then quit worrying about it and let's have some fun."

She exhaled. Clay was right. She was obsessing over every little thing. Frankly, she was surprised he hadn't already kicked her to the curb for being too much effort. She might not even be worth it.

"Okay, now," he said, lying back on the bed and pulling her into his arms. He dragged her on top of him. "Where were we?"

"You had my nipple in your mouth."

"Oh, yeah."

"You were sucking it."

He shifted her upward. "I remember. You tasted good." He lifted her nipple to his mouth.

And just like that, she fell into heat and arousal, all other thoughts fleeing her mind. Contact was an explosion of heat. She held on to his shoulders, watching him suck and lick one nipple, then the other, until she was too weak to hold herself up. She collapsed on top of him and pressed her mouth to his, her tongue diving in with a passion she'd held in reserve before.

But not now. She'd cleared her head, dismissed her reservations. It was time to focus on one thing—Clay.

He rolled her over onto her back and laid his palm on her rib cage. Again, she felt her heart pounding against his hand. She lifted her gaze to his. For some reason, watching him look at her was incredibly sobering. He seemed to be so serious, but not at all with the same intense look that he had during business meetings. Because this time, there was an underlying look of passion in his eyes, turning their normal sea blue to a dark, stormy color.

He finally skimmed his hand down her belly, his fingers tantalizingly close to her panties. He slid his fingertips just underneath. She held her breath, her gaze riveted on his face, while he tucked his hand inside to cup her sex.

She expelled her breath and sucked it in again as a whirlwind of pleasure surrounded her.

"You're wet. Hot. God, you feel good, Ella."

She fought to swallow as he moved his hand farther, sliding along her pussy lips, his fingers teasing, dipping into the wetness there and coating her. She arched against his hand and he rubbed the heel against her clit.

She gasped. Instinct forced her to grab his wrist and guide his hand to the spot that gave her the most pleasure. "Yes. Right there. Oh, Clay, that feels so good."

He pressed his lips against her temple, his warm breath teasing her ear. "I like to hear you talk, Ella. Tell me what feels good to you."

He slid a finger inside her and she lifted, still holding on to his wrist.

"That? Or do you want more?"

Another finger joined the first, and he pumped in and out. Ella tilted her head back and rocked her hips against his fingers. "Yes. Oh, God, yes, I like that."

He swirled his thumb over her clit while he finger fucked her, and the sensation was incredible. It had been too long, and she was so ready to come.

"Yeah. Squeeze my fingers with your pussy, baby. Come for me."

Tension spiraled up and through her as she held back, wanting to prolong the intensity of this pleasure. Clay continued to work her pussy and slid his hand against her clit. She turned her head and looked into his eyes, at the dark desire she saw there, and she had no hope of holding on any longer. She let go, her orgasm seizing every muscle of her body. She tightened, then released, pleasure flowing through her like the sweetest electric current, making her shake all over as rivers of sensation rocked her. And throughout, Clay tunneled his fingers in and out of her, intensifying her climax until she lay spent and limp as a rag doll on the bed.

She smiled up at him, wanting to tell him how grateful she was for what he'd just given her, but knowing it wouldn't come out right. So instead, she rolled to her side and reached for his cock, wrapping her fingers around the hot, hard center of him.

He hissed at the contact, then looked down where her hand was connected to his cock. Ella stroked him, learning the feel of him, loving every sensation from hard to velvety soft.

"Squeeze harder," he said.

She shuddered at the commanding tone of his voice and wanted to please him the way he had pleased her. She gripped him tighter and he thrust within her hand, making her imagine him inside her, doing exactly the same thing. She rolled her thumb over the soft mushroomed crest of his cock. It was slippery, moist with his fluids. She paused, never having done it with James before, but for some reason she felt bolder with Clay. She didn't know why, but wasn't about to question it. She lifted her finger to her mouth and sucked his taste from her thumb.

Clay's nostrils flared and he sucked in a breath. "Christ, Ella. Are you trying to make me come?"

She smiled as she licked his taste off her fingers. Salty, with just a hint of tart sweetness. It made her want more. "Maybe."

He rolled her over onto her back and spread her arms wide, latching onto her wrists with his hands. "I think I'd rather come while I'm fucking you. Plenty of time to play later."

She liked the sound of that. Of both ideas, actually. Fucking and playing. She wanted everything with Clay, wanted to know what it was like with him, wanted to know if she'd missed anything, if there were things he could teach her.

He climbed off the bed and returned a few seconds later with a condom. She lay there, curious, while he tore open the package and watched him roll the condom onto his cock, realizing she'd never seen a man apply one before. She and James had been each others' firsts, and she was using birth control, so they'd never used condoms.

This would be a new experience.

He kneeled between her legs and Ella raised her knees, expecting him to push inside her. Instead he dropped down and began to kiss her thighs.

"What are you doing?" she asked.

He pressed a soft kiss to her inner thigh, so close to her sex she felt his breath on her clit as he lifted his head to look up at her. "I want you ready, Ella. So close to coming you're ready to scream at me. Then I'll fuck you."

Heat rose and flared outward. She was already aroused, ready for him. How much more of this could she take?

The first lash of his tongue along the lips of her pussy brought her head up off the mattress, a soft moan escaping her lips. She didn't want to compare, didn't want to think about a man she had loved with all her heart. But James didn't go down on her, didn't really enjoy it all that much. And she hadn't pressured him to do it. She figured as long as the fucking was good, she didn't need oral sex.

Dear God in heaven, Clay had a masterful tongue. Hot, wet, licking around her clit, pressing his tongue against the sensitive nub, then sliding along her pussy lips and tucking his tongue inside her.

She might die. Could a woman die from getting oral sex? She felt these amazing sensations spiraling through her, and was shocked when her climax built so fast, especially after just having had one. She arched upward against Clay's mouth. . . . so close, so very close.

And then Clay latched onto her clit and sucked. Her orgasm hit her like a rushing freight train, barreling over her and leaving her out of control. She thrashed around on the bed, and Clay held her down by her hips while he licked her, sucking her while she came in a torrent. She unashamedly cried out her pleasure until her throat was raw and she fell back on the bed again.

Clay moved up, spread her legs and entered her while her body still pulsed with the aftereffects of her climax. He slid inside easily, her pussy gripping him in welcome. He slid one arm underneath her to tilt her hips upward and looked down at her with a smile.

Ella traced his lips—still wet from what he'd done for her. She wrapped her hand around the nape of his neck and pulled his mouth to hers for a kiss. He tasted salty—like her. She slid her tongue inside and sucked on his, the sensation overpowering to her senses. Emotion wrapped around arousal, taking her to a depth she hadn't expected.

It was so damn good to be fucked. She had no idea sex could be this good, this wild and out of control. With Clay, she felt uninhibited, as if she could actually feel his encouragement to let go. And she did, lifting her hips, widening her legs so he could power in deeper. And when he did, sliding along her G-spot, she groaned and bit his lower lip.

He only laughed in response and dug his fingers in her flesh, encouraging her to do it again.

"Give me more," she whispered against him, and he did, thrusting even harder, deeper than before.

This wasn't the sweet, gentle sex she'd grown used to with James. This was primal, wild fucking. Clay rose up and held on to her hips.

"Watch," he said, pulling partway out, forcing her to look where the two of them were connected, to see his cock slide inside her pussy.

She'd never seen anything more erotic than the look on his face as he watched them, as he watched her. She wasn't used to this intimate eye contact but found it incredibly arousing looking at him as he drove inside her, as he touched her breasts, plucked her nipples, raked his fingers along her body until he found her clit again.

They ended up partially on their sides, one of her knees bent so they could both see his cock fucking her.

"You have such a pretty pussy, Ella. Hot and wet. You make me want to come in you."

She loved that he talked to her, that he wasn't afraid to say what was on his mind, that he really seemed to enjoy fucking her. Every word he spoke, every time he looked at her, caused her to clench inside, to shiver all over. She'd never felt this connected before during sex. She felt as if the floodgates to her mind, her fantasies, were finally open and she could be, could say, anything. As a result, any inhibitions she'd had dissolved in the sea breeze.

She reached between them and began to rub her clit.

"Yeah," he said. "Touch yourself, Ella. Make yourself come again."

She wanted to. She needed it. With every thrust she drew closer and closer to the pinnacle. Clay increased his pace, powering faster now. She raised her gaze to his, strumming her clit harder as beads of sweat formed on his brow.

"Just like that," she said, struggling to breathe as she rubbed her clit, tensing as she felt the first stirrings of orgasm. "Don't stop. I'm coming, Clay."

His jaw clenched and he pumped harder inside her, then pulled her leg higher.

She splintered, climaxing with a wild cry that he absorbed with his mouth and his tongue. He groaned and shuddered against her, his fingers digging into the soft flesh of her thigh as he came, too.

That his climax was just as hard as hers meant something to her. He'd put his whole body into making love to her, had given her his full attention. And oh, had it been good.

They fell slow and easy. Clay drew her against him and stroked her hair. She ran her hands over his sweat-soaked flesh, waiting to feel . . . embarrassed or awkward.

She didn't. She moved, and their skin made squishy noises.

"We're kind of sweaty," he said.

She laughed. "Well, it was a workout."

"You complaining?"

"Not on your life."

"Come on." He dragged her from the bed to the shower—a shower big enough for more than just the two of them. The water sprayed from both ends of the shower, and it was like standing under a steamy waterfall. It was truly heaven. She decided she was never leaving this warm, misty haven, especially when Clay poured some liquid soap in his hands and washed her back. He took his time, using gentle pressure to massage her shoulders, and then skating lower to cup her buttocks.

"There are no condoms in this shower, mister," she teased, flinging him a scolding look over her shoulder.

"They're right outside, though," he whispered, nipping her lips with a kiss as he moved in closer. He slipped his hand between her legs and cupped her sex.

She thought she'd be tired, that she'd be done for, but his touch fired her up all over again. She turned around and twined her arms around his neck, lifting her face to him, to the warm spray of water.

And he kissed her, a long, arousing kiss, while his hand moved between her legs doing incredible things to her. He slid his fingers inside her, pumping her slow and easy, as if he had—they had—all the time in the world. The buildup was slow, but the end result was spectacular. She came against his hand in a hard climax that left her legs weak.

Clay stepped out of the shower for only a few seconds, returning with a condom applied to his erect cock. Ella was still pulsing, still needy for him. She spread her legs and used her hands to brace against the shower wall. He moved against her, lifted one of her legs and draped it over his hip, and bent down to slide his shaft inside her. He scooped her up by the buttocks and pushed her against the wall. And then there was no slow and easy, just fast, hard and furious as he fucked her with relentless strokes, grinding against her and bringing her close to orgasm again.

He latched onto her mouth with a desperate passion that she felt, too. And when she came, he did, too, holding tight to her and shuddering against her as he groaned his pleasure, licking at her lips and driving his tongue deep into her mouth. She took him, all of him, blinded by delights she had only fantasized about.

After, he let her down slow and easy and they rinsed; then Clay shut off the shower and grabbed towels for them both. She towel dried her hair but it was all she had energy for. He took her hand and led her to his bed. She tumbled into it and Clay followed, wrapped his big body around hers, his hand entwined with hers.

She fell asleep almost instantly.

Six

Clay woke to the feel of a warm body pressed up against him. He inhaled and Ella's scent surrounded him. He couldn't resist a smile.

Okay, this was unusual. He didn't usually spend the night with women he had sex with. Sex, yes. Snuggling and sleeping with them, no. That spelled emotion and entanglements and that just wasn't his thing. His thing was his job, and most women he dated knew he was fun and games and nothing more.

But Ella was different. This week was going to be different. He was surprised to find that he wasn't uncomfortable waking up next to Ella.

She shifted, wriggling her butt against his crotch, which not only woke him fully but definitely perked up his cock. It would be nice to slide inside her and really start the morning off well.

But for some reason he didn't want her to think this was all about sex. Though wasn't that what she wanted? Just sex?

It would be so easy to make it that. But for Ella, he wanted to do things differently. She deserved it. He slid out of bed. She burrowed under the covers and pulled the pillow over her head.

He showered, shaved and brushed his teeth. By the time he came out of the bathroom, she was sitting up in bed, her hair a tangled mess around her face. Her cheeks were pink as though she'd just woken up.

Damn, she looked cute.

"You should have nudged me."

He smiled. "I did. With my dick. You wiggled your ass against me."

She cocked a brow and cast her gaze down his body to where his lower half was covered with a towel. "Really. Was I not tantalizing enough?"

"Do you want to spend the entire day in bed as my love slave, or do you want to get out and explore the island?"

She continued to look at him.

"Well?"

"I'm still thinking about which option I like better."

He laughed and jerked the covers away. "Get out of bed. I'm hungry."

With a loud sigh, she said, "Fine. I'll be your love slave later." She pulled her dress on and grabbed her shoes. "Give me thirty minutes to shower and change."

"I'll pick you up at your condo."

While Ella was gone, Clay made a few phone calls back to the office. Tish assured him there was nothing pressing going on. He wrote down a few appointments he'd have to take care of when he got back. Other than that, everything seemed to be running smoothly. Nothing to worry about. He could focus his attention entirely on Ella.

He dressed and went to Ella's room, knocked on the door. She opened it and he sucked in a breath. She was wearing a short terry-cloth robe that barely covered the tops of her thighs. Her hair was piled up on top of her head.

She leaned against the door and frowned at him. "You didn't say what we were going to do today. What should I wear?"

He grinned. "I kind of like what you're wearing right now."

She rolled her eyes and made room for him to enter, then shut the door behind him. "Funny. Are those your swim trunks?"

"Yeah." He'd tossed on his board shorts, a sleeveless shirt and sandals. "I thought after breakfast we'd hit the beach."

"Sounds great. I'll be right back."

She came out a few minutes later wearing shorts and a tank top, the straps of what must have been her red swimsuit peeking out under the top. He liked being in Hawaii. It meant Ella bared a lot of skin, something he didn't see much of working with her on job-sites where she was usually covered neck to foot. Between last night's skimpy dress and today's outfit, he'd been treated to a lot of shoulder and legs. And oh, man, did she have great legs. Long and shapely. And he knew exactly how they'd gotten that way—hard work and not in a gym.

"What are you doing?"

She stood in the middle of the room, her bag flung over her shoulder, her head cocked to the side. One of the things he liked most about her was that she'd tossed her hair in a ponytail and she didn't have on makeup—or if she had put some on, it didn't show. So many of the women he dated were all about looking perfect. God forbid he should see them mussed up or without makeup or their hair perfect.

Ella didn't have to try. . . . Without makeup she was the girl next door, but still sexy. Not many women could pull that off. Maybe the lack of pretense was what he found so attractive about her—she never tried to be something she wasn't. Even last night's outfit—though killer sexy—was still all Ella. Simple, yet elegant.

And here he was waxing poetic about a woman he was only fucking.

"I'm just enjoying the view."

She actually looked past him and out her sliding-glass door to the balcony. "The ocean? Yes, it's breathtaking."

She had no idea. Another thing he found so appealing about her. "No, dork. I meant you."

"Me?" She looked down at herself, then back at him. "Nothing to look at here except a grumbling stomach. Let's go eat. If I don't get some coffee soon, you're going to have to carry me to the restaurant."

Ella wanted to eat at the coffee shop downstairs. Clay wanted to take her someplace special, somewhere she could enjoy the view and have a good breakfast. She'd balked, but he'd insisted, leading her instead out the front door, where his car was waiting.

"Where are we going?" she asked as the valet opened the door on the passenger side of Clay's rental car.

Clay slid into the driver's side and buckled his seat belt. "Not far."

"Good. You did hear me say I was starving, right?"

The drive was only a few miles up the coast, but the view would be worth it. The restaurant was set on a cliff. He parked and they walked the steep hill from the parking lot to the restaurant.

"Great. Making me burn what few calories I have left before you feed me."

He glanced down at Ella, who grinned up at him.

"If you faint before we get there, I'll carry you to the table."

She laughed and slipped her hand in his.

The restaurant was crowded, as he knew it would be. It was a popular spot, a lot for the great food and made even more so by the view. Floor-to-ceiling windows offered a spectacular show of the sea crashing against the rocks that made up the foundation for the restaurant, which seemed to balance precariously on the craggy cliff. If you sat at one of the front tables, which they did, it would almost seem as if you were hovering over the ocean.

"Wow," Ella said as she took her seat. "This is definitely worth waiting for."

"I thought you might like it here."

"Who wouldn't? The ocean, the breeze . . . It's breathtaking, Clay, especially to someone who's landlocked like me." She turned her gaze to him. "And you, too, of course. This is amazing."

"Yeah, I found this place on my last trip here and came back every morning for breakfast."

"I can see why. And I'm sure whoever you brought was very appreciative."

He laughed. "I didn't bring anyone with me, Ella."

She poured cream into the coffee the waitress had brought. "No? I would have thought Hawaii was a romantic destination, that you'd bring a woman."

"I come here to go fishing, not for romance."

She arched a brow. "Could have fooled me."

He laughed and leaned in, took her hand in his. "Well, not usually anyway."

"So I'm an exception."

"Definitely an exception."

"Then again, what we're doing together isn't really romance, is it?"

"What were doing together can't be labeled."

She slid her hand away and grabbed her cup, leaned back in the booth. "Sure, it can. It's just sex, right?"

"Yeah. Right. Just sex."

Why did it feel like more than that? He of all people knew that he wasn't capable of anything more than that with a woman, and especially someone like Ella, who was all about emotion and permanence and marriage. That wasn't where his life went. They'd agreed it would be sex with no strings. She seemed happy with the arrangement.

So what was irritating him?

After breakfast, they headed down to the beach, where Clay chartered a boat.

Ella stepped aboard, helped out by one of the crew. She turned to Clay. "How many others will there be?"

"Others?"

"Yes. Other people in this group excursion."

His lips lifted. "Oh. None. This trip is private. Just you, me and the crew. I thought we'd tour the island, maybe stop somewhere and snorkel."

"Really?"

He loved when she was excited and happy. Her eyes lit up like a child's. And she hadn't been pumped up about anything in a long time. He was happy to give this to her. "Yeah, really."

They sailed out of the port and onto the open sea, heading out at a leisurely pace. Clay led Ella to the front of the boat where there were cushioned seats waiting for them. The sun was out and warm, so he shed his shirt and kicked off his sandals.

"Oh, great idea," Ella said, and stood, pulled off her tank top and shucked her shorts.

Damn. Even though he'd had her naked last night, the sight of her in her bikini was enough to make his mouth water and his dick twitch. She had smooth skin, she was slender and well built, and she fit a bikini like a model. Yet she wasn't perfect. She bore scars here and there—minor injuries incurred from working construction alongside her crew. Her hands were calloused, her nails short and scraggly, and her feet looked as though they spent the day stuffed in work boots.

Maybe that was what he liked so much about her—she wasn't buffed, puffed and polished, didn't look as if she spent her days at the gym and the spa being pampered. She worked for a living, just like he did. She had a fundamental understanding of what his life was about, which was light-years away from any woman he'd ever dated. He could actually carry on a conversation with her—hell, he *wanted* to talk to her, which was rare with the women he was usually with.

She pinned him with a curious stare, her hands on her hips. The wind blew her hair across her face. "You taking inventory?"

He grinned. "Maybe."

"Well, stop it. It freaks me out. I know I'm not perfect." She slid into one of the cushioned chairs and propped her feet across the raised deck of the bow.

"I know. I was just thinking that."

She slid her sunglasses over her eyes. "Gee, thanks. You sure know how to compliment a woman. I'm amazed you get as many dates as you do."

"No, I was thinking that I can appreciate how imperfect you are, because I'm not perfect. These scars, for instance." He lifted her arm and traced his finger across the faint ridge on her forearm.

"Damn weld burn. Went right through my shirt."

"Yeah. I carry more than a few of those myself."

She leaned over and smoothed her fingers down his arm. "I recognize your battle scars."

He laid his hand over hers. "I like you touching me."

Her hand stilled. "I like touching you."

Their gazes caught and held.

"This is so . . . odd," she said.

"Yeah? Why?"

"I don't know. You, me, together. That part I'm used to. But this part?" She smoothed her hand across his arm again.

"Is that a problem?"

"Not really. I've just known you a long time. As a friend. A business associate. I'm not used to having free access to your body."

He pulled on her hand until she came over to his chair and sat on his lap.

"Get used to it. I want you to touch me."

She leaned against him, the curve of her breast so near his mouth he could have licked her. His cock rose at the thought. Instead, he buried his face in her neck and inhaled her scent. "You smell good."

Her breathing deepened. He ran his hand down her back, letting his fingers tease the material of her bikini bottom.

"You keep doing that and something scandalous is going to happen right here on this boat."

He kept doing it, letting his fingers dip just inside the material.

"Clay."

"Yeah."

"I'm pretty sure the captain and crew can see us."

"That's too bad because my dick is hard."

"Does this boat have a cabin?"

"As a matter of fact, it does."

She lifted, looked at him. "A private cabin? With a door lock?"

He laughed. "I don't think they're going to bust down the door,

Ella." He'd paid a hell of a lot of money for this private charter. And private meant just that—he expected time alone with Ella.

She slid off his lap and held out her hand. "Let's go."

He stood, hoping his erection wasn't too obvious. Not that he cared. They went downstairs, Ella leading the way. She found the door to the cabin, opened it, and Clay shut it behind them, making sure she heard him lock the door.

She was already kneeling on the bed facing him when he turned around. Her legs were spread, her fingers teasing along the front of her bikini bottom. His erection returned with a vengeance.

He came toward her and stopped just short of the bed. "What are you doing?"

"I got a little hot out there."

He palmed his cock through his board shorts, squeezing it as he watched her. "How hot?"

She seemed indecisive, chewing on her bottom lip. But then she asked, "Want me to show you?"

"Hell, yes."

Her fingers disappeared into her bikini bottom. Her eyes went glassy, her lips parted and she thrust her hips forward. Then all he could do was imagine what was going on as her hand moved.

He took a couple more steps toward her, stopping at the edge of the bed. Now he could smell her arousal, inhaling her sweet scent as her fingers did whatever the hell they were doing inside her bikini bottom.

"Tell me."

"I . . . can't."

"Yeah, you can." He untied his board shorts and let them fall to the floor, then took his cock in his hand and began to stroke it. "Look at me, Ella. Talk to me."

"Oh, God." Her gaze zeroed in on his cock. He almost lost it when she licked her lips, but he loosened his hold.

"Tell me what you're doing," he said. "Better yet, show me."

"Really?"

"Yes."

He got the idea she'd never played this game with James before. That this would be a first. And she was going to have it with him.

"Take your bikini off, Ella."

She shuddered out her next breath, reached behind and untied her top. It fell off, revealing her breasts. Her nipples were hard. He wanted to cup them, suck and lick them. It took every ounce of restraint he had to keep from going to her. But he wanted to watch. At least for the moment. Then he'd get in there and take action—later.

She moved to her hips and slid the bottoms down her thighs, stopping to look at him. He squeezed his cock, stroked it, the two of them locking gazes as Ella removed her bikini bottoms. She resumed her position on her knees, her sex visible as she widened her stance. It was probably the hottest thing he'd ever seen.

"That's good. Now I can see what you're doing."

"I've never done this before, Clay."

"It turns me on, Ella. Show me what you like. And I'll show you what I like."

He wanted her to be at ease, to let her know he didn't mind at all showing her what pleased him. He gripped his cock in a tight fist, holding the base and doing a slow glide with his hand to the tip before traveling back down again. Not fast, not too slow. Ella watched his hand, seemingly transfixed. And he got a hell of a jolt out of her looking at him.

"Now touch yourself for me."

She laid her palm flat against her lower belly, her fingertips resting just above her sex. She eased her hand down and cupped her pussy, let it rest there, her fingers lightly tapping.

Clay could tell from the look on her face that it felt good. Her eyes were half lidded, her lips parted, and her breasts rose as she breathed. And damn, watching her sure as hell felt good to his cock. He squeezed his shaft harder and pumped it once, twice—not too much—because watching Ella pleasure herself could make him go off.

She eased her hand, up, then down, caressing her pussy, her fingers teasing her lips, not quite dipping inside. And then her lips parted and a soft moan escaped them. It was enough to drop a man to his knees. She lifted her gaze to his, and he read the heat in her eyes. Heat and nervousness. He liked seeing that innocence on her face, enjoyed knowing she gave him something she hadn't yet given another man. Yeah, call him an arrogant Neanderthal, but he liked that this was just for the two of them—something special just for him. At least today.

Her hand movements quickened, her hips jutting forward. And then she tucked one finger inside her pussy.

"Oh, yeah." He stepped closer, and dropped down to his knees, putting himself at eye level to her sex. He needed to see up close, watch her finger drilling in and out of her hot sheath.

She was wet, the smell of her arousal soaking the air around him. He licked his lips and tilted his head back to look at her. Her face was dark with desire, her mouth open as she panted.

"Let me taste you."

She removed her finger and held it out for him. He grasped her wrist and brought her hand forward, wrapped his tongue around her finger and sucked it into his mouth.

Tart, tangy. Sexy, just like the woman who made him crazy.

She moaned when he sucked, and the pressure kicked higher inside him. But he could wait. He had patience. He wanted her to come first.

He pulled her finger out of his mouth and stood, leaning over the bed. "Lay down, babe."

She dropped to her back and he pulled her to the edge of the bed, then parted her legs. He took a moment to just look at her while she was naked. If someone had told him a week ago that he'd be naked in a room with Ella Hicks, he would have laughed at them, would have said that would never happen. He was glad he'd been wrong, because he couldn't think of anyone he wanted to be with more than her.

And maybe he always had, but he'd pushed the thought aside. She belonged to someone else, even if that someone else was dead.

It had always been hard for him to think of her as a woman—an available woman—because he'd always thought of James.

But for some reason, ever since he found her here in Hawaii, all those reservations had disappeared.

Because while they were here, she belonged only to him, even if it was just for a week. And he was going to enjoy having her for every minute he could.

And every which way he could.

He spread her legs and knelt, slipping his hands under her thighs so he could raise her hips. She lifted up on her elbows. Obviously she wanted to watch.

He spread kisses along the smooth skin of each inner thigh, then looked up at her and smiled, watching the tension spread across her face as he lowered his mouth to her sex.

Her skin was warm and bathed in her scent. He breathed her in and took a long, slow lick of the entire length of her pussy. She shuddered underneath him, a soft cry escaping her lips. He wanted to hear more of that and pressed his tongue against her clit. She lifted against him, moaned again, this time louder.

Oh, yeah.

She had a sweet pussy, her body so damn responsive it was all he could do not to plunge his cock inside her right now. But doing this to her—for her—was more important. He loved feeling her squirm underneath his hand, his mouth, taste her as she edged closer and closer with every lap of his tongue. He felt her tighten, knew what he needed to do. He swirled his tongue over her clit and slid one finger inside her.

"Clay. Oh, God. Yes." Her entire body vibrated when she came, her pussy squeezing his finger tight while she convulsed and thrashed against his mouth. And oh, he liked it. He liked it a lot seeing her let go like this.

He took her down easy, using slow licks and caresses, waited until her body stopped shaking before he stood, put on a condom and leaned over her.

Her eyes were glazed over and she wore a half smile that told him how much she'd enjoyed her orgasm. He'd always liked giving a woman pleasure. But making Ella come meant something more to him.

He didn't want to analyze it. It made his gut clench in a way that meant there was emotion involved in that thought. And that was dangerous territory.

Ella drew her knees up and planted her feet flat on the bed. "You going to fuck me or stare at me?"

His lips lifted. "Both, probably."

She frowned. "That freaks me out a little."

He laughed. "No, it doesn't. But if my looking at how beautiful you are when you come bothers you so much, how about we do this instead?"

He rolled her over onto her stomach and pulled her to the end of the bed, her legs dangling over the edge. That placed her ass right up against him, which made his cock dance in anticipation and his balls draw up tight.

She threw a glance over her shoulder and wiggled her butt. "Oh, I like this."

He held on to her hips, rocking against her. "Me, too. Sure you aren't going to worry I'm looking at you?"

She rolled her eyes and arched her back, rubbing her pussy against his dick. "Smartass. Are you going to fuck me or psycho-analyze me?"

This was what he liked about Ella—she was such a guy in so many ways, always throwing his sarcasm right back at him. But where it counted—the sweet softness of her—she was all woman.

He slid inside her. "Oh, I'm definitely gonna fuck you."

As he thrust to the hilt, she threw her head back, all that glorious dark hair spilling over her shoulders. He rolled his hips against her, rocking back and forth, giving her a little, then a lot, gauging the rhythm she liked.

He already knew what he liked—whatever made her moan again. And he found that the harder he powered against her, the more noises came from her—and they weren't noises of complaint.

"You want it harder?"

"Yes."

He pumped deep inside her, withdrew and thrust again. He pulled back and this time those beautiful brown locks resting against her back were too much of a lure. He wound his hand in her hair and used it to pull her head back while he drove deep. She let out a soft whimper, followed by a loud moan.

"I like that. Do it again," she said, her nails digging into the sheets.

"Which one? Pull your hair or shove my cock deep inside you?"

"Both."

Now it was his turn to groan, his cock demanding he roar to the finish line.

Not yet. Not nearly yet. Not when Ella's sweet ass bounced against him. He smoothed his free hand over her ass, keeping the other tight in her hair, and tugged while he thrust. She cried out and her pussy tightened around him.

"Clay, I'm going to come."

That was exactly what he needed to hear. He increased the pace, pumping hard and fast inside her, feeling her walls close in around him. His balls slapped her pussy with every thrust, sweat pouring off him as he powered to climax. And when she let go, when she cried out with her orgasm, he let go, too, his orgasm ripping through him like a free fall off a high cliff, taking everything he had and exploding outward, inside her, until he had nothing left, until he was shaking. He dropped on top of Ella's back, then rolled over on his side, taking her with him.

They breathed together for a while, rapid and spent at first; then both slowed to a regular rhythm. Ella put her hands over his and was doodling designs or something. He didn't know—didn't care. He just liked the feel of her touching him.

"I hope this boat has a shower," she finally said. "I'm all sweaty."

"Me, too. You make me work for it."

She giggled, then pulled away and sat up, flipping her hair out of her face. "Yeah, well, gotta get our workout in some way. We don't want to head back to work with potbellies, do we?"

She sauntered toward the bathroom. He admired her walk, waited a few minutes until he heard the shower running, then got up to join her, realizing how damned content he was with how things were going.

That content feeling surprised the hell out of him. He'd expected to like the sex. But he hadn't expected to love spending every moment with Ella. Then again, he didn't know why he was surprised. They spent a lot of time together on jobsites. Their companies often worked side by side on projects, so they invariably worked in tandem. There had always been camaraderie between them.

This, though—this was more than a camaraderie. It was a connection. And Clay felt it growing deeper.

He didn't do deep. He didn't do connections. And he'd promised Ella no strings.

So why in hell did he of all people suddenly feel as if he was tied to Ella? And why did he of all people think that wasn't such a bad thing?

Seven

"Grip it harder, Ella. That's it, babe. Oh, yeah. Just a little bit longer and you'll be there."

Ella braced her feet on the edge of the boat's stern and yanked hard, the muscles of her arms straining each time she pulled back to reel in the fish. It wasn't a marlin—the crew said it was a mahi mahi—but it would be her first big fish and she'd been excited as hell about this expedition. They'd set out before dawn this morning and had traveled to the deep part of the ocean where the best fish could be found.

Clay had caught a big one a few hours ago—a nice-sized blue marlin. Ella had been so excited watching him fight for that baby she knew she had to experience it herself. The pure power, the exhilaration of human against powerful fish—it was primal and fierce watching the two of them battle it out. And when he'd won and reeled it in, she'd seen the gleam in his eye, the pride . . . Oh, yeah, she wanted a taste of that, too.

She hadn't minded at all the hours of sitting there trolling along slow and easy with their lines in the water. It had given her time to sit and talk with Clay.

This was their last day in Hawaii, their last day together as lovers before reality—real life—set in again.

"Okay, looks like he's going to play dead in the water for a while." She looked to Clay. "What?"

"Your fish is resting. Go ahead and relax the tension in your arms. But don't let go of the rod just yet. He may decide to take off."

"Okay."

"So I just sit here. And do what exactly?"

"Well, it wouldn't be a good time to paint your toenails. Just chill. He'll come around in a few minutes."

She laughed. Talking with Clay was so easy, so natural. Not at all like talking to a stranger. They'd had conversations about work, about projects coming up and ones they were finishing. Though she hadn't broached anything personal with him. And maybe she should. After all, other than work stuff, she really didn't know all that much about his personal life.

"You've owned Mansfield Builders as long as I've been in the business," she started.

He tore his gaze away from the trolling lines and onto her. "Yeah?"

"Is that all you've ever done?"

He nodded. "Pretty much. I started out in construction as a punk when I was eighteen. My dad worked construction, said it was an honest living. It just seemed natural to do what he did. As soon as I got out of high school, I wanted to get down and dirty alongside him."

"He died young, though?"

"Yeah. When I was twenty-one."

She laid her hand on his arm. "I'm sorry."

Clay shrugged. "He'd been in the business a long time. Never wanted to move up the ranks or become a foreman. Never saw himself on the business side of things. Just liked the physical aspect of the job. It was hard on him."

"How old was he when he died?"

"Fifty-four."

"That's really young. What about your mom?"

"She died when I was sixteen. Cancer."

How had she not known these things? Because she'd been so wrapped up in her own life, and then her own grief, that she'd never bothered to find out—that was why. What kind of friend was she? "I'm sorry again."

He smiled at her. "It was a long time ago, Ella. I'm okay with it."

"You don't have any brothers or sisters?"

"No. Just me."

"So there you were at twenty-one with no family. That must have been hard."

His gaze drifted out to sea. "I managed. I had my job, my friends. I focused on those. Took college courses at night because the foreman told me I had a head for numbers and I should do something besides work my body to death like my dad had done. So I listened to him, and instead of partying my paychecks away, I went to school and got my degree. Eventually I moved up the ranks and ended up starting my own business."

"A self-made man."

He shifted his gaze back to her. "Something like that."

"I admire your drive and ambition. A lot of guys that age would have pissed away their future. You didn't."

"I didn't have a choice. I didn't want to end up like my dad."

Ella could only imagine how difficult it had been for him to lose so much at such a young age. Maybe that explained his inability to commit to any woman. Maybe he was afraid of losing someone he loved again.

She understood that way of thinking. The thought of loving someone that deeply again—and then losing them—was unfathomable.

The line tugged and she focused her attention back to the fish. So did Clay, who moved behind her.

"Give it a little line," he said, noticing she'd tensed up and was pulling against the straining fish. "You don't want it so tight that it breaks."

She unwound the reel to relax the line.

"Okay, now start reeling him in again, nice and easy this time. Bring him in closer. This is your game now."

Clay stepped back and let Ella and the crew do the rest. By the time they hauled the squirming fish on board, Ella's face was red, and she was dripping with sweat and utterly exhausted. But she grinned in triumph. She'd done it. The crew held it up and took her picture next to it. Not even half the size of Clay's marlin, but to Ella it was magnificent.

"She's a beauty," Clay said as Ella left the stern, wiping her hands and face with a towel.

"That was so much fun. And grueling. I can see why you love it."

He patted her shoulder. "You put some energy into it."

She laughed. "Yeah, my arms feel like limp noodles right now." She shook them out, needlelike tingles shooting down to her fingers.

"You're tough. You can handle it. I'll give you a massage later."

She tilted her head back to accept the kiss he offered. "I look forward to that."

After their first night together, they'd been inseparable. They'd gone snorkeling, sightseeing, bodysurfing and fishing over the past few days. And whenever they weren't doing something outside, they were inside making love with a furious intensity that left Ella exhausted and more than satisfied.

Being with Clay had been more than she'd expected out of this trip. Being with someone she knew, someone who knew her, who understood her and had no expectations about who she was—now, that was a bonus. On the work site, Clay laughed and joked with her, treated her just like another guy, which was what she expected. He treated her like a colleague, and she respected him because of that.

But this past week he'd treated her like a woman. There was a comfort level with Clay that she could never have experienced with a stranger. How foolish of her to expect that she could have come out here and chosen some random guy and had the same kind of experience she'd had this week with Clay.

It had been like a honeymoon—without the love and marriage. They'd laughed, talked, held hands, kissed, made love and talked some more. They knew each other better than any two people could. And what they didn't know they'd started to learn about each other in the past week.

It had been perfect.

Almost too perfect. Because she'd discovered she could care about a man again. That maybe love wasn't a once-in-a-lifetime thing.

Every moment she spent with Clay made her realize that the time with him had become about more than just sex.

Her no-strings week had become something more binding—at least to her. She didn't know what it had meant to Clay. Probably nothing at all. Just fun, no strings, exactly what he had promised her. Exactly what she had wanted.

At first.

After the boat docked they spent the rest of the late afternoon at the beach and the pool, just swimming and lying in the sun sipping drinks. It was relaxing and fun and, after her hard workout of marlin fishing, just what Ella needed. She even fell asleep under a shaded cabana with Clay massaging her aching shoulders. It wasn't until he pressed his lips against her neck that she woke.

"Sun's going down and you have goose bumps."

She'd been sleeping hard, hadn't even realized how tired she was.

They went upstairs—she had ended up staying the entire week in his suite—and Ella showered. She came out wrapped in a towel. Clay was on the balcony.

"What are we doing tonight?" she asked.

He turned to her, his gaze raking her body. God, she loved when he so unabashedly appreciated her like that and made no excuses for doing so. "What haven't we done already?"

She laughed. "I don't know. We've seen every inch of this island, been in the water and on top of it. We've fished, done a luau, gone to shows. . . . So, I guess we've done it all—except one thing."

"Yeah? What's that?"

"We haven't gone dancing."

He laughed. "I told you. I don't dance. I want you to leave this island with good memories of me."

Now it was her turn to laugh. "You can't be that bad."

"Really. I can."

"Okay. What would you like to do tonight?"

He stood and walked over to her, slid two fingers inside her towel between her breasts. "Maybe stay in. Order room service."

Her breasts swelled, her entire body flushed at his words and the images they conjured. Just the brush of his knuckles against the swell of her breasts was enough to fire up her arousal, make her want him. The thought of never touching him after tonight, never feeling his mouth on her again, made her fight tears.

Instead, she swallowed past the ache in her throat and managed a smile. "Staying in sounds like a really great idea."

He removed his fingers. "Let me go shower. Why don't you order us something to eat and drink?"

While he was in the shower, Ella slipped on a soft sundress. She pulled the room service menu out, scanning the dinner items, her stomach rumbling as she did. It had been a while since they'd had lunch. She hadn't realized how long they'd spent on the boat and then at the beach and pool today. The sun had already set and she was starving.

By the time Clay came out from the bathroom, she was ready to eat the sheets.

"I hope room service doesn't take long," she said, pacing the length of the room. "I'm already past hungry."

He pulled on a pair of shorts and dragged her onto the balcony. "You sure get cranky when you aren't fed regularly."

"We should have crackers in the room or something."

"There's food in the mini bar."

She cast a disgusted gaze into the room. "Please. Five bucks for a candy bar? I'll wait."

He dragged her onto his lap. "Quit bitching. Am I going to have to spank you?"

She laughed, then heated at the thought. "You wouldn't dare."

He cocked a brow. "There isn't a lot I wouldn't dare to do, Ella." He pulled her against him and rubbed her back, his fingers making a slow trek down to her rear end. "Besides, you have a great ass."

Her dress bunched up in the back and his fingers teased the globes of her buttocks. She shuddered against him. "If I wasn't starving . . ."

"Food can wait."

He bent to kiss her, her hunger taking a completely different turn.

But a knock came at the door.

"Shit," Clay said, smoothing her dress over her butt.

She giggled, her gaze traveling down over the obvious tent in his shorts. "Maybe I should get the door."

"Yeah." He went into the bathroom, shutting the door behind him.

Ella felt tons better after she'd eaten. They ate out on the balcony, because Ella couldn't seem to get enough of watching the ocean, listening to the sound of it and smelling the fresh, salty air. She was going to miss all this when she got back home to landlocked Oklahoma tomorrow, back to dirt and her crew and steel, where the only things she'd be inhaling were construction dust and the smell of the guys she worked with.

She inhaled and let out a sigh.

"What's wrong?"

She grabbed her glass of wine and leaned back in the chair. "I was just thinking how different this is from our world. Such a fantasy being here this past week."

Clay smiled, laid his napkin on the table and took a drink of wine. "So you had fun here."

"Definitely. I'm going to miss this. The blue of the ocean, the utter—forever of it. The smell of the flowers that seem to permeate the air wherever I go. The total relaxation. Yeah, I'm going to miss all of this."

And Clay. She was going to miss making love to him, feeling his body move against hers, inside her. She was going to miss the way he touched her, the way his lips slid over hers, the way her stomach tumbled whenever he looked at her.

"You can always come back. You're welcome to use my condo anytime you'd like."

But he wouldn't be in it. There was a difference. It wouldn't be the same. "Thanks. I really appreciate that."

"But you can't bring a guy."

She arched a brow. "I can't?"

"No. The thought of you fucking some random guy in my bed here just doesn't sit well with me."

She tried not to grin. "So there are conditions to me using your condo."

"Sorry. Yeah."

"I could lie."

"You could. But you won't. You don't know how to lie."

She finished her glass of wine and set it on the table. "Damn. I'm going to have to learn to be unscrupulous. Then I can have hot monkey sex in this fabulous condo anytime I can get away."

He stood and came over to her, pulled her out of the chair and dragged her against him. "Anytime you want hot monkey sex in this condo, just give me a call. I'll meet you."

Her skin prickled with chills at the same time her insides melted with heat. "Is that a firm offer? Can I get it in writing?"

"Firm offer, yes. In writing, no. But my word's good."

Okay, so he hadn't actually offered his undying love, but what had she expected? They were friends. They worked together. Not even together, really. They were competitors in business. And they'd just spent a week fucking each other like crazy. That he might want to do it again sometime was . . . nice.

Nice? Hell, it was more than nice. It was more than she expected. She knew Clay's lifestyle. He was a compulsive serial dater, and he never did repeats.

She laid her palm against his chest, somehow comforted by the steady beat of his heart. "Wow. You want to see me again. This is . . . unexpected. So rare for you."

He narrowed his gaze at her. "Are you insulting me?"

"Not intentionally. You just never see women . . . repeatedly."

"True enough. You aren't most women I know. We see each other a lot. You're an exception."

He revealed nothing in that statement. How typical for Clay. She patted his chest, trying to keep things light. "I'll keep you in mind whenever I need to scratch the itch again."

His hands slid down her back, his fingertips tantalizing her but rubbing ever so seductively above her butt. "We don't have to come back to Hawaii to have sex with each other, Ella."

She stilled. "You mean . . . back in Tulsa? You and me . . . together?"

He laughed. "You should see the look of horror on your face. It's like I just suggested we go on a murder rampage together."

She pushed away from him. "That's not what I meant." She moved to the railing, looked to the sea for its calming influence. She wished she could tell him how she felt. The problem was, she didn't know how she felt. Her feelings were mixed up inside. She needed time to sort them through before she blurted out something she might regret later.

He joined her. "I know what you meant. Sorry. I know you wanted this week to have no strings, and here I am trying to tie you up by suggesting we continue to meet once we get home. When we get back we'll pretend nothing happened between us. It'll be business as usual, just the way you wanted it."

Right. Just the way she wanted it.

Only now she wasn't sure it was what she really wanted. And the last person she could say that to was Clay.

She turned to him. "Yes, that's what I wanted."

His lips lifted and he smoothed his hand over her cheek. "So let's make tonight good."

He leaned in and brushed his lips across hers with a kiss so achingly tender she had to squeeze her eyes tight to push back the sting of tears. She shuddered as he pulled her close, wrapped his arms around her and deepened the kiss.

She would miss him. There was more to what she felt than just sex. She was afraid she was falling in love with Clay.

And she couldn't . . . wouldn't tell him that.

He'd trusted her to keep things physical between them. She wouldn't ruin this last night together by spilling out emotions when she knew damn well he wasn't interested in any of that. He was a man who enjoyed women, but didn't want any strings tying them together.

She let it all go, losing herself in his kiss, in the way he moved his hands over her body. He'd learned her body so well in the past week—where to touch her to elicit the moans she couldn't contain. He knew exactly what buttons to push and he was a damn expert at making her weak-kneed in mere minutes. The slow torture of his mouth doing sinful things to hers, his tongue sliding its velvety softness across hers, made her whimper. He moved his hands along her back, down and then up, until he tangled one hand in her hair and held on, the other continuing its slow exploration along the fabric of her dress. Her nipples tightened and pressed against his bare chest.

He pulled away, long enough for her to catch her breath and tilt her head back to gaze into his eyes—eyes that mirrored the mystery of the ocean.

He was panting, too, his full lips parted as he looked down at her, his expression so intense he almost looked as if he were angry.

But she knew those expressions now. It wasn't anger. It was pure desire.

He walked her backward several steps until her back hit the wall of the balcony.

"Raise your arms over your head."

She did, and he smoothed his hands down her arms, so damn slowly she thought she'd die in agony. The silk abraded her nipples. Her pussy was wet, her clit tingling with need. She'd worn nothing under her dress, her intent to seduce, to tease.

But now who was the one teasing? It wasn't her.

Clay used his palms to trace her body, continuing his slow assault with his hands over her shoulders, across her collarbone, then down her side, lingering when he reached her breasts. He took a few seconds to trace his thumbs over her nipples. Her breath caught and she watched, waited for him to tweak them, pull them, but he didn't, instead caressing her waist and hips, before his gaze snapped back to her face.

She swallowed, the action fruitless. Her throat had gone dry.

He grasped the material of her dress at her hips, then began to lift.

They were outside on the balcony, but it was dark. No one could see them. But the fact that Clay was baring her lower body wasn't lost on her. It was scandalous. Thrilling.

"Part your legs for me, Ella."

Her legs shook as she widened them. She braced her hands on the wall for support, found she needed it when Clay slid his hand between her thighs and cupped her sex. He palmed the wall with his other hand and kept his gaze trained on her face.

"You're wet. You want me?"

She found it hard to breathe, but managed to form words. "I think you know I do."

"I don't know," he said, sliding his hand across her sensitive flesh. "You're a mystery to me. You have to tell me what you want."

She gasped as his touch liquefied her. He slid two fingers inside her and continued his assault on her senses. "Yes. That's what I want."

He stilled. "What? Tell me."

She wanted to slide down on his fingers, to grasp more of that sweet pleasure. "Your fingers. Inside me."

The teasing smile he gave her wrecked her. "My fingers are already inside you, Ella. What do you want me to do with them?"

"Fuck me. Fuck me with them."

He did, sliding them out, then back in again. And when he swirled his thumb over her clit, she banged her head against the stone wall behind her, oblivious to anything but the sweet pleasure he gave her. And through it all, Clay watched her, kept his gaze trained on her face, while his hands performed magic.

She felt her walls tightening around his fingers as with every thrust she grew closer to orgasm. He swiveled his thumb back and forth in a steady rhythm over the tight nub of her clit, and she cried out, not caring who heard her. Her climax was swift, thunderous, and Clay covered her mouth with a deep, amazing kiss as he took her from the throes of a mighty orgasm to a languorous place where her bones felt soft and pliant, just like the way his mouth moved over her.

She was shaking, from her legs to her torso and arms. Clay continued to kiss her as he stepped in front of her, pushed down his shorts, and suddenly she heard the tearing of a condom wrapper and felt herself being lifted.

Her back scraped the wall as he thrust inside her. She didn't care, because all she knew was the feeling of being filled by his cock. His fingers dug into the soft flesh of her buttocks as he held her while he rammed into her, hard. She held on to his shoulders and rocked against him, wanting to give him exactly what he gave her.

"Yes," she said, twining her fingers up into the soft darkness of his hair. "Again."

He thrust again, and she knew she'd be bruised from this. She didn't care. She wanted marks on her, wanted to remember everything from tonight, from this last time with the man she . . .

With Clay.

And as he pumped inside her, she used her fingertips to trace the lines on his face, the fullness of his lips, to memorize everything about him, because this would be the last time she'd be this close to him.

Again he drove, deeper this time, becoming part of her. He was already part of her, would always be part of her.

Again, he thrust against her, rolling his hips this time, grinding against her clit. Her lips parted and she tightened, felt her orgasm from deep within.

"Yes," he said, his face taking on that angry quality she loved so much, the expression that said he was close to the edge.

"Come inside me," she whispered, then pulled at his hair when she came, called out his name when her orgasm hit her full force. He went with her, and this time he was as loud as she was, groaning as he pumped repeatedly against her until he shuddered, let her legs down and rested against her.

This had been the last time.

She felt his heart pounding against hers and lifted her palm to rest it against his chest.

She never thought she could love anyone again, that James had been it for her.

She'd been so wrong. She loved Clay, loved going to sleep with him at night, loved waking up with him next to her in the morning. She loved working side by side with him, arguing with him, laughing with him. She loved everything about him. He was as different from James as any man could be. James had been quiet and sweet and passive. Clay was demonstrative and brusque and such a typical alpha male, but there was something about him that she craved, that she needed.

She didn't want to let him go.

But she knew she had to.

This had been fantasy, and what they had would never work in the real world.

Eight

Being back at work was both a blessing and a curse. Ella had thrown herself into the business, which had picked up like crazy while she'd been gone. She'd spent the first few days buried in paperwork that needed addressing. By the time she'd caught up with that, she'd headed out to a few of the jobsites to catch up on the status of some of the ongoing projects, including a new startup.

Plenty to do and enough work to occupy her mind and body. She was putting in twelve-hour days, seven days a week, coming home exhausted every night, her mind and body numb. She'd strip out of her clothes, step into the shower, grab something to eat and either read a book or veg in front of the television until she crawled into bed and passed out.

Which meant she had no time to think about Clay. Or almost no time, because despite filling her days and nights, he still crept into her thoughts.

She hadn't seen him in the two weeks she'd been back. At the airport in Hawaii, she'd told him to pretend this had never happened, that he should treat her as if they'd never spent this week together.

Something odd had crossed his face. Regret, maybe? But then he'd flashed a grin at her, kissed her hard and told her if she ever wanted a repeat performance in Hawaii, he was all up for playing stud. She laughed and turned away, hurried down the gangplank so he wouldn't see the tears coating her eyes. She decided she'd seen in his eyes only what she wanted to see. He'd thought of that week in Hawaii as fun and sex and nothing more than that. And that was what she was going to think about it. Fun. Sex.

Over and done with. She was not in love with him. Her heart was not aching for him. Her body was not missing his touch.

"Woman. You avoiding me?"

Ella's head snapped up at the voice. Tish stood in her doorway, frowning at her.

Ella smiled. "Of course not. I've been buried since I got back."

Tish came in, tossed her purse on the floor and flounced into the cushioned chair in front of Ella's desk. "Okay, spill. I want to hear all about it."

Tish was the last person she was going to tell. She leaned back in her chair, thankful it was after working hours and no one else was around. "It was . . . good."

"Uh-huh. That's not exactly the level of detail I was looking for."

Ella launched into all the activities she'd done on the island.

"I don't care about shopping or snorkeling, girl. I want to hear about you and Clay."

She winced. "So you know about that."

"Who the hell do you think put you two together? Come on."

She wanted to ask Tish how he was, if he'd asked about her at all. So high school. She wasn't going to go there. She'd been the one to tell Clay to keep his distance, to keep things between them professional only.

"Well? I'm waiting."

But Tish was her friend. She had to talk to someone. "It was unlike anything I thought it would be, Tish."

Tish grinned so wide Ella was sure her cheeks would explode. "I knew it. I knew you two belonged together."

"We're not together."

Tish's smile faded. "Why the hell aren't you?"

"Because what happened between us in Hawaii can't work here."

"Again, why the hell not?"

Ella rubbed that spot in between her eyebrows where a headache was forming. "It's complicated."

"I've got time. Explain it to me."

"I don't have time. I'm really busy, Tish. Let's get together for a drink soon, okay?"

"You're putting me off because you don't have a valid reason why you and Clay can't be together."

"Yes, I do have a valid reason. Plenty of them, the least of which is he's not interested in having a relationship."

"He told you this."

"Not exactly."

"Did you tell him you're in love with him?"

Her gaze snapped to Tish's. "Of course not."

"But you are in love with him, aren't you?"

She was seconds away from denying it, but realized Tish would browbeat her mercilessly until she confessed. She sank back in her chair. "Yes. I love him."

Tish leaned forward. "Then what's the problem, honey? Tell him."

"I can't."

"Why not?"

"You know why. He doesn't want attachments in his life. Besides, I swore I'd never get involved with anyone in this industry again. Next time I fall in love it's going to be with a nice . . . accountant or something."

Tish studied her with a critical gaze.

"What?"

"You're afraid."

"I am not."

"Yes, you are. You're afraid if you fall in love again, the man you love is going to drop dead like James did."

Ella struggled to speak past the pain and fury that boiled inside her. "That's harsh."

Tish lifted her chin. "I know. And it's the damn truth. You're scared to death that you love Clay. Someone who could die on you, just like James did."

"I am not. I just know it would never work. He isn't interested."

"How do you know unless you tell him? I think you're giving bullshit excuses to ignore your fear."

Ella stood, paced the room, finally settling on looking out her window at the parking lot. "I'm not afraid. I'm strong, Tish. I withstood a lot with James's death."

"And you don't want to go through it again, so you're tossing all this on Clay, when in reality it's you who's the problem."

She kept her gaze trained on the window. "I thought you were my friend."

She heard the crackle of the leather cushion, then felt Tish behind her, her arms encircling her. "I am your friend. I love you. I went through that pain with you and never want to see you go through it again. And remember . . . I've been there, too."

Ella nodded. "I know." She wanted to say that Tish's situation was different, that her husband's cancer had been slow and debilitating. But had it really been different? They'd both lost men they loved. She was so confused.

"Ella. You can't stop living just because you lost someone. It took me a long time to get past John's death. But I did. And I'm dating again. I haven't fallen in love yet, but I'm allowing myself the opportunity to. And I know it'll happen someday when the right man comes along. You have to open your heart and let it happen for you, too."

Tears welled and she forced them back, refusing to dwell on the past, or the possible future that was riddled with terror. "You know what Clay does for a living, Tish."

"Yeah. The same thing that James did. But the construction business didn't kill your husband, Ella. An aneurysm did."

She shook her head. "I can't lose another man I love. Not again. I wouldn't survive it."

Tish squeezed her shoulders. "We're all going to lose the ones we love, Ella. You and I know that more than most people do. We just got a head start on most people. And it made us stronger. We're light-years ahead of the rest of them."

That actually made her laugh. "Yeah, I'm strong, all right. I've spent the past five years proving how goddamn strong I am."

"You're strong enough to try this again. Because you don't want to spend the rest of your life alone, without love. Without being loved."

Tears rolled down her face, the anguish tearing her up inside. Was this what she wanted for the rest of her life? To feel alone and afraid? She turned to face her best friend. "You're a real bitch, you know."

Tish's lips quirked. "Not the first time I've heard that. But you know I'm never gonna sugarcoat it for you. You love him. And I know he loves you."

Ella swiped her cheeks. "You think he loves me?"

"He's been cranky as a bear since he got back. And usually he dives right into work, happy as can be to be back there after he's been gone. Not this time."

"Have you—?"

"Asked him about you? No. I'm not poking the bear just yet. But I will."

"Oh, I don't know, Tish. I don't know about any of this. Clay just isn't the type to want to settle down with one woman."

"He wasn't the type before. My guess is he's changed his mind about that. But you'll never know unless you try."

Trying scared the shit out of her. She didn't know if she even wanted to try, because Tish was right. The thought of loving and losing someone again terrified her.

"I'll think about it."

Tish nodded and went to pick up her purse. "You do that. Oh, and the reason I came here?"

"Yeah?"

"The annual Trades charity ball is Saturday. I'm supposed to remind all the contractors about it."

She grimaced. "Do I have to go?"

"Yes. You have to go. I have to go. We all have to go. Suck it up."

"I don't have a ball gown." She hadn't been to the ball since James died. It was . . . too festive. The contractors all brought their wives or dates. It was a huge deal since it was their annual charity fund-raiser. Ella usually sent a check instead.

"No excuses. We'll go shopping because this year you're going. It'll be good for you to get out."

She sighed. "All right. Shopping? I have to go shopping?"

"Yes."

Once Tish set her mind to something, there was no getting around it. "Fine. I'll need drinks first."

"You got it. We'll go tomorrow."

After Tish left, Ella stared down at the files on her desk. Paperwork could wait until tomorrow. She needed some air. She went outside and headed toward her truck, rolled the windows down when she got in, grateful for the constantly changing Oklahoma weather that had brought a springlike day in the middle of winter. Maybe the fresh air would clear her mind and blow away thoughts of Clay.

She loved this city. Big enough for progress, for constant changing and reshaping, which meant her business thrived. Small enough for suburbs and getting from one end of town to the other in a hurry. Tulsa had growing industry and the feel of a major city without any of the congestion or drawbacks. Yet there were enough surrounding small towns that you could feel as if you really were in Middle America and get away from it all. That was what she and James had wanted, why they'd bought a house outside Tulsa. Ella had wanted the escape, had loved the small-town feeling of their little place in the suburbs with its quiet street where children played without worrying about cars zooming by.

She and James had talked about having kids, but the time had never seemed right. She had jumped into the construction business with both hands and had loved it, and the whole having-kids thing had fallen by the wayside. Someday, they kept saying. They had plenty of time. And someday never happened.

She was glad they hadn't had children. She'd been devastated when James died, couldn't imagine trying to cope and handle grieving children at the same time. She'd had to grow up herself at the age of twenty-five, had to learn to manage a business and take care of herself.

Now, five years later, she was a different person than she'd been then. When James had died her entire world had fallen apart. She had never lived alone, had never had to stand on her own. But she'd managed it, and she'd grown the company. She had the respect of every man and woman at Hicks Construction. She loved her job. It had filled her nights and days. Mostly.

And she'd managed to fall in love again, despite thinking she never would.

So maybe she didn't end up with Clay in her life. And maybe that did hurt a little. Okay, a lot. But she'd set the ground rules for their time in Hawaii. And she'd chosen the man—a man she knew didn't want strings attached to their time together.

But at least she knew now that she could love again. And she would fall in love.

Someday.

But despite Tish's insistence, it wasn't going to be with Clay.

Clay walked out of his office, surprised to find Tish still at her desk. Kind of unusual for a Friday afternoon. Usually she was gone at five o'clock sharp, ready for her weekend. He couldn't blame her.

"Workday's over. Shouldn't you be gone by now?"

Tish looked up from her computer. "Thought I'd hang out for a few minutes."

Uh-oh. That usually meant she had something to say and she didn't want to say it with the other staff around. He leaned against the desk opposite hers and folded his arms. "Okay, what's on your mind?"

"Ella."

Just the mention of her name was a gut punch. He hadn't been able to stop thinking about her since Hawaii. Oh, sure, he intended to honor her wishes, but it was damn hard not to call her, to drive over to her house, to tell her how he really felt . . . what he really wanted.

"What about her?"

"She's in love with you."

He frowned. "No, she's not." If she was in love with him, she'd have called him in the weeks since they'd been back from Hawaii. She'd have expressed some interest in getting together. She'd made things clear in Hawaii. Sex only. Onetime thing. Done and over.

"You know, for someone who's had a ton of experience with women, you are completely blind."

He pivoted and headed back to his office. "Stay out of my personal life, Tish."

He started to shut his door. Tish stopped him. "She loves you."

He whipped around to face her. "She told you this."

Tish opened her mouth, closed it, then finally said, "Why don't you ask her yourself?"

"So this is just something you've conjured up on your own. I've been on the receiving end of your misguided matchmaking skills before, Tish."

"This isn't matchmaking. The match has already been made. You two pigheaded idiots just need to open your eyes and figure out you love each other."

"Uh-huh. And you believe in fairy tales."

She smirked. "As a matter of fact, I do."

"Good night, Tish."

She shook her head. "Don't forget about the charity ball tomorrow night."

"I'm not going."

"I already rented a tux for you. It's hanging near the door. You *are* going. Key building and political contacts you need to talk to are going to be there, and like it or not, you're going."

"Shit."

"Yeah, that's what I thought," Tish said with a laugh. "See you tomorrow night."

Clay sat at his desk and looked outside at the growing darkness. The weather had been unseasonably warm for early March. Maybe spring would come early, which was a good thing. Clear, nice weather meant more construction days in the year. He'd have to map that out on his calendar, maybe bid on a few extra projects.

Yeah, right, as if he had even been thinking about work since he'd gotten back from Hawaii. All he'd thought about was Ella. How she was, what she was doing. Oh, he kept in touch work-wise through the guys, knew what jobs her crew were working on. He'd even thought about stopping by, but figured she'd be uncomfortable.

Hell, he was uncomfortable. Which really sucked because he'd never thought twice about dropping in on her before they'd had their week together in Hawaii.

But before, they'd been friends and business associates.

Now they were . . . what? What exactly were they now?

Nothing. They were exactly what they'd been before, because that was what Ella wanted. She'd gotten the sex she'd needed, and she wasn't interested in having a relationship, in falling in love, in having what she'd had with James.

Trouble was, his entire focus had changed since that week in Hawaii. And he didn't know what the hell to do about it. He'd seen what could happen when you loved someone. Love, loss. Losing his mom had hurt. It had devastated his father. And him.

Love sucked. Look what it had done to Ella. Losing James had damn near destroyed her. She'd loved James with her whole heart. And he'd sure as hell loved her. They'd been faithful to each other. James had talked about Ella as his partner, his friend. Clay hadn't understood that kind of love, to be able to feel something that deep for another person.

He did now. He wanted it now. He wanted it with Ella.

But Ella had already found the love of her life. Clay would never be able to compete with that. And he wasn't about to settle for second best.

Which left him right back where he started.

"Ah, hell," he muttered to himself, picking up the papers on his desk and setting back to work. He should have known better than to dwell on Ella. It led only to problems that had no solutions.

Nine

"Holy hell and a biscuit," Tish said.

Ella looked up. "It's okay?"

"Woman, if I wasn't straight, I'd be all over you."

Ella burst out laughing. "Thanks, I think." She moved to the mirror in her bedroom, palmed her stomach, and lifted her gaze. *Whoa.* "I can't believe you made me buy this dress. I can't breathe."

"Of course you can't breathe. It's a corset. And you'll need me to get you out of it at the end of the night, too."

Ella wasn't one to dress up, another reason she hated the annual ball. But admittedly, she felt like a princess tonight. A lot of that had to do with this dress. All black and satiny, and it hugged her body in ways Ella had never imagined. The strapless corset top was so snug her breasts nearly spilled out and over the top of the bodice. The back was laced tight—but not too tight—and it drew in at the waist, flowed over her hips, and the skirt fell in soft waves to the floor. As she moved back and forth, Ella caught sight of the high heels Tish had insisted she buy.

"I wear work boots for a living. I'll never be able to walk in these things."

"Please," Tish said, rolling her eyes. "You're a woman. Fake it for one night."

She laid her hands on her hips. "I'll try. And may I say you look ravishing?"

Tish beamed and twirled around in her red ball gown, the color enhancing her dark skin and mocha eyes. "Thanks. I'm glad you spotted this dress. It's so me."

"It's definitely you. Men will drool on you all night."

Tish laughed. "No, honey. Tonight is all about you."

They rode together to the ball, an event hosted in the ballroom of Tulsa's swankiest and most expensive hotel. Despite her initial misgivings, Ella found herself excited to attend tonight, if for no other reason than to get her mind off Clay. She knew Clay wouldn't be there. It was a dining and dancing night and she knew he didn't dance. Nor did he ever attend this ball. Like her, he always sent a nice fat contribution and skipped the festivities.

She intended to drink some wine, schmooze some politicians and bigwigs in the industry. Maybe a few people would take pity and dance with her. She'd have fun.

And not think about men or love or fear or complications.

The ballroom was packed when they got there. Tish disappeared almost immediately, having spotted some friends and rushing off to greet them.

Traitor.

Ella grabbed a glass of champagne from a passing waiter and decided to wander the room, see who she knew, then figure out where they were seated, since there seemed to be place cards with everyone's names on them. She greeted a few of her fellow contractors and their wives, people she'd known for years. Some she hadn't seen in a while—not since James had died. So of course she had to stop and answer the obligatory "How are you doing?" questions. She understood people cared, that they hadn't seen her in a long time and wanted to know how she was getting on with her life and her work. Maybe she should stop hiding out so much and attend more social functions in the future. Then she could go back to being thought of as a normal person instead of James's widow.

The ballroom was a glittering mass of tuxes and beautiful gowns. Ella could find a chair and spend the entire evening gawking at the fashion. And the jewelry . . . Dear God, some of these women definitely had money. Or their husbands did. She felt out of her element adorned only in her mother's pearl earrings, but Tish had told her the dress spoke for itself, that Ella was beautiful and she needed nothing else. Tish had insisted they get their hair done for the occasion, so she sported some kind of updo with a few tendrils swept against her face. So not her, but whatever. She supposed it was okay to play dress up every now and then. She still felt like a sham when she saw the glittering diamonds and expensive furs and even the china laid out on the starched linen tables. Wow.

But she really loved the dress and the fancy shoes, so she decided she was going to enjoy herself tonight and not care what anyone thought. Besides, she was being hypercritical. No one had batted an eyelash the wrong way at her.

It sure would have been a lot easier to send a check, though. She could be home in her pajamas right now watching television and eating something cooked in the microwave, which would be much more comfortable than this lung-squeezing dress.

And where the hell was Tish?

She wound her way through the crowd, examining each table for her name, not yet finding it. She spotted a familiar group, some of the contractors she worked with regularly. Maybe she would be sitting with them. As she approached, the crowd thinned and she caught sight of a tall, dark-haired man with broad shoulders who looked very familiar from behind.

But it couldn't be. He wouldn't come to this. Would he?

He turned, and her breath caught.

Clay. Clay in a tux. Clay looking drop-dead gorgeous in black and white. Her legs began to shake and she didn't think she could take another step. She reached for the chairback next to her and held on for support.

She hadn't expected this, wasn't ready to see him yet. Ever.

What was he doing here? And how dared he look so damn good?

He walked—no, stalked toward her.

"Ella. What are you doing here?"

He looked angry to see her. Why would he be angry? She should be angry.

"I was about to ask you the same question. Why are you here?"

He scanned the room. "There are people here I need to see."

"Same people I need to see, I imagine. That's why I'm here. And Tish made me come."

He narrowed his gaze as he searched the room. "Uh-huh. Where is Tish?"

"No clue. She dumped me as soon as we got here."

"How convenient." He returned his gaze to her, scanning her from toe to head as he had done in Hawaii. She flushed, the cool room suddenly growing warmer. "You look . . . beautiful."

"Thank you. You look pretty hot in that tux."

His lips lifted. "Thanks. It's uncomfortable as hell."

"So is this dress."

"It looks like someone sewed you into it. Turn around."

She did. She didn't know why, but she did.

"Christ. Is that a . . . corset?"

"Yes."

"Fuck me," he said in a harsh whisper.

She'd love to. Dammit, no, she wouldn't. They were over. There was nothing between them.

Oh, right. Sure they were. So why had the entire room and her body gone up in flames the second she laid eyes on him?

Chemistry. Physical attraction. She refused to deny that portion of it any longer. Why should she? She'd had ample evidence of it in Hawaii. But that was all it was. It wasn't love. She wouldn't love him.

Couldn't.

"Well, we're here. Together," he finally said.

"Yes."

"How have you been since we got back?"

"Busy."

"Ditto. You bidding on the downtown parking garage?"

"Yes."

"We will, too. I also heard there's going to be a new hotel going up on Seventh Street."

"I heard about that, too. Haven't seen any specs yet."

She hated that they'd been reduced to one-liners about business, that the ease they'd shared with each other that week had dissolved into basic business discussions.

That had been her wish, hadn't it? That they keep things business only?

But this was different. Before, they had been comfortable with each other.

They were seated at the same table together. Tish—the traitor—finally made her appearance and gave her a knowing smile throughout dinner. Ella felt trapped between Clay and Tish. She was mad at Tish, felt set up, and had nothing to say to Clay, who seemed content to spend his time talking to one of the city councilmen seated at their table. When dinner was over, she nearly leaped from her chair.

"Where are you going?" Tish asked.

The entire table looked at her.

She had no idea where she was going.

"Ladies' room," she finally managed, making a beeline out of the ballroom.

She washed her hands and took the opportunity to stare at her reflection in the opulent oversized mirror in the seating area of the restroom. Her face was flushed, pink circles dotting her cheeks. Her entire body was hot. Maybe she was coming down with something.

Yeah . . . a case of Clay. Of having to sit next to him and not touch him, not kiss him, not laugh with him, not be able to enjoy the easy conversation they'd always had with each other.

Dammit, she missed him. She wanted him back. And she wasn't going to be able to have him.

She sat on one of the chairs and stared at herself in the mirror.

Why couldn't she have him? Why did she have to be so afraid? Everyone died. Not everyone died young. Clay was strong, healthy.

She thought James had been healthy, too.

She laid her head in her hands, fighting back the ache, the memories, the fear.

"Honey, you can't spend the night in here hiding."

Her head snapped up. Tish.

"I'm not hiding."

"Yes, you are. And you have to stop." Tish crouched down and laid her hand over Ella's. "James is gone. You're still here. You have to start living again."

"I have been. I've built our company up. I've gotten up every day and worked day and night. I haven't laid around and felt sorry for myself once."

"I know. But that's work. That's distraction. That's not living. You have a chance to love someone and you're putting up any barrier you can to keep it from happening."

She started to argue, wanted to put the blame on Clay, but she knew it would be a lie. "You're right."

"So what are you going to do about it?"

Just the thought of going out there and facing him, of telling him how she felt, made her stomach clench, made her feel sick. But she had to try. "I don't really know, Tish. I guess not hiding in the bathroom would be a good start."

The tables were cleared and the room darkened by the time she had fixed her lipstick and made her way back to the ballroom. The band was playing and couples twirled together out on the sizeable dance floor. She wound her way around people milling about. Her table was empty. Everyone must be involved in conversation or dancing. She laid her bag on the table and stared out at the couples on the floor, the overhead lights shining down on them.

"Dance with me."

She pivoted and arched her brow at Clay.

"You don't dance."

"I do now." He held out his hand.

This she had to see. She slipped her hand in his and he led her to the floor. Something slow was playing, a romantic song that filled her heart with longing, especially when Clay pulled her close, laid his palm against her back and started moving her to the strains of the music.

It didn't take her long to realize he'd lied to her.

"You can dance."

He shrugged. "Maybe a little."

"You lied."

"It's not my favorite thing to do. So I just say that I can't."

"And you're making the ultimate sacrifice for me because . . . ?"

"Because I want to hold you. Because I miss you."

Her stomach clenched. "You can have sex with anybody, Clay."

"I don't want to have sex with anyone else anymore, Ella. I want to have sex with you. Just you. Only you. Forever and ever. For as long as we both shall live."

Her heart stuttered. "What?"

"I love you."

She stumbled a step and Clay's firm grip held her upright. She knew she gaped at him, at a loss for words.

"I know this isn't what you want, that you wanted no strings, someone to give you a good time in Hawaii and nothing else. I'm sorry, but I can't do that. I'm wound around you tight, just like this thing you're wearing." He tugged on the strings of her corset. "I want strings, Ella. I want to be tied to you."

Now she really couldn't breathe. "Take me out of here."

He gave a sharp nod, swept by the table so she could grab her purse, and led her out a side door where his car was parked. She slid into the passenger side, her mind awhirl in everything he'd said.

He loved her. He'd damn near proposed to her. Right there on the dance floor.

Hadn't he?

"Where do you want to go?"

"My house."

They drove in silence. Ella spent the entire time staring down at her tightly clasped hands, more unsure of herself and her feelings than ever before. When they got to her house she fumbled in her purse for her keys and ended up having to hand them over to Clay. He opened her door and she stepped in, turned on the lamp next to the door, bathing the room in soft light. She laid her purse down and he helped her out of her coat.

"Would you like something to drink?"

He shook his head. "No. I want you to talk to me."

She moved into the living room, sat on the sofa. Clay followed and picked up her hands.

"Your hands are cold. You're pale. I never thought a declaration of love would make a woman sick."

She managed a laugh. "I'm not sick. Just . . . shocked, I guess. Here I thought I'd be the one doing all the talking and you beat me to the punch."

His brow furrowed. "I don't understand."

She half turned to face him. "Ever since James died I've poured myself into work, into showing everyone how strong I was, how I was able to cope and take care of myself. But the one thing I wouldn't allow was the possibility of loving anyone ever again. Because losing him hurt me so much, Clay."

"I know."

"And then came you. And Hawaii. Probably even before that, actually, because being around you was so easy, so natural. And Hawaii proved that. I thought I could keep it physical and fun and be done with it. But I couldn't. Because you had already been in my heart even before we had that week together, only I didn't know it then. I didn't know it until after I set down those rules about no strings. I realized after Hawaii that I was in love with you."

He smiled.

"And it thrilled me and it scared me. It mostly scared me."

He nodded. "I know that feeling."

"I love you, Clay. I loved you even before Hawaii. You've been there for me since James died. You were my friend before you were my lover, and that's more important to me than anything. I don't want to lose that. I don't want to lose you. And I think I was afraid most of all of losing you."

He rubbed her hands. "I'm not going anywhere, Ella."

"I know. At least I think I know. But I'm still afraid of losing you. Either you leaving or not really wanting what I want. Or of you dying."

He gave her a slight smile. "There are no guarantees. You know that. I won't sit here and promise you I'll live forever. I can't. But I can promise you that I'll love you for as long as I live. For as long as that is."

And that would have to be good enough. Because he was right. He couldn't guarantee forty years, or fifty years, or even ten years. None of them knew how long they had. She of all people knew you had to take each moment and live it as if there would be no tomorrow. "I've been afraid to live. And I've missed out on so much. I don't want to miss out anymore. I want to love you. I want you to love me."

His eyes were as clear as the ocean. She'd always loved his eyes. Now even more so, because she saw what he felt for her.

"I do love you, Ella. I promise to always love you. It's all I can give you."

"It's enough. God, it's more than enough." She moved onto his lap and wrapped her hands around his face. She pressed her lips to his, sighing against his mouth. It felt so good to touch him again.

Clay curled his arms around her and leaned back into the couch to bring her closer against him. She loved feeling his strength pressed against her, his heart beating against her arm as he bent down to deepen his kiss.

She'd never tire of him kissing her, of the sensation of being lost in his taste, the way his mouth moved over hers with deliberate intent, as if he knew exactly what he was doing to her. She melted from the inside out, and when he moved his hand over her belly and laid it against her hip, she felt the burn there. Yeah, she had it bad for Clay, but it was so much more than physical.

Now that she'd let her fear go, she could touch him with her heart, and it was so much better than just being physical with him. She poured herself into kissing him, into roaming his chest with her hands. And suddenly there were too many clothes between them, and her corset was too constricting.

He sat her on the sofa and stood, shrugging out of his jacket and tie, then began to unbutton his shirt. She watched as he took off his shirt, kicked off his shoes and then let his pants drop, leaving him wearing only boxer briefs—briefs that outlined his erection. She leaned forward and laid her hands on his hips, then tilted her head back to see him looking down on her.

She grasped the briefs and pulled them down his legs, letting them drop to his ankles. He stepped out of them, but didn't move. His cock was right there—at her face—and she reached out with her tongue to lap at the soft-crested head.

Clay hissed at the contact. Ella's body fused with heat and desire. She dropped to her knees.

"Your dress—"

"I can't wait." She wrapped her hands around him, cupping the globes of his fine ass as she brought his cock to her mouth once again. She rolled her tongue around the tip of his cock, then brought him inside, covering his shaft with her mouth.

"Ella," he whispered, his hand coming down to rest in her hair. He pulled out pins and tangled his fingers in her hair while she sucked him, licked him, cradled his ball sac in her hands. She loved the feel of him, the taste of him, the way he responded when she loved him with her mouth.

She took his shaft at the base and guided him deep in her mouth, swallowing, squeezing the head of his cock until he groaned and pulled away.

"Enough. I want to come inside you."

He lifted her, took her mouth in a hard kiss, his tongue diving in and rasping against hers with demand, with need. By the time he broke the kiss she was panting, wet, aroused past the point of reason.

"Fuck me."

He removed the last of the pins from her hair, his gaze so intense it brought tears to her eyes.

"I've never loved anyone before, Ella," he said, nipping her bottom lip as he said it. He wound one arm behind her and pulled at the corset strings. "But I want to be tied to you. Marry me."

She stilled. Of all the places she'd ever imagined she'd be proposed to, him naked, her fully clothed, in the middle of making love, she'd never imagined. And yet it was perfect in its imperfection. It was so Clay. She cupped his face with her hands and smiled, laughed, nodded. "Yes. I love you. I'll marry you. Now make love to me."

He turned her around and they both laughed while he fumbled untying her corset.

"Damn thing. I could get my knife and cut it," he muttered.

"Don't you dare. I got proposed to in this dress. It's special."

He unzipped the skirt of her dress and let it fall to the floor, then laid his mouth on the side of her neck, murmuring to her. "Leave the corset on. I'll fuck you in it."

She sucked in a huge breath as she stepped out of the skirt and turned to him clad only in the corset, black silk panties and her stiletto heels.

His brows raised. "Now, that . . . that is a sight to behold."

He lifted her and carried her to her bedroom, laid her down on her bed and slipped off her shoes, kissed her toes, her calves and her thighs as he mapped his way up her body with his mouth. When he reached her sex, he pressed his mouth to her pussy, exhaling against her. His warm breath against the satin nearly sent her over the edge.

He slid the panties down her legs and she waited in anticipation, spreading her thighs as he returned to her, covering her sex with his mouth almost immediately, taking her to orgasm within seconds as he sucked her pussy and licked her clit with his amazingly talented mouth. She writhed underneath him while he licked her and brought her to the edge again, then stopped.

She raised her head to see him smiling up at her.

"What?"

"You're beautiful when you come."

She was way past blushing. "I'll do it again if you hurry up and get your cock inside me."

He slipped on a condom, then paused.

"I'm going to get a test. Then when it's clear I'm going to fuck you without one of these things."

She shivered, the thought of his naked cock inside her making her wet, eager to feel the slide of him. "I love you, Clay."

He gathered her into his arms, rolling her to the side and lifting her leg over his hip. He slid inside her with one easy thrust, grabbing on to the laces of her corset and tugging them tight. He bent down to lick the rim of the corset where her breasts spilled over the top. Her pussy contracted around him.

"Strings," he said as he drove against her. "Mine."

"Yes. Yours." She trembled all over at the feel of him inside her, filling her, expanding inside her every time he drove against her. Her pussy gripped him as he dragged his shaft against her sensitized tissues.

Love and lust was a powerful combination, and it drove her desire to new heights. She clung to him, kissed him, conscious of his gaze on her as she climbed to the edge. But she held back, wanting him to come with her this time. She wanted to see him, wanted this moment to be in tandem with him.

She swept her hand into his hair, held on tight, and rocked against his cock.

"Yeah," he said, his voice tight with strain. "Fuck me."

She did, sliding on and off his cock, so close she gritted her teeth to keep her orgasm at bay. And he tangled his fingers tighter in the laces of her corset.

"Fuck me harder."

His voice was gritty with strain. Ella fought to hold on, so near to orgasm she teetered on the ragged edge. But still, she held back.

"Come with me, Clay."

He rolled her over onto her back, slid his hands under her and grabbed her ass, tilting her pelvis up to meet his, then drove hard and deep, sliding against her clit and shattering her.

She couldn't hold back anymore, and neither could he. At his first guttural cry she let go, arching against him and digging her nails into his arms as her orgasm swept through her like a tidal wave of sensation and pleasure, rocketing her over and over again until she fell to the mattress, Clay with her.

She didn't know how long they lay like that, Clay on top of her, Ella caressing his back, listening to him breathe. He finally rolled them back to their sides and she opened her eyes. One by one he undid the laces on her corset until she let out an exhale of pure relief.

Clay pulled it aside and kissed her breasts. "You're beautiful in that. Wear it for me again."

"I will."

"On our honeymoon?"

She laughed.

"I love you," he said. "I hope you can get used to me saying that. A lot."

"I love you, too. And I hope you do say it a lot because I'll never tire of hearing it."

They cleaned up and Clay grabbed a pair of jeans and a T-shirt out of his car while Ella threw on sweats and a long-sleeved thermal tee. She made coffee and they sat at the table. She found it incredibly domestic, and as she did she realized she hadn't thought of James the entire time they'd been here, which was unusual.

Maybe it was time to finally lay her husband to rest. Not that she'd ever forget him, but he had been the first chapter of her life. Clay was the second.

And with putting James to rest, she put her fears to rest, too. It was time to start living again, to take a chance on love, on those strings she'd been afraid of. There were no guarantees in life. She'd just have to love Clay every day, and make sure he knew it.

"So now what?" she asked. "We both have separate businesses."

He took a sip of coffee and shrugged. "Haven't gotten that far in my thinking yet. I'm still getting used to the idea of only having one woman for the rest of my life. Give me time."

She punched him in the arm. "Asshole."

He laughed and leaned over and kissed her. "We can do it either way. Keep the companies separate or merge them."

"You're not going to demand I quit my job? You could live with us being competitors?"

"In business? Sure. It's worked fine for both of us for years. Why would we stop now?"

"You're an amazing man."

"And you're an amazing woman. I can't think of anyone else I'd rather spend the rest of my life with." He took her hand and pulled her onto his lap. "Details are details. We'll figure them out. We're together, and that's what's important. Are you sure you can handle the strings that tie us together?"

Her future. Her love. She was so lucky. "I've never wanted strings more in my life."

La Petite Mort

Jasmine Haynes

To Rita Hogan, a wonderful friend

Acknowledgments

Thanks to Jenn Cummings, Terri Schaefer, and Kathy Coatney. To my agent, Lucienne Diver, and my editor, Wendy McCurdy.

One

In her dream, she died.

She didn't wake up with a scream lodged her in her throat. She awoke with a whimper, her lashes gummed together with tears and mascara.

Forty-three years old, former model turned cosmetics executive, Sophia never retired for the night without removing her makeup and attending to her regimen of moisturizers.

But she hadn't done it last night.

And when she'd finally slept, she'd dreamed about what the doctors would do to her on Monday. Hair freshly done, makeup perfect, she'd worn a pink St. John suit with black piping and pearl buttons. They'd stripped her down to nothing, yanked her feet up into the stirrups, pumped drugs into her arm, and made her count backward from one hundred, just like in the movies. She couldn't remember past ninety-seven.

Then the dream doctors removed it while she slept. *It.* A thing. A growth. A lump attached to her uterus. They would poke it, prod it, do whatever the hell they did with those *things.* And in three days, they'd give her the results. The nebulous *they*. Malignant or benign?

Sophia knew what the answer would be. She rolled out of bed before she starting screaming for real.

⟡

She was catastrophizing. Sophia had gone from a lump to uterine cancer to death in one fell swoop. It was natural to be frightened, but things would have been easier if she'd had someone with whom to talk through her fears, help exorcise them.

But she didn't. So her thoughts kept running to the extreme.

Thank God the interminable day was almost over. Her panty hose felt too tight, her feet ached in her pointed shoes, and she'd botched her presentation. How on earth could she have forgotten the board meeting? She hadn't even practiced her talk. The night before a meeting, Sophia *always* did several run-throughs in front of the mirror, perfecting the hand gestures and facial expressions that would most effectively get her point across. Not to mention choosing the right outfit.

The only thing she'd done this morning was studiously avoid the pink St. John with black piping.

As the other VPs and board members, six men, five women—Caprice Cosmetics was gender-diversified—filed from the conference room, Ford stopped her before she could sneak off to her office to lick her wounds. "Everything all right, Sophia?"

Ford Connelly, CEO of Caprice, her boss. He was sharp, didn't miss a beat, and he'd known she was off her game.

"Everything's good, Ford." Except the acrid scent of hours-old coffee, made during the afternoon break, turned her stomach.

"You look a little tired."

Now she *looked* like her dream. She pasted on a smile. "Thank goodness it's Friday. I can have a nice restful weekend." There was rain in the forecast. February in San Francisco was usually rainy. She could light a fire, watch old movies. Her stomach plunged. After her nice restful weekend, there'd be Monday and her *procedure*. She hadn't told Ford yet that she'd be out Monday. She'd planned to tell him this morning, but she'd forgotten the board meeting, then things became too hectic.

Ford closed the boardroom door after his ever-efficient administrative aide, Constance, left. "Sit down a minute." He politely indicated the chair Sophia had just vacated.

She perched on the edge of the cushy conference chair, then jumped in to explain the disjointed delivery of her presentation. "I apologize for the few stumbles I had. It won't happen again."

God, she hated Ford seeing her as incompetent. He was handsome, intelligent, urbane, with short dark hair, penetrating hazel eyes, a chiseled jaw, and a cleft in his chin. And tall, six-three. At five-nine, she felt delicate beside him. Not that she had designs on Ford. He was her boss. She'd never cross that line. It was just that she knew she was a figurehead for Caprice, the supermodel who exemplified the products they peddled, the pretty face that illustrated how well their products worked. Unlike the other vice presidents, she didn't even have a domain; she was simply executive vice president. Of nothing. She'd wanted this position, needed it. In the throwaway world of high fashion, you might as well be dead after forty, unless you did ads for anti-aging products. She'd wanted something more. Yet her accomplishments at Caprice so far didn't amount to much. She hated for Ford to think she was totally useless. Even if she was.

He took the chair next to hers, swiveling until their knees almost touched. "Your idea is good, but we need more hard-line data before committing dollars."

Her plan was to market a new line of skin care specifically for teenage girls. Caprice dealt with that demographic only in terms of acne management, concentrating the bulk of research dollars on baby boomers. But teenage girls could be a huge market share, starting them early on a skin-care regimen that, when they reached their midforties, would cut ten years off the aging process. She knew she needed data to back up her proposal, she'd just been distracted. Since this whole thing started during her annual exam two weeks ago, there'd been the sonogram, a probe, and now the so-called "minor procedure" on Monday.

Her throat clogged up, and she couldn't get a word out for a long moment. Then she forced herself past it. "I'll have that data on your desk on . . ." Not Monday. She wasn't even sure about Tuesday. God, she wasn't sure about the rest of her *life*.

"The end of the week is fine." Ford stretched out a hand, stopped short of actually touching her. "But there's something else bothering you."

She had to tell him she'd be gone on Monday. She just hadn't decided *what* to tell him. Maybe the best approach was not to give him any explanation. "I need to take Monday off. I should be back Tuesday. I'll use a vacation day." The anesthesia would wear off quickly, and the doctor said she would have only mild soreness, if anything at all.

It seemed sacrilege that something so potentially devastating would have so little discomfort.

Ford simply stared at her.

The silence beat at her until a flush rose to her cheeks. "What?" She wasn't usually so blunt, but he unnerved her.

"In the three years you've worked for me, you have never taken a vacation day on the spur of the moment."

He remembered? She took a one-week vacation three times a year to visit her mom in Texas. Her dad had passed ten years ago, and her mother now suffered from Alzheimer's. Sophia made sure she had the best care possible.

So Ford was right. She didn't take off at the spur of the moment. "There's always a first time." She smiled brightly.

Ford held her with a steady, penetrating gaze that made her want to fidget. He obviously wasn't buying it. Sophia tried to wait out his silence. Her heart pounded, her temple throbbed. And still he didn't say a word. She should have noticed he'd used that technique in staff meetings when someone was holding back the full story on a messy issue.

"It's personal," she finally said. "Female issues." That would cut him off. Men couldn't abide discussing *female* things.

"A troublesome boyfriend?"

"Of course not." Sophia hadn't dated since she started at Caprice. She didn't have time for men. Besides, she avoided even the slightest hint of scandal like she spurned fast food. She'd had enough scandal when she was younger.

"Then what other female issues could there be?"

She couldn't believe he was so persistent. Or that he didn't get what she meant. He'd been married for twenty-five years, and had three children, two of them girls. He'd gotten divorced last year, but he still had to understand what "female issues" meant. God, this was excruciating. "I mean *physical* female issues."

"I've never known you to have *issues* before, Sophia. You're the calmest person I've met. But something's been bothering you for a couple of weeks, and we need to discuss the problem. Don't fob me off with this *female* crap."

He thought she was talking about PMS. She wanted to laugh— really, she did. Most bosses, most *men*, would have backed off long ago. Why did he have to push? Maybe she needed to hit him over the head with it. "Fine. Since you need to know before I can have even one day off, I'm having a procedure to remove a polyp from my uterus, then they'll do a biopsy." She glared at him. "Satisfied?" Her blast of anger was almost cleansing, wiping out the fear.

He sat back, his eyes serious, flecks of amber in the hazel. "I'm sorry. I've been worried about you."

"It won't affect my work." She groaned inwardly. It *had* affected her work; she wasn't prepared for the meeting today.

"I didn't mean your work. I was worried about *you*."

"Me?" She was an employee, an executive, true, but still a commodity he had to manage.

"Yes, Sophia, you." He leaned forward, his knee brushing hers, and this time, he touched her, his fingers on the back of her hand. "How soon will you get the results of the biopsy?"

Her nose prickled. Her eyes started to ache. The dream came flooding back. But she would not cry in front of Ford Connelly. "Three days. By Thursday at the latest."

"Take the time off until then."

"I don't need to." She'd spend it thinking the worst. She already was.

"You can be with your friends and family."

"My family's in Texas." Just her mom, who didn't even remember she had a daughter. "I'm fine coming back to work, Ford, but I appreciate your concern."

"All right." He tipped his head, spearing her with his gaze. "Do you have someone taking you home?"

"Of course." The surgery center wouldn't allow you to drive yourself. "I've scheduled a driver." Why was he asking? They'd worked together for three years. He was pleasant and a good boss. But he didn't *know* her. And she didn't know him.

"I'm not talking about a *driver*. I'm talking about a friend who'll get you settled and take care of you."

Her throat clogged just as it had when she'd woken from the dream. It hadn't occurred to her to call someone she *knew*. She didn't have friends, per se. She had . . . acquaintances. She was a private person. In her career, you had to be or people took advantage. There were all sorts of sycophants out there who couldn't wait to use you. Boy, didn't that sound bitter, but she'd learned that lesson the hard way when she was twenty-two. Her father had never forgiven her for the *way* she'd learned it. He hadn't spoken to her since, not relenting even the day he died, though she'd striven the last twenty years to live her life scandal free. Not even a whiff. Giving up so many things she'd wanted, even craved.

She had no *real* friends. Was that what Ford wanted her to admit?

"No," she managed. "I do not have anyone picking me up. I'll be fine." Her nose suddenly stuffed up, and her eyes hurt. If she didn't get away right now, she wouldn't be responsible for what happened. She tried to rise.

Ford didn't release her hand. "Well, I'm not letting a fucking driver take you home. I'll pick you up."

She stared at him. Why would he do that? Her heart beat so hard it set her pulse thrumming in her eardrums. "I really don't need you to do that, thank you."

He squeezed her hand, looked into her eyes. "I want to."

She sucked in a breath, held it, forced it out. Ford actually felt sorry for her. Sophia suddenly saw her life for what it was. She had no friends and no activities except those associated with her work, and even then, she was just a face on a piece of poster board. She'd never married, never had children, never truly fallen in love. She'd never even had an orgasm while a man was inside her. So many things she'd missed out on. When she died, she would die totally alone. She was so damn pathetic even her boss pitied her because she had to hire a driver to take her to and from the surgery center.

Ford shook her hand gently when she didn't answer. "Let me do this for you, Sophia."

The words overwhelmed her. His kindness made her heart ache. Her chest felt so agonizingly tight, she thought her ribs might crack from the pressure. For the first time in more than twenty years, Sophia lost control and burst into tears.

Two

Ford didn't have a clue what to do for her. Sophia was always the consummate professional, calm, controlled, never a hair out of place. She even cried without making a big mess.

But Jesus. He was a little freaked.

"Here." Wanting to touch her, he handed her a box of tissues off the coffee counter instead. She'd always been standoffish, even after his divorce. He was attracted to her, but she'd never given him an opening.

She patted her eyes, her nose. "I'm sorry. I know I'm overreacting."

"There's no need to apologize. I understand how difficult this must be." *To have that threat hanging over you.* His dad had died of lung cancer. He remembered those killing days waiting to hear test results, the radiation, the way the life had drained from him slowly yet inexorably.

"I'm trying to maintain some equilibrium. I realize I'm blowing this all out of proportion." She smiled weakly, then her face crumpled, and a fresh wave of tears pooled in her beautiful eyes.

Part of him wanted to swoop in like the proverbial knight in shining armor, bundle her into his arms, but that was taking advantage of her moment of weakness. She'd regret it later.

But he sure as hell wasn't going to let her hire a driver to bring her home. He slipped his index finger through her curled fist, and, like a child, she gripped him. "It'll be okay." He was a good dad, an effective CEO, a decent leader, but like the first time one of his daughters came to him with a broken heart, he felt completely helpless in the face of her pain.

"I know I'm overdramatizing." She sniffed, dabbed her nose, then gulped a breath.

"It's natural to be afraid of the worst, but that doesn't mean it *will* happen."

"I know." She rolled her lips between her teeth, smudging her lipstick.

He'd viewed her as unsmudgeable. Always put together. The beautiful Sophia, no last name, like Cher, an icon that didn't need two names to identify her. It was why Caprice had hired her. Her reputation, her Sophia Loren looks. Shoulder-length black hair, silky curls a man wanted to bury his face in, to steep himself in her scent. Deep coffee-colored eyes. And luscious curves. In a modeling world of stick figures, Sophia had the courage to flout convention. He knew if he requisitioned her personnel file, he'd find a last name on her W-2. But, like the rest of the world, he didn't want to know. He wanted the icon.

Until today. When the real woman sat before him.

"I've told myself not to worry about it until the biopsy comes back. I keep visualizing it's benign." She wiped her eyes. Another smudge, mascara. The woman was unraveling before him. Her long lashes shuttering her gaze, she lowered her voice. "But I'm so scared." Her bottom lip trembled.

Watching her, her pain affecting his gut, Ford felt himself unraveling right along with her. He engulfed her hand in his. "Let's get out of here."

She glanced up, eyes suddenly wide, almost as if she'd forgotten he was there for a moment. "What?"

Ford rose, tugged her hand. "Let's get dinner or a drink. Or just take a walk."

The heels of her shoes snapped together. "I can't walk in these."

"You have others in your office." He'd seen her change occasionally to go out at lunch. He didn't ask where she went or what she did, but she'd needed flats to do it.

She tipped her head back to gaze up at him, and he realized he'd revealed his obsession with her. Perhaps he should have said something months ago, after the divorce, when he'd started noticing little things about her. He hadn't let himself see because he didn't want the temptation. Even if his marriage was over long before the papers were signed, he'd never been a player. He and his wife had stayed together for the kids, but once their youngest was off to college, there'd been no point in continuing the charade.

He'd been divorced a year now. And he'd finally seen Sophia. He'd created fantasies about her, let his imagination run wild.

"A walk," she said, as if dinner or drinks was too much of a commitment, yet she needed something.

While Sophia went to her office to change her shoes, he entered his own to log off his computer, snag his coat, and lock the door. In her office outside his, Constance shut down her computer, printer, and other work devices, then grabbed her purse from the bottom desk drawer.

"Good night, Ford," she said. He didn't stand on ceremony. He was Ford to everyone. As she passed him, there was a question in her eyes if not on her lips. The same thing everyone wanted to know— *What's up with Sophia?* He simply shrugged and smiled his own good-night as she left.

Not openly gregarious, Sophia was nevertheless gracious. When Constance's daughter was in the hospital with appendicitis, Sophia had bought a pretty nightgown and asked every day how the girl was doing. She wasn't overt, but she was consistently nice to everyone. People liked her. They just didn't know her.

Maybe it was time to change that.

When Sophia reappeared, she'd fixed her makeup, lipstick, and hair, once again reconstructing the barriers she usually hid behind. They'd done an exhaustive search for an executive VP who could keep the company abreast of fashion trends and changing consumer needs, a face to epitomize what Caprice stood for: feminine beauty. The photo that decided him caught her in a field of yellow daisies, a breeze blowing through her hair. She smiled as if she were gazing at a lover the camera couldn't see. From that moment on, he imagined her that way.

Yet now he wondered who the real Sophia was. The woman in the photo. The businesswoman. The lady giving him a shy smile now and not quite meeting his eyes. A bit of them all, or none of the above.

He was determined to find out.

The board meeting had run slightly over, and when they exited the building, the San Francisco streets were teeming with commuters. Late dusk. In half an hour, it would be dark except for the millions of city lights illuminating everything. Sophia loved this time of evening. She loved living in the city. Loved walking the sidewalks at lunch. She didn't have to pretend she was someone special. She was just another San Franciscanite.

Tonight, bundled up against the cool February evening, the air sweet after a recent rain, she liked walking the streets with Ford. It was new, this sense of not being alone. He touched her arm, guiding her, and she liked that, too. It had been a long time since she'd let herself enjoy a man this way, with the simple things. Maybe it was Monday's procedure, her fears, breaking down in front of him, then feeling almost whole again, as if she'd let something go in the boardroom. Whatever it was, she thought about lacing her fingers through his, appreciating the texture of his skin, the grip of his hand, his body heat. She would have done it but for the fact they might be seen by someone from work.

He directed her toward the end of Market a few blocks away, Embarcadero Center, and the piers beyond that. The sidewalk gave way to the plaza. Ford stopped at an espresso stand.

"Two large hot chocolates with extra whipped cream."

She almost countermanded him, thinking of the calories. What the heck. If the lump was malignant, extra calories wouldn't matter.

"Thank you," she said when he handed her the steaming cup. The first sip of the delicious concoction was ecstasy. "God, that's real whipped cream." So good, she had to close her eyes to savor the scent of the cocoa and the richness of the cream.

Then the blaze in Ford's eyes as he watched her. Her belly fluttered. He'd never looked at her with . . . interest.

"Let's sit over here." Leading her to a concrete flower planter, he pulled her down beside him on the edge. The brief touch tingled long after he let go.

Not a direct route to BART or parking or restaurants, the plaza wasn't terribly crowded for a Friday evening. At the far entrance, a homeless man sat on a blanket with his dog. Couples dallied as they decided where to go for the evening, but no one was in earshot long enough to eavesdrop. She suddenly felt alone with him. Ford Connelly. It was almost too much to take in. He still wore his suit and tie from the office, an overcoat to ward off the chill. She was his direct report. Even if they were the upper echelons of Caprice management, the rules about dalliances with your boss still applied.

Steam wafted from the cup as he drank. He licked whipped cream from his lips, his gaze all over her, her eyes, cheeks, mouth, throat. God, how she'd missed a man's attentions. How he tasted, even how he smelled up close. Ford was spicy and sensual laced with hot chocolate.

"So, you've got until Monday," he said, "to do anything you want, totally worry free. What are your plans for the weekend?"

She curled her fingers in her palm. "I can't stop worrying until it's over and I know the outcome."

After a brief pause, he blinked. "Until you know otherwise, why not assume everything is situation normal?"

She laughed. "For me, situation normal *is* worrying."

"You're gorgeous when you laugh."

Versus not being gorgeous any other time? Thoughts like that were the bane of her existence. She never accepted a simple compliment without analyzing what it meant. Yet she needed Ford's compliment to warm her insides. "Thank you."

He took a longer-than-usual second to let his eyes roam her face again, the look heating her straight through. She'd worked for him for three years, respected and admired him, but never entertained a single sexual thought. He was off-limits. Until tonight. Like the lights of a Christmas tree blinking on, he suddenly lit up everything around her, inside her.

"Let's try this again," he said, a grin deepening the cleft in his chin. "If you forced yourself not to worry and did something you've never done before, what would it be?"

Have sex with you. She blushed at the thought.

He laid the backs of his fingers to her cheek. "You *really* have to tell me that one."

She laughed again, then zipped her lips. "My secret."

"Spoilsport. I know it was something nasty."

She was treading unsafe waters with him. They'd definitely edged into sexual banter. Her heart fluttered, then her pulse kicked up, beating right down to the tips of her fingers. God, the things she'd missed in her quest to be the most well-behaved celebrity. She'd missed *this*, opening up to a sexy man, the thrill of just being with him.

Suddenly she didn't want to let it go. "It was very naughty. That's why I can't tell you." Unless he begged to know. *Go on, beg, please.* She couldn't believe her boldness, yet sitting beside him made her feel more alive than she had in twenty years. She couldn't stop now.

"All right. Let's step down from *very* naughty to slightly naughty. Tell me something slightly naughty you'd like to do."

She'd had so many fantasies before she learned that if you thought them, you could accidentally let them happen. With dire consequences. Sometimes those fantasies still came to her in dreams.

Dirty, filthy, seductive, provocative, tantalizing dreams that left her crawling in her own skin when she woke.

"You're making me nuts, woman."

"I haven't said a word."

"It's written all over your face."

It was written inside her coat where her breasts felt achy, her nipples hard and sensitive.

"Tell me one of those dirty thoughts," he murmured, low, sexy, touching her with just his voice.

"It would shock you." She wondered if Ford Connelly could be shocked. Nothing ruffled him in any situation or meeting she'd attended with him.

"Try me."

God, she truly wanted to. Everything had changed. When her gynecologist found the polyp, her world tilted, then turned upside down. Next week they could find she had cancer. She could die having done nothing with her life. No children to carry on her legacy, no husband or lover, no lasting effect. She would simply be gone. She had wealth and fame, but she'd been too afraid to reach out and grab life with gusto.

Ford was offering her a taste of it even if it was only telling him a fantasy.

She skipped slightly naughty and went straight to wild. "Two men," she whispered.

He tipped his head to the left like a dog who'd picked up on the most interesting sound. Then he held up two fingers and raised one brow.

She nodded. "I want two men to make me their complete focus, their mission to give me total pleasure."

The homeless man gathered up his blanket and dog, people rushed to and fro, cars honked, laughter burst across the plaza from a group of office workers heading to the restaurants on the piers. But for all the noise and activity, she felt cocooned with Ford, the sparkle of the night's first stars overhead.

"I want an orgasm from the inside out, from a man's cock deep in me." She couldn't believe the words came out of her mouth. Yet she wouldn't, couldn't take them back. Her life had been about denial, of rich food, fun times, and hot sex. She'd made a mistake years ago, and she'd denied herself ever since.

She would stop denying right now.

Ford swallowed, his Adam's apple sliding up, down. Then his hazel eyes darkened to full-on green, and he grabbed her hand, pulling her to her feet. "Done," he said, a slight flare to his nostrils like a fine racehorse getting ready to run flat out. "Your wish is my command."

Oh, God.

Three

Sophia looked at him with wide eyes. "It's just a fantasy. I don't actually expect to do it."

If she'd said she didn't *want* to do it, he'd have stopped right there. But her word choice revealed her longing. She'd deprived herself of so many pleasures. He read that between the lines, from the fact that she didn't have a friend she could ask to drive her to the surgery to the wistfulness flitting across her face as he begged to hear her fantasies. The thought of being a part of one turned his cock to stone. He'd imagined making her come long and hard, but the thought of watching another man take her was an inconceivable bonus.

Ford squeezed her hand, stroked her with his voice. "You want it, but my offering scares the hell out of you."

"Yes," she answered, her breath a whisper of warm air in the cool night.

"What if this is your last chance?" He disliked the underhanded tactic; it was cruel, using her fears against her. But there was no way on God's green earth Sophia would have revealed that fantasy if she didn't need this as much as he wanted to give it to her. He felt the truth of that in his gut.

"I . . ." Her eyes searched his face.

He couldn't be sure what she saw. Taking her empty cup, he tossed it along with his in the trash, then pulled her close with the sash of her coat. She blinked like a frightened doe.

Sliding inside the neck of her jacket, he palmed her throat. His hand was still warm from the hot chocolate, but her skin was warmer. His entire body ached to kiss her. He'd thought about it often enough.

"Trust me," he whispered, holding his breath as he waited.

She trembled. It couldn't be from the cold. His body so close to hers gave off too much heat. She had to feel it.

"Yes."

Relief flooded his head like alcohol. Sliding his hand up, he cupped her cheek, stroked her lip with his thumb, then slowly backed off to remove his cell phone from his coat pocket.

He held it out. "I have a friend. Simon Foster."

Her deep brown eyes went black, unfathomable pools. "You've done this before?"

"No. I never cheated on my wife. I've dated since the divorce, but this is a first for me." He enjoyed sex, had a healthy drive, and a host of kinky fantasies like any other man. But he wanted this for her. "And Simon isn't shy about admitting he enjoys experiencing new things."

"Will I like him?"

"Women seem to find him attractive. He's about my age."

"Is he married?"

"No." He needed to touch her again, so he curled her hair behind her ear, stroking the delicate shell. "If you meet him and don't like him, it's off. Whenever you want to stop, you just say so." He would make it so good for her, she wouldn't want to stop.

"Is he safe?" She pursed her lips. "You know, from disease and all."

"I would never give you someone I didn't trust one hundred percent, and we'll all use protection."

She swallowed, considering. "Our secret?"

Her reputation was all-important. "No one will ever know."

Her gaze flitted over him, from eye to eye, gauging, assessing.

"I will never let anyone hurt you," he said.

Sophia believed him. Yet twenty years ago she'd trusted a man. He'd turned on her the moment her star eclipsed his and sold pictures of her to a tabloid. Photos of her performing lewd acts. Today, no one would have blinked. Even twenty years ago, it was a minor blip in her career. To her father, it had been the ultimate betrayal of everything he'd taught her. A God-fearing minister, he'd cut her out of his life like a cancer.

Sophia winced. That was what he'd died of. Maybe it was genetic. She'd paid for twenty years for her mistake, and she may well have gotten the cancer anyway.

But she would have this. She wanted this man, this tantalizing act. She'd take the memory to her grave if she had to, but at least she'd have something to remember. "Call him."

Ford punched a few buttons, held the phone to his ear, eyes on hers, fingers playing lightly in her hair.

He couldn't know how good his touch felt, how his spicy male scent teased her, how his body heat melted her on the inside. She would live her life as if there was no tomorrow because maybe there wouldn't be.

"Hey, Simon, it's Ford. Got a minute?" He paused. "I have someone I'd like you to meet." He laughed. "Yes, a woman." His gaze traveled over her. "She's gorgeous."

Sophia began to get a picture of the man. He was visual, his questions jumping first to a sexual level rather than befuddled why Ford would be bringing up some random lady.

"You're right. All women are gorgeous simply because they're women."

And Simon obviously loved all kinds.

"Very." Ford held her gaze. Very what? She couldn't be sure, but she wanted it to be something good.

"I have a proposition," he said, with a dramatic pause before adding, "I want to give her a present." Then he grinned at her. "She wants me and . . ." He trailed off, looking at her.

Sophia smiled, nodded. God, yes, she wanted him, for this night, if no other. Then she put her hand on him, his broad shoulder, sliding down his arm.

"And she wants a second. I thought of you."

Her stomach fluttered hearing it said out loud.

"Tomorrow night?" He narrowed his eyes a moment. "Okay, Sunday will be even better. As long as we don't start late. We have to be up early in the morning." He raised a brow in question.

Sophia nodded. She had to be to the surgery center by seven and couldn't drink or eat after ten on Sunday. If Ford had his way, she wouldn't have a moment to think, worry, scream, or dream the night before.

"Let's play it by ear, see how it all shakes out, no pressure." He grinned again at whatever his friend Simon said. "I know pressure isn't your style. And I need your discretion, too." He winked, as if they were talking about nothing more than a game of tennis. "I'll call you with the details when I've got it set up, but plan on meeting us in the city at about six. See ya."

Ford hit the end button and stowed the phone. Raising her hand to his lips, he kissed her knuckles. "Don't be scared. We'll go at your pace, and you can stop at any time."

She was scared, terrified. But she wanted this. "I trust you to take care of me, Ford."

He drew in a deep breath, then leaned down to lay his forehead against hers. "Good. And tomorrow we're going shopping to find the perfect outfit for you."

Her heart turned in her chest, and she laughed softly. "That's probably the most frightening thing of all."

❧❧❧

Out of the drizzle, Ford pulled her close under a striped awning. He'd picked her up at ten Saturday morning. They'd scoured Saks, Neiman Marcus, Macy's, and a host of boutiques, but they hadn't found what they wanted. Or rather, *Ford* hadn't found what he wanted to dress her in.

Despite the light rain, the streets were jammed with shoppers and tourists. A cacophony of languages drifted through Union Square, mingling with the sounds of traffic, horns, a police whistle, high heels on concrete, and the cable-car bells. The scent of tangy mustard from a nearby hot dog stand made Sophia's mouth water.

"This is the place," Ford said.

"Why is this shop any different?"

"I like that." He pointed to a pair of emerald green panties on the white drape covering the floor of the display window. Everything else was . . . normal, silk blouses and matching trousers on faceless mannequins, fluttery dresses, elegant handbags, high-heeled strappy sandals. Normal except that on closer inspection, the mannequin's areolas peeked through the dress's bodice, the blouse was see-through, and the panties lay in the back corner like a naughty reminder of what could happen when the lights went down. The advertisement was subtle; passersby would most likely miss the details. Ford, that naughty man, missed nothing. He pulled her inside.

The spacious store was relatively uncrowded at the moment, a woman in the corner going through a sale rack, another sifting through some lingerie. The blue carpeting was lush, a light yet expensive scent permeating the boutique.

Standing behind Ford as he fingered a lacy black blouse, Sophia couldn't help admiring the man's rear view. She'd never seen him in jeans. She'd never seen him in anything tight. His form was a sight to behold.

"May I help you, sir?" In her midfifties with steel gray hair, the saleslady was as elegantly dressed as the mannequins, without the naughty elements. Maybe the panties in the window really were a window dresser's joke.

Ford held out the black lace sleeve. "My girlfriend would like to try on a few things. Could you start a dressing room?"

Ha. Ford had actually shopped with a woman before. His wife? Or a more recent event? Not that it mattered.

"We have dressing areas available if you would like her to model the garments for you."

"Perfect. Thank you."

The lady tipped her head, raked her gaze over Sophia, checked a tag for sizing, and finally selected one of the black lace blouses. Sophia was well aware it would reveal her bra. Thank goodness she'd chosen black and sexy when she dressed, though she hadn't expected Ford to want her to model for him.

But then with Ford, she was learning everything about him was unexpected. He hadn't kissed her when he picked her up, but he hadn't stopped touching her either. Her body buzzed with the slide of his finger down her arm, a brush along her chin, her hand in his, an arm around her, his touch tangling in her hair.

When would he kiss her? The need was consuming.

"If you'd follow me, ma'am?"

Lost in thought and staring at Ford's buttocks, she hadn't noticed the woman waiting. She didn't want to leave Ford yet.

He gave her shoulder a little nudge. "I'm going to pick out some other things." He indicated the dressing rooms with a tip of his chin. "Go get ready for me." His eyes darkened, his lips flirting with a wicked smile.

That was exactly what he was doing. Readying her for him. For his pleasure. For Simon. The breath rushed from her lungs when she thought of tomorrow night.

Today's shopping trip was foreplay.

She couldn't wait to see what he picked out for her as she followed the salesclerk into a wide hallway. Behind a chintz curtain lay a large, nicely appointed dressing area, six smaller, curtained rooms in a circle around it with full-length mirrors in between the individual cubicles. Several cushioned chairs placed strategically made trying on clothes a spectator sport.

The lady hung the blouse on one of several hooks in a dressing room. "May I get you some coffee?"

Sophia smiled her thanks. "Milk, please. And sugar, too," she added as an afterthought. Why bother denying herself sweets?

"And the gentleman?"

"He takes it black." Odd that she'd noticed. Maybe over the years she'd absorbed more details about Ford than she'd realized. Just as he'd known she had several pairs of shoes in her office.

Alone, Sophia pulled the curtain and unbuttoned her sweater. In addition to the pretty bra, she'd opted for a top she didn't have to pull over her head and risk ruining her hair. She'd also chosen tight jeans that rode her hips and, hopefully, showcased her bottom nicely. She had to smile at her own vanity. Other than standing in front of the camera, she hadn't worried about how a man viewed her behind in ages.

She cared about a lot of things with Ford.

In the outer area, she heard him thank the clerk, the murmur of their voices, the clank of hangers, then a rustle as Ford presumably sat. "We're alone. You can come out now."

Sophia thrust the curtain aside. "I wasn't worried." Used to stripping down in front of an entire crew, she'd long since gotten over her modesty, at least in that regard.

He whistled, a low tone. "Now, *that's* hot."

She smoothed her hands down her breasts and abdomen, his eyes tracking the movement. Skin and black bra peeped through the lace blouse.

She twirled and glanced at herself in the mirror.

Ford was suddenly behind her, his warmth seeping through the thin lace. "You're buttoned up too tightly." Resting his cheek to hers, he reached around and undid the top three buttons, his fingers brushing her skin, palms skimming her nipples. "That's better."

She thought she might faint with so much heat coursing through her body, flooding the tiny capillaries along her skin.

For a long moment, Ford simply stared. Her nipples puckered. Something throbbed between her legs. She could hear her own heartbeat in her ears, feel his against her back.

He lifted his gaze to hers in the mirror. "You're fucking gorgeous."

His language titillated her. She rarely cursed. It wasn't dignified. But the word set her body tingling. "Thank you."

He shifted behind her, pressed, his hands cupping her hips, holding her still. His hard cock caressed the small of her back.

"What else shall I try on for you?"

Earlier, the saleswoman had rolled in a rack filled with several garments Ford had chosen. He stepped away, flipped through the hangers. "The black skirt."

She held it against her, full, long, hitting her midcalf, then entered the changing room and closed the curtain. She didn't undress for him. That would be too obvious. Instead, she pushed aside the curtain with each new outfit, twirled and paraded in barely there blouses, skirts with slits up to her navel, leather pants, trousers. Each time she changed, he stood behind her, viewing her in the mirror, his body close, his breath fanning her hair, hands on her, flaring a skirt, sliding his fingers over her rear covered in tight leather. She shivered, shuddered, tingled, and grew wetter with each caress.

He knew what he was doing to her, humor and heat dancing in his eyes. Then lingerie appeared magically in his hand. "I want you in stockings and a garter."

He didn't mention panties. Not even the emerald ones.

In the dressing room again, she snapped the garter belt into place over her dainty thong. Adjusting the curtain, she gave him a tantalizing view of just her leg as she rested her foot on the small vanity stool. She lifted the tight white skirt to the top of her thigh, accordioned the stocking, and glided the silk up her leg. A low male groan drifted through the curtain, and she smiled to herself.

Oh, yes, shopping was definitely foreplay.

Four

The woman would make him nuts before he finally decided on what he'd have her wear. Sophia had the longest legs, all silky smooth. He was dying to worship every inch with his tongue. She'd definitely wear the stockings. But the tight white skirt wouldn't do. Black perhaps, the first one she'd tried on.

"I think I've found what you described, sir."

Like a matador teasing a ranting bull, the saleslady flashed the latest article of clothing. Ford tore his gaze from Sophia's tasty show to finger the red satin. Oh, yeah. This was exactly what he wanted. "Thank you."

"Put the first black skirt on again," he called to Sophia as the clerk backed out of the small salon, leaving them alone.

"I thought you said that didn't show enough leg."

"I've changed my mind. We should unveil you."

She stuck her head out the curtain. "Unveil me?"

"Like a present a man gets to unwrap."

She laughed. He loved the sound. He'd gotten her to laugh a lot today. He didn't think she'd given more than two thoughts to Monday's operation. But he also needed Sophia's pleasure. It made him hot and hard to think of how pleased she'd be as Simon admired each new luscious bit of skin she revealed, her beauty reflected in his gaze.

When she pushed the curtain aside, she wore the skirt, the naughty stockings, and a white sequined blouse, her black bra beneath.

"In front of the mirror," he ordered. When it came to dressing and undressing, the woman knew how to take orders.

He took up his favorite position, right behind her. He wanted this tomorrow night, a mirror, and her sweet ass in front of him. He'd bend her over, watch his cock slide deep into her pussy. Then he'd sit back as Simon gave her the same, the sight a bigger bonus than even the mirror could offer. Ford needed to see the pleasure blossom on her face.

But he was letting himself get distracted. Pressing his cock along the crease of her ass, he started undoing the blouse's buttons.

"I could have done that myself," she said wryly.

"It's better this way." He parted the lapels, the heat of her skin warming his fingers. She had such beautiful lush breasts, he wanted to bury his cock between them.

He wanted to *see* them.

Pulling the sequined blouse down her arms, he tossed it aside. His mouth dried up. He could worship at this woman's feet. Her curves were real, beckoning, irresistible. Yet he resisted touching any of her erogenous zones. Certain things needed to be saved for tomorrow night. Like the first taste of nipple in his mouth. The first lush kiss. The first drop from her pussy on his tongue.

He deftly popped the front clasp of her bra, then held it closed a moment, teasing himself.

"I could have done that, too," she whispered.

Her hair teased his cheek, her eyes dark, sultry, and knowing. She could own him in that moment, and she knew it.

He didn't give a damn.

Slowly, revealing inch by inch. Areolas the size of quarters, dusky rose, tight, long nipples. He wanted to touch, taste, need driving him crazy.

"That woman could come back. She could bring someone." Yet Sophia didn't stop him.

He dragged the straps down her arms, the lace falling from his fingers. He drank in the sight of those perfect globes, high and pert as if she exercised every day.

He wanted his cock between those magnificent breasts, the crown popping up between them. He hadn't even begun to imagine all the things he wanted from her.

Instead of taking, he wrapped the red satin around her midriff.

"It's a corset," she murmured, fingers tracing the black lace edging.

"It's perfect to highlight your gorgeous breasts."

It would drive him to the brink of insanity watching her as they ate dinner tomorrow night. Watching Simon want her, salivate over her. Knowing what was to come.

⊗≋⊗

For their Sunday night tryst, Ford had chosen an elegant, luxurious hotel with a magnificent view of Union Square.

"Does it fit your fantasy?" Close behind her as she held the drapery aside, his breath fanned the hair at her nape.

"It's perfect." The view, the room, the menu, the man. Sophia wasn't so sure about herself. She'd started getting the jitters around four o'clock this afternoon, half an hour before he was supposed to pick her up. Hard to believe she'd agreed to do this, had actually suggested it.

What if she disappointed him?

He tugged her away from the window. "Let's pour a glass of wine and get you dressed up."

She'd worn the comfortable sweats she needed for tomorrow, and Ford brought the outfit they'd purchased yesterday. Sophia followed him down the dozen steps to the suite's lower level. Combination living room and dining area below, the bedroom and bathroom lay at the top of the short flight of stairs, the king-size bed visible from below through the metal railing.

That bed would be a reminder throughout the dinner Ford had planned. He'd spared no expense. The dining table was set, the wine already chilling when they arrived.

He handed her a glass of chardonnay, tipped his own to hers. "Here's to fulfilling your fantasy."

The wine was dry and excellent, its vibrancy tingling on her tongue. "What if I have more than one fantasy?" she teased, trying to put aside her butterflies.

"We'll work our way through them."

She laughed. "There might be way too many."

"A woman can never have too many fantasies." He saluted. "Bring your wine, I'm going to dress you."

"That's a scary thought." It was supposed to be a joke, but as she once again followed him back up the stairs, it wasn't so funny. The closer they got to the appointed hour when Simon Foster would arrive, the faster her heart started to beat.

She'd forgotten how good sex could really be. Even when she indulged in relationships, she made sure she never did anything the tabloids could use as fodder. Just in case she misjudged the man she was with. Then came the job at Caprice, and her whole focus turned to being the best she could be, impressing the executive team with her work ethic.

Ford grabbed the bag off the bed's thick burgundy comforter and sauntered into the large bathroom, crooking his finger, a wicked smile on his lips, a devilish gleam in his eyes.

If the tabloids got hold of this story? Sophia hadn't trusted a man in more than twenty years, yet she was giving Ford a veritable arsenal he could use against her. Of course, Ford had as much to lose as she did.

If Monday went against her, it wouldn't matter one way or the other. But she'd have created a spectacular memory tonight.

She braced both hands on the bathroom doorjamb. "I already showered and did my makeup and hair."

"Which is why you look fantastic and your skin smells like luscious fruit—"

"Grapefruit lotion," she offered.

"—but you're still going to get in here and let me dress you, because I've dreamed about stripping you down."

A flush rode up her skin. He knew the perfect thing to say, to do.

"Now, get in here," he whispered.

And she let herself be seduced.

He positioned her with her back to the full-length mirror on one wall of the bathroom. Ford had a thing about mirrors. Unzipping her sweat jacket, his thumb trailed down between her breasts; then he tapped the bridge of his nose. "Eyes on me."

His words stole her breath, his gaze made her wet, his touch heated her flesh.

"I love the bra."

Thin, see-through lace, it still kept her breasts high. *Touch me.* She wanted to beg. The man hadn't even kissed her yet. *When?*

He pulled the tie of her sweatpants, and she understood why he wanted her looking at him. His nostrils flared as he shoved the material over the slight roundness of her belly, past her hips. His eyes darkened as her pubic curls flirted with the elastic of her thong, then popped free the farther he pushed. A muscle tightened along his jaw as he revealed her trimmed mound, teasing himself, tantalizing, before he suddenly covered everything with the satin thong again.

That was what he wanted, she knew, for her to drink in every nuance of his reaction to her body. It had the desired effect. She forgot her jitters and fell into the moment, into wanting him.

He had her down to bra and thong in one second.

"Christ," was all he said.

It was more than enough as his gaze ate her up inch by inch. Then he reached in the bag. "Stockings first."

He turned her to the mirror, wrapped the garter belt around her waist, and clasped it at the small of her back. Her reflection was decadent, yards of bare skin, her eyes so dark she almost couldn't distinguish her pupils, Ford behind her, head bent, brow furrowed in concentration. Then he raised just his eyes and captured her with a wicked grin.

Forevermore, only Ford's face would play in her fantasies.

Turning her once again, he bent his knee and laid her foot upon it. "I can't handle the stockings. Taking 'em off, fine, but putting them on"—he quirked an eyebrow—"it'll be better watching you."

By the time she had the silk in place, she was sure his breath came a little faster.

"Beautiful," he whispered against her ear as he moved behind her to once again reach in the bag. "But now we have to cover up all that beauty."

He held out the black skirt and she stepped into it, then, just as he'd done in the boutique dressing room, he reached his arms around her to undo the clasp of her bra. "We're not going to need this." He slid the straps down her arms.

She felt herself go mad for a touch. His body, mouth, and hands had been everywhere, seducing, teasing, everywhere except the places she wanted him to touch. Her skin tingled with need, her body warm and creamy for him on the inside.

Her breasts free, he pulled her sharply against him, capturing both nipples and pinching hard. Her knees almost buckled as heat streaked to her womb and tremors shot to her clitoris. Oh, God. Opening her eyes, she met his in the mirror, then savored the sight of her tight nipples in his fingers.

He smiled. With the flat of his hand, he circled, soothing each peak. The sensation was as electric as the pinch. She'd be a puddle of gelatin before the night was over.

Ford drew the corset from the bag and wrapped it around her. Unlike an old-fashioned corset, this one fastened down the front with a row of hooks and down the back with lacings.

"This could take forever," he murmured, then he started on the front hook-and-eye fastenings. With every catch, the corset strafed her nipples in exquisite torture, followed by the warmth of his fingers. Over and over, one done, he began another, the sensations seemingly endless.

"I love sensitive nipples." He stimulated each individual nerve, lingering, making her pant with need.

Sophia shifted her hips, rubbing him. His cock surged against her backside.

"Naughty, naughty girl."

"Well, get on with it."

He held her gaze in the mirror. "Slow is so much better."

He was right. Yet she enjoyed getting feisty. Finally he was done, and he stepped back to peruse his handiwork. Her breasts swelled above the lace, her skin creamy against the red satin, her dark hair striking. The bones of the corset forced her to stand straight, the front arrow resting provocatively on her abdomen, as if it were pointing the way for him. The look in his eyes left her amazingly wet.

He tipped his head side to side. "Tighter, Scarlett." He tugged on the back laces.

She sucked in a breath. "Not tighter, Mammy."

But Ford did what he wanted, cinching her waist and plumping her breasts, the slightest hint of areola revealed. "That's what I like."

She loved the effect, and honestly, it was comfortable. Not that comfort mattered. She'd have borne a lot less to inspire that heated look as his gaze roamed her reflection, not to mention the delicious rasp of material on her skin.

"You're too fucking hot," he said, running his palm along the lace edging above her breasts, touching her skin with nothing more than the heat of his hand.

Stepping back completely, he swept his arm out. "What do you think?"

In red and black, her shoulders bared, she felt sexy and decadent yet elegant and classy.

"Simon's going to feast on you."

She wanted Ford to feast.

As if he read her mind or the expression in her eyes, he raised the full skirt. Above her knees, over her thighs, to the lace top of her stockings, her thong, the garter.

"You've got on too many clothes."

She laughed. "You just dressed me."

"I made a mistake." He backed her up against the counter. "Hold this." Folding the skirt into her grasp, he went to his knees before her to unsnap the garter's fastenings, then rolled her panties past her hips. The thong's crotch clung a moment to her pussy, then pulled free. Ford closed his eyes and inhaled. "Christ, you smell good."

His mouth so close, she was too entranced to utter a word.

He whisked the panties over her stockings and down her legs, lifting one foot, then the other, to remove them.

He stroked her with his eyes. "Your pussy is so plump and pink and pretty."

She laughed.

"I want this." He blew on her, and Sophia gasped. Moisture flooded her. Her pussy contracted almost as if she were orgasming. His touch as he refastened the garters tantalized the skin of her thighs.

Rising to his full height above her, he cupped her face in his palms. "I will make sure tonight is the best thing you've ever had." Then he dipped his head to take her mouth.

The first touch, the first taste. Electrifying. She felt him in every cell of her body as he held her face. She parted her lips. He delved deeper, seeking, taking, his taste sweet yet sparkling with a hint of wine. Then he backed off to lick, nip, and tease, before going deep once again.

She couldn't breathe when he let her go, losing herself in his gaze. Incredible yet terrifying. And utterly exciting. They hadn't even dated. Now she was supposed to take on him and another man. It was sex with a stranger yet there was safety in being with Ford. He was giving her the best of both worlds.

She wouldn't forget tonight. Ever. She almost wished it could end with this perfect moment, so that she could never, ever forget it.

A bell tinkled through the suite.

Oh, God.

Simon Foster had arrived.

Five

Sophia hadn't spoken much during dinner, nor had she eaten more than a few bites of the scallops Ford had ordered for her. She barely looked at Simon. In the bathroom, she'd been hot, wet, and pliable. Ford lost her the moment the bell rang.

Her regret lay in the middle of the table between them all. It was on the tip of Ford's tongue to get rid of Simon and start over with her. Alone.

Then Simon yanked the bottle of wine from the bucket. "Your glass is empty." He filled Sophia's for her.

Getting her drunk wasn't how Ford wanted this to happen.

Simon was decent-looking, thick graying hair, six feet, wide shoulders, a toned bulk women seemed to like, and a ready smile. Looks weren't enough. Sophia was elegant and refined. The guy was a little rough around the edges even if he had worn a suit and tie. Had Ford made a mistake in his choice?

Sophia picked up the glass, actually looked at Simon, and smiled for the first time. One of her real smiles, not the pasted-on stretching of lips she used in board meetings.

"Thank you." She tipped the wine to Simon, to Ford, sipped. Then she stood, glass in her hand. "I'm sorry, Simon."

Shit. Ford pushed back his chair. She'd changed her mind. He'd have to win her trust all over again. Dammit. He shouldn't have moved so fast. He should have fantasized with her, worked his way from drinks to dinner to her bed, like a normal relationship. Instead, he'd jumped on her fantasy, made her put on a show for him in a dressing room, then hadn't even had the decency to let her wear panties tonight. But Christ, she was luscious in that corset.

"I've been rude," she went on. "You came all this way for me." She slowly rounded the table, stopping behind Ford, her image tantalizing him in the gold-speckled, floor-to-ceiling mirror tiles on the wall. In the flowing black skirt and red satin corset against her dark, curly hair, she was as exotic as a gypsy.

Her hand on his shoulder shot all the way to his cock.

"I had a little attack of nerves." She smiled. "But I'm over that now. I think you're incredibly sexy, and we should get this naughty show on the road."

Simon barked out a laugh. Ford didn't shock easily, but the queen of diplomats managed to shock the hell out of him with her bluntness. Her reflection distanced her too much for him to gauge her expression.

Ford turned, bracing his hands on the back of the chair.

"I think you're irresistibly sexy, too." She fluttered her eyelashes at him.

Yet he worried there was still a trace of shadow in her eyes. "You don't have to do this."

"Hell, yes, she does, buddy." Simon chuckled. "I've got a hard-on for her you wouldn't believe. That bustier is hellaciously sexy. I've been hoping her nipples would suddenly pop free."

Laughter danced in her eyes, eclipsing the shadow. Simon was out there, direct. It was one of the things Ford liked about the man.

She pointed with her wineglass. "I'm terribly curious how you two met."

"I worked on his house," Simon supplied.

Ford snorted. "Why don't you tell her the *whole* story?"

Simon grinned. "I had a hot little journeyman electrician working for me. She really knew her way around a man's wiring."

"I caught them in the electrical closet." Ford shook his head with mock disgust.

"Your wife and kids were away on vacation." Simon spread his hands. "No harm would have been done if you hadn't come home early from your golfing party."

Sophia leaned down to Ford's ear. "What were they doing?"

"Oral sex," Ford mouthed dramatically.

Simon guffawed. "She was blowing me, and damn, but that lady could suck."

Sophia raised a brow at Ford. "You didn't fire him?"

"He swore he didn't put the three minutes on the bill."

She laughed. His heart turned over in his chest, then righted itself. "Only three minutes?" she asked.

Simon downed a gulp of wine, set aside his glass. "She was very, very good. Three minutes was all it took."

"Well, I do hope you take a little longer tonight." Standing behind Ford, she drove her fingers up through his hair, then raked back down with her nails. He damn near shivered.

He couldn't see into her mind. He wasn't sure why it took her forty-five minutes to overcome her jitters or, after the hot kiss they'd shared in the bathroom, why nerves even attacked at all. Damn if he cared now. The lioness had come out to play.

"I'll take as long as you need." Simon stood, shoved his chair back, and undid his suit jacket. "This is all about you. Just tell us what you'd like first, princess."

Ford's gut knotted. It was a he-man, primeval sensation, but he didn't want Simon getting anything first, not before he did. First kiss, first lick of her nipples, first taste of her come, first clench of her pussy around his cock.

In a blink, Sophia rounded Ford's chair, raised her skirt, and, with a flash of delectable pussy, climbed aboard his lap.

Holy hell. He almost lost his senses.

The corset forced her to sit tall, straight. A gorgeous Amazon. "What do we want first, Ford?" she whispered, giving her lower lip a sexy swipe of her tongue. She smiled, a naughty half smile he never would have dreamed her capable of.

His fingers spasmed at her waist. *Fuck me.* That was what he wanted, deep male instinct needing to conquer and claim.

Too soon, though. The fantasy would be over before it got started. "You should come first."

"Ooh," she cooed. "Right out of the gate?"

"After the first one, your body will be primed. You'll come faster, easier, and harder. All night long."

She clutched his shoulders, squeezed, held his gaze with those lovely dark cocoa eyes. "Simon," she said, "would you like Ford to make me come?"

Simon pulled his chair around for a better view. "Hell, yes."

She shifted back on Ford's thighs slightly, braced the high heels he'd bought for her on the carpet. "Then I'm ready for you to perform," she intoned regally.

Christ, she was getting off on it now, having two men to do whatever she wanted. He'd unleashed a . . . queen bee.

He raised her skirt, revealing tasty thighs, pretty trimmed bush, and lush pink flesh. Her sensual musk rose to intoxicate him. He should have made her come in the bathroom, licked her to orgasm, just between the two of them. Yet this was what she wanted, two men to focus their undivided attention on her.

"That is one damn fine pussy," Simon said.

She preened. Ford tunneled between her legs. Then he tasted her on his hand. "God, you're good," he whispered. Ambrosia. It was so damn hot and sweet the way she smiled at him then. He needed her to come by his touch. Now. She bit down on her lip, tipped her head back, moaned as he penetrated her with one finger only.

"How wet is she?"

Ford flicked her clit until she opened her eyes again. "Touch yourself," he told her.

Her eyelashes drifted down until she was looking at his hand between her thighs, his fingers caressing her. Then she added her own touch, covering herself in her sweet cream.

"Put out your hand and let him taste how wet you are."

Her pupils dilated. She had fantasies, but he doubted she'd done anywhere near the things she'd imagined. Like letting a man lick her come from her fingers. Had she ever even masturbated for someone?

Mesmerized by his gaze, she lifted her hand, held it out for Simon. He knew the moment the man sucked her into his mouth. Her lips parted, she drew in a sharp breath, closed her eyes. Then swallowed.

A rush of moisture flooded his hand.

"She tastes sweet," Simon murmured.

His cock twitched. Ford wanted to bury his face in her pussy, lick her to kingdom come. "Here's the first of many orgasms."

He spread his legs, drawing her thighs fully apart, then strummed her little button as if it were an instrument.

"Ford." She dug her fingers into his jacket, arched. He loved his name on her lips. "Please."

He slid two fingers in her to find her tight and slick. "Pinch her nipples hard. She loves that."

Simon chuckled. "She's a naughty one."

Her gaze flicked between the two of them as Simon rose. She panted as Ford hit a particularly sweet spot.

Simon ran his fingers across the swell of her breasts. "Fucking gorgeous," he said with a touch of awe. Then he dipped down beneath the corset's lace edge, popped a nipple free, then her breast. Sophia hissed when he pinched her, the areola turning a rich, deep red, as succulent as a cherry.

"The other one," Ford demanded. Her body clenched around his fingers. He pulled out to circle her clit with all her moisture as Simon gave ministration to her other breast.

The sight, long, pert nipples, breasts plumped above the corset, Simon's blunt, callused fingers working her—Christ, it was too fucking hot. Ford's cock throbbed like a jackhammer in his pants.

Then Simon pulled back her head by the ends of her hair and took her mouth. Her perfume's intoxicating scent rose from the hollow of her throat. Her body tightened, clenched, jerked, and soft sounds purred in her throat. Tension built in her thighs, her pussy milked his fingers, and she shoved Simon away, crying out. After long, heavenly moments, she threw herself against Ford's chest to catch her breath.

It was too damn good for words.

Ford didn't give her more than five seconds to gather herself. He pushed her off his lap, backed her up against the table, and lifted her skirt.

"Dessert now," he said, his voice harsh. His eyes glittered with the hardness of amber.

With his tongue on her, Sophia had barely recovered from the last as a second orgasm shot to the surface. She'd wanted attention; Ford gave her more than she could handle.

Her body shuddered. Simon tore off his suit jacket and yanked on his tie, holding her gaze as Ford buried his mouth against her. There was something so indefinably sexy and decadent about looking in a man's eyes while someone else's tongue swirled her closer to orgasm.

Simon was hot, tall, big hands, sculpted muscles, and a sexy, shit-eating grin. She didn't cuss, but there was no other word for it. Ford hummed against her pussy. Oh, God. She was going to do it again.

"Let me make her come this time," Simon growled.

Ford laughed against her, pulled away, twisted the chair he'd been sitting in, and positioned her in his lap, her back to his chest. "I want to watch it from here," he whispered against her ear, resting his chin on her shoulder to peer down.

Then he tugged her legs, settling her knees to the outside of his, and spreading her wide for Simon's view.

"Man, that's too fucking pretty to resist." Simon went to his knees before her and parted her folds with his fingers.

"Oh, God, Ford." She didn't know what she meant by the plea.

It was too much, terrifyingly fast. She'd gone manic, jumping from nerves to exhilaration and back again. During dinner, she'd almost called it off. Then chastised herself for being chicken. Again. As she'd been for years. Yet even in deciding, she'd envisioned hours of working up to such intimate things. But giving herself over to Ford, he took her at his pace. And God, she needed to come again so badly her pulse pounded in her ears.

He kissed her neck as if he understood every fear, every emotion driving through her. "It's okay, baby. Let him make you feel good." Ford held her skirt high, exposing her trimmed pussy, pink flesh, and turgid clitoris. "Beg him to suck you, baby. Talk dirty."

She couldn't resist doing whatever he asked, wanting to please him as much as she needed her own pleasure. "Please lick me, Simon."

Simon rubbed the edge of his finger up and down, sliding inside her pussy briefly, then watched her with smoky gray eyes as he circled her clitoris.

"Dirtier," Ford urged.

She inhaled, let it out. "Eat me," she whispered, then raised her voice. "Suck my pussy, fuck me with your fingers, make me come."

Simon attacked her with gusto. Ford's cock surged against her bottom. A silver head between her legs, her white skin against the navy of Ford's slacks, a tidal wave of sensation. Simon swiped her clit with his tongue, sucked the button, worked it, then dipped down to drink from her pussy, shoving his tongue deep inside. She panted, felt herself losing her mind, Ford whispering irresistibly in her ear. He took hold of her chin, turned her slightly, pulling her mouth to his, then he kissed her with lips, tongue, teeth, everything. The two of them took her over, dragged her under, and when Simon's blunt fingers entered her, as he played her with his tongue, she came, moaning against Ford's mouth. He drank her in, every sound, every gasp.

When she opened her eyes, Simon gazed up at her with eyes the color of ashed coal. "I need to fuck her, Ford, now."

Ford buried his face against her neck. "You want that?"

"Don't ask me what I want; just do whatever you need." She was high as a kite, on drugs, soaring. She didn't know what she wanted except to give him anything he asked.

Ford simply lifted her as if she weighed nothing, set her on her feet, bracing her hands on the table. Instead of giving her to Simon, he fished a condom from his pocket, unzipped, and pulled himself free.

Glancing over her shoulder, her body pulsed. God, he was long, thick, beautiful, and terrifying. She hadn't taken a man in three years.

Ford covered her body with his. "Watch us. I need you to see me." He tipped her head to the mirror.

He had such a thing about mirrors. A vein throbbed along his shaft, the head plum-colored, the skin stretched, a short nest of pubic curls at his root. He rolled on the condom, grabbed her hip, and watched every move in the mirror, catching her eyes in the reflection. Then he guided himself to her opening. God, as his cock breached her, she understood why he loved to watch. He was so tall, so big. She felt so delicate, so beautiful in the red corset. It seemed to set her skin on fire, and the exotic, erotic feel of it against the underside of her breasts was heaven.

Then his cock broke through. In a moment of pain, she flexed her fingers. He soothed her with a kiss at her nape, and the ache vanished as he eased deeper.

"Fuck, that's awesome."

She glanced at Simon. He'd unzipped and stroked a massive erection, the crown a voluptuous bulb begging for her mouth. He gathered a bead of come from the tip and used it as lubrication, stroking down to his shaved balls, twisting his hand on the way back up. Her blood heated, her pulse raced. The musky aroma of precome swirled in the air. She'd forgotten that sex was sight, sound, and scent as well as sensation. Maybe she'd never known it. Not until Ford showed her tonight.

But God, the feeling. Indescribable. So full, right up to her heart, her throat, tears at her eyes. She'd forgotten. Or maybe it was Ford, how perfectly he fit her. Going to her elbows on the table, she pushed back on him, taking him deeper.

He groaned. "Yeah, baby." He stroked slowly, leisurely, watching his cock in the mirror, then spearing her with his eyes. "I don't want to come yet. Not this time. Later."

She blinked a question.

He answered. "I just wanted to be first to make you feel how fucking good it's going to be when we really get going."

And God, it did feel good. She had no clue how much her body had needed this.

"Simon's turn," he whispered.

She realized then that he needed to be first in everything. The first kiss, the first orgasm, the first cock. He could let anything be done to her as long as he got to be first. The knowledge lodged in her heart.

He tossed a condom to Simon, pulled from her depths, and got rid of the rubber. "How do you want him?"

She tipped her head over her shoulder. "Facing you."

He kissed her hard. Sensation exploded in her chest.

Simon sat in Ford's chair, patted his lap, his cock high.

"I want to watch him enter you." Ford helped her climb on top, spread her legs, placed her, as if he were giving the other man a precious gift. "You are so beautiful," he whispered as Simon slipped past her opening.

Ford held her legs open, stroked her thighs, slipped in to caress her clit as Simon slowly pulled her down.

She'd thought how sexy it was meeting Simon's eyes as Ford put his mouth to her. It was nothing compared to this.

Ford watched and it felt as if he'd entered her. His eyes darkened, shifted, dropping to Simon's cock inside her, flitting back to her face.

"How does it feel?"

She was filled beyond imagining. No man could do that alone. It was as much Ford's gaze, his voice, as it was another man's cock, another man's hands at her hips, guiding. She marveled that she could do this, allow this, be a part of it. Her own boldness shot her higher.

Ford put his finger to her clit, rubbed as she rode, then he said one word: "Come."

Her body clenched, her pussy clamped down on the hard cock inside her, and she climaxed with a hoarse gasp and tears leaking from her eyes. God, so good.

Yet it was too quick. She needed more time, more of Ford inside her. She hadn't even tasted him, and now it was over.

"That was just the beginning, baby," his voice soothed, as if she'd said all that out loud. Maybe she had.

"I wanted you to have a taste of everything. Now we're gonna get naked and make you come all night long."

Six

The corset was the last thing to go. Simon sat in the chair opposite the bed, lazily stroking his cock as Ford unlaced the last binding and let the bustier fall past her hips. He helped her step out of it. Until Sophia stood splendidly naked before them.

"Those are the most perfect tatas I've ever seen." Simon rose, sauntered close, bent, and kissed one pearled peak of her breast, tugging the nipple into his mouth.

Ford's cock throbbed as she closed her eyes, resting her fingertips lightly on Simon's head.

The pleasure riding the planes of her face was glorious. He'd reveled in it downstairs as Simon's cock stretched her, filled her. He'd steeped himself in it as he slid into her tight channel himself.

She had so much more pleasure to receive. They'd given her a fast, hard ride, providing a taste of everything he wanted to do to her. Ford had loved that even as Simon made her come, it was his own name on her lips. Now he wanted slow and luxurious.

"On the bed, baby." When she didn't move, Ford picked her up and tossed her.

She squealed and laughed. His breath whooshed out at the lighthearted tone. Sophia was regal and elegant, anything but light-hearted. Until now. For him. Because of him.

He crawled across the bed. "You take that breast, I'll take this one," he told Simon before he licked, sucked, pinched, and drove her crazy.

"Oh, my God," she said, laughter tinkling through the words. "Every woman should have this."

They kissed every inch of her body, her neck, her belly, her hips, as she writhed beneath their attentions. Then they rolled her to her stomach and did the same to her back. Simon licked the crease of her ass, and she squirmed. Ford trailed his tongue up her spine, and she sighed. Her flesh quivered beneath his touch as he tunneled a hand between her legs to find her creamy center.

Simon raised his head from the butt cheek he'd been nibbling. "I think the lady needs to be flat on her back again for us, don't you?"

"Sure do," Ford agreed. Turning her, he parted her thighs and nestled between her legs. "How are your G-spot orgasms?"

She moaned, lifted her head, barely opened her eyes. "The G-spot is a myth."

He and Simon exchanged a look.

"No way in hell it's a myth," Ford said.

"You poor, poor princess," Simon added, kissing her hip.

"You're men. How would you really know?"

Simon raised one brow. "I think I hear a challenge."

Ford smiled. "I know I do." Holy hell, this woman needed him. He eased one finger inside her, pushed until he felt the slight bump of her G-spot.

She sighed.

"Is that it?"

"I don't know, but it felt nice." Eyes closed, a smile danced on her lips.

Oh, yeah, it was nice. Especially combined with the fact that Simon climbed her body to take a nipple into his mouth.

Ford added another finger, worked her slowly until her body

began to ebb and flow with his movements. She almost purred when he dropped his lips to her clit. Her skin flushed a rosy hue, and her taste flooded his mouth. God, she was sweet.

She stretched her arms above her head, arched, then drew her knees up to give him better access.

He looked at Simon, and he knew the perfect thing.

"Here, come down and lick her."

Stretching out across the bed, Simon took over, wrapping his arm around her waist and coming at her clit from the top. Rising, Ford changed the angle of his manual penetration and hit her just right. She bucked, cried out his name. He knew it was a mere touch of what she would have when the orgasm finally hit.

"Here, princess, help me out." Simon pulled her hand down, started her circling her clit. Past the point of modesty, she did it without word, without protest, arching into her own touch, moaning as Simon added his tongue to the ménage.

Ford took her hard with his fingers along the ridge of her G-spot. She writhed in ecstasy, outside of herself, overcome. Christ, this was what he'd wanted to give her, a complete unleashing of her inhibitions. A night to make her forget tomorrow, an experience like no other, better than any fantasy.

Her pussy clamped down on his fingers, hands grabbing for the rung of the headboard, her body rising, pumping in rhythm to his fingers fucking her. Till finally she cried out, long, loud, the loveliest wail of pleasure he'd ever heard.

And in there somewhere, Ford was sure he heard his name.

❧

She came apart and couldn't figure out how to put herself back together again. Her body coiled in on itself, shoving them away until she curled in a fetal ball facing the window. Two tongues, two mouths, multiple fingers and hands. It wasn't merely double the pleasure. It was too much, too good, too everything.

She started to laugh, not because she wanted to. She simply couldn't help herself. Ford flopped down in front of her, stroking the hair back from her face. She'd already memorized his spicy scent. Simon's was earthier.

"So what was that about the G-spot being a myth?" Simon's voice rumbled behind her. Caressing her bare hip, he dropped a kiss on her backside.

"It's definitely not a myth," she managed amidst another laugh. Her bones had liquefied, her core imploded, her limbs incapable of movement, and she could sleep for days.

Except that she needed to tell Ford something. After a deep breath, she forced her eyelids open. He was so beautiful up close, right in her face, his hazel eyes flecked with amber, his lashes long. "Thank you."

"We're not done." He smiled. The man had the most adorably wicked smile, lighting a tiny spark in her exhausted, well-used body.

She hadn't tasted the salty-sweet ambrosia of his come. He was right. They couldn't possibly be done. Not before she'd taken him on her tongue. "Taste you," she whispered.

The amber in his gaze outshone the hazel. "I'm all yours." He took her lips, her mouth, then licked the salt of a tear from her temple. She'd cried as he wrenched that climax from her.

"Not *that* taste." She closed her fist around his erection. So big. She wasn't sure how he'd fit inside her. Yet he had, and she wanted that again. But first: "This taste."

He smiled again, captivating her. "If you insist, I suppose I'll be forced to let you."

Squeezing, she ran her hand once up, once down. His nostrils flared. Rising to his knees beside her, he cupped the back of her head and lifted her to receive his cock.

The first sip of precome was like the finest of wines, sharp, clearing her head, making her crave more.

"Eyes on me," he murmured, just as he had when he was dressing her earlier.

She sucked hard on the crown, drawing another drop of come, then eased down his length, taking as much as she could. With the flex of muscle in his jaw, his changing expressions, she relished the sight of how her mouth affected him. Watching made his salty taste and silky texture that much more potent.

God, he was exquisite. Holding her head, he fed her more, touching the back of her throat. There was so much of him left that she couldn't swallow. Sliding back up, she let him slip loose, then teased with her teeth along the underside until she reached his testicles. She sucked one into her mouth.

Ford swore, fisted his fingers in her hair.

"Share the wealth, buddy." Simon's body heated her back, then he, too, rose to his knees beside her.

She lay flat, and his cock bobbed invitingly. "Take him," Ford urged. He'd given his taste first, now he could watch. Sophia loved that. Somehow it made them a couple, and Simon the third, though a very delectable third.

She slid her lips down Simon's cock. He was a tad thicker than Ford, but a bit shorter. His chest was smooth while Ford's was lightly matted. Their individuality heightened the experience beyond what she could have imagined. She took Simon deep, his scent pleasantly pungent, his taste saltier.

Ford wrapped her hand around his cock, and she stroked him while sucking Simon. It was a feeling like no other, the differences in their sizes, scents, tastes, Simon's smooth length versus the vein throbbing along the side of Ford's cock. Even the way they licked and sucked her clitoris had been unique to each.

How she'd missed indulging in men.

Sliding Simon from her mouth, she said, "I could get used to this." Then she took Ford again. Sweeter. Better? Only for the emotion she had about him. Everything with him was more than with Simon simply because of her undeniable emotions.

Ford had rescued her from tomorrow. From twenty years of denying her needs.

How many times she switched, Sophia didn't know, didn't care. Their tastes mingled, became one. Until Ford straddled her, the underside of his testicles caressing her abdomen.

"I need these breasts." Plumping them around his cock, he

stroked in, out, the plum-colored crown beckoning her lips. "Suck Simon while I do this."

She closed her eyes, pulled Simon into the depths of her mouth, and reveled in the sensation of skin on skin, Simon's balls shaved smooth, Ford's sac scratchy with five o'clock shadow. She would have laughed if her mouth wasn't full.

"Fuck, that's good, princess."

She sucked harder, and Simon groaned, pumped faster, his rhythm slightly off tempo with Ford's.

"She going to make me come, buddy," Simon punctuated with a growl.

"Not yet." Ford sighed. "This is too damn good to stop."

They talked over her, about her, compliments, curses. Ford's spicy scent filled her head as Simon's taste teased her tongue.

"Shit. Enough or I'm gonna come." Simon pulled free, nostrils flared, his lips parted as he dragged in air.

Ford had closed his eyes, lost in the plump flesh of her breasts. Lazily he lifted his lids and gazed at her. "Do you know how hot it is to see your lips wet with his come?"

He made her feel so perfect, she couldn't utter a word. She'd wanted all the attention, for everything to be about her, but pleasing them, making their cocks hard, their balls heavy with the need to climax—that was just as important.

"I need to watch him fuck you, baby." Ford stroked her cheek tenderly.

"Yes." She needed him to watch.

"Oh, goodie," Simon said, rubbing his hands together and breaking the sudden needy tension between them.

"How do you want it?" She didn't ask Simon, she spoke to Ford.

"On your hands and knees, doggie style."

In her staid relationships, the position was undignified; even the name was. Now she wanted it more than she could say. God help her, she didn't even care which man gave it to her, who took or who watched, because they were both a part of it.

"Come on, baby." Ford helped her up. From the bedside table

where he'd left them, he tossed Simon a condom. Holding her chin, he promised, "This will be so fucking hot."

Simon touched her backside, cupped her hip with one big hand, his fingers sliding into the crease of her leg and groin.

"Take her slowly," Ford ordered.

"You're gonna kill me, man." Simon's cock rested at her center, then he slid forward, over her clit, rubbing himself in her moisture, lubricating the condom. "She's so damn wet."

Sophia heard the chuckle in his voice, adored the matching grin on Ford's face. She'd never been with men so vocal.

"Fuck her, Simon. Fuck her good." Ford's eyes blazed.

Simon pushed, a shallow penetration.

"Deeper," she begged.

He gave her another couple of inches. "That deep enough for you, princess?"

She snorted inelegantly. "You know it's not."

"Just don't want to take you too fast," he said, giving yet another mere inch or two.

"Tease," she threw over her shoulder, glancing at him.

His smoky gray eyes sparkled, and she imagined him in the closet with his journeyman, laughing down at her as she took his cock deep into her mouth, then groaning as she sucked hard.

He slammed home, and she cried out. "Oh, God, so good."

Ford stroked her chin. "You okay, baby?"

"Make him go faster," she begged.

"You heard the lady."

Simon pulled out, thrust deep, his cock grazing the sensitive G-spot deliciously.

"I need you," she murmured to Ford.

"In a minute. Just a little more Simon for you."

"I need your cock now." She folded him into her hand and sucked him down. Lord, there was nothing like it, Ford's flavor tantalizing her taste buds, his aroused scent flooding her nose, Simon's thick cock drilling high.

Then Ford groaned belly deep, his penis flexing, pulsing. Holding her head, he fucked her mouth, his rhythm matching each stroke of Simon's cock inside her. A mini orgasm rippled through her, like the preshock of a mighty earthquake.

"Shit." That was Ford.

"Fuck," Simon followed. "Let me come, Ford," he added with a grunt, as if he needed Ford's permission.

"Do it."

Simon's cock spasmed with the hot pulse of semen, his fingers bruising her flesh deliciously in his throes.

Ford held out until Simon gave a last gasp, then he pulled from her mouth, still hard, dripping precome, and sat back on his haunches, his breathing harsh. "My turn," he whispered.

Retreating, Simon stroked a hand over her hip, then climbed off the bed, heading for the bathroom to dispose of the condom.

For a moment, it was just her, just Ford. While every woman should have two men at least once in her life, Ford was all she needed now.

"On top," she said. "I need you on me." Another thing she'd missed, the weight of a man pinning her to the mattress.

Putting his lips to her mouth, he kissed deep but swift, then trailed a hand from her cheek, down her throat, between her breasts. He dropped a kiss on her nipple, then licked his way down her belly, ending with another kiss on the rise of her pubic bone. He lifted his head, spearing her with a look. "Whatever you want, baby, you shall have."

It felt like a vow. She wondered if it would last past Monday. Then she didn't care as he rolled a condom down over his magnificent cock, spread her legs, and climbed between them. Leaning forward, he braced himself with one hand. "Ready?"

"Fuck me, Ford, please."

He grinned. "I thought you'd never ask."

"I've been asking all night."

"Not like that."

"Get on with it, man," Simon growled from the doorway.

And Ford plunged home. She arched her neck, savored the fullness, then his weight as he laid on her, rubbing her breasts with the light mat of hair on his chest.

The bed dipped as Simon climbed on, stretching out on his side close enough for her to sense his body heat. "Does he feel as good as I did, princess?"

"Better," she said, holding Ford's gaze.

"Better how?" Simon asked with a feigned tone of affront.

She cupped Ford's face as he pumped inside her, stroking her G-spot. "I don't know why it's better." She didn't care, nor did she believe it offended Simon in the least.

Ford's cock swelled, caressing the spot more thoroughly until she put her head back, closed her eyes, and gasped her pleasure. He eased off, rising so she could see straight down her abdomen to his beautiful cock taking her. Holding her hip altered the angle of his penetration higher, and she moaned. Oh, God. There'd never been *anything* like this.

Then Simon put his finger to her clitoris.

She arched, soared out of herself, watched the amazing tableau as if she were floating, Ford's cock pounding her, her breasts bouncing, Simon's big hand massaging in slow circles. Her climax sparked deep inside, sizzling through every vein, every vessel and capillary, tingling in every muscle. Ford shouted, his cock throbbed, beating against that glorious mythical G-spot she'd been sure didn't exist, and Sophia splintered into a million pieces.

What did they call it? *La petite mort*, the little death. Well, if this was what dying and going to heaven meant, she just might be okay with whatever tomorrow's outcome turned out to be.

Seven

Waking with Sophia in his arms felt natural, right. Making love to her in the early hours bore more a tender side versus the wild abandon of last night, between just the two of them, Simon having left long before midnight.

Yet in the morning, on the way to the surgery center, Sophia huddled close to the passenger door, staring out the window at the warehouses and buildings flashing by along the freeway. It was early, the commute far from full swing. The traffic was light, yet infinitely interesting to her. From the moment they'd risen, she'd been quiet, remote, withdrawn.

Ford picked up her hand, brushed his lips across her knuckles. "Don't worry. Everything's going to be fine today." Mere words, but they were all he had to offer right now.

"Oh, I'm not worried," she said too quickly. "I'm just mortified wondering what the people in the next room must have thought because I screamed so loudly last night."

Little liar. But he wouldn't push her. She needed to get through this in any way that was best for her. "I'm sure they were jealous as hell."

She laughed. The sound was one note off. "I'm surprised they didn't call the hotel management."

"That would have been a crime in itself." He held her hand firmly when she would have pulled away. "Simon said to tell you thank you for the most memorable experience of his life."

She blushed.

The words were his, not Simon's. They'd exhausted her by the time Simon dressed, and she'd barely mumbled thank you and good-bye when he'd kissed her on the temple before leaving.

"Was it what you expected?"

A gentle smile creased her lips. "It was more." She squeezed his fingers. "Thank you, Ford. I won't ever forget what you did for me."

The sentiment felt uncomfortable, as if last night was a one and only. It didn't have to be. He wanted to argue the matter, but again, he'd leave it for later. After Thursday when her results came back.

The exit for the center loomed all too soon. Her fingers seemed to chill in his grasp.

"I'll be waiting for you when you wake up."

It was the only promise he thought she'd let him make right now.

She woke in a coffin, the sides draped with blue cloth. Oh, God, just as her dreams predicted, she'd died right there on the table, doctors all around, needles stuck in her arms, feet imprisoned in the stirrups, and her legs spread. What a way to go. The perfect epitaph: She died with her legs wide-open.

Sophia tried to scream, but her throat was paralyzed.

Something warm, human, and comforting touched her forehead, and she opened her eyes.

"Here you go, hon. Have a drink."

A nurse in a turquoise smock held a juice box with a straw.

She wasn't dead. She was in the recovery room surrounded by blue curtains separating her from the rest of the patients. Sophia pulled the straw between her lips and sucked. God, yes, she'd been thirsty, nothing to drink since last night. She should have had a glass of water after drinking the wine, but she hadn't even thought about it until after ten and too late because of the surgery in the morning.

The pretty young nurse patted her shoulder. "You just lie there for a little bit, okay? Then you can get dressed and your husband's waiting outside." She flitted off to another patient.

Husband? Sophia felt as if her head were wrapped in wads of tissue paper. She didn't remember having a husband. Oh, silly girl, the nurse meant Ford. So sweet. She smiled dreamily. He'd stayed with her in the admitting area until the attendant called her name. He'd talked and talked, trying to take her mind off her fears, not requiring an answer, letting her sit quietly as he filled the silence.

She would have gone mad if not for him.

The juice box was empty. She was still thirsty. But she wanted to get out of there. Sitting up, her stomach turned over, and her head swam. Her sweats, purse, and shoes lay in a gray plastic bin on a chair by the bed. She stared at them for the longest time, willing her stomach to settle.

The nurse returned. "You okay, hon?"

"May I have some water?"

"Sure. You can get dressed if you feel up to it."

"Thank you." Sophia stared at the bin of clothing, then finally swung her legs over the side of the bed. It was little more than a gurney and low to the floor so her feet rested on the linoleum. She still wore the paper booties and polka-dot hospital gown.

One breath, two, her stomach felt a little better. She didn't want to keep Ford waiting. He'd already wasted most of his morning.

Oh, God. He'd see her like *this*. She couldn't even think about how horrible she looked. She shouldn't have worn any makeup because then at least it wouldn't be smudged all over her face. There was no mirror to check herself in. She wanted Ford to see her as she'd been last night. Sexy, seductive, uninhibited. She'd lied in the car this morning. She hadn't been embarrassed about being overheard. She loved the idea.

She just didn't want to tell him how scared she was. He'd given her last night so that she wouldn't be frightened. She hated that the morning light brought back all her fears, ruining the perfect weekend he'd given her.

But she was still so fucking scared. Yes, *fucking* scared.

The nurse brought her water. Sophia thanked her and sipped. The juice had been too sweet, unsettling her stomach.

"Need any help?"

Clutching the gown closed over her bare rear, Sophia stood gingerly, her legs a little wobbly. "I think I'm okay."

"Call if you need me."

Sophia smiled her thanks, and the woman left her alone. A sip of water calmed her stomach, then she was so thirsty, she gulped down almost half. Fishing through the bin, she found her underwear buried beneath her sweats.

When the nurse poked her head back between the curtains, Sophia was dressed.

"Good. Your hubby's right outside." Steadying Sophia by the arm, she led her to a door at the far end of the room, past the nurse's station and several curtained patient areas.

Other people having *things* done to them.

Pushing open a door, the nurse handed her through. And there was Ford in a small anteroom with four chairs and a table heaped with magazines.

Oh, God. She wanted to cry, he looked so good. Dark suit, red tie, crisp white shirt, smooth-shaven jaw, and that gorgeous cleft in his chin. She felt all weepy just looking at him.

"Hey, baby."

What if she died? What if she never saw his face again, never felt his lips on her or drew his spicy scent deep into her lungs, filling herself with him?

The nurse handed him a list of after-surgery instructions, patted her shoulder as if she were a child, and left them.

"Do you hurt?" he asked, taking her arm and leading her to the car parked right outside the door.

She was numb. Physically and mentally. "I'm okay. Just tired." The anesthesia left her slightly groggy. She didn't remember anything about the procedure after hitting ninety-seven on her countdown.

"I'll get you home in a jiffy and settled in bed. You can sleep all you want."

He drove capably, yet her stomach pitched and rolled with every turn. She closed her eyes and leaned her forehead against the cool window glass beside her. Woozy and light-headed, she just wanted to crawl into bed and sleep for a million years.

She wasn't even aware they'd pulled into her condo's underground parking until he shut off the engine.

"Stay there. I'll come round and get you."

He was so solicitous. She was so out of it. It was too much effort even to thank him. The poor man.

In her flat, she headed straight for the bedroom and the bed. All she did was slip off her shoes and climb beneath the covers he held for her.

"I'll get you some water."

Lying down was worse, her head spinning as if she were drunk. She pushed to her elbow, her stomach flipping. Oh, God. "Ford?" Panic edged her voice.

He was there in a moment.

"The bathroom."

She barely made it to the toilet, heaving the juice and water she'd drunk, searing her throat, tears leaking from her eyes, and Ford's hand holding her hair out of the way.

He left her long enough to fetch a washcloth, heated with warm water. Dabbing her forehead, then her lips, he murmured words she didn't quite understand. Nonsense words maybe. His tenderness brought fresh tears.

Tomorrow she'd be mortified, but today, she clung to him like a lifeline.

<hr />

Ford called the doctor and got the nurse. The nausea was either a reaction to the anesthesia or dehydration. They recommended consistent sips of water, not too much at once. It was the equivalent of "take an aspirin and call me in the morning," but after he got Sophia to drink the liquids slowly, her stomach did calm down.

He tossed his suit jacket and tie, toed off his shoes, and watched her while she slept, the TV on low volume, a news program drifting into a couple of sitcoms. It was barely nine when his eyelids started to droop. They'd been up early, not to mention the previous night's activity. Removing the remainder of his clothes haphazardly, he crawled into bed with her.

It might be pathetic, but caring for her gave him the sweetest bite of pleasure. He wanted more bites, longer, sweeter, hotter, lots of them. Taking care of her, laughing with her, talking to her, making love to her.

One short weekend wasn't going to be anywhere near enough.

❧

Sophia closed the bathroom door gently so she wouldn't wake Ford, then flipped on the light and checked herself in the mirror. She looked like Joan Rivers after too many surgeries. Wiping off her makeup, washing her face, and moisturizing fixed most of the damage. A glass of water did the rest.

She felt marvelous. It wasn't like having a cold or the flu where today you were a little better than yesterday. This was bam, she was a whole lot better, the contrast between now and this afternoon punching up how darn good she felt. She had no discomfort either. Okay, she wouldn't try calisthenics, but she would like . . . something. More aptly put, she'd like to give Ford something. Right now.

They couldn't make love, the doctor having suggested she wait a few days after the procedure. But intercourse wasn't the only sex act.

The clock glowed two a.m. as she burrowed back beneath the covers. Ford was big, warm, and naked. Their time together was almost over. She needed one more taste to remember him by. He stirred as she pushed the blankets aside to trail a finger down his arm. Sighing, he shifted to his back. She continued her travels to the base of his cock, then his testicles, scratching lightly. He murmured, and his cock flexed. In the dim light of a quarter moon, she could see his erection rise.

She played lightly, teased gently, until his cock was a flagpole stretching across his belly. Her mouth watered for a taste of him.

Licking him from root to tip with a long, wet swipe, she lifted him with one finger to slip him into her mouth. The salty-sweet zest of come sizzled on her tongue. She'd never allowed a man to come in her mouth, but she wanted to swallow Ford whole. She sucked lightly on the crown, wondering if she could get him to climax in his sleep. Tonguing the tiny slit, she gathered more droplets of come.

Three days ago, she'd have denied to anyone that taking a man's cock in her mouth could feel so powerful and beautiful, yet Ford turned her thinking upside down. His cock was gorgeous, his taste divine. She drew him all the way in, as far as she could, then grazed her teeth along him as she trailed back up, fisting her hand at his base.

He moaned and arched, forcing himself back inside the heat of her mouth. She sucked hard on the head, and he swore.

"You're supposed to be asleep," she said, squeezing him in her hand, stroking.

"It's the best damn wet dream I've had since I was a teenager." Laughter laced his voice, followed by a groan as she slid him to the back of her throat. "God, don't stop."

He was thick and delicious, and she tried every position and speed—a hard, fast suck; a slow, leisurely glide; just her tongue along the outside; then her teeth, a light nip, a swipe along his ball sac, sucking his testicles in her mouth, tongue swirling, then always back to the crown to lick off the precome.

He writhed on the bed, tangled his fingers in her hair, swore, groaned, begged. "Please, baby, please, baby."

His legs began to tremble, and his body rose to pump in her mouth as he held her down. She loved it, the need, the pulse, the taste, then his hoarse cry as he shot against her tongue.

It was the tastiest of meals. How she'd allowed herself to miss out on this, she'd never know. But then, it was Ford, and everything was better with him.

When the tremors died, he pulled her up against him, rolled her over, his chest to her back, his cock along her spine, an arm wrapped beneath her breast.

"Wench," he whispered. "I can't do anything in return."

"All I needed was that."

Oddly, despite no orgasm, her body felt replete and satisfied. She could awaken this way every morning.

Eight

Sophia thought the wait would be interminable, but the three days came and went in the blink of an eye, and on Thursday morning, she was sitting in her office staring at the phone, willing it to ring.

Worried she'd worry herself sick—that was a whole lot of worrying going on—Ford had barely left her alone. After her lovely performance Monday night—make that Tuesday morning—Ford agreed she was in fine form to go back to work. He arrived at her door Tuesday and Wednesday evening, too, armed with delicious takeout. They hadn't made love, but she was developing a taste for the man. Could a man's come be considered a drug? Because she definitely felt the beginnings of an addiction.

She was living a fantasy she didn't want to end. But of course it would end today when she got the results. The thing was she hadn't been able to think past today. She was terrified to think past today.

"Have you called yet?" Ford stood in her doorway, tapping the jamb with his fingers.

"I was waiting for them to call."

Closing the door behind him, he settled in the chair opposite. "Call."

The muscles in her legs tensed. Fear was a debilitating thing. You knew exactly what to do to alleviate it, but you couldn't bring yourself to act because you were afraid what you heard wouldn't be what you wanted. If you ignored it, it would go away.

"The answer's going to be the same whether you hear it now or you hear it later."

She admired Ford's intuition about people and situations. Except now. It pointed out the differences between them. He was a doer. She was the one who got done. So to speak.

He raised a brow. "You want me to call?"

She realized she hadn't said a word since he sat down. "No, I'll call." She was being ridiculous. Pulling the card from the desk drawer, she laid it by her office phone, then carefully punched the numbers in with the end of a pencil.

Ford blinked, the lines of his face overly tense. Or maybe that was her imagination.

She went through the rigmarole, giving her name, confirming her birth date, yadda yadda. Tapping the card, she concentrated on the voice rather than on Ford sitting in front of her, but her heart pounded as if an eighteen-wheeler were bearing down.

"We were just about to call you," the nurse said, her voice bright.

She was too cheery for bad news. Sophia held her breath.

"Everything was fine. The biopsy was negative."

The breath whooshed from her lungs like a deflating balloon. She didn't realize she'd closed her eyes until she opened them to find Ford standing by her side.

"Thank you," she managed, making some idle chitchat noises about how she was feeling, fine, wonderful, then finally good-bye. She hugged the receiver, the dial tone vibrating against her chest. "I'm okay," she whispered.

Ford grabbed the back of her head and took her mouth with the sweetest, most delicious kiss she'd ever known. A taste of tongue, the softness of his lips, the scent of skin.

Then he leaned his forehead against hers. "Thank God." His minty breath caressed her cheek.

They stayed that way forever. Or maybe a minute. Her chest hurt. She couldn't breathe. But she wasn't going to die. At least not this year.

Ford stroked a thumb beneath her eye, his fingers brushing up into the hair at her temple. "Feel better?"

There were some things words couldn't describe. The depth of emotion she'd felt as he filled her that night. The strength of her orgasm. The taste of that first amazing kiss. The zest of his semen in her mouth. And this moment, all the more potent because she shared it with him.

"Better," she whispered. Life had taken a sharp right turn off a cliff two weeks ago, and she'd hit bottom, hard. Now it had made a complete U-turn. She could start over. She could make plans. She could stop dreaming she was in a coffin.

Ford took the receiver from her hand and set it back in the cradle. Damn if it didn't ring immediately. "Yes," she said, eyes drinking in Ford so close to her.

What did it mean for them now?

The voice on the phone broke through her reverie. "Sophia, it's Constance. Could you tell Ford his eleven o'clock, Schuman from Price Waterhouse, rescheduled for two this afternoon?"

"Sure, Constance." *And may I tell you I don't have cancer.* She felt a giddy need to shout it out loud. Thank God Constance had already hung up before she could make a fool of herself. "Schuman will be here at two instead."

"Great." Ford hauled her to her feet. "That means we can have a celebration lunch. Get your coat."

"I'd love to." God. He still wanted to see her. "Where shall we go? I'll meet you there."

"Let's do John's Grill. They've got fantastic lamb chops. And we can go together."

Lamb chops. Yes. Perfect. She was going to celebrate by eating whatever she damn well wanted. "Sure, why not? We can go together."

She stepped around him, heading to the coatrack for her jacket. "It'll look like a business lunch." Of course, they hadn't had a business lunch since the day she started, but that was okay. No one would think anything.

He pulled her back with a hand on her arm. "I don't care if it looks like a business lunch or not."

She shrugged. "Well, we don't want people to think we're personally involved."

A line furrowed his brow as he stared down at her. "We *are* personally involved. I fucked you nine ways to Sunday and held you while you puked."

God. Why did he have to remind her about Monday? It was mortifying. "I realize we're personally involved." She wanted more of it, of course. God, why wouldn't she? "But we shouldn't advertise it since you're the CEO and I'm a VP."

Ford snorted. "What happened to living out your fantasies?"

"Of course I want to live out more fantasies. We just need to be discreet about it."

Ford stepped around her, locking her office door. "Fuck discreet."

A blush bloomed on Sophia's cheeks. Embarrassment or excitement? Ford didn't give a damn. He was not going to let her go back to the persona she'd worn last week. She was a hot, passionate woman, and he would not let her deny it anymore.

"What are you doing?" She gasped as he backed her up against the desk.

He tugged her knee-length skirt up her thighs. "I'm showing you how indiscreet we're going to be. And how much you're going to like it."

She shoved at his hand. "Ford, we can't do this here."

Despite her efforts, he found the tops of her thigh-highs. "Look at that. You're wearing the naughty stockings and garter again." He glanced up. "You don't want to be discreet any more than I do." Palming the crotch of her panties, he found her damp, her sexy, aroused musk rising to his nostrils.

Her semisweet eyes became pure dark chocolate. "This is bad."

He slipped beneath the elastic of her thong. "This is oh so good."

She clutched his arms, her fingernails digging in despite the layers of his jacket and shirt. When he found her clit, she moaned. He circled, and she sucked in a breath, closed her eyes, her head falling back.

"I'd love to fuck you right now, but your doctor's instructions said to refrain for a week."

"Ford." She moaned.

The way she said his name made him crazy. He would not allow her to keep him her naughty little secret. Instead he'd make her scream.

Ford went to his knees in front of her and pulled her thong to the side. Her sweet, plump pussy beckoned. "Beg me, Sophia. Beg me to lick you and suck you until you explode."

She gazed down at him with liquid eyes. "Please."

He parted her folds and took her clit with his tongue, swirling around in her juice. Damn, she was wet, hot. He felt her lean back on the desk, widening her stance.

He sucked her clit into his mouth and reveled in her soft cry, the way she threaded a hand through his hair, then clenched her fingers, holding him against her. She chanted his name, "Ford, Ford."

He licked harder, faster. Her legs trembled. Then he took her with two fingers. Her sweet cream flooded his tongue. He didn't let up when her pussy clenched around his fingers, riding out the orgasm, taking her higher, feeling every bump and grind, loving even the way her fingers yanked on his hair.

When the quakes thinned out to aftershocks, then even those faded, he opened his eyes to look at her. Her breasts rose and fell rapidly. Lipstick stained her parted lips. Her eyes appeared dazed.

Ford gently patted her thong back in place, straightened the garter belt, her stockings, smoothed her skirt to her knees.

Then he rose. "I'm not letting you end this or keep it a secret. I'm not hiding in corners with you and copping a feel when no one's looking. I want dinner with you, the theater, the symphony, parties, events, and quiet nights watching action movies on the big screen."

"I hate action movies," Sophia whispered, her heart thudding in her ears, her legs wobbly.

"We'll compromise. A chick flick, then an action movie."

"Isn't this against company policy?"

"There is no policy regarding movies."

She sighed. "You know what I mean."

He bracketed her throat with his hand, forcing her to look at him. "Screw company policy. I won't waste a moment with you. I'm not going to hide what we have. That's another fucking waste. Haven't you learned anything?"

She closed her eyes. She'd looked her mortality in the face. She'd dreamed her own death. And she'd wanted to create a memory. Well, she had. She would forever remember all those glorious moments with Ford, even with Simon. She would never regret a thing they'd done. But they were back to reality now.

"Take a chance, Sophia."

He took her mouth, tasting of her, reminding her of all the naughty things they had yet to do.

"If we cause a scandal," he murmured against her lips, "we'll weather it together." He rubbed his nose against her cheek as if he were marking her. "If we get fired"—he threaded his fingers through the hair at her nape—"we'll find other jobs." Finally he pulled back, pinning her down with his gaze. "Tell me you're not going to let your fears stop you."

Her fears. She'd lived her life by her fears. When she thought she was going to die, she thrust them aside to grab for something she wanted. Somewhere along the way, hadn't she sworn to herself that she would live her life, whatever was left, to the fullest? But the moment she was given a reprieve, she'd reverted, letting her fears resurface to drive her underground again.

Ford was right. She could weather a scandal. She could find another job. In fact, she didn't need one; she had sound investments despite the economy. But she needed Ford. He was the most important thing to enter her life in twenty years.

"Fine," she said, glee beating in her heart, "we'll date."

His eyes heated to that delicious amber shade as he grasped exactly what she was saying. "Dating is good."

"But we really shouldn't have sex in the office."

He grinned. "How about if it's after hours?"

"Anywhere but at the office."

"Anywhere?"

"I've always wanted to do it in a hot-air balloon."

He hooked an arm around her back, yanking her closer. "That could be risky."

"I think I'm going to like a little risk in my life."

"Baby, letting me into your life is not going to be a risk at all, I promise."

She cupped his cheek and let all the seriousness in her heart seep into her voice. "I want you in my life, Ford. For a very long time."

She would not waste another second.

Jasmine Haynes has been penning stories for as long as she's been able to write. With a bachelor's degree in accounting from Cal Poly San Luis Obispo, she has worked in the high-tech Silicon Valley for the last twenty years and hasn't met a boring accountant yet! Well, maybe a few. She and her husband live with Star, their mighty moose-hunting dog (if she weren't afraid of her own shadow), plus numerous wild cats (who have discovered that food out of a bowl is easier than slaying gophers and birds, though it would be great if they got rid of the gophers, but no such luck). Jasmine's pastimes, when not writing her heart out, are speedwalking through the Redwoods, hanging out with writer friends in coffee shops, and watching classic movies. Jasmine also writes as Jennifer Skully and JB Skully. She loves to hear from readers. Please e-mail her at skully@skullybuzz.com or visit www.jasminehaynes.com and www.jasminehaynes.blogspot.com. And don't miss her exciting new novel, *Hers for the Evening,* coming in May 2010 from Berkley Heat. Turn to the back of this book for a sneak preview.

Honor Bound

JOEY W. HILL

Acknowledgments

My sincere thanks to Phil and Kris. As a soldier who has done multiple tours in Iraq, Phil provided invaluable insight into the story details related to Peter and Dana's service in the military. Kris, his wife, was kind enough to let me pick Phil's brain right after his return home from an Iraq tour, which was incredibly generous. Any factual errors remaining are entirely my own.

I also want to thank wonderful fellow authors Kimberly Kaye Terry and Taige Crenshaw for reassuring me that a romance about two people who happen to be of different races *can* focus first and foremost on the love story. Ladies, if I screwed it up, that's also all on me!

One

"I can't believe you broke out the 1939 Macallan." Peter examined the bottle of whiskey. "You must think I'm going to die this time."

Ben slanted him a grin. "Well, it is your second tour. Two strikes."

"Man has that much luck, it's got to run out," Lucas agreed. The athletic CFO dodged Peter's affable punch, leaning back in the spacious VIP booth that allowed plenty of room for the five men, all at or above six feet tall, with shoulder spans to match.

"You guys are terrible," their waitress decided, a dark-eyed Spanish beauty with a name tag that said *Maria*. With extreme pleasure, Peter noted the lushness of her breasts, presented with mouthwatering appeal over the tight hold of her velvet blue corset. Nothing got him going like a corset, the way it held a woman's body, the subtle implications of restraint. The guys knew him well. There was no better place than an upscale BDSM club to bring him the week before he shipped out.

"Honey, where you going?" she asked.

"Afghanistan."

"Iraq's too tame for him," Matt put in. "He'd be bored."

"He'll get slack, cozy up to some doe-eyed beauty with an IED under her burka. One a lot like you, gorgeous." Ben raised his empty glass, giving her a lazy, appreciative look.

She snorted delicately at the green-eyed, dark-haired lawyer and flipped a corkscrew out of her short apron. "I better get a good tip from a group guzzling down Macallan. This goes for about ten grand, last I heard."

"Yeah, but he blew his entire wad on it," Jon said. "He's trying to compensate for spiritual emptiness with material goods."

Even as Jon spoke, Peter noted the engineering genius of their five-man team was gazing absently around the club, which probably meant Jon was solving physics equations, creating the next great invention, and meditating on the meaning of the universe, all while determining which woman he'd take to Nirvana with him tonight.

"Bullshit," Ben snorted. "You can be right with the universe *and* enjoy the finer parts of it. Like our gorgeous server. Want to share a sip with us, darling? There's room on Peter's lap, though you'll find far more to satisfy you on mine."

Peter kicked him under the table, but Maria laughed, expertly removing the cork. "Tempting, but not allowed, *precioso*. Do you like toffee?" she asked Peter.

As he nodded, she poured a draught and handed it to him. "Must be why your friend chose it. Despite his *mierda*, I think he knows a lot about you."

Ben raised a brow. "You've had Macallan before."

"You think you're the only high roller who's ever come through, *precioso*? This is The Zone, the most upscale fetish club in the South. And I do drink. When I'm off duty, and if the company's worthwhile." She gave him a saucy look, checking him out just as outrageously. "We're delighted to have you here. You call me if you need anything."

As she sauntered away in the skintight latex black pants, a diamond pendant dangling provocatively at her nape from the choker she wore, Ben leaned out. Peter gave Jon a nod and he shifted right, hard. Too late, Ben grabbed for the table, ending up on his ass on the floor as the men burst out laughing.

"All right, keep it up. Next time you guys get yourself in a legal snarl, this lawyer'll keep his mouth shut."

Matt Kensington, their boss, but as much a part of their group as the alpha wolf was part of the pack, bared his teeth in a grin. "You might not have a job for long."

"I know too much about all of you." Ben, unimpressed, put himself back in the booth with retaliation in his gaze. "Plus, no one else will put up with your crap. What do you think, soldier?"

Peter had taken a swallow. He closed his eyes. "Hell, Ben. This is the shit."

"I beg to differ. It is definitely not shit." But Ben smiled, poured for himself and the other three men. When they lifted glasses and brought them together, for a while nothing further was said, each contemplating the whiskey and why they'd brought Peter here.

None of them would talk about it tonight. Nothing serious, anyway, because Peter wouldn't want them to. They worked together in Baton Rouge as the management team of Kensington & Associates, the manufacturing acquisition company Matt Kensington had founded and made successful through their combined talents, but an unshakable bond existed between them whether they were around a boardroom table or a poker table.

There were a lot of things that went into that—shared experiences, ups and downs—but the fact that every one of them was an experienced sexual Dominant, preferring to use control and varying levels of pain to bring a woman mind-boggling pleasure, was the one that would hold the upper hand tonight.

That bond had only grown stronger when the dynamic changed. Lucas and Matt were both married now, but Peter wore a St. Christopher's medal that Matt's wife, Savannah, had given him for his last Afghanistan tour. He always wore it, like a favor from his monarch's queen. No one at the table would laugh at the thought. It didn't matter that they were hell and gone from those part-fantasy times of medieval chivalry—there was a code of behavior they exercised in business as well as personal life. A female journalist for one business magazine had picked up on it, coining them the Knights of the Boardroom. Or Soul-Sucking Predators of the Bayou, depending on who wrote it. Suppressing a smile, he glanced around the table.

Matt Kensington was every inch their leader, with his hawk features, dark, piercing eyes and powerful build. Savannah, who of course was not present for this guys' night out, was a golden match for him, delicate as a princess but a tough-as-nails CEO herself, such that Matt had had to employ all their sensual talents to take her down and make her his. After he cut his heart out of his chest and offered it to her as a fair trade.

Lucas, K&A's CFO, was hell on wheels with numbers and identifying unprofitable acquisitions that could become moneymakers. He was also an amateur cyclist, which had stumbled him over Cassandra Moira on a cycling trip a year ago. He'd conducted her takeover as relentlessly as any Peter had seen him implement on their unfortunate targets, only his methods had been far more pleasurable and persuasive.

He envied both men their happiness, but was glad for them. Maybe the proximity of all that marital bliss was a contagious disease that couldn't help but make a man think about the possibility of permanence with a woman. But hell, you needed the right woman for that, and he believed in fate. He didn't worry about making it happen.

Jon would agree with that. He was the most spiritual of the crowd, into ancient history and philosophies, Tantra and meditation, despite their merciless male ribbing about stretchy shorts and yoga sessions. He would be amused to find Peter had such a Zen take on relationships, but there it was.

Recruiting a family wasn't in his immediate future, anyway, because being in the National Guard, seeking overseas assignments, was one of the ways he'd decided to give back. He didn't care if people thought it was old-fashioned or misguided honor bullshit. He liked bringing and enforcing the peace necessary for people to self-actualize. Having a front-row seat when and if they learned not to live in fear, seeing their kids play in the streets without being blown up . . . It made it all worthwhile.

He'd have time for a family or he wouldn't, but he was living the life he wanted to live. And Matt was more than supportive. Peter had no qualms about saying the men at this table were his family, Matt most of all. Peter's parents had died when he was in his teens. He'd had a rough time of it, but had entered the army young, done a three-year stint, and then, when he'd sought his degree, Matt had interned him at his burgeoning company, bringing a kid with blue-collar manufacturing aptitude and white-collar business systems understanding into this interior circle, an unconditional acceptance that he'd needed when the bottom fell out of his life.

Ah, hell. He hadn't drunk enough to be getting this sloppy sentimental. Shifting his thoughts, he focused on the prospect of comfortably slaking his lust on a willing submissive. As Ben made another smartass comment and Jon came back with unruffled transcendentalism, Peter lifted the Macallan to his lips with a smile.

Dana stood in the shadows to the right of the bar as Maria returned. When she glanced at the waitress, Maria gave her a smile, following the direction of her interest. "They're something, aren't they? Every one of them handsome as sin. Flew in from Louisiana to give their buddy a send-off. He's going to Afghanistan next week."

"The one at the end." Dana noted the military hairstyle, the way the dark blond man held himself upright, even as he enjoyed the male companionship.

"Appears so." Maria gave her a considering look. "They're all Doms, sweet. If you're looking for a hookup, you could do a lot worse. They wouldn't be allowed in here if they weren't decent guys, but my impression is they're a cut above decent. The two on the inside are married. Wearing the rings and everything, and made it crystal clear they're just enjoying the view and here for their friend."

Dana nodded. The waitress's reassuring tone suggested she saw how nervous Dana was. But it was stupid, because she'd blown a wad of money on a temporary membership to The Zone for her two-week leave. She'd looked forward to this night for a while. It had been her decision to come alone. Not really the smartest idea, going to a new fetish club by yourself, but The Zone's rep was untarnished. Security inside and out, an intense vetting process that had taken the temp membership a couple months in advance to be approved, and she wore a slim bracelet that told staff she was new, so they'd keep an extra eye on her, help her know the ropes. Her lips curved. A good metaphor for a BDSM club. Her newness might be another reason Maria was giving her the pep talk.

She'd been a sexual submissive since her teens, but of course it had taken some mistakes and tears to figure it out. Once she did, she'd discovered the scene and never looked back. Though unfortunately, accepting and exploring her own sexual nature hadn't led to the immediate relief of frustration she'd hoped. It was a lot harder to find a compatible Dom worthy of her trust than she'd expected. Ironically, the same thing that made her crave a man's dominance was the same thing that made her keep them at arm's length. Most didn't put off the right vibe, or left her lukewarm. Subs at her club back home in Atlanta had told her it was like dating. You had to try on a few Doms, see what worked, what didn't. You couldn't keep holding out for the perfect one, the one that would take command of her senses from the very first second. You had to work at it.

So she'd tried harder, with fairly disastrous consequences. The Doms close to what she wanted were rife with those who could take it too far. Not because they were bad men, but because what she wanted was a lot like Goldilocks—rough, but not too rough. Her wants and needs were a moving target. She'd know it was right when it *felt* right. She couldn't describe it. She wanted to be completely taken over, but she resisted it at the same time. While she knew that was unreasonable, it didn't make it any less true.

Well, this was the freaking best fetish club ever, from what she'd heard. She had nothing to lose tonight. Because she'd chosen to come alone, no one knew her. What happened here would stay here, so she should stop skulking and do something, right? So—deep breath. She'd let her inhibitions go and . . . retreat while she still had a scrap of personal dignity.

C'mon, Dana. Get your shit together.

Her eyes went back to the soldier. When his hair grew out, did the sun lighten that wheat color? His eyes, thanks to the angle of the club lighting, showed storm-cloud gray, which might could become steel, like the line of his jaw. He was on the end, probably not only because he was trained to be readily mobile, but because he had the widest shoulders and longest legs. Not one of her absolute requirements for a good Dom, but man, it sure added to the fantasy. The white shirt he wore with his jeans had to be tailored for those shoulders. As Maria had said, all of them reeked of money. And a man who sat like that had to be an officer. But she wasn't after the boy's cash. Just one night of his time. If she ever got up the courage to leave the corner.

"Are you having a good time?"

She started out of her mental struggle to find herself facing another tall and powerful man. He had dark, close-cropped hair and intense amber eyes that fairly screamed Dominant, causing a shiver to run over her skin. She could tell he noticed, but he remained smooth, professional. "I'm Tyler Winterman, one of the owners here. I wanted to make sure we were treating you right."

"Yes, sir." Only hours with a drill sergeant made Sergeant Dana Smith manage not to stutter the response. The "sir" was an instinctive deference to his status here that he seemed to take as his due, which everything about him said he should.

"Good." He ran a light, reassuring hand down her arm. "You look beautiful. A fortunate person should be very happy to meet you tonight. Would you like an introduction to someone?"

"I . . . um. Well, he might not . . . I don't know him." Her gaze flickered, a brief flash. Still, Tyler shifted and determined exactly whom she'd been looking at.

"Hmm. Why don't I leave it in his hands, then? You chose well, Dana. Let us know if you need anything."

He moved onward, leaving her gaping like a trout because he'd known her name. That surprise didn't keep her from noting he had a fine, fine walk. Slacks fitted right, shirt tucked in, thank you, Jesus. As a rep of the female gender, she was obligated to watch that tight ass, the predatory grace of a sex-on-Gucci-soles prowl.

Stopping at one booth, he stroked a proprietary hand over the moonlight-colored hair of a tall blue-eyed woman there. From the way her gaze warmed, whatever he said to her was obviously intimate. The amber eyes flamed in response. Giving a lock of her hair a tug, he moved away. Straight toward the table where Dana's blond soldier was sitting.

"Oh, no, don't. Don't you dare . . ." She stood, mesmerized, as he put a hand on her guy's shoulder, spoke low to him. If every man at that table turned around and stared at her, she was going to respond as if a grenade was hurled in her proximity. She'd dive behind the bar.

The blond stilled, glancing up at Tyler. Then he shifted his gaze right to her.

In those few milliseconds, Dana turned over thoughts of whether to meet his eyes, not meet his eyes. Smile, not smile. *Oh, crap.* This was what she always did. Worried about what she should or shouldn't do, when all she wanted was to be completely swept away, where no choices were hers, except the one where she needed to say good night at the end of the incredible experience and head back to her real life. Even if she found her fucking romance novel, she had no delusions that it could be more than a one-night-only engagement.

This guy was perfect, because he had nothing in common with her—white, wealthy, likely an officer—but there was that irresistible vibe coming off of him. Drawing her like a bug to a zapper, which meant she might get disastrously burned. She wasn't complaining—*I promise, Grams*—but nothing in her life had been a fairy tale. Was it too much to ask for one solitary night that *was* like one?

She got her answer when his eyes locked with hers. While she knew she was standing by the bar, people moving past her, music vibrating the floor beneath her feet, dim light strobing, it all disappeared. She'd had that spark of sexual connection with Masters before. It was always thrilling, a toe-curling, delicious shot of anticipation. But this . . . Her breath went short, and she suddenly wanted nothing more than to be near him. It was scary as hell. And yet she stood stock-still, like some dumbass golden-haired princess, waiting to see if the prince would take command, bring her out of stasis into full, vibrant life.

"There's someone worth your attention at your two o'clock."

When Tyler Winterman, part-owner of The Zone, put his hand on Peter's shoulder, bent, and murmured that statement into his ear, Peter blinked. There'd been plenty of available women hovering since they arrived, and of course Ben had hinted they had someone special lined up for him. While Peter was down with that, he knew Tyler wouldn't draw his attention to just anyone. So he looked. And the second glass of Macallan he'd been lifting to his lips stopped halfway there.

Holy shit.

For a second, he thought he was looking at Ben's special arrangement, but because Ben knew Peter's tastes, he wouldn't have arranged for this girl. Not unless he'd reached ass deep inside of Peter and pulled out some unconscious dream he hadn't realized he had. All the attributes that Peter usually sought weren't obvious in this one. In fact, she wasn't *anything* like the women who usually attracted his attention. Yet here he was, unable to look away.

She was a black woman, for one thing. While the beauty of dark skin had teased his gaze before, he'd never felt pulled toward it as he did now. He had the taste of toffee on his tongue, making it easy to imagine her skin tasting like a complementary caramel, or a swirling chocolate. Or perhaps something spicy, exotic.

He liked his women tall and well endowed, with tits that he could fuck with his cock, lubricated with his pre-come. Or watch the curves move with generous abandon while he fucked her from behind, in front of a wide, well-lit mirror. This woman was petite, with an athlete's lean, hard muscle. The elegant slimness of her bearing made him wonder if there was Ethiopian in her background. She had a proud slope to her high forehead, the suggestion of sculpted cheekbones and a precise chin, though the rest was hidden beneath a mask. When light strobed over her face, he saw the mask was deep purple and green with dangles of amethyst and emerald beads framing the delicate jaw.

A simple, short sheath covered her body, the black fabric translucent, fluttering as she breathed. Despite the fabric and dim light, he could tell her breasts were a small but pretty set, the curves likely a good fit for his hands. She wore a jeweled harness that included nipple clamps, such that he could imagine those stimulated peaks pressing into his palms. A chain ran between the clamps, down to a navel glittering with a temporary catch bead that hooked another delicate chain low on her hips, traveling around to the back. The scrap of dark thong made her look almost naked until he took a closer look, and lingered in that tempting shadowy area.

When he eventually raised his gaze, he took it to her neck. All available subs wore a collar of some form, with an attached ring so that a Master might leash and claim them for the night, if both parties were willing. Hers was a high-neck ring collar, triple stacked, with a single steel diamond-shaped loop on it for the attachment.

As she waited, obviously knowing she was being evaluated, her eyes glittered behind the mask. Her lips parted. Slowly, she pivoted on one high heel. The five-inch stilettos made him bare his teeth in a feral smile at her clever attempt to add to her height. As she turned to face the wall, light shimmered across skin dusted with glitter powder. The sheath had an open back, draping down so he saw the delicate waist chain dropped a single teardrop pearl in the tender dimple of her tight, round ass. But it was what was tattooed across the small of her back, as precisely curved and sweet as a porcelain teapot, that got him to his feet. "Guys, I really appreciate the girl you got me, but there's been a change of plans."

As he moved across the room, he couldn't take his eyes from it. The boldness of the tat was too masculine for her feminine frame, but it showed well against her copper skin in the club's dim light. A twisted American flag, held in an eagle's talons, with a script beneath it.

Your freedom, my life. Armed services ink.

When he reached her, he stepped in close. He could say it was because the music was loud, but he wanted to be damn sure that signal was for him. Keeping her cheek pressed to the wall, she left her lashes lowered in that shy invitation. As he moved in, she shifted her legs apart. Offering to be evaluated further. Peter suppressed a growl.

She had short, close-cropped hair, and that high ring collar went from the base of her neck to the point of her skull. It limited her head's mobility, requiring an upright posture and dependence on a Master's direction. That, and the automatic spread of her toned, lean legs, which tilted up her delectable backside, confirmed she was an extreme player, firing his blood further.

Peter knew a woman gave up a piece of her soul every time she gave her body. Usually he let them decide how much of a piece to give, because his desires ran toward the more hard-core, the ones who had it deeper in their nature than just adding kink to their lives. But getting into the mind of a full-natured sub meant tapping into more-than-inside-the-club-walls fantasies. So he usually settled for a club-only sub, had a good time fantasizing about the possibility of more, and then went on his way.

Until this moment. For some reason, this slim creature made him think of what really fired his blood—a woman that was all his, for always. A woman whose submissive nature was a match for his Dominant one.

Drawing a steadying breath, he touched her nape, drifted down her spine toward that marking that had called to him, though he noted she had a couple other tattoos as well, shadowed by the sheath. Trembling under his touch, she made a quiet noise. He leaned in, pressing his thigh against her ass, the sensitive crease, the hint of his knee finding treasure between her parted thighs. Her breath caught.

With that closely shorn hair, he could see the shape of her ears.

Delicate and perfect, like the rest of her. "So what's your rank, sweetheart?"

"Sergeant."

He'd meant it as a jest, assuming the tattoo to be a leftover from an ex-boyfriend. At least he hoped so, because he didn't mess with a woman who was still attached. But as he glanced over her again, he registered that the body he was looking at wasn't aerobically fit. It was combat fit. "Well, seeing as I'm a captain, I outrank you."

A smile teased her soft, full mouth, so moist from a burgundy lip gloss it made him think of an entirely different set of lips. "Yes, sir," she murmured.

Unable to resist and wanting to test, he didn't ask. He slid a hand between her spread legs. Soaking wet against the panel of those nearly nonexistent thong panties. She let out a harsh gasp, and his eyes sharpened. "Not used to a man just taking you over, are you, sweetheart? But that's what you crave."

She closed her eyes, biting her lip. Nodded, and his blood went to full boil.

"I want you tonight." He usually had more finesse, but he made it a rough demand, no question, request or games. The urgency that gripped him now had nothing to do with the limits of time. "I want the collar and jewels off. They're not mine."

When she removed them, taking in a breath at the tug to the nipple clamps, she laid them on the bar for an efficient Maria to tag and place beneath it. Then she lifted her chin. Peter slid his fingers over the fragile network of arteries pumping at an accelerated rate and tightened slightly, creating a collar of flesh and bone. Her pulse elevated. "Good. Look at me."

She did, and he was caught by that gaze, a pale green like summer grass, quiet lagoons and women's springtime lawn dresses. Overwhelmed by dark, hungry pupils.

"Give me your hands." He took out the short tether he'd been given as a guest Dom at the club and unwound it.

She held them out, but as he looped the tether around her wrists, the slim fingers found him under his untucked shirt, hooked in the waistband of his jeans, knuckles brushing his abdomen intimately. His lips twisted. "Interpreted that order in your own way, didn't you? That'll earn you some disciplinary action."

When her eyes sparked, he knotted the tether to bind her to him. She kept her fingers where they were, and his aching cock was already chafing, straining toward that touch. Maybe she felt his heat, but her rising desire was as palpable as his own. He wasn't going to take her back by his table, but straight to a room where he could see how much of a fight she liked. If her need to make a man work to be her Master matched his desire to prove he could acquire that target, it was going to be a hell of an experience.

"Is this a first time for you, sweetheart?"

Her voice was throaty, velvet sin. "I sure hope so."

Two

The advantage to two strangers hooking up in a BDSM club, versus in a bar, was there wasn't a lot of awkward small talk, the need to get to know each other. One led, one followed, the basic rules established, and the game began. Dana preferred that, though it was yet another ludicrous paradox about what she wanted. It was impossible to achieve the emotional rapport she wanted with a Master that way.

So she'd thought.

This one was keeping her off balance. He'd brought her to a private playroom, but not a dungeon, a Victorian drawing room or a stable, some of the more hard-core settings. It was an honest-to-God garden, with plants and sod, and lights that could be darkened to show a holographic heavy moon and glittering stars above.

If she didn't know for sure they were still within The Zone, she would have thought he'd taken her outside. The silver light reflected on her skin like moonlight in truth. Gleaming in that same light was a statue of Aphrodite, and a fountain with prancing unicorn sculptures around it. No whips, chains or restraints that she could see. While she was impressed with the production, the exorbitant temporary membership fee worth every dime for props alone, it seemed like a soft setting. She liked it hard. Had she chosen wrong? Of course, it wasn't the first time she'd had to steer a new Master in the right direction.

She lowered her voice to a practiced persuasive purr. "Perhaps my Master thinks his new slave can't handle it rough and dark. Perhaps he'd like to ask her the types of things she's willing to do for him."

Her Master-for-the-night turned. The storm-cloud eyes were dark in the dim light, but the moonlight sculpted the planes of his face, giving him an implacable look of irresistibly cruel sensuality, vibrating life and power.

"Take off your shoes."

Most Masters wanted the stilettos to remain on, and she liked it that way, too. When you were five foot nothing, the shoes gave that sense of stature, the fuck-me sway of the hips and elongated calves that drew a man's gaze. Without them, she felt a little too close to the "short scrapper" she'd been dubbed as a kid, because of the day she'd beaten up two boys on the corner who'd tried to take Robbie's lunch money. It had taken Robbie a couple years to forgive her for that. But of course now he was dead, and forgiveness was out of her hands.

Damn, two seconds with the guy and she was already tapping family shit? She needed to take control of this, get out of this environment and into one where she was more comfortable.

She'd kicked off the shoes, but before she could draw a breath, he'd stepped forward and scooped her up with graceful, easy power. His hands were big and warm on her thighs and back. His hard abdomen muscles flexed as he walked, body shifting under the point of her hip. Taking her to the fountain, he studied it and then sat her down on the edge, letting her feet curl into the thick grass. The fountain wall was embedded with smooth stones like goose eggs, pressing intimately into the valley between her thighs, the seam of her buttocks. A fragrance in the water's mist teased her nose. Behind the rush of the water, she could hear crickets and frogs.

"You'll speak only when spoken to," he said with deceptive mildness. "And your safe word is 'freedom.' Don't move from where I've placed you." As he released her, he passed his fingers along the eagle tattoo, grazing the dress's low back, making her shiver. Despite her doubts, she thought "freedom" might be the last word she said to him.

Straightening, he propped a foot on the wall. His leg flanked her, his body dwarfing her with his sheer size. As he undid the cuffs of his shirt, he examined her, slow and easy. When he began to unbutton it down the front, her mouth went dry, but she didn't get the feeling he was performing for her. Everything about his body language said *she* was the center-stage show, there to serve as his entertainment. As he took his time, her lower belly was drawing tighter, an odd quake in her thighs because she didn't know what he planned. Even if she was the woman regularly in his bed, she thought she still wouldn't know with a man like this. He'd keep the control, and he'd keep her guessing.

The moonlight caught the silver of his dog tags, as well as a St. Christopher's medallion that fell above them. It captivated her, seeing her Master's personal things. *Winston, Peter R.* That was his name.

Wanting to break the strange feeling knowing his name evoked, as well as the sense of helplessness he'd imposed on her, she reached out to help him unbutton the last two buttons of his shirt. As her fingertips grazed the cotton, her lips parted, tongue touching them in anticipation.

In one swift movement, he captured her hands in one of his, pushed them down so they were cupped between her legs. The contact, her own hands against her pussy, the pressure of his hand against them, arched her up. Her head fell naturally into the cup of his other palm as he brought his mouth onto hers.

Men kissed all different ways, and she'd sampled quite a few of them. Despite that, she had no way of classifying this one. It was a command in a kiss. He didn't ask to take over; he just did, as if he knew he could take anything he wanted from her. Whether she said yes or no was irrelevant to him. He'd brought her into this kind of setting for a reason. *He* was the hard-core trappings, the dungeon, the spanking bench and whips. If he'd taken her into a dungeon, she might have been terrified down to her toes. She probably still was, but the setting helped balance what he was putting her through now, kept the danger to a thrilling edge, on the near side of the teetering plunge where she'd lose her mind.

His tongue went deep, exploring teeth and moist flesh, the roof of her mouth and all the hot crevices in a flexible, stroking way that said he was quite aware of which part of a woman's body was most closely related to her mouth. As he rocked her backward, he released his hold on her hands. She would have grabbed on to his biceps for support, but something told her to keep her hands where they were, and she was smart enough not to move them against herself without his permission. But it was difficult.

When gravity took her down farther, he moved right with her, his arm locked securely on her lower back, fingers spread to hold her buttock tight. As he held her over the fountain's gurgling waters, the aromatic mist touched her skin. She wanted to touch his corded throat and short hair. While the shirt wasn't open all the way, the muscled and broad expanse she'd glimpsed had a scattering of fine gold hair dusted across it.

He increased his grip on her buttock, making her mewl. She gasped into his mouth as his thigh insinuated itself between her legs, pressed against her wet heat. It also pushed her back farther, so her ass was hanging over the edge of that wall. He pulled up the bottom of her sheath dress, catching the thin ribbon of her thong in his clever fingers. He moved both out of the way an instant before two well-placed jets of water surged up from the fountain pool, hitting her clit and anus with insistent pressure. The water was cool enough to be a shock, warm enough to make her squirm against it, creating friction. Now she understood why he'd placed her exactly where he had.

"Be still," he warned her, those eyes close, the mouth gone from sensual to stern and uncompromising. Though he hadn't touched her mask, it felt stripped away, his gaze boring into hers. "You going to keep trying to run things, Sergeant?"

A girl from her usual club had told her there were two types of Dominants: the mechanical and the psychological. *The good ones mix it, you know. The setting, the toys, the mind games. But the really psychological Doms, they're rare. I've met one or two, and girl, they're the scariest and most tempting of all. They seem like they know everything about you from the get-go, and they don't need to do a single thing to have you licking their boots.*

She wasn't sure she was into boot licking, but that wasn't what her girlfriend had meant anyhow. It meant something way more than that. She had a feeling she was confronting it at close-quarters distance. Actually, make that point-blank.

He'd told her to be still, but those water jets made it impossible. Her body had to jitter and squirm in response.

"I'm sorry, sir," she gasped. "I can't."

"Like I thought. A discipline problem." He lifted her away from the jets and, with that same effortless strength, flipped her over. Now he was sitting on the wall and she was on his lap, her wet, glistening bottom perched high. She couldn't help herself. She gripped the tough denim over his calf and put her mouth on him, biting into the fabric. God, he smelled edible. A man with money and good grooming knew how to seduce a woman's nose with the right aftershave and soap, keeping the earthy scent of male as the perfect complement to the mix.

"Five feet and a hundred pounds of trouble."

A hundred fifteen, but who was arguing? Most of that fifteen was in her ass and tits. No man Dana knew had ever complained about that.

"Lift your arms straight out in front of you."

Not an easy feat when you were folded over a man's thighs, but she locked her stomach muscles and that shapely ass to comply, and earned a noticeable twitch from the iron bar of his cock, pressed hard against her belly as an incentive. Blessing every agonizing workout where she'd pushed herself on strength training, she threw in a not-so-subtle rub against him.

He smacked her ass, and it wasn't some passing swat. Holy God, the man had some power behind that arm. The wobble of her buttock in response rocked up her spine. "You're going to piss me off, little girl, and that's not something you want to do. You haven't chosen a Master who can be led around by his cock tonight."

Uncertainty and indignation flooded her. She didn't do that. She was looking for a Master who would take the reins. It wasn't her fault most of them didn't.

He reached down, making her realize there were compartments in the fountain wall. Because of her position, she couldn't see, but after the sound of a hydraulic door closing, he straightened. While she suspected he could hold her with perfect balance, he shifted so she rocked, caught off guard, and had to grab at him again.

"Arms out, soldier," he barked, and gave her a matching handprint on the opposite cheek.

"I was falling, sir."

He put his hand on the back of her neck, exerting enough pressure that she had to strain to keep her upper body up and arms out as he'd demanded. This was bringing back some harrowing memories of Basic Combat Training. But Basic was about breaking the person down, remaking and retraining them, wasn't it? She swallowed.

Leaning down so his breath was against her ear, he had that implacable hand suddenly caress her nape in a way that sent nerves yearning toward his touch. "If you're falling, trust me to catch you, Sergeant."

Before she could respond to that, he'd straightened and clasped her wrists. He'd retrieved gauntlets with lacings, so he could tie her arms together, wrists to elbows. As he worked the fabric down over her forearms and then began to thread and draw the lacings tight, her stomach and ass muscles quivered. The lifted position was becoming excruciating. But he'd ordered her to do it, and damn it, she'd do it.

His dog tags plinked against her back. The cool metal against her flesh was in contrast to the burning in her stomach and shoulder muscles, the ache in her neck. He was taking his damn time, even though he never faltered, weaving those two gauntlets with smooth precision. Every time he pulled a section taut, the increased restraint coiled up the need in her pussy the same way.

"You like that, don't you, sweetheart? What would you think of a full corset, one of those cruel hourglass makers that robs you of breath and puts your pretty tits on high display, drawing a Master's gaze to your accessible ass?"

She shuddered, thinking of how deliciously restrictive it would be. How did he know she'd fantasized about that? She had a couple, but Masters had unlaced her out of them, never into them. Not as if she was their possession, a gift they prepared for themselves. When she'd fantasized about it, she'd also fantasized about a Master like this one appeared to be.

"Yeah, you like that idea, I can tell. I like a corset on my slave. It shows off how beautiful she is, all those womanly curves, the boning keeping her straight and proud, knowing she's got nothing to worry about. Because she's mine."

She closed her eyes, lost in the pleasure of the thought. She wasn't a woman who sought the shelter of a man, but for some reason the idea of being his like that gave her a welcome sense of sanctuary, a place she could count on when she needed it. It was a dangerous thought, because loneliness, dwelling on the fact she had no family left, could too often take her down the wrong road.

The leftover lacing was wrapped over the hand he put beneath her curled fingers, as though he were offering a branch to a bird. "Rest your weight now."

She wanted to hold out longer to prove she could, but her straining body overrode her, her gasping muscles letting out a cry of relief. Then the movement of his body told her he'd pulled his dog tags over his head. He broke the latch, wrapped the chain around her neck twice and snapped it shut again one-handed, an impressive feat. The beaded chain tightened on her throat when he cupped her

chin, stroked his thumb along the corner of her mouth to get her to
open up, and then slid the tags onto her tongue.

"Close your teeth on them."

She did, so the edge of one was visible between her lips, the
chain swinging against her chin. He stroked her back. "Good girl.
You drop them, and I'll be very displeased. You think this is a cushy
environment, don't you? No dungeon, no clever, cruel metal devices
made to torture flesh. It's too soft. Isn't that right, Sergeant?"

His voice had that dangerous purr to it again, so she nodded her
head, a quick jerk. She didn't even think about lying.

"You know your Bible? 'And out of the ground made the Lord
God to grow every tree that is pleasant to the sight . . .'"

She did know her Bible, but was surprised that he would use it
here. Her curiosity about that was short-lived, however. Apparently
those compartments held more than man-made items. He brought
a thin, whiplike branch into her line of sight. Not a polished switch,
lacquered and placed for sale in The Zone's diverse gift shop. This
was one that had been cut and peeled, much as someone might have
done in ages past to take a child behind the woodshed. Or an errant
wife, in the days of the "one-inch thick" rule.

Holy God, switches hurt. She didn't know if she could . . .

He was sliding it along her buttocks. "I'm going to teach you
that when I give you an order, you follow it, Sergeant. I don't care
how hot you are, how wet your cunt. What you want to happen or
you're nervous about. I'm your Master and you trust and obey everything I tell you, to the letter. When I tell you not to move, you
don't move. When I tell you to move, you move your ass as if it's on
fire." The tip teased her pussy and she wiggled before she thought,
then froze, but it was too late.

"Fire it is."

He brought down the switch. *Holy Jesus, Gram, forgive me.* Three
successive strikes and she was yelping against those metal tags, feeling the edges against her tongue, but she wouldn't let them go.
She'd learned her lesson. He'd given them to her; she was going to
hold on to them.

He ran his hand over her smarting ass. She was shaking. God, when was the last time she'd shaken like a newbie during a session?

"You want your freedom, Sergeant?"

She was blowing like a winded horse around the outsides of those tags, saliva escaping in an embarrassing display. But she shook her head. Tears she didn't understand clogged her throat.

"There you are, baby," he murmured. "That's the sub in you, rising to the top like cream. Like this kind of cream." His fingers passed through the honey of her pussy. "You just needed some focus. Got to get your mind on your proper business." He traced the eagle tattoo again, following the ripple of the gathered flag; then he made a wide loop to cruise up her back. She had two other tats, not as visible through the sheath's mesh, because they were simple pen and inks. He was resting on one now: the Lord's Hands. Dog tags were inked in a wrap around them, inscribed with *In God We Trust*.

Doms usually stayed away from that one. Too spiritual or personal, and the clubs weren't a place for strangers to get close in that kind of way. Only for pain and pleasure, and losing yourself in a place far beyond the mundane.

"Looks like you made a promise to your grandmother." His touch descended to the script below it. *I'll never forget, Gram.* "No matter what shit you see, you told her you'd keep Jesus and His teachings in mind. Let Him help you with every hard decision a soldier has to make. I like that."

Breath shuddered through her lungs as he moved to her final tattoo, a rendering of Athena. "This one's all for you, though. You call on her to forget the fear, give you a warrior's courage. Mixing the Christian and pagan together, because a soldier needs tactical support wherever she can get it. The devil never lacks for representation out in the field."

What was he doing to her? Slow, sensuous circles on her stung buttocks, words that were stripping away shields most Doms never touched. But she'd known, hadn't she? He didn't need the dungeon. This was what he did to a woman. He flayed away the skin, left her completely exposed. Was this what she'd signed up for?

Apparently so. Because despite the fear and uncertainty, "freedom" had never felt more unappealing to her. Her fingers closed infinitesimally where they were hooked over his. So slight, it might be taken for a simple involuntary twitch of her body. She cursed herself for a coward. She had that Athena tat for a reason. Closing her eyes, she tightened her grip, passed her fingers back and forth over his knuckles. If she was being the sub she was used to being, she'd provoke him with a grip suggesting what those fingers would do if they were on his cock. Instead, she moved in a tender caress on his curved fingers, tracing the calluses, the tough male skin.

"Oh, sweetheart, you're a treasure. You don't even realize it, which makes me harder." He turned her, lifting her in the cradle of his arms again, and stepped right into the fountain, unconcerned about his jeans or the scuffed-looking cowboy boots he wore under them.

He took her to the Aphrodite, which Dana realized was not sinuously posed without purpose. Peter set her down against the statue, so her bottom rested on the goddess's bent knee. Stretching her arms up and back, he laced the extra gauntlet ties to a discreet ring embedded at Aphrodite's throat, part of her jewelry. The alabaster folds of her artful dress formed hard curves through which he threaded Dana's feet, pointing her toes with fingers caressing her arches and the sensitive ankles. When he stepped back, gravity and resistance kept Dana firmly restrained. Aphrodite's ample cleavage pressed into her back so her own breasts jutted out.

When his hands closed on her there, she could tell in his absorption and touch that her captain was an avid breast man, making her wish she had more to offer him there. But he was so thorough, exploring the way they molded into his palms, testing their weight, tugging the nipple clamps and staring at her stimulated nipples in a way that had them aching. It left her feeling as though they were more than enough for him.

"My favorite thing, sweetheart," he murmured. "Suckling pretty tits until I make you come. But there are some other things we need to handle first."

He shrugged his shirt off his shoulders, his gaze drifting up to her mouth, the way she continued to hold his tags. But when he turned to toss the shirt over the fountain wall, letting it flutter to the grass, she drank him in greedily, glad he wasn't a Dom who required her to lower her eyes. One set of biceps bore the *Don't Tread on Me* flag with its coiled serpent. Celtic styled letters formed an arch over the massive breadth of his shoulders. *PEACE.*

She understood why he'd put it there, because it had the same meaning the Lord's Hands did to her. They fought to protect and preserve, but any soldier who'd seen the carnage of war yearned for the day when love would prevail. And hoped there'd be some recognizable vestige of himself left when it finally arrived.

The soul of this man was strong, strong enough to surround her and carry her through anything. The unexpected thought startled her. She'd heard from subs who'd been broken down to the point their most vulnerable needs and truths were revealed. She hadn't thought she was there, but her heart was telling her something different. He'd barely touched her physically, but she already felt owned by him, through and through.

He hadn't moved, holding her gaze as if he knew something intense was going on with her. Maybe for him as well. Reaching out, he traced her mouth, taking away embarrassing saliva with a knuckle. There was a softness in his gray eyes, something that made the coil in her lower belly pull in two directions, toward her heart as much as the throbbing need between her legs.

Please do something. Hurt me. Fuck me. I don't care. Just don't strip me like this so fast. She should spit out the tags, take whatever punishment he could dish out. Anything but this freakish scenario straight from a romance novel, offering love at first sight and everything that went with that improbable scenario.

Yeah, in the middle of a BDSM club with your legs spread and your tits thrust out. Get a grip, Dana. Had she deluded herself to make her fantasy a reality?

He'd picked up a small remote from an alcove to the right of the statue. When he pressed it, water started flowing off the branches of the palm tree draping over Aphrodite's head. It poured down, filtering under her eye mask so she had to turn her face into Aphrodite's cheek. The water spread out, taking a dozen different routes along her throat and over her curves. That flood, as well as the fragrant mist rising, soaked through the thin fabric of her sheath, pasting it to her body.

On the bottom of the pool was an artful scroll design, but when he bent in an attractive ripple of muscle, a pull of denim at groin and thigh, she saw through her wet lashes that not all of them were decoration. Some were long, thin hoses. He straightened one, and the pinpoint nozzle on the end warned her ahead of time. Her clit spasmed in remembrance, her already moist pussy beginning to prepare for him anew.

"If you come without my permission, I'll give you ten more lashes with that switch," he said. "You keep a Master at arm's length, suck his dick and let him paddle your cute butt, call you a naughty girl. You think you're a badass. But on the inside you're a total pussy, sweetheart."

Her reaction wasn't calculated. She snarled and almost dropped the tags, showing her teeth. He showed her his in return, a devastating smile, but there was a heat in his eyes, a hardness to his jaw that told her the intensity wasn't all one-sided.

"You want way more than that. That's why those tags are in your mouth. Remember who you belong to."

The words were a somersault, from outright combat to lovemaking. Helpless here, tied and spread before him, that water licking down her body, she knew the pasted sheath highlighted every crevice and curve, the jut of her nipples. He hadn't taken anything off her but her shoes, and she'd never felt so naked. He hadn't taken off the mask because he didn't need to do so. He was laughing at her attempts to mask who and what she was.

He started at her nipples, playing with them like a cold, forked tongue, making her gasp with need, then washed the water over the high curve, hitting the crease beneath. Her body undulated, breasts quivering for him. Then he dropped and the water jet hit her clit

dead on, shuddering through her body like voltage. No, no, no . . .
Oh, God. From the first second, she lost. No matter how much she
wanted to do so, she couldn't control her body's reaction, because he
was flicking his fingers through the spray, idle movements changing
the friction. She bucked against the hold of the restraints, her ass
slapping hard against Aphrodite's unrelenting knee. She bit down
on the metal, felt the raised type of his name and rank, who he was.
Her Master.

She wouldn't whimper, wouldn't plead. Son of a bitch thought
he could get under her skin, into her head. She didn't want that.
She wanted . . . God, she didn't know what the hell she wanted. She
couldn't think, immersed in sheer, tsunami-powered feeling.

She wanted to lose. It would give him pleasure to switch her ass.
That was what he wanted. He was her Master. She wanted to do
whatever made him hard, whatever would make him want only her.

But in the end, it didn't matter what she wanted. He already
knew, and he took away all choices. The orgasm hit her like a tidal
wave, so intense it was painful. Though her clit was oversensitized,
she wasn't in a position to move away from the stimulation. She
screamed and screamed and screamed, the only thing left in her tumbling mind the need to keep a pit-bull grip on those tags, though
more saliva pooled, slipping out around them. Fortunately the water
washed it away, while the orgasm took everything else.

As she slowly descended to occasional, spasmodic jerks, she was
mumbling around the tags, trying to clear the water from her eyes,
her body shaking so hard. She needed his arms, his body, his heat.
Please, Master. Master. That was what she was mumbling, though it
registered only in a far-distant part of her floating head.

When he came to her, bringing the hard heat of his bare chest
against her, tears spilled out without reservation this time. Locking
his hands over her laced wrists, he pressed his mouth to her cheek
below the mask. Though the water continued to flow over them,
over her face, she was sure he knew she was crying.

He pulled back, but she kept her eyes closed, unsure if she could
handle whatever he had planned next. She couldn't hear anything

over the rush of water, and her body was vibrating so violently it provided its own low roar in her mind, clouding everything else.

When he returned to her, she moaned against the tags. He was blissfully naked, his knees against her thighs as he leaned into her, taking hold of her wrists again and bringing that fine chest closer to her face, so she could press into it, wishing she could open her mouth, taste water and heat.

His cock pressed between her legs, the head finding her with unerring accuracy. She was so slick and wet, she sucked him in like her mouth, but Jesus, he was a big man all over. She couldn't raise her legs, couldn't control anything as he pushed into her, slow and inexorable, refusing to be denied, no matter the tightness of her entry in this position. With the water running over her face, her sight and hearing were limited. But that made every sensation more excruciatingly noticeable. The shape of his broad head, the hard but delicious malleability of his cock, learning the unique feminine shape of her channel. He'd used a condom, since the club allowed nothing less, but she wondered what bareback would have felt like with this much heat and hardness. Her hold on the tags had increased to the point the chain had constricted on her neck, biting in, a collar he'd created only for her.

She wanted to hold on to his taut ass as he pounded into her, feel the flex of it. His thighs pressed to the insides of hers, his sheer size widening her, despite the ankle restraints. Her body was still going, moving with every movement of his, her aftershocks as strong as some orgasms she'd had with other lovers.

Please, please come. She begged him in her mind. She wanted to give him that release, give him anything. He was gorgeous, strong, everything she desired. Totally merciless and totally protective, all at once. She didn't know how to explain that thought, but it was in everything he was doing.

Tilting up as much as she could to give him even more access, she stroked his cock with her inner muscles to tell him how she felt. His fingers bruised where they gripped her wrists, and yet she saw his gaze flicker over her face with infinite desire and something deeper as she risked a look. She'd relish every mark he left on her, trace the dark smudges for days afterward.

"You want me to come, baby?"

She nodded, fast, quick, spoke the garbled words against water and metal. "Please, Master."

"Squeeze me harder with that sweet cunt. Tell me how much you want it."

She put everything she had into it, despite the fact she felt weak as a newborn kitten. However, it was enough. He leaned in, seized her mouth again. It was exquisite torture, the tip of his tongue on the seam of her closed lips, licking at her the way he might lick at her pussy, teasing those lips into full, puffy arousal.

She squeezed harder than she ever had, and started working herself as much as her bonds allowed, stroking, moving faster, though her lungs fought for air and her body strained at the limits of exhaustion. She'd give him everything; she just wanted him to . . .

With a deep, guttural noise, total male animal in rut, he let go. His face stretched into that sexy rictus of pleasure, lips baring back from strong teeth, nostrils flared and eyes glazing and yet firing at once, the brow drawing down to emphasize the fierceness of his response. She reveled in it, her body trying to keep up, but she had no reservoir left. She sank down on him, grunting at every powerful thrust, telling him she wanted more, more, more. He'd left her lips, her nose pressing into the hollow of his throat, burrowing as he used her body for his release.

When at last he slowed, he brought her face up for a lingering tease of her lips again, his eyes open and holding hers as he did it. He kept doing it until a slow liquid heat began to unfurl in her. She didn't think it possible, but she was unable to control her reaction. A true Dom, he knew when he had her juices resurging, because he slid back from her then, releasing the restraints that held her to the statue.

This time she didn't try to catch herself or control her descent, and she sagged into his waiting arms. When he carried her out of the fountain, plush towels already laid out on the sod made her wonder what Zone employee had seen her being pleasured. Had that enviable employee seen him ramming into her, that magnificent ass flexing?

As he laid her down on the towels, he continued to treat her as if she was his in all ways. He positioned her arms over her head and then, with one casual jerk, he ripped the thin dress she wore. Spreading it out to either side, he tenderly removed the nipple clamps, even though the blood rushed back to them painfully. He knew, for he bent and closed a warm, soothing mouth over one, making her whimper again, everything in her weak and out of control. He took his time about it, slow, methodical licks of his tongue, soft suckling, then moved to the other until she couldn't help but move restlessly beneath him.

All barriers to her body gone, he picked up a towel from the additional stack next to him and began to massage terry cloth over her skin, making her whimper when he ran it across her breasts, her breath sucking in at the sensitivity of the area.

Then he reached her pussy and her legs loosened automatically for him, earning an approving nod. Setting the towel aside at last, he leaned down, used his mouth to clasp the chain, slowly draw the tags from her lips. For a moment she held on to them, locking her jaw. His brow rose, a glint coming to his gaze. When at last she released them, he removed them, his fingers caressing, and returned the tags to his neck. She saw she'd left tooth marks, and was thrilled that he'd carry a reminder of her.

Since she was already there, it was a natural desire to look even lower, but she hesitated, looked back up at him.

"Look your fill, sweetheart." He put his thumb to the corner of her mouth. "You didn't cut yourself, did you?"

She shook her head, and looked. Down that powerful chest, to the sectioned abs, the conditioned body of a trained soldier. His cock was impressive even in semi-resting state, lying on the corded thigh muscles. She saw scarring in the abdomen area, though, scarring she recognized. A bullet injury, as well as some strikes that could have come from narrow brushes with explosions.

"Afghanistan," he provided. "I'm pleased to see you aren't marked that way."

"Yet," she whispered.

Gray clouds could become steel in an instant, she realized, as he leaned close again, his heated breath on her face. It made her lips yearn to taste, even as she trembled at what was in his face. Something no man had ever shown her with such undeniable clarity. Possessiveness.

"You'll keep your head and this fine ass down, Sergeant, so it stays that way. And I haven't forgotten those ten strikes with the switch. I'll make sure I send you off with a reminder to obey me in that."

She swallowed, fearing and anticipating that switching, her fingers curling into the sod above her head, even as her pussy moistened further. He went to one hip next to her, propping his head on his fist, and stroked his fingers over her clit, watching her reaction. "Tell me your name. Your real name."

Three

Dana Esther Smith. Her voice had been soft but strong as well, like the flow of a river current he could feel on all his extremities, and perhaps even deeper than that.

Hours later, he'd escorted her back past his table, headed for the locker area. Matt and Lucas had been holding the fort. Matt had raised his glass, giving him his blessing. If Ben had still been there, he knew the lawyer's eyes would have lingered a little too long on Dana's tempting backside. That was Ben, always trying to get something started. Hell, he and Ben had shared a willing submissive before. But this time the thought raised his hackles, made him glad Ben was otherwise occupied.

The whole night had been full of unexpected surprises. He normally preferred a woman with no ink, but the three she had were such tantalizing clues into her head. Despite a jaded, sophisticated world, they suggested she was up-front about her gut convictions, like him. But emotionally there was shielding, complexity. It was what made a woman so damn appealing and frustrating at once.

He'd done what he'd promised, switched her pretty butt good, though a part of him didn't want to mark that delectable flesh with such angry red stripes. While he'd wanted to play more with her sweet tits, his focus had been getting past those shields. Afterward, he'd made her kneel, take him in her mouth, a true submissive's favorite posture, and had her suck him back to life with that skillful, devil-blessed mouth. She'd tried to sass him a couple times when the feelings they conjured in that magical room overcame her. He'd taken care of that. Repeatedly. But he couldn't claim to be any less shaken up. With Dana, he'd not only wanted more; he'd taken it, forced her to that brink with him.

She came toward him now, because they'd agreed to meet at the entrance before she took off. She'd changed into jeans and a snug black tee. The little tease had left off a bra, probably realizing he couldn't keep his eyes off a woman's breasts. The jut of her nipples and wobble of her small curves were damn distracting, but he didn't miss that she was trying to play it cool. She'd left the purple and green mask on. Giving him a friendly but distant smile, she went to her toes and brushed his mouth with hers. "It was a great night, Captain. A once-in-a-lifetime, God's truth."

Astonishingly, she was pulling away, intending to head for one of the waiting taxis. Catching her wrist, he yanked her back to him. Pushing her up against the wall, he treated himself to a rough squeezing of those curves while he kissed her hard and deep, no passing brush of lips. When he lifted his head, her eyes were glazed behind the mask, her lips parted and heart beating fast.

"Trying to play me again, Sergeant?"

She swallowed, shook her head, but he was satisfied to see he'd broken that calm exterior. "I just . . . I can't give you more than tonight, Captain. I want to, but I've got to keep my head on straight. I'm only on leave. Maybe another time, another place . . . I won't be back for a year."

Fuck, what was he doing? He was leaving for Afghanistan next week himself. How could he demand more? Because there was a hell of a lot more there, and no man in his right mind turned his back on that much treasure. He forced himself to look past his own feelings and at her stiff body language, registering the thready pulse. It didn't matter if she was knocked off her axis, too; Dana obviously hadn't intended to take her Zone experience any further than this. When a woman got spooked, she needed her space, time to think. He couldn't push her now, no matter how much he wanted to. The problem was, by the time she thought it through, he'd be on a plane, and she'd be God knew where.

Damn it, earlier he'd calmly accepted fate's direction for his future relationships. If fate was true, he'd see her again. Right? Tonight, he had to let it go.

Releasing her reluctantly, his hands lingering, he nodded. Fought back something that made no sense, that told him to fuck fate, to keep her here with him. Always. "Take care of yourself, Sergeant."

She hesitated, maybe because she felt that resistance from him, or maybe because he was crazy enough to think she felt it from herself. Then she nodded, her fingertips grazing his forearm. Her breasts moved in that quivering, sexy rhythm as she moved to the cab. When he held the door for her, he noticed the slender nape of her neck still bore the faint imprint of his dog tag chain. After he shut the door, she put her hand up to the glass. He tried to meet her palm to palm, but then the cab pulled into traffic and his fingers slipped off. At last glimpse, he could tell she was taking off her mask, a shadow disappearing into the night.

It took a full five minutes of staring into the empty street, his mind circling itself, before he shook himself out of it, turned and went back to the club.

For the next hour and one additional bottle of Macallan, he managed to convince himself he'd done what he should. He responded automatically to Matt and Lucas, shutting out their curious glances. Sure, fate would bring them back together. That and electronics. She was in the military; he was in the military. He could find her. But a year was a fucking long time. He'd left it pretty open-ended, but it had to be. Right?

He recalled how she'd taken off the mask after she'd gotten into the cab. That last smile, light and easy only in appearance. Her eyes had said so much more. She'd pushed him away, taken control to protect herself. He'd walked right into it, because he didn't want to hurt or scare her. But by doing so, he'd sent her the opposite message he'd wanted to send. Who the fuck cared where they would both be in a week? It was what he wanted her to carry around with her for the next year that was important.

"Matt," he said abruptly, slamming down his glass. "I need your help."

There were many reasons to appreciate having lots of money, and the ability to find information quickly was one of them. By waking one of Matt's contacts, they'd found out she was flying back to Fort Bragg in the morning. From there she would return to Iraq. She was with the 18th Theater Support Command, a Supply Sergeant.

Peter's heart had flipped at that news. While he treated women soldiers with respect, at heart level, he preferred women not to serve in combat areas. It went against his deepest instincts to put a woman in harm's way. Protecting them was a man's job.

Ruefully, he'd imagined what colorful things Dana would say to that. He was sure she had a mouth on her. Anyone who'd been out in that godforsaken heat, with sand in every crevice and crack, was comfortably fluent in swearing. But of course thinking about her mouth got him hard again, thinking what he'd done with those moist, accommodating lips.

So here he was, standing in the airport at the security check-in point. He'd gotten there four hours ahead of schedule to be sure, and been scoping it ever since. As intently as he was scanning very face, he was surprised airport security hadn't questioned him.

Though he hadn't seen her face without the mask, he knew her the second he saw her. She had only one carry-on, one of those bags women wore slung across their chests to carry all their girl stuff.

Probably a paperback book or some other way to pass the time on the flight. He wondered what she read, what she liked. She was in the jeans he'd seen last night, but now she wore a long-sleeved, snug knit shirt over it with a vee neck that showed the right amount of cleavage. Whatever bra she was wearing was holding her high and firm. A small silver cross nestled into her collarbone.

The face he hadn't demanded to see last night was delicate and determined. She carried her head with graceful dignity on the slim neck, her closely shorn hair only emphasizing the beauty of her skull shape, the sharp slope of cheekbones. A straight nose and lush, soft lips. The conditioning of her body made her movements graceful, confident. Men and women alike couldn't help a second look, because confidence turned a handsome, petite woman into a beautiful, elegant one. With amusement, he saw she was wearing sizeable wedges. He wondered if she put platforms in her combat boots to give her the extra five inches she'd tried to use as one of her many defenses last night.

Maybe he was lucky that he'd had so much experience with women, though if she was feeling an ounce of the possessiveness he was, Dana might not think so. All the submissives whose company he'd enjoyed, even the longer relationships he'd had, had taught him not to confuse hormones with his heart. But he saw her and, God, it was exactly like last night. Everything he'd learn about this particular woman would fascinate him; he was sure of it. He'd want to learn more and more. This was real. But that lack of doubt couldn't erase the panicked pressure in his chest, knowing he needed more time. He'd take anything, even thirty minutes in a coffee shop, but she was running late. So he'd have to treat the next ten minutes as the most important of his life—without scaring the shit out of her.

She saw him. As she slowed, cocking her head, her eyes bright with a mixture of curiosity and not a little apprehension, he straightened off the column where he'd been leaning.

"Come here," he mouthed, need burning through him like an oil fire.

How had he found her? Had she conjured him? For the past twelve
hours, she'd tried to shake it off. Finally, she'd given up, basking in
the freaking glow of the most amazing experience she'd ever had.
Why hadn't she given him her address, asked for his?

Because it was best to leave it at one magical night, not spoil it.
The fact that it was the most earth-shattering experience she'd ever
had sexually, on a deep, emotional level, didn't mean that could
translate outside of the club walls. The things that were different
about the two of them were still different. Last night had over-
flowed with magical trappings, perfect timing, everything. That
wasn't real. In a real world, Cinderella had to go back to being Cinderella the next day.

She was depressingly aware that such internal arguments said
more about her than the experience. Maybe the reason she hadn't
found the Dom she'd been seeking was she wasn't brave enough for
that risk. She couldn't bear to lose someone she loved again, whether
it was from a relationship disintegrating or something far worse. So
one night and one night only. That was the best thing.

She'd almost convinced herself of it; then she saw him there.
That look, the way he called her to him, those firm lips mouthing
the command, and her mind went AWOL.

She didn't know if she walked or ran. She just knew within three
seconds she was pressed up against him, on her toes to reach that
mouth. *This is crazy, this is crazy, this is crazy. But God, so wonderful.* He
cinched his arm around her waist and hauled her up so she could lock
her arms around his neck, drink deep, pull him inside her one more
time. Leaning back against the column to give them both an anchor,
he cupped her head, taking control of the kiss. All that tall, hard
body, so broad and strong, and now she could grip his biceps, run her
fingernails over the *Don't Tread on Me* tattoo, scrape his skin. He
growled in her mouth but she couldn't resist trailing her fingers
through the short hair at his nape as well, letting her hand slide down
along his jaw. He made that kiss last a good long time, so long that

it was she who had to break it, reluctantly. When he at last let her down to her feet, he kept his hands at her waist, thrilling her with the possessive grip.

"I'm already late for check-in," she said, cursing the fact she was late. "I can't miss this one. I'm due back at the base."

"I know." His mouth became a determined line. "Dana, I expect to see you again."

From the flicker in his gaze, she wondered if he'd intended to use more charm, though the raw honesty hit her low and hard. She knew so little of him. Maybe his cock was just tied up with his head. Maybe her mind was no better, spinning with hormones. She couldn't make this leap right now. She couldn't. She wasn't ready.

But the feelings swelling up now at the look in his gray eyes, the feel of his hands on her body, had her rattled down to her toes. She'd been blown away last night. Didn't matter if it was hormones or not—she couldn't deny that she'd never reacted to a man like this, not in her whole life. She'd fantasized about a Master like him, right? So how much could she risk of herself to see if he was the real deal? How far would he go to prove it?

"Okay," she said softly. "Then write to me. Not e-mail. Letters." Old-fashioned love letters, like the ones Gram had gotten from Grandpa when he was in Vietnam. She'd requested those letters be buried with her.

He studied her, his expression intent, fathomless. "You going to give me an address?"

"You knew to find me here. I expect you can find that easily enough."

"You're not going to write me back, are you?" At her quick negative shake, his gaze darkened, that chin getting an obstinate look she knew she'd be powerless to resist.

"I'll look forward to every one you send me. If it's meant to be, I'll see you again. Please," she added desperately as he slid his touch up her waist, his thumbs pressing into her rib cage beneath her breasts. "It's too much, too soon. I . . . can't handle it any other way." *Please, please write to me.*

Leaning down, he brushed her nose with his lips, gave her a close-up of those intense eyes once more. "A test. You want me to prove something to you, protect yourself, okay. I'll let you have your way this once, because I don't want you rattled where you're going. But in a year or so, when they let you come home again, you'd better be ready for me, little girl. We're not done. Not by a long shot. And you won't be calling the shots then."

Dana ran her knuckles down his jaw, loving his words, loving that he thought of her safety at the same time he wouldn't let her think she'd gotten away with anything. "Thanks, Captain," she whispered.

So many things she wanted came bubbling up, closing her throat. Maybe if she had enough faith, she would give him everything about her, inside and out. Despite the family she no longer had, she wanted to believe the crazy idea that this virtual stranger could be her new family. She wanted someone in the world to know her down to the deepest level of her soul, be connected to her in a way that even death couldn't take. She wanted him to be that someone.

God. Which was exactly why it was best to do it this way. If he was the real deal, blurting all that out right now would surely send him into full retreat, back out to the overpriced parking. Right? When he put his hand to her face, that thought vanished. Turning her cheek into that tender gesture, she leaned into his hand, letting him hold her that way, hoping she was conveying . . . something to him. Something that would make it worth it to him to keep writing, even when she wouldn't let herself write back, the most unfair test possible.

"I hate this." His jaw flexed. "I want to keep you safe."

Giving him a smile, she picked up his other hand, opened it. She bent his middle and index fingers inward, leaving the other fingers straight. Tapping those two fingers on her chest, she curled her hand over his. Her fist barely covered his, but she squeezed him hard nevertheless.

"That's sign language for heart. You'll hold my heart safe until I see you again." She swallowed, whispered the next word. "Master."

His eyes became molten at the title, spoken outside the restrictions of the club, making her glad she'd dared that much. Rising on her toes, she pressed her cheek to his strong jaw, closed her eyes and let herself be totally vulnerable this blink in time, holding their locked hands between them. "Keep your ass down, too. I haven't seen nearly as much of it as I want to. But . . . if you change your mind about us, thanks for everything."

"I'm not changing my mind."

"I hope so. But no obligations, Captain Peter Winston."

It was so hard to move out of that embrace. Somehow it tied into everyone and everything to whom she'd ever had to say good-bye. She was blinking back freaking tears. Shouldering her bag, she gave him a quick nod and moved toward check-in.

Instead of making forward progress, however, she was brought up short, the strap of her bag used to haul her back up against him one more time. He invaded her with a kiss that reached all the way to her toes, caused her to cling and sigh into his mouth, perilously close to saying words that would make her a romantic fool.

When he let her up for air, he held her gaze like an oath.

"You got an obligation to me, Sergeant. And I won't be forgetting it."

Four

Two months later

"Man, I can't believe I'm in this fucking oven on wheels with you two when Gary Sinise is coming to visit our platoon today. I wanted to squeeze Lieutenant Dan's fine, tight ass." Specialist Leslie Sykes peered out over the rocky desert terrain. "I see you snickering back there, O'Neill. I know you're still chasing that tail up at Battalion, so don't think you're better than me."

"Nope. No more. I realized a man has to be an idiot to get involved with a heavily armed woman."

"Good thinking. No woman in her right mind could hang out with you for more than ten minutes and not want to shoot you," Dana said, keeping her eye on their right perimeter, tracking the vehicles behind them. "Of course, you'd best remember women are resourceful. If they don't have a gun, a blunt object works mighty fine. More personal that way."

Leslie laughed. "Sounds like you might be better off switching sides of the fence, O'Neill. Come squeeze Lieutenant Dan's ass with me."

"Hey, hey, hey . . ." O'Neill gave her a mock scowl. "Don't ask, don't tell, soldier." He jerked his chin at Dana. "She's just running a diversion. She doesn't want us poking at her about that guy she's been mooning over ever since she got back."

Dana shifted in the passenger seat, adjusting her helmet. "I only want you poking at me, Sergeant O'Neill. You and all your fine manly stuff."

Leslie snorted. "Like I believe that. I think he's got your number, girlfriend. What's this boy like?"

Dana smirked. "A tall, blond captain with an ass that would put anything you've ever imagined to shame. The ass of all asses."

"Ooh, she's gone to the white-boy side." Leslie chuckled. "Your grandma would be spinning."

"No. I think she would have liked him."

Her own certainty about that surprised her. He'd written her, as he'd promised. Once a week, without fail. While those letters should have come with a fire-hazard warning, they were devastating for far more than the sexual innuendoes. . . .

I can't believe I agreed to this shit. One minute I feel like some lovesick fool; then I remember that kiss, the way you ran to me at the airport, and I can barely breathe. Yeah, it's crazy. I know you're trying to convince yourself it's hormones, that I'm writing this because I'm seeing way too many sweaty guys and not enough soft, female flesh, but it's you, Dana. I don't want to be a dick, but that night was far from the first time for me. But it was the first time I was left with this hurting ache inside. Letting you go was a mistake, leaving an emptiness that won't be filled until I see you again. Are we both crazy? I want to find out. I intend to find out.

I know you were scared, and that's part of why you decided to make us do it this way. I don't want you to be scared, sweetheart. I want to know everything about you, why you're so scared of loving and losing. But I'm thinking you're also pretty smart, because I'm writing all sorts of things I wouldn't normally share with a woman, especially if I want her to remain impressed with me. For example, I like little dogs. Particlarly the scrapper ones, the Jack Russells, who won't give up and are so tough they won't back down from anything. Kittens are pretty irresistible, too. My buddy Lucas and his wife, Cass, just got a couple from the shelter and they're maniacs, tearing up everything while making them laugh their asses off.

I guess I'm pretty predictable. Beer and pizza is my favorite meal, and I like falling asleep in my boat on the bayou. I once woke up beached on a sand spit next to a couple alligators. They apparently figured I was too dumb to mess with. I'd like to fall asleep in my boat with you in my arms, let the sun bake us and not wake up until the mosquitoes try to drive us in . . . no alligators that trip, though.

If I told you I started falling in love with you the first moment I saw you, the kind of fall that could turn into a long, spiraling lifetime of love worth having, it would scare you to death, wouldn't it? So I won't say it. I'll just think it.

Her lips curved in a small smile, remembering. They'd had nothing more than sex between them, right? But as if that was a battle already fought and won, his letters cut right past the bullshit, letting her into his mind, telling her his thoughts. He was drawing her in, making her want to be with him on all levels so bad that it hurt, just like he said.

I've always wanted to drive across the country, stop wherever we wanted. See those sights that nobody ever takes the time to see. The best ice cream shop in a small town in the middle of Iowa, run by two people who started it back during the fifties. Or a historical marker where some famous Civil War general watered his horse and sat under a tree, writing a letter to his wife. I think you find out a lot about someone when you travel with them. And though

our initial trip was way too short, I already know I'd like to take
a much, much longer one together. Don't shake your head. I know
that's what you're doing. So how about it? I'm going to finish
every letter with a question, because I want you to have all sorts of
answers for me when next we see each other . . . but one will be
more important than any of the others.

"I've got movement to the left," O'Neill said sharply.

Dana's attention snapped fully back to the present, though even with the distraction of Peter's letters, the forefront of her mind had never left off surveillance of their surroundings. Vehicles moving supplies between towns were too rich of a target, and Combat Logistic Patrols ran every day to supply Combat Outpost Posts. The up-armored FMTV lumbering behind them carried medical and food supplies. In front of their vehicle was Sergeant Sinclair's up-armored Humvee, and two more followed behind the FMTV.

"Where?" Leslie asked, and then the question became moot. Dana shouted out the warning as the RPG round whistled through the air. The rear vehicle of their convoy exploded, the flash illuminating the area.

In a matter of seconds, everything was chaos. They'd hit a straight stretch between two curves, and the insurgents had set their ambush well. The sergeant and his detail ahead barely made it out before their vehicle exploded, blockading forward progress. A hail of AK-47 gunfire rained down from the ridge on their three o'clock. It was a sure bet they'd mined the sides of the road with IEDs to keep them from going around.

Fortunately, they hadn't gotten the Humvee that mounted a 50-cal, right behind the FMTV. Those guys were firing hot and heavy up into that ridge.

"Go, go, go," O'Neill was barking. Dana slid out after Leslie and they hit the hard-packed ground, running for the meager ditch on the opposite side of the road.

"Straighten up." Dana grabbed Leslie's vest and hauled her along. Leslie rarely got out of the Battalion S4 shop and had made a newbie mistake, trying to crouch down as she ran. The body armor was too heavy to allow for that. She'd trip and land on her face. "Move your ass!"

The dirt kicked up around them as they ran, but Dana heard the M-4 fire as O'Neill covered their six. In the corner of her eye, she saw the men in the Humvee and supply truck doing the same, a gradual fall back to this ditch line.

"Targets ahead." Dana heard the shout, saw the insurgents waiting in the ditch, guns raised, dark eyes wild, faces wet with nervous sweat. She swung her own gun around, braced for recoil and let it go, sending them scattering. One got punched through the head and flipped back, and then she and Leslie were in the ditch and she was shoving the body out of the way.

"Breathe, girl, breathe," she counseled Leslie, hunkering down. "Just keep it together, shoot straight and wait for orders. They'll call for air support."

And please God, let them get here in time.

"God, no women in combat. Yeah, right." Though Leslie's voice was cracking, Dana was glad to see she was keeping it together, checking her ammo with shaking fingers. Then her gaze landed on something else sharing the ditch with them.

"Les, look."

Her friend followed her gaze, saw the RPG left behind by the fleeing insurgents on this side. "I've never shot one."

"Me neither." Dana firmed her chin. "We'll sure as hell figure it out. That Humvee only has a few minutes before someone throws a mortar on it."

"Us, too, probably. Fuck. God, this is crazy."

Thankfully it wasn't Dana's first firefight, so the rapid change of circumstances and incredible noise wasn't new to her. There was no communication down the line yet, the sergeant likely trying to raise that air support and relying on their knowledge of how to stay down until he decided how to form their defensive line. Right now, this was likely the best they could do.

Snatching up the weapon, Dana examined it closely, figured out the dual trigger. She had to wiggle up the side of the ditch. Bullets cut through the ground at the edge. But setting her teeth, she went to her knees, lifted her helmeted head and took aim.

The missile shot up. She'd aimed lower than her target. As she'd anticipated, it went higher than she'd intended, but not too high. It hit the ridge a couple feet below the edge. Dirt and rock exploded, sending an avalanche of debris and flailing bodies down.

"O'Neill," Leslie screamed.

Dana tossed the RPG aside. O'Neill had gotten briefly pinned down at the vehicles, providing additional cover fire for the drivers. When he made a run for it, a round hit him from the insurgents who'd come out from the hidden curve ahead. He dropped like a stone.

The two women didn't hesitate, coming up over the edge of the ditch shoulder to shoulder. "Get him to cover," Dana shouted, turning the M-4 toward that group of targets along with the others who came to back her up. Leslie grabbed hold of him, tried to get him onto his feet, but O'Neill was six feet of muscle. Another soldier went to help. Dana backpedaled in front of them, bullets whistling around her, kicking up dirt. Thank God, the insurgents were probably jacked up on adrenaline shots or Khat, not shooting worth shit, but it was close enough. Any second she expected one to punch through her. Noise and AK-47 fire, hell on earth.

She had been in active engagement before because of situations like this, but nothing this intense. She'd trained for it, though, and kept training for it, even more so than the guys who got field experience far more often. The enemy didn't give a damn if you were a woman or not when it came to shooting U.S. soldiers, and this situation made all those extra grueling hours of practice worth it, even if her heart was pounding up in her ears.

Think about the targets, and a gorgeous captain who will be so *pissed if you don't come home and take that cross-country trip with him. Nap in that boat together. He'd probably chase you to the Pearly Gates with those alligators just to beat your ass.*

She stumbled over something, saw a Pepsi bottle roll away wildly. A second later, the world exploded in bright light and pain.

Five

Peter got out of the taxi and breathed deep of the bayou that backed up to his Baton Rouge home. Jon had been coming here regularly while Peter was on tour so it didn't get an empty feeling to it. While that meant he'd probably burned some weird incense or had one of his tranquil and oh-so-centered bedmates chant over the front door, that was okay. Whatever he did, Peter had no doubt it would feel as comfortable as when he left. This time it was going to feel better than it ever had. Not only because it was home, but because now he could go after Dana.

Fourteen months had gone by, and his feelings ran as strong for her as they had that night. Worse, even. It was the damnedest thing, but why should he be surprised? Matt and Lucas had known the minute they met Savannah and Cass, respectively. He'd seen it happen, but hadn't realized it felt like this.

He couldn't believe he'd agreed to her terms, satisfying himself with a one-way stream of letters until the end of their tour. As he'd told her, sometimes he'd felt like a lovesick fool, putting his thoughts in that vacuum. But he kept himself going by reviewing, again and again, every detail of their short time together. Particularly how she'd seen him in the airport and run to him like water in the desert. She'd surrendered to him that night at The Zone, and not merely her flesh. When she kissed him, there'd been forever in that girl's grip.

The second he got stateside, he'd called Jon, asking him to find out where she was and have Matt's admin make travel arrangements for him. He didn't care if she considered that cheating. *His* tour was done. He was going to have a shower and a nap, but twenty-four hours weren't going to pass before he was on his way to her. Thank God for the Taliban and dangerous missions. They'd kept him from going crazy this past year.

Smiling wryly, he opened the front door, and found Jon sitting in his living room. With Matt, Lucas and Ben, suggesting they'd all ridden together in Jon's car out front.

Peter stopped. They would have met up tonight for beers and celebrated his return, but they wouldn't have come like this. Not unless . . .

When Jon rose, the expression in his somber face twisted Peter's gut. "She's dead." Peter forced out the words, but a heartbeat later cursed himself for being the one to say what he least wanted to hear. "That's not possible. The letters didn't come back."

"They were forwarded. She's not dead, Peter." Jon took a step forward. Peter held his ground, his fists clenching. Waiting. "She was injured in southern Iraq twelve months ago. She's been stateside ever since."

"Is she . . . What happened to her? Is her family . . ."

He should have done everything to keep her off that plane, sacrificed a lifetime of principles and patriotism to keep her safe. He was going to shake Jon like a rag doll if he didn't start talking. *Now.*

"It was a firefight, a pretty bad one," Jon said, holding him with his steady gaze as Lucas moved to Peter's side. "She got caught in an explosion when she was laying down cover fire."

Damn it, Sergeant. You're not supposed to be in combat. But women never did as they were told, did they? He'd seen the jut of the stubborn chin, the firm muscle of that lean, prepared body. She wouldn't walk away from a fight. No more than he would.

"What's happened to her?"

"She's blind." Peter closed his eyes, but Jon pressed on, knowing him well enough to give him all of it, fast as possible. "She lost the ability to hear in one ear. The other has diminished capacity. She's badly scarred, but my understanding is most can be repaired with reconstructive surgery. Some of it has already been done. But the main thing is she's alive, she can walk and she has all fingers, toes and limbs. . . . Focus on that."

"Okay." Peter nodded, his lips folded together tight. While he told his heart to stop thundering, the other men drew closer, forming a half ring around him. That, plus the hesitation in Jon's voice, tipped him off to the fact he hadn't heard it all.

"Tell me the rest." Peter shifted his gaze to Matt, standing directly in front of him. Years ago, Matt had been the one to come and tell the younger man his parents had been killed in a car crash. The steady look in his gaze had been the same then, despite the fact Matt had barely been out of college himself. Kensington would do whatever it took to get a job done. To make things right. He'd honed the same quality in Peter.

"Dana has no living family," Matt said quietly. "She had no support system to deal with this."

"You tell me she's on the street talking to herself, living out of the garbage, and I'm going to have to kill somebody."

"No." Lucas put a hand on his shoulder. "She didn't have much in the way of a bank account, but she got full disability and benefits, enough to rent a small place near a VA hospital and cover her living expenses. She's not going to be vacationing in Tahiti every year, but she's not starving. She's high up on the list for care at a residential facility, but they're crowded, and in truth, the specialist I talked to said she doesn't need that."

Peter's pulse thudded anew against his throat. "So why's she on the list?"

Jon shook his head. "She's doing the minimum required to learn new skills, improve the compensatory use of her other senses. The specialist confided that it was the nurses who coordinated the duplex unit where she's living. They found a lady, a nurse, to stay next door and take care of her. I'm sorry, Peter, but I know you'd want to know. He said if not for those steps, she might very well have ended up on the street. She has no interest in anything other than sitting in a chair."

"Damn it, they have all sorts of resources for PTSD shit. Why didn't they—?"

"The patient has to be willing. And you know how irreplaceable a family support network is for dealing with those kinds of issues." Jon swept a meaningful glance among the men standing before him. "Which is why we're here now."

Peter swallowed, pushing down the fury, the knowledge that still had his pulse accelerated. Lucas squeezed his shoulder, a reminder of support. Taking a deep breath, he thought it through, closing his eyes again to focus.

They waited him out. He was the hands-on guy, the one who went and straightened out snarls at plants in their Central and South American locations, dealing with a wide variety of concerns in unexpected, sometimes volatile, environments. If he approached it that way, he wouldn't lose his head, get mired down in thoughts about how she needed him and he wasn't at her side right now.

He opened his eyes. "I need to know everything you know, Jon. I want to talk to this specialist myself. I'm bringing her home."

Ben raised a brow. "You knew her for one night."

"It doesn't matter," Matt answered for Peter, gazing into his face. "She's the one, isn't she?"

Peter nodded. All those months, he hadn't doubted his emotions, but their strength had baffled him. But now, on a tidal surge of those feelings, thinking about where she was, how she needed him, he knew what it was. The men around him, they were the family he'd chosen, but she was like a part of his heart that had been missing since he'd lost his blood family. A part sent by fate, so he'd recognized her from that first second.

He shook his head, pushing back the wave before it unmanned him. "Since she's coming back here with me, whether she likes the idea or not, it's likely I'll need some wheels greased."

"Always happy to keep you out of jail for kidnapping," Ben said dryly.

Matt moved forward then. Lucas withdrew so Matt's hand could replace his, grip Peter's shoulder with hard reassurance. "We'll take care of both of you. Bring her home."

Six

As individuals, they were relentless. As a team, they couldn't be stopped. It had taken a few nerve-racking days to get it all together, but if they could pull off an aggressive takeover of a floundering multinational corporation, they could handle the relocation of one female soldier, unwilling or not. Paperwork of course wasn't a problem for Ben. But then they hit an unexpected snag. A determined, caring woman.

Christina Lawson was a retired RN, a former Vietnam field nurse. Her husband had killed himself years ago, never able to leave Vietnam behind. She was the one who lived in the other side of the duplex, checking in on Dana daily. She rebuffed Ben's legal bullshit, veiled threats and charming persuasions alike.

So Jon stepped in, because Peter's impatience made diplomacy impossible. While he didn't know what Jon had said to her, she at last agreed to their plan to relocate her charge. *If* she had a face-to-face meeting with Peter first, and *if* Dana consented to leave with him.

Peter wasn't going to fault the woman for being protective of Dana. But when he got out of the rental car in front of the small duplex, a nondescript housing unit located adjacent to the hospital acreage, he was vibrating with the need to kick in the door of whichever side held Dana, and say to hell with any more delays. Since Christina Lawson was planted on the porch, arms akimbo, his plan might have to include a wrestling match with a woman his grandmother's age.

As he came up the walk, the nurse studied him from head to toe, her expression suggesting she was considering whether she needed a broom or a shotgun. He cleared his throat, made a considerable effort to look affable and charming, despite the fact the ache that had been building inside him these interminable five days threatened to hemorrhage.

"Mr. Winston?" Christina offered a hand and he closed his over it, noting fingers swollen with early arthritis, but there was strength there still. She nodded toward the porch swing. "We can talk here."

No "Glad to meet you," or other bland courtesies that would mean nothing to either one of them. He could appreciate that, but the knot in his stomach didn't loosen.

"Won't she . . . ?"

Christina shook her head. "I told her I was going to be on the porch, visiting with a friend of mine. She rarely gets out of her day chair, so I knew we'd have enough time for privacy. She wears her hearing aid grudgingly, so she won't hear us, either. Even if she has it on, she has to concentrate on what's being said and the person must speak clearly, toward the functioning ear, for her to detect and understand. Unfortunately, visual clues and lip reading are what helps a person with hearing loss the most, and those are aids her blindness denies her."

"I'll get her upgraded to a top-of-the-line hearing aid," he said immediately. Jon had already told him about advances in technology, which he'd heard with only half an ear, but Peter remembered the basics nonetheless.

Christina cocked her head. "The problem isn't money, Mr. Winston. Money undoubtedly helps, but there are impoverished children blind and deaf as Helen Keller that adapt to their handicaps. The problem is her. I think you already know that, though. Please sit."

He took a seat, bracing the swing when his weight tipped it forward. A tight smile touched Christina's features, but he wasn't sure if he could be encouraged by it.

"You are a big man, that's for certain. Mr. Forte said you were a businessman, but you have military written all over you."

"I just got back from my Afghanistan tour."

"I know that. I know a lot more about you than you realize, Mr. Winston." She was on her hip on the swing, her sneakered feet swaying lightly over the boards as he unconsciously moved the swing in an agitated rhythm. Noticing it, he stopped, but she continued to study him, saying nothing.

Goddamn it, he was going to go insane. "Tell me what you need to know, Mrs. Lawson." Turning to face her dead-on, he dropped any pretense at hiding how he felt. "How do I get past you? I've waited fourteen months to be back with her again. She may not have said a single word about me, but I can tell you, right before I shipped out, she opened her heart to me, and I'm sure she's as much mine as I'm hers. I won't do anything to hurt her. I swear it to you on everything I am. You want blood, a written guarantee—"

He stopped, his jaw flexing. "I'm sorry. I know I sound like an obsessive stalker. I'm just . . . I'm going fu— I'm going insane not being close to her, able to help her. You've done a great job; I'm grateful, but—"

"That's fine, Mr. Winston," Christina said abruptly. "I've seen what I need to know. Here are my terms. You can stay the night here with Dana. In the morning, if she tells me she wants to go with you, she can of course go wherever she wishes."

Now it was his turn to stare at her. "That's it?"

The nurse nodded. He blinked, ran a hand over his face. "Well, I'm sorry, Mrs. Lawson. The way you were over the phone with Jon . . . Hell, the way you looked when I pulled up, I was expecting a hell of a lot more than that."

"You expected me to pull out the interrogation techniques I

learned in Saigon?" She twinkled at him then, but the humor didn't reach her eyes.

"Yeah, a little. So do you mind if I ask what miracle changed your mind?"

"It was not so much what you did to change my mind, as what you did to confirm the decision I'd already made. Can I trust you to stay here?"

Under that penetrating maternal stare, he was hard-pressed not to squirm, but he nodded. Pursing her lips together, she rose and disappeared into the right-hand side, taking care not to let the screen door slam. When she returned, she held a decorative photo box. As she opened the top, Peter saw his letters, neatly filed. At his stunned look, Christina nodded.

"I can't get her to do much. Not even basic navigation of her surroundings, but she always knows where this box is. She shows no interest in anything, but she'll do almost anything I ask, if I agree to read one to her. Though I don't know why that matters, because her lips move as I read them. She knows them all by heart."

Peter's gaze strayed back to the box. There were worn places in the glossy veneer, where it looked as though fingers had gripped the box. Christina watched him. "Some nights, when I'm wandering about out here, smoking a cigarette—a terrible habit I've never kicked—I'll see her sitting in her bedroom, dark but for the television. She'll be holding that box, or have one of your letters in her hand, stroking her fingers over the words she can't see."

Because Peter remembered some of the things he'd put in those letters, it was an effort to hold that knowing gaze, but she was continuing. "I've cared for many soldiers since my husband. I have no degree in psychology. Sometimes I think all that learning can interfere with seeing with your heart, using your common sense. But I do know when they lose interest in everything, turn so deep inside themselves that not even the ones who love them most can reach them, they're already in the grave." Her voice wavered, old shadows rising in her eyes, but she firmed her chin.

"Dana is like that in so many ways, except for this. You are her one lifeline, Peter. For the chance that it can save her, I will risk throwing that line to you, a man I only know through these letters, but who has come to me and spoken from his heart."

Her green light made him want to leap up, shove through that door, but she was his best key to reaching Dana's mind. "Why do you think she's drawn into herself?"

She shook her head. "It's hard enough when you have family to support you. But when you go through this and wake up so alone and isolated . . . Her grandmother was her last living family, and she died three years ago. Dana had two brothers, both killed in gang wars on the streets, though apparently she was the eldest and tried to keep them out of trouble. Her mother ran off on them and she didn't know her father. A common enough tale for a girl born in bad circumstances. Thanks to her grandmother, she made something of herself."

The nurse glanced over the quiet neighborhood street again. "Our girl in there protected a fallen comrade under heavy fire. She didn't have to do it, but she did it anyway. She was given a medal at Walter Reed. The nurses packed it with her belongings, but she hasn't touched it." She sighed. "I'd lay money she's never been a whiner or shirker in her whole life. But a woman who's had to be so self-reliant can break when she's pushed hard enough. When she thinks she's all alone."

"She had you."

"There's a difference between that, and having someone who's close to her heart, someone who *knows* her heart, to help her heal. That is what I got from your letters, Captain Winston. I think you know her heart, by instinct if not experience. I honestly feel that all that Dana needs is someone with a key to her. I don't think she's in a deep depression, the kind that they treat with chemicals. She's angry a lot, and anger means passion. Apathy and indifference are much worse signs. If you can get to her, and she puts half the energy to getting out of her chair that she dedicates to staying in it, she'll do as much as she ever planned to do, and probably more. All she needs is someone to help her find herself again. Once she does that, the rest—learning new skills, rehabilitation—it's all waiting for her. I expect you'll help her through that, but if you need guidance, I'm always willing to point you in the right direction."

She rose as abruptly as she'd done everything else, a woman of decisive action. Peter expected she'd been a hell of a field nurse. "All right, then. She's all yours. Unless you come and get me next door, you won't be disturbed until tomorrow morning."

"But—" Sudden panic invaded him.

Christina reached out, took his hand in an unexpected reassurance, her brisk voice gentling. "There's nothing medically wrong with her, Peter. Except for the fact she barely eats or moves out of that chair, she's as healthy as you are. And she knows enough about her handicaps to let you know before you take a misstep. You'll be fine."

She withdrew her touch and straightened. "Be what you know she needs you to be. Kick her ass into gear again. She doesn't need any pity. She's had way too much of that. I'm going to go grocery shopping now, but I'll be back in a while. Trial by fire. I understand that's your specialty."

Giving him one more direct look, she put the box quietly inside Dana's door, retrieved purse and keys from her own unit, and headed down the walkway to her car.

She doesn't need any pity. Jesus. He understood that, but all he wanted to do was scoop Dana up, rock her in his lap and tell her he was going to take care of everything. He was still wrestling with it when he stepped into her unit, made his way through a bland front room and functional kitchen, to the back den where Christina had indicated she spent most of her daylight hours.

When he stepped into the room, his conflicting emotions swamped him.

Except for what was filtering through the sheer panels, there was

no light. It made it a soft, sad atmosphere, adding to what vibrated
from the woman curled up on an oversized recliner. Since she appeared to be staring toward the window, he suspected she had some
sense of the light, or perhaps she felt the sun's heat. Though it was
afternoon, she wore pajama bottoms and a sweatshirt that swallowed her. She looked clean and showered, however. Since she still
kept her hair short, the filtered light gleamed off the slender tube
that wound around the shell of her ear to hold the hearing aid in
place.

She'd turned into a mole. Burrowing down in her clothes, her
recliner, her featureless home, digging a hole to bury herself here.
Jesus Christ. Christina was right. He didn't need a shrink's license to
understand the less-than-subtle message.

I wish I'd died, rather than having to face this alone.

In that revelation, pity got shoved to the side by something
much stronger in him. Anger. It didn't matter that it wasn't at her,
or that it might be misplaced. He'd use it.

There was plenty of room for him on the recliner, so he settled
his hip there, his thigh close to the tips of her bare brown toes. They
were painted deep burgundy. That had to be Christina's doing. Laying his palm over them, he closed his hand instinctively over the
small, cold digits, passing his thumb over her sole.

Her head lifted and turned toward him, the light from the window showing him more of her face. The sightless eyes wrenched his
gut, made him want to weep. As Jon had said, they'd done their
best to repair the extensive scarring in her face, but it would take
time for the surgical scars to heal and disappear. She would never
again have the fresh, sculpted beauty she'd had that night, replaced
by a hard, tortured thinness. But as much as that and the lack of
vision in her eyes concerned him, it was the lack of fire that bothered him most. Her gaze wasn't merely sightless, but also lifeless.

No. Christina had said she had passion, anger. That fire was only
dormant. He would accept nothing less. *Know her heart by instinct.* He
was no Prince Charming, but he'd spent a great deal of his sexually
mature years learning to uncover a woman's inner sensuality and fan

it to a raging inferno. For a submissive, that reaction was so closely linked to her soul, both had to be ignited to give her everything she needed. So maybe he did have the key. Because from their one night together, he knew what kind of submissive she was.

Reaching out, he slid his palm to the side of her face. As she had at the airport, she tilted her head into it, her eyes closing. No matter the scars, her sweet mouth, the curve of her cheek, her slim neck, they were all the same. Tracing her lips with his thumb, he teased them open to caress her teeth, graze her tongue. She tasted him with the tip of it, and he saw a lethargic desire flicker across her face.

"I keep dreaming about you." Her voice was a bit raspy. There'd been some damage to her vocal cords, but if he hadn't known, it would have passed as a sexy purr. The volume was a little low, the pronunciation slurred, as if she were sleepy. "That night. I want to be back there with you, so much. God. It was all so physical, and so much more than that. I ache when I think about you, Master." She swallowed and became a smaller ball, as if compressing her thighs and the need there. "I'd rather dream about being with you forever, than live another single day, you know?"

She used his hand as a pillow, nestling down farther. With her other hand she splayed his fingers, ran them over her mouth, one at a time, slow, tasting, nuzzling. Peter felt his groin tighten, even as he was appalled at himself. She's . . .

There's nothing medically wrong with her, Peter. Christina's admonition, her knowing look. Wow, he was slow on the uptake. But he was still warring with it, the need to nurture and yet take her over at once. Hold her close and spank her within an inch of her life for scaring him. Well, hell, there was time for both, wasn't there?

Her brow was crinkling, mouth pressing together as if holding back emotion. "God, it smells like you, feels like you. The heat in your skin. Gram used to tell me I could have anything I wanted bad enough, do whatever I wanted to do." A bitter chuckle. "That's what we tell kids, don't we? It gives them the courage to try. But what do we say when they end up like this? No 'Be All You Can Be' Army slogan now, hmm?"

Peter pressed his lips together. Taking his hand away, he bracketed her with an arm, leaned in until the heat of his breath touched her face and she lifted hers, startled at his proximity.

"It's time to cut this shit out, Sergeant."

She jerked up. He was quick enough she didn't slam into his chin, but he didn't go far. Paling, she touched the front of his shirt, then moved to his arms, feeling the cant of his body over hers. "Peter? Oh, fucking hell, I thought . . ."

"Been talking to me a lot without me being here? Living in your own reality?" He caught one of her seeking hands, squeezed it a little harder than he wanted to.

"You can't be here." She snatched her hand back, retreated as much as the cushioning would allow, as if she was trying to burrow in truth. "You don't want this."

He kept her caged between his arms, made her feel the energy of his immovable presence. When he brushed his lips against her cheek, he registered the satisfying ripple of reaction, the pant of her nervous breath. "Telling me what I want isn't your job, Sergeant. That's the problem you had the night we met. You tried to control the uncontrollable."

Her lip curled, but he smelled fear behind the sudden anger. "What's my job, Captain? School crossing guard? Airline pilot?"

"That's self-pitying crap. There's more than that out there. But for right now, you only have one job. Doing whatever I tell you to do. You're going home with me."

Shock flitted across her face, followed by desperation, warring between fury and frustration. Hope dodged in between, so ghostlike it broke his heart. But he also saw something else, a lick of lust, his order igniting something deeper and more primal in her, something that had made her surrender to him months ago. But now her fingers curled into tight balls, fighting him.

"Not much difference between my self-pity and your pity. You're not taking me home like some kind of stray that needs your help. You don't want an invalid."

"No." He answered with a calm he didn't feel. "But that's not what you are. There's a difference between an invalid and a person who thinks she's one."

She shoved at him. He let her get out of the chair, but he noted she didn't go far, swaying uncertainly. Damn if Christina wasn't right. Dana had lived here for months, and yet she was barely familiar with her surroundings. When he rose and she lifted her face, he could tell she could gauge his height. Her senses were there. Just waiting for her to fucking use them. She'd said he didn't want her. He noted she hadn't said she didn't want *him* or what he was offering.

"We had a deal, Sergeant, and I'm not letting you out of it," he said sharply. He'd communicated in battle and on a busy manufacturing floor. He had no problem being heard by a woman with hearing aids. "You can't see, or hear as well as you could before. But you can smell, taste . . . touch. If you've been dreaming about me the way I've been dreaming about you, I know exactly what you've been thinking about. We're going to start there."

He caught her hand. Before she could pull away, he brought it to the front of his jeans, letting her touch wake to life the beast he hadn't sated since he last saw her.

It shocked the hell out of her; he could tell that right off. She hadn't been treated as a woman in a while, a woman from whom a man might demand things like this. A hard-core submissive's desire went beyond sex, into some deeper, psychological matters. He'd use his knowledge of that unapologetically. Maybe knowing less about her personally would help, because it would keep his focus on the one thing that might break her out of this self-imposed funk of hers. Then he could sate his overwhelming desire to give her the tenderness and comfort he had stored to overflowing in him, learn everything he wanted to know about her.

Her face was a study in mixed emotions, but the parted lips, the tension strumming in her body, told him she was reluctantly aroused. Surprised, he watched her sink down before him, her hands slipping to his upper thighs. Though staying still was excruciating, he waited, seeing what she would do.

Her lips twisted, and now he saw that anger simmering that Christina had warned was there. "I don't have to see to give great head, do I? Even with this face I can be a pretty good whore. Hell, better, because I won't rely on my looks."

Before he gave himself too much time to think it through, Peter pushed her backward onto her ass. She landed hard.

"Ouch," she yelped. When he yanked her up by the front of the shirt, thank God she reacted as he'd hoped. Twisting to break free, she kicked, taking him below the knee. If she'd been in shape, she might have caused him real damage, but in this case it barely registered. Making sure she had her feet under her, he pushed her off him.

She stumbled back and went rigid, stretching her hands out around her, floundering. It killed him, but he forced himself to remain ruthless. "This is what you learned in basic combat training. This weak-assed shit."

Shock coursed her features, but then her face hardened like a weathered statue. "I haven't exactly been keeping combat ready," she snapped.

"Yeah, I noticed. You've been sitting on your ever-widening butt—"

Her temper didn't ignite. It exploded, frustration uncapped in a way he didn't anticipate. Snarling like a wild animal, she swung and overbalanced. He caught her as she fell into him, but immediately tossed her back to her feet rather than gathering her to him the way every cell of him craved to do.

Despite the disorientation, she whirled, baring her teeth. He saw the flash of fire he wanted and kept pushing, ignoring the ache in his own chest. "You can fight. You just won't. You've given up. You're lucky—"

"Not the fucking 'You're lucky' speech again. I swear to God, the next person that says that to me—"

"Will what? Get a tap from that little-girl fist of yours? I'm getting a hard-on from it. Come tickle me some more."

She screamed and lashed out again, but this time she focused.

Her fist landed against his palm, held square in front of his face. His jaw set in satisfaction. *There's my girl. Would have snapped my head back.* His fingers closed over her tense fingers, holding them as she quivered.

"Damn it. I can't . . ."

"Yeah." He touched her neck carefully, cupped the side of it, then squeezed, hard. "Yeah, sweetheart, you can. But you need help."

"Not you." She shook her head, and tears seeped out, destroying him. "Not from you. Damn it, Peter, I want to have some pride left."

"You're pissing it away, every day you sit in that chair. You smell like this room, not a human being. You're becoming part of the furniture." He brought her chin up to him, glad she couldn't see the anguish in his face as he made his voice rough. "And you gave up the choice by not accepting help from anyone else. If you *ever* make a crack like that about being a whore again, I will fuck you up ten ways to Sunday. You won't sit comfortably for a month. You're no one's whore."

"I can feel the scars. I look like a monster."

"No, you don't." He moved his palms to her face, to the healing lines at her cheek and forehead, teasing her lashes. "Your eyes are still that pale green, like marsh grass. You've got a surgical scar here, and here . . . healing. Your skin is still so soft, your lips so full. . . ." He placed one of his hands over her heart, cognizant of the rise and fall of her breast, and one against her temple, stroking the short hair there. "Heart and head. That's all you need to heal, Dana. The rest doesn't matter. It's just skin. You're beautiful to me, inside and out."

"You don't even know me."

"Yeah, I do. That's what scares the shit out of you. I can bust your comfort zone wide-open. I'm not going to leave you alone. I want you to live again."

Her breathing elevated, the tracks of her tears widening. "I want you to leave," she said brokenly.

"No, you don't." He swallowed, hoping it was the truth. "You've always taken care of yourself. You hate depending on others. You think you have to run the whole damn world without help. The only time you let it go is when you follow orders or put on a leash and collar and hand it to the right Master. But even that you had to control, and that's why you never found him, thank God. Until you found me. I'm not going to let you control me. I'm going to help you, no matter how hard you try to drive me away. Starting right now, I'm going to prove that to you."

"How?"

She didn't have a comfort zone anymore. She had a big, dark hole in which she lived, the definition of isolation. But his presence seemed to shoot light into that hole, and he was right about that part—it scared the shit out of her. She wanted to cringe in the shadows, stay away from those spears of illumination and the pain they could bring. She needed him to be gone. He was supposed to be her fondest memory, not part of her desolate reality.

Instead, he shoved all her wishes aside when he answered her frightened question with action. He caught her under the arms, pushed her against the wall and put his body flush against her, lifting her off her feet.

Oh, God, he felt even better than she remembered. Those same broad shoulders, corded neck. His smell . . . Oh, she hadn't savored his smell the way she should have. Aftershave, soap, heated, angry male. His testosterone was at boiling point, and having someone angry at her felt incomprehensibly good. She wanted to fight with him some more, draw blood, so much rage boiling to the surface. The passive-aggressive anger she spewed in fits and starts at Christina was nowhere near the clean, white-hot fury that Peter drew to the surface, simmering darkly for so long with no outlet.

He might kiss her. The very thought ignited spiraling pleasure in her lower belly, its potential heat capable of burning the rest away like a big trash burn, the shit that had been roiling in her gut for months. Instead, though, he hiked her up against his body so she had to wrap her stiff, tired legs around his hips. She wasn't sure where he was taking her until he laid her down on her bed. Before she could anticipate him, he'd stripped her of her pajama bottoms and the cotton panties beneath.

Holy shit. She wasn't ready for this, and she defended herself the only way a helpless animal under attack could. Rolling into a ball, she wrapped her hands in the base of the sweatshirt so he couldn't take it off. She shook her head, knew she was saying "No, no, no" in that muted, hateful whine that echoed off the inside of her skull.

He was strong enough to uncurl her, so she was braced to lose, panic threatening to make her hyperventilate. But he settled next to her. His fingers caressed her ear, her nape, a soothing stroke. Once, twice . . . until nerve endings stopped cowering and reached for his touch instead. Then his lips were there, teasing flesh that had not forgotten that wonderful, free-fall feeling of arousal, those nerves strumming to life. He reclined on his hip behind her, his large hand stroking down the length of her thigh, his denim-covered groin cradling her bare ass. She stayed still, barely breathing, a rabbit hiding as he went down to her knee, then back up, tracing the curve of buttock as she quivered and a breath escaped her.

She hadn't been touched by anyone but doctors and nurses for months. They examined, poked, prodded. Even though they made every effort to put her at ease, to be gentle, it was always as if they came from every direction, like an enemy attack. She refused to go back to the therapy sessions to learn "how to be blind." She pretty much had a grasp of it. It sucked, and since she could barely hear what most people said to her, being around people at all was exhausting. She'd stopped paying attention. The dark void was quiet and dull, and attempts to draw her out of it made her angry and vicious, as she'd just demonstrated in such an embarrassing way. When she couldn't see or hear people's reactions, she'd found she didn't give a rat's ass if she pissed them off or hurt their feelings.

Peter's every emotional reaction was physical and immediate. And they mattered to her, damn it. Whatever decibel he was using, she could hear him without strain. It was good but frustrating as well. He wasn't going to be ignored.

Curling into a ball had not been a well-thought-out plan, either, for his fingers followed the curve of her buttock to her pussy, teasing the petals with gentle, light but inexorable fingers.

"Peter . . ." She couldn't help the whimper, the tears that squeezed out at being touched in such an intimate way, after everything else. If her body aroused like a normal healthy woman's, when she was anything but, she might shatter. "I can't bear it."

"Shh . . . let me hold you. I've burned to hold you, sweetheart."

His other arm tunneled beneath her, wrapping around her chest so she automatically latched her hands onto his forearm. Because of that, he brought her fetal-curved body farther into the shelter of his body. But he changed that altogether paternal image when he collared her throat with a large hand, forcing her head up and back against his shoulder.

Every nerve ending detonated, and not merely the physical ones. Damn him for knowing a submissive's mind too well. The shudder went all the way from that point of contact to her toes, and her thighs loosened a little more. His fingers dipped in, found moisture and spread it over those lips like honey. She mewled, gasped some more.

"You won't call me by my name without permission, sweetheart. You know who I am. Tell me."

She couldn't call him Master. She wasn't that person anymore, couldn't pretend she was. Whatever this moment was, he deserved better, more, and that was a road she could no longer travel with him. She had nothing to give. So she shook her head against his hold, even though she couldn't change the thundering of her heart, the aching hardness of her nipples, needing his mouth and touch, the ruthless tug of his fingers. Ah, God, she'd thought a million times about the things he'd done to her breasts.

Two fingers entered her pussy, stroked, thrust. One leg shifted over hers, keeping her legs in their folded position, thwarting her desire to open them. His thumb passed over her clit again and she cried out. She wanted to fight this, wanted to shut everything down, shut him out, but he wasn't letting her. If she could shut down her emotions, maybe she'd dare to perform like a whore in truth. He'd know, and be pissed off enough to leave her alone. But she couldn't.

Every good thing she'd had in the past months had revolved around thoughts of that night, of those letters Dana had long ago committed to memory.

Even though I'd love to hear your sweet voice, even if it was only words on a page, it doesn't matter. When I sleep, I share dreams with you. You're right next to me in this cot. I hear your breathing, and feel peace; at the same time I ache because you're also so far away. I think loving you, having you in my life, will be like that. A never-ending craving and peace at once.

"Dana, say it."

She shook her head again. She couldn't give herself that dream. Not for real.

He rolled her to her back. She clutched the shirt, but she'd defended the wrong perimeter. Putting her legs over his shoulders, he knelt and put his mouth between her legs.

The minute those clever lips touched her pussy, she bowed up, nearly swallowing her tongue. After the surgeries and healing of her physical injuries, there'd been no extremes of pain or pleasure, everything a straight, monotone highway, the unrelenting fires of hell her mental horizon. This was cold water in desert heat, a miracle and painful shock at once, potentially dangerous if taken too fast or at too extreme a temperature.

He seized her wrists, held them to her sides. *Stop, stop, stop.* Those bottled emotions were rising so fast, the pressure capable of detonating within the sexual response, tearing her apart from the inside. She'd be incapable of distinguishing the emotional torment from the physical. But his tongue knew how to drive thought away. He scraped and teased her cunt, plunged his tongue deep, sucked on her labia, rubbed his face against her so she felt the five-o'clock stubble on her tender inner thighs and the prickle against her sex as he made wide circles, then tight ones, licked and bit.

Her body couldn't care less about the turmoil in her mind. She worked herself against his mouth now, her fingernails digging into his wrists. "Oh, God . . ."

Her body strained for that pinnacle like an out-of-shape runner. Helping or torturing her, he slowed the pace, lapping at her like a wolf tasting blood, learning her particular flavor. Her foot pressed into his back, heel sliding over the muscled skin beneath his shirt. She thought of the fountain and how he'd laid her on the grass, placing his bare body on hers, the blissful artistry of skin and muscle.

Peter . . . The sad mental cry of loss washed down the tunnel of memory, a flood of anguish wrenched from deep inside of her. The orgasm turned it into a powerful, mind-shattering force, ripping a scream from her throat. She fought against him, fought the climax. She needed to get free. It was too much and she couldn't handle any more. No more . . .

When his hands left her at last, she went back into a protective ball, rocking, the aftershocks still shuddering through her in small jerks. He curled around her again, but this time to hold her tightly, his legs coming up under hers, his wide back curved around her so she was a sea creature safely ensconced in its shell. His breath against her ear became the sound of the ocean, a soft rush that carried her wherever it would. He was stroking her head, a firm, reassuring touch, slow and massaging at once, his thumb caressing the sensitive occipital bone.

"That's it, sweetheart. Let it out."

It was different when someone was holding you, when you mattered specifically to them, not a faceless nurse or VA volunteer being painfully kind. It offered a terrifying glimpse of new possibilities. She couldn't depend on him this way.

That was, unless he didn't give her any other choice. For the first time in months, that thought—not having control—didn't bring bowel-loosening fear. In fact, the kind of anxiety that gripped her now dared to include an emotion she hadn't felt in a while.

Hope.

Seven

Peter set Dana's suitcase outside the screen door, with a defining smack intended to catch her attention. It did, her head tilting in response. She was backed up into the corner formed by the entertainment center in her front room, her feet braced. He studied her, the set of the chin, the faint quiver in the hands she clenched against herself. All it had taken was the idea of leaving this hole and she was back in panic mode, digging in. He'd already seen enough to know he wasn't going to get her to agree to anything by morning. But he'd also seen she still had fight and spirit in her, and knew in his gut the most important thing was to get her out of this bleak cave. Even if he had to take her right now, in the middle of night, when Christina was sleeping. He'd written a note and left it on the front table, so the nurse wouldn't call the cops. Hopefully.

"I'm not going with you, Peter," Dana said. Her voice was one octave away from shrill. "I have no interest in being your little project. I'm fine here, doing just fine."

Yeah, if her life's ambition was to be a mushroom.

When he heard her voice break, saw her too-cold hands grip

themselves, he fought his protective instincts for patience. Control. When she'd gripped the hem of her sweatshirt, not wanting him to see what was beneath it, that had been bad enough, but when he stripped off her sweatpants he'd seen the left leg. The scar tissue so twisted and virulent, from knee up to her thigh, a few pings on her shin. And the way she'd shaken under his touch, wanting touch so desperately, but so afraid of it, too, feeling everything he touched as if she was reliving it again.

The longer he stayed quiet now, the more her hands shook. It was epidemic, sweeping through her body. As he approached, she tensed, shrank back against the television. She could feel the floor's vibration, or had detected his scent, his heat. Putting his palms on either side of her, he intensified it.

"Just go away, Peter. Please. Please don't do this to me. Don't destroy that good memory of our night together with some pathetic attempt to pretend there can be more now. Maybe there couldn't ever have been. I mean, what do we have in common, really? Except sex."

He leaned in. "Look up at me."

"I can't see you. What's the point?"

"Because I told you to do it. And because you can feel what's coming off of me. You know what's in my eyes, Dana. What do we have in common? Maybe not much. Hell, my mother was a Yale graduate, and my dad was a Texas roughneck, working rigs out in the ocean. When they died, when I was fifteen, they were as crazy in love as ever. People aren't jigsaw puzzles, Dana. Sometimes people don't fit until they rub up against each other, chisel the rough edges and the shields away. The more they want it to work, the more willing they are to do that rubbing."

She tightened her arms across herself. "I don't want to try, Peter. I don't want anything. I just want you to go."

He stared down into her face; then he nodded, straightened. "Okay. I'll just do one more thing." He went to the front door, found what he was looking for and returned. Moving to the side table by the couch, he flipped open the top of the decorative box so it clattered loudly against the cheap wood.

Dana's head went up. "What are you doing?"

"I'm burning these letters. You don't want anything, so they don't mean anything, right? I mean, if what's in them isn't strong enough to weather one of us getting hurt, what's the point? Hell, I guess I'm glad it wasn't me who got blown up, because you would have ditched my ass in a heartbeat."

"Peter, we don't have a relationship. I'm not going to tie you to me because—"

"You're not going to do anything to me, sweetheart. I came here on my own. If there's any tying to be done, I'm the one who'll be doing it." Lighting the edge of one envelope, he waved it to let the smoke drift her way.

Her face transformed. She hadn't thought he'd do it, obviously, but he hadn't realized she'd charge across the room toward him, a thin scream tearing loose from her throat. She hit the coffee table full throttle, slamming it against the sofa as she stumbled forward.

"Shit." Dropping the paper into the metal ash bucket he'd brought in, he leaped for her, catching her right before she fell onto the glass top. But she twisted, making him follow her down as she writhed to the floor, turning on him like a wild animal.

"Those aren't yours. You can't burn them. *Stop*." She scrambled to her feet, trying to fight past him, trying to get to them, even though she was facing a different direction, disoriented. The expression on her face was horrific. Twisted, desolate, enraged. Hanging on grimly and praying Christina was a heavy sleeper, he raised his voice to catch Dana's attention.

"Dana, settle down. I didn't burn them. They're fine. Listen to me, damn it."

She stopped, panting, her clawed fingers clutching his arms, her muscles still banded in full resistance. She was so weak, though. Her attempts to push against him were comparable to village kids he'd playfully wrestled in Afghanistan. The thought snapped his control and he brought her to her back on the carpet, looming over her.

"I burned some blank stationery Christina left on the table. But goddamn it, I will not leave you here. I don't care if I have to fucking carry you, kicking and screaming, between here and Baton Rouge. I will do it. You're not staying here. This isn't living."

"I don't want to go. Doesn't that matter? Freedom, freedom, freedom. That's my safe word to let me go and *fuck off.*" She snarled it in his face, and then lost it, all those nerves strung tight beneath him spasming as she disintegrated into a full-blown thrashing, screaming tantrum. He had no choice but to pin her full-body, keep his hands cupped behind her head so that she couldn't slam her skull repeatedly against the wood floor. She beat at him, tried to kick, sank her teeth into his shoulder through his T-shirt. Like one of those terriers he'd written her about. Small, tough and honest.

She was broken into a hundred pieces, and couldn't see to pick any of them up. But he could see every one of them. He *would* figure out how to bring them back together. Pressing his face into the side of her head, he squeezed his lids tight, not wanting to let unmanly tears fall when her screams became sobs, a keening wail of pain.

He expected Christina to burst in, but when she didn't, he remembered her words. *She's angry. A lot.* This wasn't the first meltdown she'd heard. It made him relieved and furious at once. He pushed the latter aside with effort.

"It's all right, sweetheart," he said roughly. "I've got you. I'm not letting you go."

"You can't. . . . I'm already gone."

"No, you're not, damn it." He fished for something, anything. "I asked you a question at the end of every one of those letters. You remember?"

It took a while, but at last she nodded. When he warily lifted some of his weight off her, her nose was running. She worked her hand up underneath the weight of him to wipe at it gracelessly, her eyes still streaming in silent anguish. He swallowed.

"I asked you if you'd ever thought about a different career, other than the army. What was your answer to that?"

She sniffled, shook her head. "I . . . I can't do that anymore."

"What was it?" He wouldn't reassure her yet. If it was something that required sight and hearing, well, they'd figure out something else she could do and love.

She squeezed her eyes shut, as if she could still see, another way she could hide. "I wanted to be a minister. Give people . . . faith, and hope, that life could be better."

He stared down at her as the tears increased. She turned her face into the carpet to let the sobs take her anew. Setting his jaw, Peter rose and lifted her off the carpet in one motion.

"We're going," he said.

"You owe me such an astronomical favor, I could demand your first-born. I've met Middle Eastern terrorist leaders less intimidating than that nurse friend of yours. She agreed to three days before calling the cops, but only because I said you'd call her with progress reports and let her talk to Dana whenever she wanted to. She said either way she's going to have a piece of your hide for reneging on your original agreement."

"Dana wouldn't agree to go with me, but she refused for the wrong reason. She doesn't think she deserves me."

"Smart girl. No decent human being deserves you."

Peter offered a suitable hand gesture, which Ben returned, the videoconferencing connection making it a slow-motion movement. The signal at his bayou home was a little broken up at times. Then Ben shrugged. "Seriously, I think you're okay. Christina knows you're good folk. In fact, between you and me, I think she actually expected you to do something like this. Did Jon make the changes you wanted before you got home?"

"Yeah. I've got to go. Give Christina my cell number so she can call me anytime."

"Will do. We still on for tomorrow night?" Ben lifted a brow at Peter's pause. "You rethinking this?"

"Yes. No. Hell, it's been a stressful few hours. Haven't slept since yesterday. Getting an unwilling woman on a flight, even a private one, is a bitch."

"Get some rest," Ben advised, studying him in a way that told Peter he saw that the exhaustion was more than physical. "When you need someone to spell you, give us a buzz. If she'd be more comfortable with a woman, Savannah or Cassie is more than willing to take a shift. Good luck."

Peter nodded and cut the line, returning to his living room to face his mutinous houseguest. Her unreasoning rage from hours before had morphed into a woman's silent anger. He wanted to interpret it as an improvement, now more about not wanting to be told what to do, rather than a complete unwillingness to believe there was a good reason to be here.

Fortunately, she'd exhausted herself by the time he'd put her in his car, belting her in. They'd been almost to the airport when she rallied. Getting her out of the rental had been a bit of a scuffle, alarming the attendant. Dana informed him that Peter was a complete overbearing bastard, but then thankfully subsided without a demand for police intervention. The attendant had given him an askance look, to which Peter gave him a bland "you know women" look that earned a grin and forward progress.

It gave him hope that, deep inside, she did want to come here. Of course, she'd been scared shitless and he was her only familiar link. As angry as she was, she clung to his side, shaking as he took the shuttle to the private hangar. He described everything as they went, told her what was going to happen before it happened. While she didn't respond, her fingers held on to his as though she were hanging off the side of a cliff. Fuck, had she been out of that house at *all*?

She'd fallen asleep on the plane. While part of it was emotional exhaustion, he knew it was more than that. Ben wasn't the only K&A man he owed. He made a mental note to send Lucas a case of his favorite Scotch. The CFO was a master at pleasuring women with his mouth. The techniques he'd shared with Peter, in a variety of memorable past experiences, were what had sent Dana into that spinning pleasure, which likely had knocked her off balance enough for him to get this far.

He'd carried her to the K&A limo that had met them at their private hangar in Baton Rouge. When she woke in his lap, she'd kept her cheek pressed to his chest. He'd seen the slow movement of her lashes as she blinked. They'd been thick and lustrous that night long ago. He wondered if the injuries made them thinner and more delicate-looking now, or she'd had on more mascara than he'd realized. He'd touched those tiny hairs with his fingers, stroked them. While the car drove toward the outskirts of Baton Rouge, he thought about all the things he wanted to know about her, to give her.

When they reached his house, he'd guided her through the basic landmarks of the different rooms, then settled her in a chair in the main room as he called Ben. She'd remained there, unmoving, her face telling him nothing, though he sensed a cauldron brewing.

He could deal with that. What he couldn't accept was leaving her there another minute. Every tear she'd shed after her climax, the storm of emotion it and his misguided attempt to burn the letters had unleashed, had felt like acid on his insides. He was responsive to women's tears, yes, but this woman affected him differently. She had that first night, and she did now. The vicious pounding in his head was unrelenting. As unreasonable as he knew it was, he should have been there to protect her. He hadn't been, so he was going to help her now.

Despite what she thought, it wasn't charity. He needed to see that fire in her eyes again, see the courage that came with her submission to him, that willingness to surrender that was a gift, not a defeat. She'd dreamed of him for months, she'd said so, while he'd been haunted by her. She haunted him even now, the ghost of a woman hovering over the shell she'd become.

"I'm thirsty," she said abruptly. "Do I have to beg for food and water?"

"I might make you beg for everything, sweetheart. If I remember correctly, the way you begged had a sweet sound to it."

She pressed those luscious lips together, but he saw her swallow.

There were women who were submissives only within the defined boundaries of a sexual situation, but for some that undercurrent could run under a wide variety of things, and he knew she was one of them. That would help here. He knew it, if he could figure out how to tip the scales away from her fears. He was banking on the fact her passion for life would be inextricably tangled with the desires of the flesh. And her response earlier said she hadn't yet cut those ties, thank God.

While he'd been content to be a Dom within other women's boundaries, this was the kind of submissive he'd wanted. One who had that tantalizing undercurrent. Savannah and Cassie were similar, another way the K&A men were alike in their needs and desires. When Jon and Ben found their own women, he'd lay money it would be the same.

He went to a squat by the straight chair in which she sat so rigid, wearing the baggy jeans he'd put on under her sweatshirt. He'd left most of her clothes there, because he wanted her to leave that persona behind. As soon as he could get her out of these, he'd probably burn them.

"If you're hungry or thirsty, Dana"—he traced her lips with a forefinger—"ask your Master for food and something to drink."

That same painful and rigid expression crossed her face. "Peter, please don't. I'm feeling too vulnerable right now, you know?"

"I know. But here's the deal, sweetheart." He shifted so his splayed knees were bracketing her calves. His one hand closed over both of hers, clenched in her lap. "Give me three days. Be what you would have wanted to be to me, and trust me to help you do that. On day three, if you want to go back to that damn box, I'll take you there myself. But give me that. What do you have to lose?"

He was lying, of course. Even when K&A did their negotiations, he was the floor man, the guy who went in and evaluated a plant's assets and their production processes. He wasn't the poker player like the others. But he put everything into his voice to convince her he meant it, that he would take her back to that pointless existence if he couldn't get through to her. Even though she had no one else.

Yeah, right.

There were times that lying in a relationship was the best thing. He had no qualms that this was one of those moments, whether he was lying to her or she was lying to herself about believing him. But in the space of a held breath, she gave a short, barely there nod. "Okay," she whispered.

Dana felt his hand tighten over hers, an approval. She knew this was wrong, but he'd brought her here, his will irresistible. How was she going to say no in three days, when she couldn't say no now? And why *wasn't* she saying no? Was it a pathetic reason, letting her destiny be decided like a broken branch carried by whitewater? Or was there a kernel of hope left inside of her, a hope that some will to live that had escaped her these many months still existed in her heart and soul, and he could find it? She didn't know. But for now, she'd made her decision. She'd be that broken branch and see where she ended up, as long as she didn't take him over the falls with her. She was just afraid that she wouldn't care, that she'd cling to him so she wouldn't fall alone. And she'd never been pathetic like that.

"All right." His fingers caressed her palm. "Let me show you a few more things."

He rose, and drew her up with him. She didn't like being in unfamiliar surroundings, but with his arm around her waist, guiding her, she tried to relax, somehow knowing he wouldn't let her stumble over things. "What's that scent?"

"Jasmine, from my front yard. Jon had some cut. Mixed with lavender." He guided her to the pottery vase that held them, molded her palms over it. There were smooth rolls, curves, not like a normal bulb vase. She took over the investigation, her brow furrowing as she worked her way up it, then sideways, and back up again, until she found the flowers, the thin stems and nodding blossoms. He had a fan going, and they were swaying in the faint breeze. He had a screen open as well, because she could hear shrill birds crying out over what he said was the bayou. She could smell it, the damp vegetation and salt.

"It's a person, isn't it?"

He closed his hands over hers, leading her to the clay features, distracting her with the brush of his fingers on her knuckles. "It's an abstract reclining nude. She's lying on her hip, her hands folded under her face. Her skin is texturized like a tree's bark, the flowers forming the canopy." He paused. "It's a piece by a famous local Louisiana artist. The finish is ebony. Jon bought it while I was away. Thought I'd like it."

"Oh, yeah? You got a thing for black girls, Captain?"

"Lately. One in particular." He caressed the sensitive bone of her forefinger, his intent obviously sensual. Dana swallowed, her fingers spasming against the curve of the sculpture's head and slim neck.

"He didn't include hair."

"No. He wanted the beautiful line of her skull. Long hair would interfere with that." He touched her ear with his other hand, moved to the erogenous zone at the base of her own skull, massaging, slow. "If you decide to stay, I'll take you to some of the galleries here. I bet you can give me a different perspective on the pieces."

She stiffened, drew back. "Sure. I'll write up reviews for the local paper. Don't give me the blindness-heightens-your-other-senses bullshit."

"The fact it pisses you off doesn't make it less true. As responsive as you were that first night, I can tell that you're hypersensitive to every inch I move over your skin now. And you want more of it, are about to go crazy for it. I know I am."

There was no boast, simply quiet fact. She folded her arms over her chest, but she wanted to move away, and couldn't do that without using her arms. As much as she knew he wouldn't let her fall or run into anything, it was an instinct when she couldn't see. So she dropped them with an annoyed sigh and moved away from him. Her thigh pressed the edge of an easy chair, and when she glided her fingers along it, she found something even softer than the cushion-ing. And furry. She lifted it to her face. "A stuffed animal?"

"A kitten. It was a housewarming gift from Ben when I moved in." He cleared his throat. "Said if I moved out into the sticks, it was the only pussy I'd get out here."

"It sounds like he cares about you." The wary smile tickled her cheeks, muscles she hadn't used in a while. "He's not harboring some secret lust for you, right?"

Peter snorted. "If I was the last fuckable thing in the universe, and then only because he has to stick his cock into something every twenty-four hours or he thinks it will self-destruct. If it came to that, I'd break it off for him."

"You love him, too," she realized. She moved on before he could reply, trailing her fingers along the silky surface of an end table. A tall house plant, a palm, brushed her face with scratchy edges. The walls she touched to the right of the open window were beadboard, the drapes a clean-smelling cotton. As she made her way around his living room, she noted he didn't have enormous amounts of furni-ture, but what he did have held a plethora of objects to discover. At one small table there was a chess game. In process, if the positioning of the pieces were any indication. Her brow furrowed again. "This isn't a traditional set. It's pewter, and the figures are . . ."

"Toy soldiers. That one was Lucas's gift. They all look really GI Joe—ish. Except the Queen figure is Barbie. Carrying an M-16." There was a smile in his voice. "It's an older set."

"They're your family."

"Yes. Once you decide someone's your family, you watch after each other." He let it hang there, the significance obvious. Since Dana didn't know what to say to such an absurd implication, she kept moving, but she knew she was orbiting around his scent and heat, keeping him close. He was right about the hypersensitiv-ity. Those few inches of her flesh he'd brushed with his were still tingling.

It had been so long since she'd reached out to explore her surroundings, as if she were a scared, lost camper who couldn't appreciate the woods, preferring to huddle over the fire and stare down at the small tin of provisions she had left. But in his presence, where she felt absurdly safe, she was absorbing smells, seeking to touch, to recognize things. She'd been cold a lot, but now she was warm in the sweatshirt. The room apparently received plenty of sun, so it must have west-facing windows, given the time of day. If she could see, she imagined she would be bathed in light.

What the hell was the matter with her? She should be majorly pissed off, keeping her ass in that chair until he took her back. But that last tantrum had been her worst yet, and they'd been occurring more frequently lately, as if her body were screaming to split away from her damaged soul, get out and run, blindness or no blindness. She couldn't deny it felt . . . different to be somewhere new, somewhere not about herself.

"Can I borrow a T-shirt?" she said, trying to hold on to her sullen tone. "Or did your loyal minions arrange for me to have a wardrobe?"

"The idea of keeping you naked is appealing, but they did actually bring some things by. Let's get you a shower first."

As distracting as the image was, him compelling her to stay in his home without anything to warm her but himself, when his hands settled on the hem of her shirt again, she automatically latched onto his wrists to hold it down.

She could feel the weight of his stare in the silence. "Let go of me, Dana."

She knew that voice. Even with her degraded hearing, she knew the sound of a Master taking command. From the second he'd come to her place, he'd been proceeding under the assumption she desired that, even outside of a club. Like so many other things, he was right, before even she'd realized how much. She hadn't ever indulged it that way, not trusting any Master enough. Before her accident, she'd wanted to do so, enough that her skin rippled with gooseflesh at the sound of it now. The idea had been terrifying to

her then. While she was surprised at how little fear she had of relin-
quishing herself into his hands, when she had so little control to
relinquish, she still couldn't release him, because of other fears.

"I'm afraid of what you'll see." The rawness of it resounded in
her head.

"You don't have to be afraid of anything with me." The steel was
still there, but as implacable tenderness. "Lift your arms."

Slowly, she released her hold, one finger at a time. When she
lifted trembling arms above her head, he pulled the sweatshirt
free.

She hadn't been wearing a bra, so moist marsh air touched her
bare flesh, making her nipples peak. He opened the jeans he'd had
her don at the duplex, made her step out of her shoes, then stripped
them off with her panties, leaving her completely naked.

The scar tissue marked the left side of her torso and leg like a
crazy quilt design. Sick of dealing with doctors, she hadn't scheduled any more cosmetic surgery since her face. At the time she made
that decision, she didn't care about how she looked. Now she desperately wished she'd done it. She supposed Peter would consider
that progress, but resentment and terror warred inside of her at his
lack of immediate response.

He'd settled his hands on her upper arms, keeping her squarely
facing him. His breath was slow, steady. Too slow and steady. Something about it suggested . . . barely suppressed anger. His palms
were heating with it. Part of her was intimidated, another part en-
thralled by the dangerous power of him, so near. He was angry at
faceless enemies, she realized, at someone who would dare hurt her,
leave her looking like a toy someone had broken and should have
cast away.

His finger traced the mark beneath her left breast. "Does any of
it hurt?"

"Not really. The ribs and arm hurt some when it gets too cold,
but the scars don't hurt anymore." At least not the way he meant.
She was pathetic. There were people far worse off than her. She
should be able to handle this, but all she wanted to do when she

thought about it, touched it, was cry like a little girl over what she'd lost. She'd had pretty, unblemished skin. She'd liked the line of her hip, the smooth roundness of her shoulder, the unmarked perfection of her left breast. While she couldn't see it, she could feel it, the rough texture. Maybe that was why the "heightened senses" platitude made her so angry. Heightened senses could be a curse, because she could feel every scar like the surface of the moon. She told herself to be glad she didn't have eyes to confirm it. Though she'd never see the wide, wide ocean again. Or Peter's smile.

"Please speak. If you don't speak, I'm going to lose my mind."

"I'm looking at a beautiful, brave and foolish woman. One whom I'm very, very glad is alive."

Eight

She bit her lip, overcome, but he didn't require her words. He reached away from her, and she heard the slide of something like metal across a table surface. When he brought it up, it brushed her sternum. Jewelry. Or . . . Her heart rate started accelerating.

As he put the collar on her throat, she followed it there, passing her fingers over his wrist, then down to the wide strap, lined so it wouldn't chafe. A waterfall of decorative chains fell from it. It had a D-ring loop, with a pendant. Touching the oblong disk, she realized it was a medallion. Because she'd replayed every detail she remembered about him that night, her throat closed, already knowing.

"It's the St. Christopher's I wear." He increased the collar's constriction, resulting in a violent contraction low in her belly. Her fingers trembled where they rested on his thick wrist. "You know the rules, Dana. While you wear this, I'm your Master. You're mine. You follow my orders; you do what I tell you."

"But I didn't . . . I refused to call you that."

He touched her chin, lifted her face, and she sensed him so close, the idea of his mouth hovering so near overwhelming her. "Are you going to refuse now?" he asked.

She swallowed. A hundred denials leaped to mind, but it wasn't her rational mind running things now. "No."

"No, what?" His tone sharpened, making her jump. She responded automatically, pushing all worries and concerns aside.

"No, Master."

"Good." The deep, sensual pleasure in his voice rippled through her. "Because we have some business to handle before I bathe and dress you the way I want."

Taking her arm, he guided her back toward the main source of that marsh breeze. She heard the creak of a screen door opening, and he was leading her out before she could balk.

She hated it, but her legs started to tremble. The give of the boards suggested she was being led onto a boat dock. That meant they were surrounded by water, and she was completely naked. One misstep, and she'd be in the water. Her fingers crept up to hold his hand at her waist, knuckles burrowing into his palm. She was thankful he didn't admonish her for lack of trust, but squeezed that hand, reassuring her without words.

She started when something dragged against her skin. Before she could panic, he stopped, guided her hand to touch long, waving grass. It apparently grew up along the sides of this part of the dock, tall enough to tease her bare ankles. As the strands moved under her palm, she took a deep breath, focused on their motion. Her nostrils flared, bringing her the aroma secreted in their sun-soaked stalks and darker, moist places near the waterline.

"The smell is so vivid, you can almost see it, can't you? C'mon, sweetheart. I want to take you to the end of the dock."

When she straightened, he led her onward, no hesitation, a smooth pace that had her stomach jumping like the frogs she could faintly hear croaking, which meant they were making quite a racket near the dock. At the end, he let her feel the edge of the dock with her toes, then put her hands on a piling. The wood had a worn texture under her palms.

"Now, if I vanished all of a sudden"—he stroked a hand along her tense shoulder—"which is *not* going to happen, there's one of these every five feet or so, and a rope runs between them. If you want to come out here, you can follow that rope, sit on these boards, get some sun. When you reach this one"—his grip increased over hers—"you'll know it's the end, because there's a knot to the rope." He showed her that, his fingers sure on hers. "Below that is the water, and my boat. I'll take you out on it soon."

"Great. I'll probably get seasick." She was having trouble enough walking on solid surfaces. She wasn't sure she wanted to think about the unstable glide of a boat.

"It's a smooth, easy ride. I paddle it most times. A lot of nights, I sit out here and drink a beer after work. Listen to the frogs, all the night sounds, until the bugs outnumber my zappers and drive me back into the screened porch."

She yelped as something ice-cold touched her, and he caught her waist before she instinctively leaped right, which would have taken her into the water. She grabbed his biceps anyway, cursing him. He chuckled. "Language, sweetheart. It's a beer. There's an outdoor mini fridge here. Want a sip of mine?"

She tried to draw a steadying breath, wondering if she was the only who realized she was completely naked in broad daylight. "Not going to offer me one?"

His hand, cool and wet from the beer's condensation, drew a line down the outer curve of her breast, slow and easy. "No. You'll drink from mine, if you ask nice."

Yeah, he knew she was naked. As flustered as she was, she detected full awareness of it in the sexy intensity of his voice. "But first, we're going to get that business out of the way I was talking about."

He shifted to set down the beer, then straightened to bring both her hands up to the piling. Looping a coil of line around her wrists, he guided her hands to a metal hook embedded in the piling before he drew up the slack, locking her wrists against it.

Well, at least if she was tied here, she couldn't fall into the water.

But her breath was still getting short, the restraint doing funny things to her insides, anticipating what he was planning.

"I'm not sure I'm ready for this."

He let his hand slide down her arm to her back, down to the curve of her buttock. Then, as he had the night in the club, without preamble or permission, he eased his fingers between her legs. She gasped as he stroked the wetness there, brought it back out and painted the moisture over her lips before he took her hand to his mouth, let her feel him taste his own fingers, a quick swipe of his tongue. "You're ready, Sergeant. Now, I gave you one clear order when you left. What was it? You'd better remember it."

A few hours ago, she'd been huddled in a dark room. In a way that didn't ignore or minimize her physical limitations, he was nevertheless acting as though they had no bearing on how he intended their relationship to progress, as if she'd returned whole and wanted to try out a 24/7 Master/sub relationship with him.

Holy God. She yelped as a strip of heat sizzled down her backside. The switch.

"Yep." His voice held dark satisfaction, a thick stew of lust. "Liked the results so much last time, decided to get my own. Answer me quick, Sergeant."

"You told me to keep my ass down, sir."

"And did you?"

"No, sir."

"There are a couple soldiers who likely wouldn't be alive if you had. You did your duty as a soldier, but you overrode your Master's command. You did right, but you still have to be punished, don't you?"

"Yes, Master." Her fingers gripped the post, her mind whirling.

"How many lashes do you think you deserve for risking what belongs to me?"

She swallowed again, feeling a fear different from any she'd felt in the past long months, fear wrapped up in building need. Slick arousal was trickling down her thigh.

"Five," she stammered out, sensing that hand getting ready to flick again. With his strength, she didn't think she'd last more than five before screaming her lungs out. How close was the nearest neighbor?

"Really? Hmm." He shifted to her other side, and when his hand ran down her flank, she jumped, anticipating the switch. "I'll ask you the question again, after I give you the five *you* prefer."

Oh, son of a bitch. She was wrong. Not only in her answer, but in how many stripes of that branch she could take without screaming. Her skin was tender from too much sitting, too few workouts, and the next one felt like bacon grease in an open wound. Two, three . . . The cry ripped from her throat, so loud she heard the echo. The faint frog and bird sounds disappeared. He didn't pause. Four and five.

Gasping for breath, she whimpered with shock and relief as he rolled the cold brew over her buttock, slow, easy, taking out the stinging throb. Back and forth, as the hand holding the switch took a firm grip of the other cheek, kneaded it with casual, indulgent pleasure. "It's softer, Sergeant, but it's still a nice ass. Now, you going to try for the *right* answer to that question?"

She nodded. "However many my Master feels I deserve."

"Bingo, sweetheart." He pressed against her back then, and she sucked in a startled breath as the switch bent across her throat, below the collar, hauling her head up against the side of his jaw. He pressed his groin against her aching backside, and he was hard as a rock, making her want to widen her stance. Her nipples ached below that restraint, every reaction she had responding to the demand of his body.

"That suspended second in time, when I didn't know if Jon was going to tell me if you were dead? There aren't enough lashes in the world to make up for that feeling. Then there's not telling me what was happening, not calling for my help. I could stripe your ass bloody in a heartbeat, Sergeant, for those things. I mean that."

"I didn't want you to come to me out of pity, damn it." His anger goaded her pain, her heart wrenched between emotions and lust.

"I would have come because you belonged to me the second you met my gaze at The Zone. Which is why, tomorrow night, you and I are going to visit my local club here. I'm going to remind you of that, open those eyes of yours to what you're more than capable of seeing. If you do that, maybe, finally, you'll be ready to take cautious steps toward embracing a new life for yourself. The way you should have been doing, all these months."

A fetish club? Was he crazy? With lots of people and noise, and ways to fall and run into things and not know where she was or . . .

His hand settled on the collar. "You're already worrying. Dana, how long have you been a sexual submissive?"

"Most of my life," she whispered. "I've known about it since high school."

"And like a lot of them, you have trust issues, until the right Master takes you in hand." One of those large hands dropped, squeezed a sore buttock again, earning a gasp. "Between now and tomorrow, you'll feel better about that. You're going to serve me the way a slave should. I'm going to keep you hot and wanting, all day long. You're going to talk, a lot, and tell me everything going on in that head or heart of yours. You'll trust me with everything. If you hold anything back, if I suspect at any time you're hiding anything from me, I bring you back out here, and we go again. Believe me, I'm pissed enough to take pleasure in beating your ass a few more times."

She heard the rough emotion under the hard words. He was controlled, but that roughness, what it implied, was harder to face than a hundred more times at his whipping post. She didn't want to care how he felt. She'd kept herself walled up, feeling as if she'd fucking tear the world apart if she let loose, but he was strong. Maybe tougher than her. Right? He could handle it. But that itself was too damn appealing, too fast.

She rested her temple against the piling, fingers digging in again. "What will it change?" she asked, unable to keep the bitterness out of her voice.

His hand slid around her front, cupping her hip bone. When his tone softened, she choked on a sob. "Why don't we see, sweetheart?

I know you're scared about tomorrow night. But I'm going to have a gift for you, something that will help you embrace your own pleasure without fear. I promise. So I don't want you to worry about that, about anything. Okay? Can you do that for your Master? Will you trust me that much?"

I want to. Oh, how easy he made it sound, and yet she felt as if he'd put her on a roller coaster before she was ready to go to dizzying heights at such speeds. But there was an amazing, small part of her mind that didn't want to cower, a burning light that made her summon up a scrap of courage, and speak. "You said something about a sip of your beer?"

He gave it to her with her hands still tied, so she had to lay her head in the cup of his palm, trust him to guide the fluid into her mouth. As she swallowed, he stroked her throat, then down over her sternum, teasing the tops of her breasts as if he saw no scar tissue at all. They didn't behave as if they were anything less than they'd always been, nerves awakening under his hands, the curves swelling and nipples hardening further.

When he finally released her from the hook, he took her back to the bench, keeping her hands tied. As he sat down, holding her between his knees, she imagined how he looked there, in a pair of jeans fitting just right, maybe his arm stretched across the bench. She could sit down next to him, or on that knee, but her mind turned to what she'd almost done in the apartment, the way she'd gone to her knees. She'd been goaded by darker feelings then, but now . . .

She realized she was trailing one of the fingers of her bound hands along his knee, a two- or three-inch stretch, a nervous movement back and forth. "My slave appears to know what I like best with my evening beer."

His voice was husky, and she swallowed at the sound of a loosened belt buckle hitting the bench, imagining the purr of a zipper. She envisioned his cock stretching up in all its hard, thick glory, him leaning back against the rail, sipping the beer as she serviced him with her mouth. That organ glistening with her saliva, her ass red with his punishment. Her knees were already folding beneath her, without conscious direction. His hands were there, though, guiding her down, and he held her weight until he'd put a cushion on the boards for her knees. His touch lingered on her nape as both sets of her fingers crept up his inner thighs, accommodating her tied wrists.

She hadn't had the opportunity to touch him much that first night, or even last night. Now he indulged her pace, letting her explore the texture of the light mat of hair on his muscled thighs, the smooth flesh of the insides, the encroaching heat of his groin as she drew closer to his testicles, working her way to what she knew awaited her.

When her hand closed greedily over the hot, hard base, she felt him suck in a breath, a gratifying one. Dominance and submission were all about power and control, a perfect state of trust and surrender. By taking away so many of her decisions right now, Peter was giving her the chance to fully evaluate the one decision that would be hers to make when three days were over.

Before her injury, she'd wanted that perfect state handed to her on a platter. Ironically, blindness and Peter's arrival had shown her the devastating truth. It was a leap of faith. Had she lost her ability to leap that far, though? How could she even know the right direction to leap when she couldn't see him, couldn't hear the sound of his heart calling to hers?

"Shh, sweetheart. Stop thinking."

The reassurance and warning in his tone returned her attention to the weight of him in her hand. Heated, silken skin over steel, the musky, aroused aroma as she brought her mouth down, stretched her lips over the broad head, tasted the salt of him, fluid already gathered on the tip.

He stroked the shell of her ear that had the hearing aid. He didn't dislodge it, the movement easy and familiar, not the exaggerated care that would have distracted her. It brought her back to thinking about what had changed since they'd last seen each other. And yet, she liked it when his fingers convulsed abruptly as she went down, relaxing her throat to take him deep. Skills that didn't rely on her sight and hearing were enhanced by this singular focus on taste and smell, his physical reaction. For the first time, she felt a tiny trickle of satisfaction with the thought. Something within her power to give.

While the idea of him drinking his beer excited her, this casual use of his slave, she also liked the idea of him being too aroused to do anything other than dig in for the ride, so she put all her effort into it.

His thighs trembled, and he thrust up. She scored him with her teeth, swirled her tongue over the base, found his heavy testicle sac and squeezed it, caressing the sensitive perineum. She knew how to slide a finger slow and easy up his backside and make him see stars, but for now she focused on this.

She did miss hearing him, the guttural whispers an aroused Master would make, the murmured command to suck his cock harder, faster. As if he knew that, the clutch of his hand and the thrust of his hips communicated that message, making her wetter. She wanted him between her legs, wanted to feel whole and real. She also craved the spurt of his seed into the back of her throat, his roar of release vibrating through her touch, breaking that muted sound barrier.

When he came, it was all that and more, his hand clenching on the back of her neck, his cock thrusting into her mouth so hard it was all she could do to keep in rhythm, drawing it out as seed flooded her throat and tongue. She heard his male groan of satisfaction, the animal sound of it thrilling her to her toes, her calves slick with her arousal. She didn't slow down until he started twitching with the sensitivity. Licking him, teasing him with small kisses and nips, she savored his shudders. He caught her chin and pulled her up, lifted her in an amazing display of strength to straddle his lap. He kept her off his cock, despite her moan of protest. Instead, he cradled her face and cleaned his fluids from her lips with his T-shirt, wiping the moisture from her eyes, caused by the strain of powerful thrusts. Finding his abdomen beneath the raised cotton, she dug into his muscles with needy fingers.

"God, your cunt is so flushed and swollen. You want your Master to fuck you, don't you?"

When she nodded, he claimed her lips, tasted himself and her at once. He gripped her ass, made her writhe against him, whimper as he prolonged the wet, sucking pleasure of his mouth. But then he drew back and held her, his hand on her throat where the collar was, a reminder. "Not right now, but soon. First, I'm giving you that bath."

She'd tried to protest, explain she did know how to shower herself, but that had won her a stinging swat on the bottom before he shepherded her into the garden tub. He'd given her a very thorough bath, embarrassing and arousing at once. Sliding his fingers into her pussy as well as her anus, he left her on the cusp of climax before he turned to rinsing her, stimulating her nipples with the sprayer.

God, she wanted him inside her, but the frustrating fact was that she wasn't used to so much physical exertion, and he was far too intuitive. "It's bedtime, sweetheart," he said after he dried her gently, cupped her face. "There'll be time for the rest."

He even carried her to his bedroom, a sign that she couldn't conceal her utter lassitude. It had a quiet, tranquil feel to it, an aroma of wood and Peter. The bed's cushiony quilt and abundance of pillows also bore his reassuring scent. He lay down with her, a consolation prize, and while she lay with her head on his chest, he described everything in the room in detail, from the overflowing bowl of change he had on the dresser, to his pictures, snapshots of his travels for his company and with the military, and the view of the bayou out the open screened window. He did so well she couldn't help but see it all, imagine herself as part of it, him wrapped around her.

When he at last went quiet, probably to give her the chance to doze off, she remembered what he'd said out on the dock. *Tell*

*me everything going on in that head or heart of yours. Trust me with
everything.*

"Can I ask you something?"

"You can ask me anything."

She nodded, rubbing the firm pectorals beneath her cheek.
Reaching up, she stroked the curve of one, found the bump of his
nipple. "Were my tattoos ruined?"

His hand drifted down her back, traced the eagle and flag. "No,
sweetheart. Your promise to your grandmother is still there."

She wondered why it didn't surprise her that he understood the
most important one to her. "When I got it, she said only trashy
women got tattoos. And she worried that it might be blasphemous.
But I think she liked it. She put her palm on it, said a prayer for
me. So I've always felt her hand there, too."

"I'm sorry she died, Dana. She sounds like a wonderful woman.
Do you think she would have liked me?"

She would have loved him. But for form's sake, Dana sniffed.
"She'd have said you need to be taken down a peg or two. But she
would have tolerated you."

He chuckled, and the warmth of it slid through her, thickened
her throat as she imagined him and Grams together, the banter they
would have shared. How gently Peter would have treated her. She
sought another subject before tears made her foolish. "Why did you
decide to be a soldier? I bet you were an adrenaline junkie."

"It was probably some of that," he admitted. "But eventually I
matured enough to realize how damn lucky I am to live here, to
be given the blessings I have. So I pay it forward, hoping to give
those choices to others. I know how that sounds these days. People
make fun of it, think a guy like me is stupid."

"I don't," she said, and he stilled, their hands intertwined. "I
hate what happened to me, Peter. But I believed in what I was
doing, despite some of the bullshit we deal with. I had a purpose."
But what was her purpose now?

As if sensing her mood trying to slide downward again, he gave
her a playful squeeze, shifted to speak closer to her ear, tease her

with his breath. "I admit, I throw in the pay-it-forward thing to make me sound sensitive, rather than a macho chauvinist Rambo. Impress the girls."

"I like Rambo." She smiled against his muscular heat, brushed her lips there. "And you've already blown your cover. I know you're a macho chauvinist. Sitting out on your dock, making your woman give you head while you drink beer and watch alligators."

"You passed the audition with flying colors. Most I interview fail miserably, though I give a few of them points for enthusiasm."

She thumped him, but when he caught her fist, the humor had disappeared from his voice, leaving a rough note that told her she wasn't the only one vibrating with need. "My woman. I like the sound of that."

So did she, fool that she was. "You are sensitive, in some ways," she said. *The way a man should be sensitive.* She could hear the reassuring beat of his heart so easily this way, her cheek pressed to his chest. "A little heavy-handed and possessive, but there's nothing mean about you. You're determined, and you believe in what's right and wrong. You'd tear your heart out if someone really needed it." She traced his pectoral again, let her fingers start to drift downward.

"Using flattery to have your way with me?" But despite the teasing, there was a strained quality to his voice.

"I know you're hard, Master. Why won't you fuck your slave?" She made it a whisper and felt the jump under her hand where she'd managed to inch down to his cock, slide it over the head, straining against fabric. He caught her hand.

"Because she's tired, and my first job is to take care of her. So she'll be up for serving my needs later." He brushed his lips across her brow. "Though I'm pleased you're thinking about wanting to please me."

She was. She was also surprised by how urgent her need was to perform that role for him, no matter her exhaustion. Before her accident happened, she'd realized that the night between them had gone far beyond roles and performances. Her need for him, to be his submissive, had only gotten fiercer the longer she was away from him. The craving was as relentless now, practically blood and bone deep. She'd been so quick to believe it was gone, beyond her reach, but a need like this didn't evaporate on command. Every time she'd thought of him or heard one of his letters, it had stirred, but at his reappearance, it had flared high and hot, restored to full, vibrant life. Vibrant anything was something she'd thought beyond her reach as well.

He held her like a velvet cuff, relentless and gentle both, and she relaxed into that hold. When she slid into the warm waters of a dreamless sleep, she was still confused, but for the first time in a long time, she lacked the jagged ache in her throat, the lonely sense of isolation squeezing her heart. He was here, and she could sleep in his arms.

Nine

She didn't wake until the next morning. While the loss of time chagrined her, she was amazed she'd slept so deeply. She woke as she'd fallen asleep, secure in his arms, and wondered if he'd moved at all. His body was warm and strong beneath hers, his thigh still tangled with both of hers, which initiated all sorts of prurient thoughts. He wasn't going to be deterred, however. He pressed a kiss to her temple before she could push for something more, and lifted her out of the bed.

"We'll do a workout, and then have some breakfast. I've got a sports bra and shorts here for you."

The man had a damn Gold's Gym in his house. Within no time, she was sure he must have been a drill sergeant before he was an officer. He put her on his treadmill, guiding her hands to the supports, and then worked her up to some god-awful speed guaranteed to send her into cardiac arrest. Right before that red zone, he put her into cooldown. While she listened to the faint clink and thud of weights as he did his lifting near her, she could smell the pleasant aroma of male sweat, and imagined him there, on his back, lifting the bar over his head.

"How much do you press?" she asked, fumbling for the towel he'd left on the treadmill arm to pat her sweaty neck. Now that she was thinking about it, she realized the speed and incline probably weren't that hard—she was just so damn out of shape.

"Two hundred this morning. I do about four hundred in a dead-weight lift. You did good. Pull the tab out and the treadmill will stop. Then come over here."

A clank and shudder through the floor suggested he'd dropped the weights into their cradle. She stepped off the treadmill, lifted her hands, seeking the weight set or him. She located him, or rather his bare, slick chest. Her fingers drifted, finding from his loose waistband that he was wearing only a pair of jeans. She wondered if he was barefoot, liking that picture. His short hair maybe a little rumpled, since neither of them had showered yet. Lifting her hand to his face, she traced his jaw, felt the morning shadow. "Is it gold, like your chest?"

"Yeah, sweetheart. Or as Lucas calls it, baby hair."

She smiled. "You know there's an inverse relationship between how much men care about one another and how much they insult one another."

"That's why we have girls. So we can be emotional and wimpy with someone who won't hold it against us."

"Yeah, right. You big pussy."

He chuckled. "Not a good idea to insult your personal trainer this morning. Not if you want pancakes for breakfast."

He took her through the machines and again pushed her to her limits, though she found that severely below where she'd once been. It didn't matter that she'd been part of the cause, unwilling to move out of a chair for months. She couldn't help resenting it, how quickly she exhausted, the weakness of the left side. For some perverse reason, it underscored how handicapped she felt, even though this was some-thing she knew she *could* change. She was biting back tears by the time she worked her way around to all the machines and found she could barely meet the minimum recommended reps.

It didn't make it any easier that he held all the control, holding himself away from her like a damn animated piñata she couldn't see, taunting her with his proximity.

"Sweetheart, you're getting there. Here." He guided her hands up to the triceps pull, even though her arms were shaking. "Hold on to these."

"I can't do any more. I'm—"

He closed his hands over hers, holding her grip, but instead of getting tougher with her, he bent to her throat to suck off the beads of sweat gathered in the tender pocket formed by her collarbone, right under her collar. Her rapid breath caught in her throat, and she let out a moan he answered by following the track down to her cleavage. The sports bra was tight, too tight. When he cupped her, she wanted to feel the callused palms against her female flesh. He answered her unspoken desire, pushing up the plastic band and letting it constrict over the curves, baring her nipples to the air.

"Oh, God . . ." He was fondling her, slow kneading, strokes and pinches of the nipple, as if he had all the time in the world. Her hands convulsed on the pulleys. How did he know to shift his attention from the weight of the curve, to tracing the shape, to teasing the nipple, and alternating the stimulation in myriad delicious ways, making her rock against him, gasp and groan at the torture? He didn't have to say how much he adored her breasts. She felt it in every touch, in his heated attention to every inch of them, but then he spoke, making her crazier.

"I'd love to do breast bondage on you, sweetheart. Use rope to lift and squeeze these beauties, put a bar clamp on them so when I removed it you'd feel tingling through every nerve ending, make you come when the blood rushes back into the nipples. Get them pierced so I could keep you in jewels, tug on them whenever I want."

The military didn't allow body piercings. But that wasn't a problem anymore, was it? Though that brought a shot of pain, it was balanced by the image of what he was suggesting. "I bet you like sparkling things, don't you, Dana? I'd put you in diamonds, maybe some gorgeous emeralds, like your eyes."

She tried to use her stomach muscles to lift her legs and wrap them around his hips, but she couldn't do it without his help, and he wouldn't let her get that close. "You want me to touch your pussy so bad, don't you?"

"Please . . ." she whispered.

"I love your begging, but you don't want it bad enough yet." Adjusting her sports bra back over her breasts, he smoothed his palms over the aching nipples. Before she could say something nasty she was sure would get her into all the right sorts of trouble, he had her doing triceps pulls. Christ. Then hip abductions, the seam of her shorts rubbing against a very wet pussy. But she was using her other senses, and she noted that when he counted off for her, his voice had a tight note. When he went into the next room to get them some more water, the rhythm of his steps through the vibrations of the wood floor was uneven. She curled her lip in feline satisfaction.

"Your gait sounds a little off there, Captain. Hauling something heavy?"

Coming to her side, he helped her find the weight blocks and showed her where to put the pin for the next rep. As he did, he bumped her hip in warning, bouncing her off him a couple feet. "Keep it up, Sergeant."

When she snorted, she heard his sexy, self-deprecating chuckle. "Yeah, yeah, I know. You are. Behave and I'll give you some water."

The bottle had a straw, which he guided to her lips as he drew her close within his arm span. As his palm smoothed over the curve of her ass, he let her rest her hand on his bare chest, though she itched to drop her touch to explore straining denim. "Ready for another rep?"

"No." She suppressed a sigh. "Everything's harder. My joints hurt and my balance isn't for shit. I feel like such a damned girl." God, she was whining.

"You are a girl." He gave the back of her head a quick stroke. A soldier's reassurance, not a caress. A brisk gesture that said, *You can do this.* "You know, there's a great yoga person who can help you improve your flexibility and balance. She's a PT as well. We think Jon has the hots for her, so he could charm her into a discount rate."

That should sound like a good idea, but instead it irritated her. She didn't want to go through all this. She just wanted to be herself again, now. She chose not to respond, since she knew she would only sound waspish, but Peter wouldn't let her get away with that. He passed his thumb over her lips. "What're you thinking, sweetheart?"

"I feel like giving up," she confessed after a long moment, the truth of it shuddering through her. "I'm afraid to test my limits, see where they actually are. Maybe it's better not to know. I'm not sure I can handle knowing. I know I'm chickenshit."

She hadn't said things like this to anyone. Maybe not even to herself. Hearing the words resound in her head now made her afraid as well, wanting to take them back. But he kept that gentle stroke on her face, soothing the scars, lulling the memory of them.

"Yeah, you are a little bit. Hell, anybody would be. But you know what? You could have busted my ass at the car rental place. You didn't. You were brave enough to do this, Dana. I know you felt like it was easier to jump into a firefight with your sight and hearing, knowing who and what you are, than to face the uncertainty of where you're going now, what you can be."

"How would you know that?" she managed.

Pressing his forehead to hers, he cupped her face with both hands as she lifted hers to close on his wrists. "Because it's how I would feel. Only I'd be a lot more scared, because guys always think we have to be the biggest and the strongest."

She stifled a half chuckle, half sob. "Yeah, you called that right." But she kept her forehead pressed to his, and for now, he seemed content to stay there, tracing her ears, letting her get her emotions under control, until she straightened on her own. She set her jaw, moved back to the bench, though it was hard to leave the proximity of those long, clever fingers. "Let's set the pin higher for the next one."

"No. Once you do a full workout at this range without it exhausting you so much, we go up. Maybe in a few days. You do it gradual, sweetheart."

But in two days, she'd be gone. Unless she decided to stay.

"Believe me, I'm just as eager for you to get back into shape." His tone changed. "I don't want anyone making fun of your ass. I'd have to beat them up, even though I kind of agree that your ass is a little spongy right now."

Picking up the two-pound girly weight she was sure he'd dug up for her, unless he did finger or toe lifts, she hurled it in the direction of his voice. At his satisfying grunt, she put her hands on her hips. "You don't know what a fine ass is, white boy."

"Oh, yeah? I know an attack on a superior officer when I feel it."

She recognized the mock threat in his voice, and was off the bench, backing up into a more open space. He'd given her the room's layout, and unlike the apartment, she could recall everything. Her hand followed the wall as she anticipated his approach, though of course she couldn't hear his steps unless he approached like a clog dancer.

It didn't matter. Launching the sparring match with a frontal attack, he kept her moving, back and forth across the mats. He called out his moves beforehand, letting her know when they were approaching the boundaries of the room, but like everything else, he pushed her a little past where she thought she could go. Whiny, pathetic Dana might have wanted to drop to the mat and surrender. But a stronger, older Dana surfaced, remembering her training, refusing to get cowed when she lost her balance from her hearing or sight loss handicap. Every time she did, he was there, catching her, bringing her back to her feet, keeping her going until she was winded again.

And feeling better, despite it all.

An hour later they sat side by side on the screened porch, eating breakfast. Well, he sat, while she wilted into a chair like a limp rag. She had managed to help him in the kitchen, bringing him things and getting familiar with the layout there. Despite her weariness, she was ravenous, probably for the first time in months.

"You a good cook?"

She stopped in midbite. "Yes. Well, I was."

"What, you don't think you are anymore? Did you lose your memory?"

"Yes, I can cook," she grated, tearing the toast in half and finding the jelly.

"Make me one of those as well." He put his slice of toast next to her hand, guiding her fingers to it. "I like it pretty thick."

"Why do you want to know if I can cook?"

"Well, if you only want to sit in a house for the rest of your life, I figured you could cook and clean for me, be my sex slave. It'll be a win-win."

She bared her teeth in his direction. "Fuck off, Captain."

"Feisty. Your mouth gets you in trouble a lot, Sergeant." He touched her lips, though, brushed her cheek with his knuckles in a tender gesture that made her want to dip her head into his hand again. Feel his pulse and strength through his fingers, the warmth and support. Instead she cleared her throat and returned to her breakfast.

"So, I'm doing better this morning. Maybe we shouldn't go out tonight, you know. No need to rush things."

As the silence drew out, she cursed her mistake, even as her toes curled at the pause. She swallowed, something new rising up in her. "I'm sorry, Master. I'm trying to control things again."

"Yes, you are. Let it happen again and you'll finish up your work-out with your glutes smarting from something other than squats."

He'd said it wasn't her job to worry. She was supposed to follow orders. He was right. She'd gone, eyes wide-open, into a firefight. Why going into a BDSM club could so terrify her, she didn't know, but it had been this way since her injury. Without her eyes, her hearing so diminished, things frightened her so much more easily. But in a short time, he'd shown her there were things she could detect that others couldn't, and those senses could help her. But she still feared the helplessness, the possible abyss that could yawn before her, swallowing her before she knew it was there.

She put down her sandwich, reached out. He was sitting next to her, and yet it was still a gratifying surprise to feel his hand close over hers instantly. "I'm scared, Master. Really, really scared."

It was hard to admit, even without seeing his face. The words nearly strangled her. But then his arms were around her, sliding her onto his lap so he could rock her.

"I know, sweetheart. I wish I could take away your fear, but the only way I know to do it is to help you face it. I'd face it for you if I could."

The truth of it was in the fierceness in his voice, a depth of feeling she wasn't sure she could handle, let alone believe. He tightened his grip on her. "It takes years for a Master to earn the trust I'm asking for from you. But I know how tough you are, deep inside. I know you want to trust me. I'm not going to do anything to let you down, all right?" He pressed a kiss to her temple; then she felt his lips curve. "What if I promise to keep your mind and luscious body so occupied with terribly sinful thoughts, fear won't have a chance of sliding into your mind?"

She wasn't sure anything could eliminate all worry from her mind, but she was more than willing for him to try. When she managed another nod, he slid his hands down her back, squeezed a buttock. "Finish your breakfast. Time to take you on a boat ride."

❧❧❧

Peter knew she was afraid. He ached to tell her that she didn't have to do anything, that he'd protect her from everything. Every instance of pain or fear she had tore him apart inside. She'd had months, but it was still new to him. He wanted to grieve with her for what she'd lost, let her know the utter terror he'd felt at the idea of her being gone from his life before she'd really fully entered it.

Instead, he went back into the bedroom, took a few steadying breaths, and then brought her jeans to her, along with a long-sleeved knit cotton top borrowed from Cass's younger sister, who was a similar size to Dana. Next he applied bug spray, a necessary preparation for poling through the bayou abutting his property. The lemon insecticide had a smell strong enough to make her nose wrinkle, but helping her smooth it into her forearms, the slim neck and her ankles above the socks of her small sneakers, made him want to touch her more. Though he'd found an avenue through her wary shields through Dominance and submission, he wasn't playing kung fu Master to her Grasshopper. He wanted to fuck her senseless, detonate an emotional and physical explosion that would deplete both of them. He wasn't a saint, for Christ's sake.

Getting outside on the boat dock and into the boat helped settle him, though things far deeper than his cock were stirred by their drifting progress as they poled away from the pilings. She hadn't felt comfortable sitting on the opposite bench, so he eased her to her knees in the bottom of the wooden craft, between his feet. As he moved through the marshland he loved, she pillowed her head on his knee, her hands loosely wrapped around his calf. Dana noted the myriad bird and insect life, asked him to identify the calls and warbles that were loud enough for her to hear. He told her about the others, tried to imitate them and almost coaxed a laugh out of her. She registered humidity and temperature, depending on whether they were poling through quiet shadows or bright, lazy sun patches.

Though she'd sneered at the compensatory benefit of her heightened senses, she unconsciously reached for those abilities. As they passed under the branches hanging over the water, she felt the lace of Spanish moss teasing their shoulders. When she trailed her fingers in the water, he watched the flow through the slim digits, the pull of cotton across her breasts as she twisted. He'd refused to let her wear a bra, wanting the pleasure of her nipples. The temptation of those peaks made him want to press her back on the bench, lift the shirt and suckle her, let her sigh and squirm as the boat drifted.

But her head was back on his knee, her fingers idly playing with the seam of his jeans' leg. She was getting sleepy, and that was okay. He wanted every day to be like this. He wanted to go to work, knowing she was going to be part of his life at the end of the day, on the weekends. Maybe she'd call him at lunch, from whatever job she'd be doing. He knew she was too damn smart to settle for sitting in a chair listening to the piercing shrieks of swamp birds, though there were few things more pleasurable to do on a lazy afternoon than that.

He wanted her to have her own life. Even so, a part of him liked the image he'd painted earlier, a 24/7 sex slave. It appealed to his protective side. Of course, a smart Master knew that a fully Dominant nature had to be reined in, the same way a submissive couldn't allow her own cravings to overwhelm her self-determination. Right now, he had to hold on to that balance for both of them. When she got her feet back under her, she could help him keep his urges in check, with that smart mouth he knew she had.

The thought warmed him, made him smile. Tenderness swamped him as he saw she'd fallen asleep. He held her cradled between his knees, moving slow and steady through the waters she'd feared earlier. One step at a time, one fear at a time.

Despite her murmured protest that she could walk, when he tied them off at the dock, he carried her up the boardwalk, into the house and to their bedroom, laying her on the covers. "I'll go run you a bath while you wake up a bit, sweetheart."

"My own personal servant," she said groggily, but there was an impudent quirk to her lips. "Isn't it supposed to be the other way around?"

"When a Master demands it, a slave serves, and serves him well. But a Master takes good care of his slave. That's the way it works."

Her lips pressed together. While her green gaze was sadly vacant, a yearning expression filled it abruptly. "We want you, Master," she said in a throaty voice. "Please. Soft and quiet, here on the bed. Let me know you're here, a part of me."

That expression reflected a desperate desire to believe in what he was offering, spoken and unspoken. It was also a painful reminder that, as much as he wanted to do so, he couldn't heal everything within her in a couple days. Even the goals he'd set, to pull her back from the desolate edge of darkness and help her find the courage to stay with him, might be more than could be accomplished in the time he had.

No. If that was all the time he had, he *would* make it work.

He could tease her, play with her, drive her to screaming climax, but in the face of that appeal for lovemaking, he was the one at her mercy. Unfastening her jeans, he took them off her legs, along with socks and shoes. He kept the tee on, liking the way her nipples pushed against the fabric, the points sharp in their arousal. If she curled her arms around him, would he lose all control? Bury himself in her, surround her and never let her be a foot away from him?

"I'm not sure this is the right time for this," he said quietly.

"No one's touched me for so long, Peter. Not like this. Like I'm real and . . ."

"Not broken?"

Reaching up, she touched his face. "Yeah. But I am broken, aren't I?"

She was killing him. He circled her wrist, held it and turned his mouth into her palm, nuzzling. "You're wounded, sweetheart. That's all. You'll heal, if you give yourself a chance."

Her fingers curled into his shirt, nails biting in. "I need you so badly right now. All the way into my heart."

"I want to give you that. But . . . I don't want to piss you off, sweetheart, but I really don't think you're ready. I also think it'll be better for you tonight, if we hold off, build it up in you." In the face of her whispered plea, the emotions she was tearing loose in his chest, he couldn't hold on to the stern Master he knew he should be. Blowing out a breath, he drew her hand down so she could feel she wasn't alone in her desire. "Hell, this is a bitch for me, too."

Dana swallowed at the size of him. "Do you have to be so damned honorable?"

"Believe me, honorable is not the deal here." He molded her fingers over him, held her grip there tight. "I don't want to win the battle, Dana. I want to take the field, win the war. When I make love to you in this bed, it's going to be because you've accepted you're with the man and the Master you want for the rest of your life."

"Peter, there's no way. . . . We barely know each other."

"That ground's already been covered, sweetheart. Come on. Let's get that bug spray off of you and start getting you pampered and prepped for later tonight."

"You promised . . . that you'd give me something to make me not afraid."

"I will. After a bath. Now, stop being all puppyish or I'll give you a spanking for turning your Master into a big softy."

He wondered if she realized how close he was to his own edge, particularly as he watched her struggle to rein it back in. Then her chin lifted. "I bet you cry at Hallmark movies."

"To even suggest I watch Hallmark movies is pushing past the line, little girl." Lifting her and taking a quick nip at her quivering mouth, he took her to the tub. As he ran the water, he removed her T-shirt, grazing his knuckles over the taut peaks.

"You do like tits, don't you?" she gasped.

"More than God and country," he said gravely. "And yours are gorgeous." He guided her in, helped her sit and adjusted the temperature. "Open your legs."

Surprise crossed her face, but she complied. Removing the small waterproof dual-headed vibrator from a drawer, he caressed her inner thighs with it, letting her get a sense of what he was doing before easing it into her pussy and her anus. She had gorgeous legs, and though they were out of shape now, the skin was still silky, giving. He couldn't help thinking of how they'd feel wrapped around his back. He teased dark curls before he positioned the device and she bit her lip, her nipples hardening further.

It had no more than an inch of penetration, slim straps anchoring it in place and allowing him to position the clit teaser. She did that little breath-caught-in-the-throat thing while he made the adjustment, but when he turned it on a low level, her response was gratifying. She arched up, water sloshing against the sides, her nipples jutting further, challenging him to prove the truth of his convictions. Sliding his hand beneath her back, he brought his mouth to the closest one, taking it in like a small, swollen grape, suckling it so that she pushed her feet against the end of the tub, moving rhythmically against the vibrator. He laid his hands on her hips, stilling her.

"Enough of that. You stay still, move only as I need you to move. Your pretty pussy is going to weep and ache for my cock and the release I'll grant it later tonight. This is all about preparing you to serve me tonight, any way I demand. I know you haven't forgotten how to serve a Master."

Her pulse elevated in her throat, her fingers curling under the water against her trembling thighs. God, she was going to kill him. She responded to his every order. Whether with sass and fire or soft entreaties, or tentative trust, she responded. And whether or not she realized it, by responding as a submissive, she was responding as the unwounded spirit he knew still lay within her.

It was a cynical world, one that had long ago abandoned love-at-first-sight to the very young and foolish. But his gut didn't lie to him, and her response to him told him he was right. It connected to things down deep in both their souls; he was sure of it. If she'd come back whole, he would have pursued her surrender as fiercely as he was doing now. Could he convince her of that, in less than forty-eight hours?

⁂

By the time he let Dana out of the tub, she was very clean and completely mindless. Since she had to clutch his shirt for balance as he walked her backward into the bedroom, she eagerly traced the way his waist muscles shifted with the movement, his abdomen tensing with self-restraint. When he left her standing in the middle of the room, he squeezed her hands, held on to them to the full reach of their arms before regretfully letting her go. It might be how aroused she was, but as she listened to him rustle in the closet, Dana actually felt as if he might be seeing a beautiful submissive standing in the center of his bedroom, her ass cocked in a provocative manner, the slim line of spine and nape so tempting, particularly with his collar still on her throat. He hadn't yet taken it off, and she didn't want him to do so.

She still wore his toy, though he'd added a harness to hold it in place. The dual vibrator changed speeds and sensations frequently, keeping her at a high peak. If his intent was to prepare her for tonight, she was ready. Hell, at this point, she might do a whole football team, if it meant Peter's cock would slide into her at the end, bringing her home inside herself.

The unexpected thought brought a lurch of emotion.

"Come stand over here, by the bed." When he got her there, he sat down on it, trapping her between his knees, settling his hands on her hips. That mere touch made her moan, thrust toward him shamelessly. He kneaded her buttocks, soothing and stirring at once. "That's it, baby. You're so hot for me now, aren't you?" Spreading his fingers, he tapped on the anal plug, making her grab hold of him for balance. "Tonight there are a couple things I want you to do for me. One, accept that you're beautiful. No hunching over, hiding yourself. Second, remember that you can trust me completely. I promise I'll keep you safe. There will be nothing for you to fear. All right?"

Though she jerked her head in a nod, she couldn't help the frisson of worry that shivered across her skin. His hands tightened on her. "I know it's going to be difficult. Which is why I think an additional training aid is necessary to focus your mind where it should be focused."

His hands left her as he picked something up. "We talked about this, that first night. I'm going to wrap you in a physical reminder of your Master's protection, my demand for your obedience to my will."

The stiff satin caressed her flesh, laces feathering across her skin.

A corset.

※

. . . keeping her straight and proud, knowing she's got nothing to worry about. Because she's mine.

"You liked that idea, wanted it bad. I could tell, enough that I wished I'd had one around that night. I even started a letter that would give you a play-by-play of how I'd lace you into one, but two paragraphs in, I was so hard I knew I couldn't finish it without embarrassing myself. This one isn't as custom fitted as I like, but we'll get you one that is soon. Lift your arms over your head."

Dana didn't think she could get more aroused, but the constriction of a corset made the impossible possible. As he wrapped it around her and began hooking it down the front, his knuckles teased her breasts. Clear desire trickled over her thighs, earning an approving growl from him. He took his time, as he had earlier with the fondling and suckling of her breasts, working his way down, finishing mere inches above her pubic bone. Then he turned her and went to work on the laces.

He told her the strapless corset was a copper color. As he tightened the laces, her breasts were bound and displayed at once, in that high pillow-top way that men found irresistible. Risking punishment, she lowered one hand to feel it, and suppressed a smile when he grunted a rebuke, one with a growl of lust in it. She raised the hand again. She couldn't stop herself from responding to his every touch. Her enhanced sense of taste and smell made it worse. If he grazed her breast, she arched. If he slid a palm over her buttock, she pushed back into his hand, wishing she could grind down on him. Every lacing made her feel more restrained, and *his*, at once, and damned if he wasn't right. Being encased in it lifted her body, straightened her spine, made her feel as if she could do anything. Including be beautiful. Her Master would cherish her, keep her from harm.

A long time ago, she'd wished for one night of a fairy tale. She'd gotten her desire, but she wondered if tonight would truly be the answer to her dreams, in the gods' sometimes tragic way of granting wishes. It didn't matter; she'd take it.

Let me be lost in this, if only for tonight. Forget everything else and believe I can see. She could already imagine how he looked in every detail. Somehow she knew his every expression, though she hadn't had the opportunity to see many. Maybe it was because she'd fantasized so much about him, all those many months. But she wanted the opportunity to put her fingers on his face, actually feel what his facial muscles did as he smiled, laughed, frowned, concentrated . . . came.

She mewled as he removed the vibrator and harness, caressing her before setting them aside. "You're so fucking hot and sexy, sweetheart. I wish you could see yourself. Every man there's going to wish you were his to fuck."

The unadorned male evaluation, spoken straight from his cock, was more believable than a hundred praises calculated to charm. When nylon rope stroked against her cheek, he let her touch it, follow it to the end to find the metal fastener. Without a command, she dropped her head back so he could attach the tether to the ring on the collar, above the St. Christopher's pendant.

He placed his lips there first, the sensitized skin above the collar, and she cried out, but kept her hands above her head as he'd ordered. When he drew back, he made an approving noise. "This is yours, sweetheart. When we get there, you'll wear this at all times. You'll feel my touch through it. It's ten feet long. Inside any range I pay out, you can touch and explore without fear."

When his fingers collared her even above the strap, she dipped her head, touched the tip of her tongue to his knuckle. "I intend to show you off, and take fierce pleasure in knowing you're mine. Mine to fuck in front of them if I want, or have you suck me off at a table while I share a drink with my friends. Sit you on my lap and let you go to sleep when you get tired. Dwell on the pleasure of having you in my bed."

She'd never had a Master she trusted enough to go quite that public. So the searing pleasure of the idea with Peter surprised her. Belonging to him, serving him in front of others. She would feel their eyes upon her, the heat of their lust pressing on her as she served her Master.

As if he could follow her thoughts—and maybe he could, because she was sure her face reflected her arousal—he spoke in a voice laden with demanding lust. "Practice being on this leash. Give me the lap dance of my life, as if I'd ordered you to do it there. Grind yourself down on me the way I know you want to, showing those other guys what they're missing. And always remember—you belong to me."

She'd been a good dancer, but that had been then. Self-consciousness arose, but at an encouraging murmur, she grasped for confidence. It didn't hurt that he had her so jacked up from his touch and that vibrator, she was a creature of pure sex right now.

He must have had a remote on the bed, because though he hadn't moved, the reverberation of a bass line came through her soles seconds before the music reached her ears, drowning out everything but what he wanted her to do. It was a hard rock piece with lots of drums, a blatant pounding sex rhythm. Letting the music penetrate, she swayed, shifting from one hip to the other, getting the sense of it. She visualized nightclubs where she'd worn silky, scanty dresses, danced with friends, or found a good-looking boy and enjoyed rubbing herself against him in some outrageous dance moves.

But even then she hadn't wanted just hot, sweaty sex. She wanted the guy who would tolerate only so much teasing, the flashes of ass and leg goading him to take her over, take her in hand, make her feel the invisible bonds he had on her at all times, with or without a collar.

Of course, if that boy had been Peter, she would have let the strap of her dress drop off her shoulder, the neckline of the dress getting dangerously low, drawing his eye to the wobble of the breasts in danger of full exposure.

Now, though, she didn't have to imagine such a thing. She wore his corset, binding her from breast to low on her hips, making her hyperaware of her exposed cleavage, the curve of her buttocks. All on display for him.

She let desire flow through her like water, guiding her body into the first steps. As she rocked into it, she backed up, putting her hand on the leash. Letting it slide through her fingers, she registered how it drew taut as she reached the limits. She liked the idea of using the leash, knowing the man on the other end of it was holding on to the control, his attention on her as tensile as that strap. Turning, she wrapped herself in it, let it bind her arms and upper torso, augment the corset's constriction. When she reached him, her hands were trapped at her sides. One restrained hand found his spread knees and she turned, slid her backside low, down his abdomen, then lower. She put her ass in his lap and executed a rotation that gave her a mouthwatering idea of how hard his cock was.

Straddling his thigh, she teased her wet pussy along the line of the denim, then turned in a relatively lithe move she might not have been able to pull off before the morning's workout. Or tomorrow, when every muscle would be sore. Now she brought her thigh up against his testicles, shimmying down and up against them, imagining his eyes on her breasts, nearly in his face. She could feel his hot breath on them. Then she turned again, dancing back from him, unwrapping herself, only to follow the leash back in, her slim fingers teasing along it until she found him again.

She liked how the corset restricted her breathing, all of it a reminder she had nothing to fear, that he had her heart and soul encased in that satin cage. She sat herself down in his lap again, and this time used her hands braced on his knees to grind and bump herself against him.

"There's a mirror in front of you, sweetheart. I'm getting the best fucking view of your tits in that corset, the way you're bent over like that. Keep working your ass against my cock. I'm going to explode." A stinging slap on her thigh resulted in a pleasurable spasm in her pussy. "Not too much of the same rhythm, now. You keep your mind on pleasing me and not getting yourself off. That's for later."

Easier said than done. Damn, he was too intuitive. She varied the rhythm, but kept on with the dancing, switched back to a front strad-dle and rocked herself in front of his face. Holding on to his shoulders, she got her knees up onto the bed, her back immediately supported by his hands as she leaned back into his strength and figure-eighted her way across his cock. She had to be dampening his jeans, because she was soaked again.

Before her accident, she would have had the stomach muscles to hold the position for a longer time. Now, though, her muscles burn-ing, she had to back off, but he slid her down and around, to cradle her in his lap. Closing his hand on the strap, he tugged on it near the D-ring, his fingers playing in her deep cleavage.

"Whose sweet slave are you?"

"Yours, Master," she said hoarsely. God, she remembered how she'd wondered if she'd ever find this, the one who could chain her, yet make her feel like her wings could stretch farther than she'd ever thought possible. Was it still possible to fly if you had to see your-self another way, through another's eyes?

Lust suddenly torn between something more serious, she touched his face, the slope of tough jaw. Felt him still as he picked up on her mood. "If I'd known it was going to be the last time I was going to see you . . ."

"It wasn't." Cupping her hands, he pressed them harder to him. "If you let me into your soul, let yourself be inside mine, you'll al-ways see me more clearly than anyone."

"How do you know that?"

He brought his mouth close, touched hers. "You were miles and miles away for over a year, but I saw you every day, sweetheart. Every fucking day."

Ten

They were meeting at Lucas and Cassandra Adler's home, and taking a limo from there to the club. Peter had helped her don a wraparound short black dress that was open in the front to show the corset's tenuous grasp on her breasts, and stockings with slim garters. He'd also left the collar on. She was a little discomfited, but he told her she looked like a sexy woman with a penchant for Goth jewelry. From his possessive, lingering touch on her thighs as he helped her don the stockings, she realized he'd integrated them for her confidence, not because he felt any part of her needed concealment. When his hands touched her, all she felt was his desire and pleasure in touching her flesh.

As he handed her into his car and made sure her seat belt was secure, then dropped a kiss on the top of one breast, she drew in a shaky breath. The butterflies in her stomach were throwing rock grenades. She inhaled Peter's aftershave as he got in, a big man getting behind the wheel, making the car rock. He'd already turned on the seat heater for her, and she was grateful for the warmth coming through the upholstery, since the evening air had a nip.

"What kind of car is this?"

"You after my money now? Gold digger."

"Gram always said a good man with money was as easy to love as a good man with none." She sniffed. "But I'm only after your body, Captain."

"Well, then." He covered her cold hand with his, squeezed. As he rubbed a soothing thumb over her knuckles, he leaned over, brushed a kiss along the back of her ear, nuzzling there. Sliding his fingers into the seam of her thighs, he pressed until she parted them. "Leave them like that," he whispered into the microphone of her hearing aid so she caught the sensual purr close up. "I want to play with your pussy while I drive. I'm going to keep you talking the whole way, so I can hear your voice break as I get you hotter and hotter."

As a distraction technique, it was unbeatable, tangling her nerves back up into full-blown lust until she could barely think. By the time they pulled into the Adlers' driveway, her breath was fast and shallow. The tiny thong was in danger of dripping, she was sure. But she heard a console opening, a moment before he pressed an absorbent cloth against her, making her start up against his hand and grind herself there like a wanton, her hand falling onto his forearm, gripping it for an anchor.

"I'm making you into a mindless little slut, aren't I?" He murmured it against her ear again, his body close and hard next to her. Lunging, she met his lips in hot, openmouthed need, and thank God, he didn't deny her. He captured her movement, controlling it with a hand to her nape. Sucking on her tongue, he thrust his in with a demand that incinerated even hers. When his hand sealed over her pussy, not to stroke but to grip, a reminder of his possession, she moaned against his lips.

"Remember," he growled as he broke free at last, "that you're *my* mindless little slut."

"Yes, Master," she breathed, even as she trembled. Her fantasies hadn't done justice to a Master this dominant, one so overwhelming. The healthy, whole Dana would have loved it, but this Dana

wondered if it would be too easy to give in to it, damn him to a life
of watching after her physical shortcomings. In truth he seemed
completely comfortable—or totally oblivious—to such shortcomings. That might be dangerous, too, because his confidence might
make her crazy enough to start believing this was possible.

Peter Winston was as sure as hell of himself, which made her
hope all the more painful. Two days didn't a new life make. It was
only the start, and maybe he really didn't realize everything that
was involved. If she agreed to stay longer, could she handle the
agony if he changed his mind? How long would it take before she
was strong enough to handle a setback like that? And if he realized
it was a mistake, and tried to stay with her out of pity, she'd just
die. It was easy to say she wasn't a coward; far harder to prove it to
herself.

He was taking her around the back, through a pool area. Though
she smelled the chlorine, he described the area to her in precise
military detail. His friends were at a tiki bar about forty feet away,
mixing drinks. Vaguely, she picked up greetings, and clearly heard
Peter's response. As he guided her along the concrete, he had a hand
at the small of her back, one of her hands in his. Despite that, she
tucked her other hand back to touch his fingertips on her hip, trying not to cling or show fear of tripping.

Then another, uncomfortably familiar scent came to her nostrils.
Her steps slowed and she cocked her head. "Is there someone to our
left?"

"Yes. Cassandra's brother, Jeremy. He's sitting in one of the pool
loungers, about ten feet from you. I was going to introduce you to
him, but he appears to be dozing." The cautionary note in Peter's
voice needed no translation. She'd been in a hospital long enough
to recognize the stench of medical treatments, IVs, and sickly sweat.
A combination impossible to erase, no matter how often the nurse
bathed her.

"I'm awake." She heard a sluggish voice, raised to catch his attention and therefore reaching her ears. Then a murmur of sound
that Peter translated.

"Jeremy said it's nice to meet you, Dana."

God, she hated that, when someone had to repeat something to her. But she supposed it wasn't the end of the world. Following an impulse, she moved toward the lounger, taking Peter with her by holding on to his hands. He stopped her, guided her around something in her way. Another lounger, according to what brushed her thigh.

Leaning down as the scent grew stronger, she found a thin leg, a drape of cloth that might be a robe. "I'm fine, Jeremy," she said. "It's nice to meet you." *See, Gram, I remembered my manners, even while being led around like a cart horse.*

"You might not want to touch me." Jeremy cleared his throat, spoke a little more loudly. "AIDS leper here. In fact, I could kick off at any time. Sis has to check with a mirror to see if I'm breathing, or if it's time to take out the garbage."

Peter winced at Jeremy's usual caustic take on things. Though he could tell Dana had heard him clearly, her hand had not moved from its position on his leg. Cassandra was walking toward them. From her expression of quiet pain, he knew she'd heard her brother's comment, though he was sure she'd heard his cynical humor before.

Lucas came with her, sliding a hand around her waist. He shot Jeremy a guys-giving-each-other-shit look. Peter thanked God for his sensitive friends when Lucas took his voice up several octaves. "Yeah, knowing his inconsiderate ass, he'll stay alive a day after the usual trash pickup, so we have to put him on ice for a week."

Dana sank down on the edge of the lounger, found Jeremy's sleeve, followed it to his hand, and slid her fingers in between his. "Your voice," she mused. "It sounds a bit like my brother's. You're too young."

"You're too pretty to be a jarhead."

"That's a Marine term," she said primly. "But thanks."

As Peter watched her, the way her hand moved carefully over Jeremy's thin fingers, he suspected his curiosity mirrored Jeremy's. The young man stared at their hands.

"You must really like your brother. You're touching me, and you don't even know me."

"He died some time ago. That's why I needed to touch you." A faint smile crossed her face, but there was no humor in it. "Sometimes when you can't see, you have to touch to be sure. I hear his voice sometimes. I heard his voice for a while. . . ." Her voice drifted off and Peter saw the moisture gather in her eyes, but even as he stepped closer, she shook it off, gave Jeremy an arch look, despite her inability to look directly at him. "You think after being blown up, I'm really worried about you sneezing on me? If someone wanted to kill me, they've already tried hard enough. I could show you some scary scars."

"Though I much rather you didn't," Peter put in, instigating a competitive spark in Jeremy's face, cynicism briefly replaced by wry humor.

"Hey, she may find the emaciated look sexy, versus your beef-cake routine."

"No doubt," Peter said dryly.

Aside from Jeremy's sickly aroma, the subtle sadness in Peter's tone told Dana the boy looked bad. It was amazing how much she could pick up from voices, even when she couldn't always hear the words clearly. Ironically, her comprehension improved when she stopped worrying about hearing the response, instead focusing on the emotions she was hearing. Jeremy was frightened. Perhaps that was why, though he was obviously close to slipping into sleep again, he'd wanted to be out here, around people, voices and light, because darkness was closing in.

She'd had the opposite reaction, wanting to withdraw when she knew the loss of light would be a permanent fact of her life, not a transition to death. Gram had always said, "People ain't happy with nothing. God blesses them, they complain. Bad things happen, they complain. They can't think about nothing but themselves, though the whole world's full of people worse off they could be helping to feel better."

Following impulse, she found Jeremy's face with her fingertips, leaned in to press her lips against the gaunt cheek, holding herself there. His hand came up, gripped her arm. Long, skinny fingers. Cold. The boy was so cold. He needed another blanket.

"There's nothing to fear," she whispered. "All you're doing is stepping into God's arms." Gram had said that, too, when her brothers were killed. *Stepping into God's arms.*

"I'm not all that religious," he said, voice breaking.

She'd found the right crevice. People were all cracks and crevices. Since people got more of those as they lived and lost, it was sometimes hard to find the right opening to a young heart. But for this boy, it was one large Grand Canyon, easy for someone—she swallowed—easy for someone with the eyes to see it.

I wanted to be a minister. . . .

"My gram said religion only matters to men, not to God. Your heart belongs to Him, and He's always there to welcome it back, like a mama's arms. Or a sister's," she added, remembering what Peter had told her in the car. Cassandra had raised her siblings.

Jeremy's breath was a little uneven, his hands gripping her arms hard, a wordless thanks. As she eased him back, stroked his brow, she could tell even that little exertion had depleted him. He relaxed, sleeping again. When Peter's hand covered hers, she let him lift her to her feet, guide her away from the lounge chair. His fingers grazed her cheek. "There you are," he murmured. "The girl I met in that club. As far as *my* heart goes, you have it, sweetheart. God's going to have to fight you for it."

"Not the only one." A deep timbre reached out to her along with another male hand, giving hers a squeeze. "Lucas Adler. I'm pleased to meet you, Dana."

"I'm Cassandra."

Before Dana expected it, she was eased into a friendly female hug, one with some heavy emotion behind it. Long hair brushed her cheek, smooth skin against the faint texture of her healing scars. "Thank you for what you just did. Because of Peter, you were already welcome here, but consider yourself welcome anytime."

"Even without his deadbeat ass," another voice put in, and her hand was taken in a new strong grasp. "I'm Ben."

She didn't need eyes to know the two men were tall, a little dangerous and a lot sexy. With the sensory overload Peter had inflicted on her up to now, her body fairly vibrated in response to any stimulus. It hadn't occurred to her eye candy would still have an effect on her, but apparently it was misnamed. A good-looking man had a way of appealing to more than one sense. Of course, Peter had already proven that to her. She cleared her throat, tried to rally the spirit belonging to that girl Peter remembered.

"You must be the slick lawyer."

"I see he's already set you against me. He's insecure that way. Afraid I'll take you right out from under his nose."

O'Neill crossed her mind. His teasing, the playful sexual innuendos. He'd come to see her when they'd both been at Walter Reed. She gave him kudos for coming more than once, because she'd been a bitch most of the time. She should have been kinder, more responsive, because in hindsight, she realized he suffered guilt over her injuries. He'd healed, with only a harrowing scar to impress the girls, but psychological wounds could fester. Maybe she'd write or e-mail him. Peter would help her.

Now, though, she tuned back in to her immediate surroundings, lifting a brow in Ben's direction. "Men tend to underestimate a short woman's ability to kick their balls into the back of their throat. Lower center of gravity and all."

"Ouch," Ben responded, a grin in his voice. "Peter, I'm definitely going to take my shot."

"I'm sure," her escort said. Peter's touch slid down her back, giving her buttock a caress. The pressure of his hand against the stiff corset, giving way to the thin fabric and her accessible flesh beneath it, riveted all her nerve endings toward that point. The caress made her already aroused body even more so, such that she was glad another introduction was forthcoming, letting her catch her breath.

"I'm Matt Kensington, Dana. It's a pleasure to have you join us. This is my wife, Savannah."

There was a charisma to that voice, a rolling power to the grip that confirmed he was the leader of this pack, because the position of Peter's body changed, a shift as if he was presenting her for approval. Then she felt Savannah's cool, slim fingers, a welcoming, firm hold. Aside from that, the brace of diamonds on her wedding ring was enough to tempt a closer investigation, because Peter was right. Dana *did* like jewelry.

"Thank you for what you did in Iraq," Savannah said quietly. "Your sacrifice means so much to us all. If you need anything, you need only ask."

She wasn't sure what to do with that, but then she met the last member of Peter's unusual circle of close friends.

"Jon." This voice was tranquil, a sexy almost-like-a-dream quality to it. "Dana, when you're comfortable, I've been studying some impressive advances in sensory technology that may interest you."

"Jon's our mechanical genius." Peter's caress again. "In a variety of ways. The device you experienced earlier today is one of his far simpler ones."

Dana cleared her throat, glad for once she couldn't see because she was sure she'd blush up to her roots meeting Jon's knowing gaze. "It was . . . effective."

"Glad you enjoyed it." Jon's sensitive, clever fingers enclosed hers, stroking her palm, an easy intimacy that seemed to reflect the way they'd all touched her. As if somehow by being Peter's, she was part of an inner circle, provocative and calming at once.

In the car, Peter had reminded her all four men were sexual Dominants, their attitudes and preferences like his own. She hadn't really believed it, but now, in their presence, there was no doubt. In another situation fear might have trickled through her, wondering how much she really knew about Peter, taking her to a BDSM club with his friends. But, despite the different quality and mannerisms to each, they had that same humming undercurrent that Peter had.

Firm, confident sexuality with an underlying . . . tenderness. Protective. It acknowledged the fears she might be facing, and yet sent them a message: *Nothing's going to happen to you while we have anything to say about it.*

On top of that, in Cass's and Savannah's voices, she heard the purring ease that reflected well-loved women. And finally, even if she was putting too much stock in this test flight of her other senses, it didn't change one inexplicable fact—she trusted Peter.

He'd plunged right into her shit without any invitation. He'd been overbearing and pushy, a bully in every sensual, protective way. There wasn't anything cruel about him. He might frustrate the hell out of her, such that, if she had any intention of accepting his ludicrous offer to stay, she'd occasionally have to hit him in the head with a blunt object while he slept. But he'd never let anything hurt her. Even if she was too uncertain of her handicap for her irrational mind to accept it, her rational mind did.

"Let's have a drink and get to know one another before we go," Matt suggested, the masculine Texas drawl in his voice as alluring to a woman's senses as she suspected the rest of him was. "Then we'll go."

※

While Peter and Lucas lifted the sleeping Jeremy and carried him back to his room, where his younger sister Marcie would tend him that evening, Cass and Savannah guided Dana to a circular sofa arrangement. Used to being self-conscious, worried about what sentences she might miss, she found it amazing that this group of strangers so quickly dispelled her anxiety, on those issues at least.

Dana felt no catty or pitying vibes from Cassandra and Savannah at all. They integrated her into the conversation, drawing out information on her interests and pointing her toward shopping and recreational activities in the area they'd love to visit with her. She hadn't felt so easily accepted since basic training.

When Peter returned and settled next to her, the group delved into cocktails, catching up on business, some social talk. As the men moved around, it brought her the distracting, pleasurable scents of male heat, cologne, aftershave, dry-cleaned silk and cotton. The first one to touch her was Jon. A casual brush of her knee accompanied the courteous, "Would you like another drink, Dana?"

As Ben and Lucas stood behind the couch, exchanging opinions with Peter on some business matter, Lucas's thumb and forefinger circled her nape, a light pressure as he leaned over to respond to his wife's gentle reproof about talking business. Ben followed it up with a joke about being henpecked, and his knuckles slid along the point of Dana's shoulder.

During the mixture of conversations, it happened several times, each of the men apparently taking turns with the sensual but respectful caresses. It was when Matt Kensington did it, taking brief hold of her foot in a large hand to straighten the strap of her sandal for her, awakening the highly sensitive nerve endings along her ankle, she realized, with shock, what they were doing.

They were marking her. Identifying her with the pack, but also helping her to recognize them as well. She could be crazy, but she was almost certain she wasn't. Instead, she was impressed by their intuitive understanding of how it reassured her, to have tactile imprints to anchor and center her.

Beyond that noble purpose, it enhanced the charge of sexual anticipation flavoring the air, since they all knew where they were going tonight. Peter had his arm stretched behind her, and she was hyperaware whenever he dropped his hand from the couch to tease her collarbone. Once, his other hand settled on her leg, gliding up her thigh. Just a brief, sweet caress to the inside, and before she thought, she'd started to spread her legs, a submissive's automatic response to a Master's touch there. He gripped her smoothly, stopping her, but before she could get discomfited, his lips brushed her ear in approval.

Cassandra and Savannah were both submissives, she reminded herself. Since she knew the nature of a submissive, she wasn't surprised they were successful businesswomen. The fact they gave their men a lot of playful shit was a bonus, one that had her laughing and joining in the banter herself. Peter threatened to take her home before they taught her bad habits.

Home. It didn't sound as odd as she would expect. She let that thought bolster her when they finally headed out to the club.

More conversation, the scent of champagne and truffles, and then a chocolate-covered strawberry Peter fed to her directly from his own mouth, settling his lips over hers as she laid back in the cradle of his arm in the spacious limo. The taste of the fruit and confection melted her body into the insistent strength of his.

"Hell," Ben groused from the seat across from them. "Way to get my dick hard before we get there, Peter. Ease up or I'm going to jump the first pretty ass I see."

"Like you need an excuse," Jon observed wryly. "When we went to St. Bart's, I thought they were going to kick us off the island."

As Peter lifted his head at last, Dana drew in a ragged breath. "Just how rich are you all?"

"Peter's a poor cousin, really." Ben's knee grazed hers, then his calf as he stretched out a long leg on the side opposite of Peter. "One of those hangers-on that sponges off his betters. We tolerate him because his whole soldier routine attracts women. You'd be much better off with a lawyer."

"Particularly a castrated one," Peter said.

"Peter is quite well-off, Dana," Savannah reassured her. "You don't have to worry about working two or three jobs to support him."

Dana let herself smile. "Well, as long as he's not after *my* fortune. I have two or three of these kind of limos lying around, you know."

Then her stomach was jumping again, because the limo pulled in the club parking lot. She tried to calm it, focusing on Peter's reassuring grip on her hand. While Surreal was not as upscale as The Zone, Peter had said it was still one of Louisiana's best fetish clubs, doing its best to emulate The Zone's example on the more limited budget it had. As the others got out, she was hit by a wave of loud voices and white noise. Heat and a flicker at the corners of her dark vision suggested a lot of flashing light. "It's busy tonight," Jon mentioned, as he exited the limo last.

She hadn't moved, both hands clutched around Peter's one large one, resting in her lap. His fingers bracketed her thigh, squeezed. "You trust me, sweetheart?"

"I want to. I'm scared, though. And I hate it. I don't think I can do this. Please don't make me do this." Her breath was starting to come faster. Fuck being calm. That wasn't going to work. She'd been crazy to agree to this.

For months, being blind and mostly deaf had made her unsure of herself, frightened by new things in a way she'd never been. It was easier and safer to stay within her comfort zone, with people she knew, places that were familiar. People could call it a crutch, but they didn't fucking know what it was like. What had she been thinking? Her good sense had been fogged by sex—that was what it was. Hell, she'd hardly known she still had a libido until Peter came to find her. Okay, yeah, she'd fantasized about him all the time, but like a dream, not a reality. This was reality, big-time, up close and way too freaking personal.

"Hey, hey." He cupped her face. "Focus on me, sweetheart. Breathe. Breathe slow and deep. There is nothing to be scared of here. You remember why?"

She swallowed. "No, no, I don't. Peter, please—"

"Because I'm not going to let anything happen to you. Say it."

His fingers were stroking her face and she could feel how close he was. Hell, he'd pulled her into his lap, was cradling her, holding her . . . Well, she'd say like a child, except his fingers had slipped between her legs, and she was amazed as he used her earlier arousal to simply slide the tips of his fingers partway into her, past the thong. It centered everything there, throbbing, anxiety and lust tangled into a ball. "Say it, Dana."

"You're not going to let anything happen to me," she whispered, and gasped as his fingers twitched, sending pleasure spiraling hard and tight through her clit.

"Damn straight." Snapping the leash on, he gave her a tug, a sensual reminder of their afternoon. "Ten feet, remember?"

"It's a club, Peter. There will be people I don't know all around. . . ." He'd said she should feel comfortable touching, but what about being touched? And strangers? His friends were okay; she'd met them, but—

"You've known you were a sub since you were a teen. Remember telling me that? Trust in that, Dana. Trust your Master."

When he brushed his lips over her temple, she pressed into that touch, squeezing her eyes shut. "I've got you." He said it against her ear, a habit she was beginning to like, particularly when he took a little nip at the earpiece of her hearing aid, an unexpected sexy caress. "Let's get you out of this." Moving slow and easy, his fingers drifted down her sternum, molding over her left breast before he dipped down to the tie of the dress, loosened it and slid it off her shoulders. She'd be leaving it in the car, wearing only the corset, thong panties, stockings and low pair of heels he'd given her.

She'd worn as little the night she'd met him, less even, but she'd felt nowhere near as vulnerable as she did this night. Despite that, though, strangely, the removal of the outer garment almost seemed to help, because it truly left no doubt whose and what she was here. His slave. His submissive, under his guidance and protection.

"Here you go." When he bracketed her face, a mask slid down over it, one that fit her nose and around her eyes, but stopped there, leaving her mouth and chin free of encumbrance. Lifting her hands to it, she realized it was a remarkable likeness to the mask she'd worn for him that night.

"Now"—he found her right nipple beneath the corset, began to do a slow pinch and roll that had her mouth dry—"be whatever you want to be tonight, sweetheart, as long as you remember you're mine. This is your fairy tale, however you want it told. Anything that worries you, you tell me and I'll fix it. You hear?"

Tears threatened as she touched the mask, smoothed it under her fingers. "Peter, we can't live in a fairy tale."

Easing his touch up under her jaw, he cradled her face, and then she was close in his arms again. They wrapped around her back, her hands settling on his chest, curling into the cotton oxford he was wearing, the silk of his tie. "I'm giving you one tonight, Dana. I'm going to convince you that you *are* my happily ever after. I want to be yours, if you'll give me the chance."

She wasn't sure if he was teasing, and if she was crazy for wanting him not to be. So she summoned an indifferent smile, struggling for their earlier banter. "I don't know. I'll have to compare your portfolio to Ben's. You know I'm a gold digger."

"Hmm. Then let me give you something else to think about."

Catching her lips in an unexpectedly aggressive kiss, he put his hand back between her legs, massaging her clit, delving deep inside with devilishly clever and aggressive fingers that demanded nothing less than full surrender. The ambush caught her off guard. In less than five seconds, the climax took her like a fast rush of machine-gun fire, jerking her back against the cushions, her hands clutching at him for an anchor as he continued to kiss her senseless, her ass rubbing in frantic rhythm against him and the plush fabric of the seat.

He milked her to the end of it, took her down to a gasping, shuddering aftermath, and then nipped at her lips. "That's the last I want to hear about Ben's fucking portfolio."

"Sure," she said faintly. Though, privately, she thought if she ever wanted to be overwhelmed with a mindless climax within seconds, she'd shamelessly chant, "Ben, Ben, Ben," to elicit that reaction from her captain again.

She bit her lip, shuddering with an aftershock as he used a handkerchief to clean her, holding her thong to the side, rubbing her as she clutched his jacket sleeve. When he readjusted her clothes, she wondered if the handkerchief was his. If he left it on the seat with her scent, or put it back in his pocket to carry. Then he was getting out of the limo.

Her legs were trembling now for more reasons than nervousness, so he supported her as she emerged. She blessed him for thinking of the mask, which would conceal that her eyes were sightless. Taking a deep breath, she tried to imagine how she looked. The nightclub lights would gleam off the curves of breast, hip and waist encased in copper corset, most of her scars beneath the garment and stockings. Her ass would be shown to good advantage in heels that were flattering but not ice pick or too high, Peter's sensitivity to her balance. She was going to have to look into that yoga instructor, and practicing walking. She did like how stilettos made her ass look. She thought Peter would, too, if she got the confidence for that fuck-me-if-you-dare pendulum swing she'd had down pat before.

The clothes helped. Lord God, did they help, as every child who'd ever played dress up knew. Instead of being in a dark room in a sweat suit and mindless stupor, indifferent to her life, wallowed down in fearful misery, she stood in front of a BDSM club, in the company of a man who'd made it clear he thought her capable of anything. Who, despite what scars might be showing, thought she was sexy, gorgeous. His.

It wasn't the clothes. It was him. The corset was his weapon, one he'd deployed with maximum devastating effect. With that Master's intuition he had, he'd discerned its power over her from nothing more than her brief reaction to the suggestion, on one far-too-short night, more than a year ago.

Before this had happened, she'd always believed in herself, her own strength. It shamed her, the way she'd faltered. In the army, she'd accepted certain things couldn't be accomplished alone. She just hadn't realized she might need someone to stand at her back even when it didn't involve AK-47s and insurgents.

Could she dare to hope he stood there for the right reasons, or was it pity? Powerful, deceptive nostalgia goaded by a titillating memory, instead of present reality? She wondered if it was a sign her perspective was changing, that she was more worried about what was going on in his heart than her own. Was that good or bad?

His hand was on her hip, stroking the top of her buttock, his thigh pressed to the back of hers. Reaching down, she curled her fingers over his. They overlapped hers, his lips touching her throat below the collar, so that she tilted her head back to his shoulder, giving him immediate access.

"We're going inside now," he said. "It's going to be impossible to hear in certain places, okay? Pay attention to the leash, to my touch. If you get confused or disoriented, don't worry. I'm right here."

She nodded. Leaning down, he brushed his cheek against hers once more. "We're going to have fun tonight, sweetheart. Right?"

She latched on to the relaxed quality of his voice, tried to take it into herself, despite the fact she was all too aware that the human world was a very visual and auditory one, not one that encouraged touch. Even fetish clubs had stringent rules about touching anyone without invitation, though if there was a large segment that liked to play public, there were often a lot of invitations. But she couldn't see or hear any of those invitations.

Peter promised they would have fun, that he was here. She had to trust him to keep her out of trouble. Still, her pulse was pounding in her throat as he took her up the ramp toward the entrance, steadying her at the change in angle. He'd described it in detail on the way, so she focused on the image. Blue and silver lights outlining the main doorway, people in all manner of fetish garbs inside, paying their cover fee, having their IDs checked. Of course Peter and his friends were already members, so they passed through that area. It was crowded, though. Peter's hand was wrapped in the leash, lying on her hip, keeping her close, but she still bumped people. A brush of velvet from a cloak, smells of latex and leather, that humming vibration of arousal. Music from the approaching dance floor resonated through her feet. Realizing they must be passing through the public play area, she heard snatches of things. A muted, rhythmic sound she realized was a flogger. A cry of pain laced with pleasure, the plea to a Mistress for more.

Perhaps Peter would take her to a booth with his friends, get a drink. She could kneel at his feet. She wouldn't have to move, to fight the overwhelming urge to stretch out her arms and pinwheel, trying to figure out her surroundings.

When the crowd let up so she could breathe, move more freely, Peter eased away from her, letting the leash lengthen and slacken. Immediately she reached after him, but he was already beyond her fingertips. Before she could panic, the tether twitched. Not pulling her in that direction, merely letting her know he was there.

He was giving her ten feet to do as she pleased, but she didn't want to move. This spot was safe because she knew it. Ground solidly beneath her feet. It was way too soon. While the people were no longer crushed against her, there were still too many of them, stepping in and out of that personal space buffer. Too many scents, sounds, sensations, not the arousing mélange she'd experienced at the Adler home. It was too overwhelming.

Reaching up to grip the tether, she drew in the slack so she could determine and move in Peter's direction with slow, uncertain steps. She walked out of the shoes, needing to grip the floor with her toes, health laws be damned. Damn it, he kept moving, staying out of range. He wasn't going to let her cling to him. Frustration shot sparks through the anxiety. If she could see, this wouldn't scare her at all, not even if she was alone. But she wasn't alone. That light tug again. A reminder he was here. Nothing would harm her.

Then something unexpected happened. She had more space to breathe. Those strangers who'd been so close no longer were, though she still sensed a crush of people in the noise and air movement. Had they figured out she was handicapped in some way and moved back? Were they staring at her? No. She wore her mask and leash, so she was no more of a spectacle than any other submissive. Submissives were here to be seen, to serve.

Too many unknown variables. She struggled for calm, but even the reassurances weren't enough. *Oh, hell. I can't do this. I can't.* Here she was in the middle of vast amounts of people, a fish alone in an indifferent ocean carrying her where it would. Isolated, where sound was a distant cacophony she couldn't understand. How could he bring her here, when she'd been in virtual isolation for so long?

Why was he doing this to her? He should know better. She wasn't that same fucking Dana, was she?

"I can't do this," she said aloud, and then she shouted it, anxiety clawing raw at her throat. But her voice would simply be swallowed in all the other noise. That was the way the public areas could be. With a snarl, she wrapped her hands on the leash and jerked, a terrified, angry child wanting to bring him to her physically.

It came free in her hands, the strap slapping against her calves in gentle rhythm. Dana froze, her hands clutched on it. She'd pulled the leash from her Master's hands.

Eleven

He couldn't be more than eight feet from her, right? A staccato of heartbeats later, however, she still didn't feel his reassuring touch, or a tug indicating the end of the leash had been picked up.

But then, he wouldn't, would he? He was there, but he was waiting on her. With Masters she'd had in the past, her interactions might have been fun, occasionally intense, but that deep, soul-level bonding she'd sought with the right Master, who touched her submissive soul and achieved a link that went beyond posted rules, the one who understood it was a part of who she was and not just a way to liven up her sex life, had not appeared. Until Peter. He'd already proven he had a deeper understanding of her need to be dominated than even she'd admitted. She trusted him on instinct, not experience.

The rules were now specific to the two of them, not what was laid out on the wall. She'd pulled the leash from his hands, so it was up to her to give it back to him and accept his punishment. If that was what she wanted.

She'd broken out in a sweat, holding that tether in clammy palms. When she made the first step, she had to stop and steady her wobbling knees. But in his home, even at the Adlers', she could feel him, separate from everyone else. If she could calm down, and focus, she somehow knew she could feel him, find him. He was watching her intently; she was sure of it. He'd promised to be no farther away than ten feet. He wouldn't break his word. He just wouldn't give in to her fear. Everyone else had, all these months, but he was ruthless, ruthless as only the Master of her dreams could be. He believed the submissive in her was stronger than the wounded creature she thought she'd become. He wouldn't abandon her, but he would force her to trust that he was there, to find him and hand him the leash again.

She wanted to trust him that way, but she hadn't let herself face the fear that came with increased dependency. She'd hidden in her room, let her ability to trust get as weak and flaccid as her muscles. Taking one step forward was harder than anything she'd ever done. Her heart rate accelerated. She had no idea what was in front of her. She should crouch down, go to hands and knees to feel her way along the floor like a groveling animal. But Gram would be appalled, clucking about hygiene, hundreds of feet that had been God knew where traipsing across the carpet.

A half laugh, half sob choked out of her. As if that mattered right now. The pulse of the music drummed through her feet, loud enough that she could hear the song and words. Sade. "Nothing Can Come Between Us." It had been one of her favorites. It *was* one of her favorites. Taking a step, she breathed. One step, one breath. She could have been any sub whose Master had blindfolded her beneath her mask, a sensory deprivation to increase the intensity of the experience.

Intense was definitely the right word. She took another step, and brushed cloth.

A suit jacket. Her knuckles grazed a shirt's small, smooth buttons, then moved to a lapel. It wasn't Peter. She'd known that as soon as she came within range, because she knew his scent, his heat. But this man wasn't unfamiliar. Jon Sage, a smell she'd associated with him, mixed with the whiskey he'd been drinking. When he'd asked her what drink she'd like, he'd taken her hand in an easy motion, pressed her knuckles to his chest, so she recognized the texture of the jacket. He passed his own knuckles over her cheek now, below the mask, and grazed her lips with . . . chocolate?

Chocolate and brandy, a cordial. When she parted her lips, he placed it on her tongue, caressing her throat as she took it. While she was occupied with savoring the unique, rich taste, he let her feel that he was holding something soft, almost like a clay, in his other hand. It had a form to it, as though there were wires beneath the malleable substance. He leaned in, his mouth against her ear.

"Peter's demand. I'm going to put these two things on you, dearest. Draw a breath in, so I have a little room. He's got you laced quite tight, the sadist."

That voice was pitched exactly as she'd suspected. Despite his tone of gentle amusement, Jon was quite capable of issuing a command as a Master. Whatever bound these men together, it made it impossible for her to feel threatened by him now.

Peter had reminded her in the car that she'd been a submissive for as long as she could remember. The relief that could come from obedience to a man she knew could handle her, that she could trust and test by turns, was an elusive but familiar shadow she wanted to chase down, pull into herself and leave fear behind. *Peter's demand . . .*

Holding still, she took a breath, the chocolate melting on her tongue. Jon's long, clever fingers slid into the corset, worked across to her nipples and then pinched that disk of clay over each. He had a sensual touch, functional and caressing at once, so that the pressure made her catch his sleeves, steadying herself at the rocket of sensation. Then his hands slid free, resting on her shoulders. It was like Play-Doh. Her lips curved at the ridiculous thought; then something began to happen that drove away any thought of a child's toy.

It was warming. Warming, and something else. It penetrated her nerve endings and . . . Holy God, her nipples were getting terribly aroused, as if Peter were suckling them, tugging, creating a liquid pool in her lower belly that had her off balance.

While her body shuddered with arousal, Jon turned her, sending her from him with a gentle nudge. With fear being supplanted by physical desire, she dared a few more steps, wondering if he'd sent her toward Peter.

Instead, she stumbled over her shoes, but someone caught her from behind as she gasped. Ben. He was easy, so larger-than-life sexy, his aftershave a rich, teasing scent.

"Need to get you back in those shoes to protect your feet, darling."

. . . *you can touch or explore anything within your range* . . . It was too much to resist. Rather than complying, she reached back, found the knot of his silky tie, and threaded it through her fingers. His hands closed on her hips, steadying her. She arched, her tongue teasing her own lips at the additional stimulation to her nipples. The movement brought her ass fully against his groin, and holy God. Talk about a portfolio. Ben had gotten extra blessings from the cock fairy. She couldn't help it, not with that stimulation happening to her nipples. Thinking about Peter watching, remembering their lap dance, she made a slow, sensual circle, her lips curving at an expulsion of air on her nape that suggested she'd inspired a half chuckle, or a muttered curse. Ben tightened his fingers, made her step into those shoes.

"You're trouble, darling. That's for sure. Go on with you, now."

Since she'd let Ben's tie drape over her shoulder, the silk passed over the high top of her breast as she moved away. This time she attempted that pendulum saunter, biting her lips at the sensations that sparked through her nipples like electricity. Straight ahead she went, not at all surprised to come up against Lucas. This was why she could move ten feet however she wanted. Peter's friends had formed a loose circle around her.

How they were doing it in a crowded club environment, she had no idea, but she was learning not to question the miracles Peter could pull off. She wouldn't run into anything, touch anything Peter knew she shouldn't. Of course, he might have something to say about that little tease she'd given Ben, but if he reacted the way he had in the car, she'd go back and give Ben a full lap dance to experience that punishment again.

But now there was Lucas. Broad shoulders, tight, athletic body. An amateur cyclist, according to the earlier small talk. Intriguing choice, all of them wearing suits or more formal attire. His shirt was probably some impressive brand like Armani, with that soft, feel-me texture, though the chest beneath had its own appeal. His hands were holding her firmly under her elbows, a Master's hands. His knee brushed against her bare leg, making her hyperaware of how easy it would be for him to shift, widen her stance so he could press a bicycle-hard thigh between her legs. His lips were against her ear now, though, feeding her eagerness to have more pleasures woven into her lust-fogged mind.

"We all have our specialties, sweet Dana. If Ben had his way with you, he'd take you in the ass, keep you screaming and climaxing at once. Jon has his many clever devices, and my specialty . . ."

He took her hand to his mouth, and enclosed two fingers there, making her gasp at the artful way his tongue swept between the knuckles, such an obvious representation of the way he might penetrate a woman's pussy that her pulse sped up when he let them slide slowly out and then took them down to her panties. He pressed her fingers over her soaked thong. "Those might be my lips there, if Peter allows us the pleasure and opportunity at some future time. But tonight is just for you to feel the possibilities."

Holy crap, her knees were weak. If Peter willed it, these men might do even more, bring her pleasure in multiple ways at once. She wondered if they'd ever shared Cassandra or Savannah, if those women craved such extreme play the way she had. The way she *did*. An erotic shiver went through her at the certainty of it.

When Lucas let her go, he didn't nudge her in a specific direction as the others had. He simply stepped back, letting her decide where she would go. She'd wrapped the leash around one arm to keep from tripping on it, but she'd preferred it taut, one end in Peter's hand. Her anger had dissipated. She was anxious, aroused, her mind spinning, but she moved forward without fear now, convinced they wouldn't allow any missteps. As such, the next obstacle surprised her, because it wasn't male. Or a familiar body.

She'd walked into an occupied St. Andrew's cross. Exploring, Dana found lovely, thick hair that tumbled down soft shoulders. She drew back when she brushed what was obviously a bare breast. A female slave. If she was in the public area, her Master or Mistress was likely encouraging a limited amount of touching. No one had stopped her yet, so cautiously, Dana reached out again, investigated a pair of breasts far heavier and fuller than her own. Aroused nipples, despite the raised welts on the generous curves. A hard-core pain slave. Despite that, in sympathy, she bent, kissed the abraded flesh. The woman quivered beneath her mouth. She couldn't hear her reaction, which meant either it was below her hearing threshold or, more likely, she was gagged. The shudder was pleasure, though, so she continued to investigate, finding the restrained submissive had a curved belly and Venus's thighs to match the breasts. A voluptuous woman. She liked that, liked the woman's smooth skin. She bit back a helpless little moan of her own as the strobing feel of whatever Jon had put on her nipples increased, responding to her own elevating arousal. She pinched this woman's nipples, a reflection of how much she wanted her own teased. She thought of what Peter had said about the breast bondage, imagined it in detail. She wanted that. She wanted Peter.

What she was doing must be pleasing him, so she decided to push it further, see how much he could take before he got involved. Coming closer to the woman, she ran her hands over the curvy body, learning her, grazing her knuckles over a puffy clit. The restrained slave hadn't come yet, or had been built back up to mindless heights again. Dana pressed her corseted breasts against the woman's and whimpered at the sensation against her stiff nipples. She rubbed herself there, trying to get relief, even as she found the woman's stretched mouth with her fingertips and kissed her over the ball gag, kissing her like she wanted Peter to kiss her. Hard, demanding. She rubbed her silk-clad pussy against one of those pillowy thighs, across the woman's mound, and clung to the posts above her as the

woman shuddered and cried out. Rotating her hips and then thrusting forward, she brought pressure and friction against the woman's
mound. From the back she knew it looked as though she was fucking the woman as a man would, all the while giving them a generous display of her ass.

Was the blindness making her abandon all inhibitions, or was it
the overstimulation of her nipples, the feast to the senses his men
had just given her? She didn't know, but she was yearning toward
what all subs sought, that subspace where rational thinking meant
nothing and responding to one's Master was everything, giving
pleasure and receiving it.

Peter was a breast man. Turning, she leaned back against the
woman's body and plucked at the front of her own corset, unhooking the top several eyelets, then cupped her breasts, displaying
them. When her ensconced nipples brushed the top edge, she bit
back a cry at the near-climactic sensation, arching back into the
woman. Oh, God, if her Master or Mistress freed her hands, but not
her legs, that woman could cinch an arm around Dana's waist, reach
around to Dana's pussy, bring her to climax while the men watched,
growing harder and harder.

She liked the idea, felt the power of it, desire and lust pulsing
toward her. She wondered how much of an audience she had. Now
she felt no fear of it, because she knew that protected circle was
around her. What were Cassandra and Savannah doing? Were they
watching, or doing similar things? Or did these Dominants bring
their women here for arousal and voyeurism only, confining their
play to more semiprivate methods? Was that another reason this
circle of men were around her? The message being that she was here
to serve Peter's pleasure, but not available to others except someone
like this restrained slave, who'd become another enhancement to
their private pleasures?

When they'd wanted to touch her, with Peter's consent, it had
only been more stimulating, fuel thrown on the fire. It was all about
her pleasure, as he'd said. She didn't feel handicapped or pitiful. She
felt cared for, not as someone who needed protection, but as some-

one who'd been given it because they didn't want to share. The idea swept her with feminine power. But she also burned with a craving want, and that want had a specific target. She'd wanted him to come to her.

But he was her Master. She'd pulled the leash from *his* hand.

Sliding away from the woman, she stopped, trying to concentrate past her arousal. It wasn't only their intoxicating combinations of male scents that told her they were close to her. She could detect body heat, some kind of pulsing . . . energy. For the first time in nearly a year, she didn't notice that she couldn't see or hear. Her other senses were giving her so much, she could see them around her in every way that mattered. She felt the hold of the corset keenly, the power it gave her through its possession, and responded to it. Lifting her head, she straightened her shoulders further. Using her heart and soul, she found the unique signature, the male scent she wanted, the one for whom she wore the corset. Adjusting her direction, she walked six steps, and knelt, bowing her head and holding up the leash. "Forgive me, Master."

It was noisy, but not that noisy. He heard her. Peter stared down at her bowed head, the offered leash. She'd driven them all crazy with that performance. Hard as a rock, he was raging to put his claim on her. Lucas, Jon and Ben had all done what came naturally to them, and Peter had been satisfied with how it increased her desire. These men were capable of giving any woman the most intense orgasms of her life. He'd love to give her that gift . . . another night. She hadn't been his long enough, and there was still too much ground to cover, before he would be willing to share more than this.

He'd had a bad moment when she jerked the leash away. He'd known she was more hardcore, but that had been before. Afraid he'd gone too far, something in him had broken loose. Fuck, he didn't care what the right thing was to do. He was going to do what he'd wanted from the first. Scoop her up, take her away, protect her from everything. He couldn't stand doing this to her, seeing her fear and pain.

It had been Jon who'd steadied him, placing a hand on his arm, giving him a steadying look before he stepped out and let Dana run into him first. And now, in those six steps she'd taken toward him, Dana had given *herself* a glimpse of what she could choose for herself. Maybe it would lead her to trusting him, not just for this scenario, but to the deepest levels of her soul, so eventually she might choose him. Then he could spend his life ensuring she never regretted that choice.

Taking the leash from her hand, he wrapped it around her wrists, holding on to them for a few long moments, tracing the fragile bone and smooth skin. When he at last drew her to her feet, he brought her to him, keeping the leash taut this time. The bare brush of her body against him, the near embrace, the tremble that swept through her as a result, almost broke him. But with a light squeeze of her hands, he guided her through the circle of the other K&A men, to the opposite wall where a favorite device waited.

⊰⊱

Guiding her hands to it, he let her explore the breast stock while he released the sliding adjustment. As he found the right size, her fingers drifted down his back, grazing his arms. Most Masters had firm rules about their subs touching them without permission, but he liked how she used him as an anchor in unfamiliar surroundings. He couldn't get enough of it. But eventually he turned her square to him and opened up the hooks of her corset until it gapped below her breasts. When he removed Jon's invention, he bit back a groan, seeing how distended the nipples were. The boning of the corset was stiff, but he was able to fold it back enough that he could guide her breasts into the two spaced circles in the smooth mahogany wood. Tightening the metal adjustments inside the circles diminished their size, so that it held her fast. Her blood vessels would constrict, enlarging her breasts and making them more sensitive.

He raised the height of the stock, so she was straining on her toes. Then he placed the nipple clamps on her. She cried out at the stimulation, biting her lip at the pain that came with it. Easing the screws, he found that balance where she was on the knife-edge, her tremor from intense arousal, not unbearable pain. Then he connected the clamps with a chain, meeting in the middle with a padlock he held in his palm. Guiding her bound hands up to feel where he'd placed her, he saw her register how the stock worked, like one of old, only instead of arms, its torturous focus was on a woman's luscious curves. The circle adjustments kept her there with a snug hold, but as an added psychological measure, the locked chain between the nipple clamps underscored how impossible it was for her to pull away and free herself. When he let the padlock fall out of his hand, she jerked hard, a cry wrenching from her throat at the shock of the sudden pull against the clamps and her already hugely aroused nipples. Beautiful, mauve, impossibly aroused peaks.

"Oh, God, Master . . ."

She was so wet that her thighs glistened with it, the thong useless to absorb her arousal. He loved it, couldn't wait to strip her out of it and take her in only the stockings, corset and collar. If he had his way, that was what he'd always have her wear when she was in his house, in his bed.

"Now for what I promised you." He made the words wet, covering her ear with his lips, dipping in with his tongue to trace the crevices around her hearing aid. "I'm going to make you come by sucking your pretty tits, sweetheart. You're going to gush like a man. I know you want my cock, but you'll wait for that, as punishment for pulling the leash out of my hands, until you'll never do that again, will you?"

She shook her head wildly, eyes glazed and mouth parted. "Please . . . Master."

Jon had had a staff person bring Peter a chair, so now he sat to study the display in front of him, stretching out his legs under the stock so they pressed against her calves on either side. She shifted on her toes, making the muscles in her thighs and that heart-shaped ass strain. Her gorgeous tits looked round and heavy. The lock was dragging her bare nipples down, which he knew were tingling like a son of a bitch. Taking his time, he leaned forward and blew on one.

She screamed, convulsed in aroused reaction. He wanted to do this forever, but because he didn't want to damage those tender blood vessels with prolonged constriction, he closed in, put his mouth over one nipple and the clamp.

"Oh, God, oh, God . . ." It was a chant. On another night, he'd ask Lucas to lick the fluids trickling down her leg, all the way back up to her cunt, start drinking that nectar he liked so much, while Ben slid a few nicely lubricated things in and out of her pretty little puckered anus. She'd come again and again, until she was so exhausted they'd have to carry her. But tonight, he wanted her to come from his mouth on her nipples only, a reminder that he could command her response. That he could take care of her in all ways.

Oh, fuck, she tasted like butterscotch. Jon thought of everything. He suckled her, so gently, because hard would have been way too much right now. It was the thing he'd learned first about pleasuring a woman, and it remained the most important. Take it slow and easy, keep it slow and easy, until she was begging mindlessly for it rough, and then the time was right to let loose his own needs. That was fine; he was so hard, he wasn't getting out of the chair until the very second he intended to ram his cock into her.

Her head thrashed this way and that, fighting her restraint not because she wanted to be freed, but because her body had to move in response to the stimulus. He moved to the other nipple, teasing that one, swirling, nipping, then slow, long drags of his tongue. He brought his hands into it, adding to the squeezing sensation, milking her breasts into his mouth while she became animal and savage, her words reflecting the fact he'd put his claim on a soldier as well as a good churchgoing girl.

"Oh . . . fuck. Please fuck me . . . Let me fucking come . . . Oh, God . . . love you sucking my tits . . . Please, Master . . . My cunt needs you . . ."

He kept sucking, licking, biting. Her legs were shaking, but he didn't need to worry about her falling against the restraint and hurting herself. Ben materialized out of the shadows and slid a capable arm around her waist, holding her steady. He met Peter's eyes, gave him a nod, and Peter kept doing his magic on her breasts. Ben had to be light on his toes, because in her state, her pussy was seeking his hard thigh to rub and hump. He kept his leg away from what was Peter's alone tonight as a flush rose along her throat and the expanse of smooth flesh above his mouth. Her face was straining, lips pulled back in a pre-orgasmic snarl. Peter bit, sucked harder now, and squeezed one last time, pushing her over.

Her shrieks could have been heard in the lobby, as if he hadn't already attracted a sizeable crowd. He and the other K&A men weren't normally public players. Cassandra and Savannah were sitting up in a mezzanine seat with Matt, where they had a good view of the display, but were not part of it. Peter liked keeping his woman to himself as well, but he'd known Dana needed the more hard-core, the sensory overload. It would push her into the mindless ecstasy state that was a Master's drug, where nothing stood in the way of her true self and desires.

As her climax rocked her against the stock, her hips pumped wildly. Ben was intent on her reaction, his jaw tight and eyes green fire. Some girl was going to get the ass-fucking of her life tonight. Ben would make Peter pick up the tab, because he'd likely use one of the house submissives who could handle his rougher needs. That was okay. He'd gladly pay it.

Peter rose, circled around. Ben held her until Peter opened his slacks, slid a condom on, and then the lawyer stepped out of the way. Perfectly in sync, Peter's arm slid around her waist as Ben's was sliding away. As she collapsed back against Peter, he slammed into her cunt, into rippling, slick-as-an-ocean flesh. She was still coming, her pussy oozing sweet honey as he plunged into it.

She cried out again, a deeper, animal cry of satisfaction. Digging his fingers into the back of her collar, he held her head up, drawing the tether taut between its hold on the D-ring and her hands as he worked his hips against her ass, striving for deeper, harder. "Fuck . . ." He came as violently, ramming her so her tits pressed harder through those holes, the lock swinging in a way that had her flinching even through her pleasure. Jon moved into Peter's chair, catching the lock so it couldn't cause her further pain. As she whimpered through aftershocks and Peter's final thrusts, Jon removed it, as well as the nipple clamps. Knowing the blood surge could be intense, he brought his fingers into play, massaging her sore breasts as he loosened the stock. She moaned at the additional stimulation, but stayed where she was, good little slave that she was.

Peter shuddered with her through their aftermath, even though he wanted to be where Jon was, making sure she didn't experience the terrible pain that could sometimes come with the returning blood flow. Damn, he wanted to be everywhere at once. Jon gave him a wry smile, backing off as Peter's hands came around and took over, earning another dove's cry of need from his sweet girl. She was near full collapse; he could feel it. There was nothing medically wrong with her, no, but the workout this morning had told him what her conditioning was, where her limits were. He had promised he'd always take care of her, and he wasn't going to fall down on the job.

Glancing up at the viewing mezzanine, he saw there was no space between Matt and Savannah and Cassandra, the women sitting on either side of him. Though of course Cassandra was all Lucas's, that odd code that bound them permitted some liberties in such an arousing environment. So Cassandra leaned into Matt's support, her fingers working up and down his thigh in a needy little gesture while Matt had his hand discreetly up Savannah's tight skirt, probably fingering her beautiful pussy in slow circles. Her lips were already parted, her throat working. He had his other arm around Cassandra's shoulders, fingers lightly running up and down her upper arm. His knuckles grazed the side of her breast, which displayed a very attractively jutting nipple through the hold of her snug knit dress, since Lucas had had her shed the bra in the shadows of the limo.

As Peter expected, Lucas appeared beside them. Cass was up and in his arms, nearly climbing up his body such that he hitched her up, let her wind her legs around him as he cupped her ass and took her away toward a private room. Matt and Savannah rose, Matt supporting Savannah around the waist as they followed. They'd been known to take the same room, and enjoy the pleasure of watching one another, though they didn't often invite the single members of the group to such displays. That was all right. Jon and Ben were already seeking their own partners, seeing Peter had things well in hand, literally.

He was now alone with his remarkable woman, trembling with reactions as strong as what he himself was feeling. Removing his condom, he eased her back from the stock. Before he could arrange his clothes and lift her in his arms, she'd turned and dropped to her knees. With hardly a hesitation, she found him, closed her mouth around his drained cock, licking and cleaning him, a desperate gratitude that pierced his heart as he saw the tears. Withdrawing gently, he fastened his slacks and bent, lifting her. She nestled into him, her wrists still bound, else he suspected she would have wrapped herself around his shoulders.

He wasn't going to one of the rooms, he realized. He was taking her home. He wanted to be with her at home.

Twelve

The limo would return for the others. Peter had told her that, but said little else. It wasn't an awkward silence. She didn't say anything, because she couldn't speak. She'd never had an orgasm like that—hell, an experience—in her life. She'd shuddered and jerked for a good half hour now, so that Peter had moved her into his lap, holding her close, pressing kisses into her brow and murmuring to her. Her nipples were still vibrating, and occasionally he would touch them, stroke and massage in a way that kept a low simmer of arousal swirling.

"I don't understand," she said at last. She could hear the broken tone in her voice, echoing in her head, knew it reflected what was shattering inside her.

"What?" He tipped up her chin, traced her cheek, telling her he was looking into her face. He'd removed the mask, but now his hand passed over where it had pressed into her skin, reminding her of it. Her tears fell without her permission all the time, so why she ducked her head now, embarrassed, she didn't know. But he kept her face up. "Tell me, sweetheart. Don't cry. Your tears will destroy me."

She heard it again, that mysterious dark lake of his emotions that kept reaching toward her and then withdrawing before she could grasp it. She gripped his wrist. "It's too intense. I know it's not just sex between us, Peter. But how can I . . . I can't wrap my mind around this in a couple days, make any kind of decision about anything. I'm terrified to rely on you, to be disappointed, or to disappoint you. I mean, hell, if I'd come back whole and we'd dated, I would have been in a position of strength. Not needy and dependent. How do I know you know what you're getting into? How do I know any of this is real, for either of us?"

He was silent for a bit, silent enough to make her worry, to make her wish she'd said nothing. See, she was already too clingy. God, what had happened to the woman who'd plunged into a firefight?

"First," he said at last, "I completely agree. There's no way you can make a decision about us in two days. I never expected you to do that. What I want is for you to decide that we're worth a shot, and stay with me. See how it goes."

"I don't want you paying for stuff and—"

"Then we make a damn budget and cut it down the middle. If you want to eventually get your own place nearby, to prove something to yourself, fine." The spark of temper was oddly reassuring. "That's not what this is about and you know it. What if you *had* come back healthy and whole? Do you think you'd want me any less? Do you think I'd want you any less than I do now? How did you feel about me before that bomb exploded, Dana? Tell me."

She wanted to resist him, but she couldn't fight her own honesty. "I couldn't wait to see you again." The unconscious word choice formed a lump in her throat. "I dreamed of you. Wanted you so much it hurt."

His fingers slid over the ache, caressing the throat bound in his collar. "You do see me, Dana. And I see the woman I met a year ago. The woman I still want, the woman I can't wait to discover more about every day."

She blinked back tears. "How do I know you aren't staying with me out of pity? I do know you, Peter. You're honor bound to save the damsel in distress. You don't know anything else."

"I'm honor bound to stand by the woman I love," he responded. When a little sob escaped her, he traced her tears, kissed them away. Dana had to hold on to him, so hard her nails dug through his shirt. Maybe she imagined it, but the voice that spoke against her ear had a suspicious break to it. "I'm only scared shitless that you might not want to stay. I've never held a woman against her will."

"Oh, really?" she managed. "What do you call forced into a cab and flown off in the middle of the night? You have a problem with 'no means no,' Captain."

He gave a shaky half laugh. "Don't change the subject. You're so worried about what's happening in *my* head. How do I know you aren't staying with me out of some weak-assed dependency?"

She swatted at him. "Peter Winston. I haven't said I'm doing *anything* yet."

"If we trust each other, we'll both know the truth in time. We'll know it's love, real and true." Guiding her now-captured hand to his jaw, he let her feel the resolve in his mouth, touch his lips, so she couldn't mistake his meaning. "In the long run, the doubts won't matter, Dana. You're going to become more self-reliant every day, and one day you'll know for sure why you're with me. I know how important that is. You'll start giving me shit about being overprotective, and I'll shout back. We'll fight, make up, the way couples do. But you'll always admit I'm right, because you want me to be happy."

It startled a snort out of her. "I wouldn't count on that one, Captain."

He shifted beneath her, tightened his arms. "You've lost your sight, some of your hearing. You haven't lost your brain, your sense of touch, smell, your inner strength. Your soul." His fingers touched the Lord's Hands, sliding along her shoulder blade. "Every time a soldier goes into battle, he's believing in something more than his physical body. Whether he calls it God, luck or his own damn gut, he does. The body's a crutch, sweetheart."

He put her hand on his heart, and did the same with his own, the heel pressed to the high curve of her breast. "This is the real deal, what we all rely on when everything else is taken away. Tonight, for a few precious seconds, you knew that. I saw it in the way you held yourself, the way you walked to me and handed me that leash back, regal as a princess."

Because of him. His refusal to let her hide from herself, his willingness to use his friends and all their seductive talents, as well as his own, to tap into the deepest part of herself, a part that wasn't destroyed by that bomb. A path to re-creating the rest. And he was asking her to rely on his heart while she took that journey.

Closing her eyes, she pressed her lips together. "Peter . . . my family is gone. Gram died I guess the way a person's supposed to go, but my parents, my brothers . . . They were taken, in a way. I've never considered myself damaged, just good at getting along and doing what needs to be done. But you're offering your heart to me. Even if I could look past any worries I have about whether or not that's real, I've got a terrible fear about that."

Despite her best attempt, her voice broke. She tried to steady it, trying not to fall apart, but here were the damn tears again. "That fear says, 'How much more do I have to lose? How much more can I take?' I feel all alone, anticipating the day you'll be gone, like everyone else."

"Damn it, you're not alone." He tucked her head underneath his chin, his arms becoming steel bands, every muscle hard and sure against her. "I knew you for one night, went off to damn Afghanistan for a year and couldn't shake you. Your scent, your voice, everything you are. I'm willing to take the chance that fate knows something I don't, that it's going to give us a long time together, time to make this thing we've got deeper, harder and more powerful and peaceful than we can imagine. So that if we do lose one another to something in the future, even if it's old age, we'll know every second was worth it."

He lifted her up, so she felt his gaze on her face again. "As for how much you have to take, you have to take it all. Every bit of love and life you're given. I bet that's what your gram taught you."

⨳

She thought of that, all the way home.

Home. When he opened the door, guided her through it, Dana took a couple steps, stopped and breathed it in. His home, one he wanted to share with her. One he wanted her to be a part of, to make it theirs.

Thinking about that now, she moved forward, using her fingertips to find her way, drifting along the easy chair with the stuffed kitten, the side table, the table with the vase and chess set. She already knew more about where everything was here than she had in the place she'd stayed for months. As if she *wanted* to know this place. Or already knew it, somehow. Just as she seemed to know him. He moved behind her, slow. He was keeping pace with her, but remaining silent, as if he understood she was debating something important.

She felt his tension, that murky undercurrent she'd felt off and on from the first moment he'd darkened her door again. Those were the emotions that would tell her what he was truly thinking and feeling. Would he give her those if she asked, or did he think she couldn't handle whatever they were? And was he right?

But he kept following her. Slow steps. Each time she stopped, he did as well, always a little closer to her, closing that distance, ratcheting up that tension. Her pulse elevated with the increase in heat, from him or her, she couldn't tell. When she got to his bedroom, she turned at the foot of his bed. He hadn't put the dress back on her, but he'd wrapped her in his suit coat. The hem of it brushed her thighs. Letting the jacket slip off her shoulders, she stepped out of her shoes. Then, after a brief hesitation, she turned her back to him and removed the thong, then the stockings, a slow slide of silk down quivering thighs.

He'd given her a safe word. Freedom. The implications of the word hit her, the word he'd chosen so randomly a lifetime ago.

Under his restraint, she'd soared higher that night at The Zone than she ever had in her life. Until tonight. Or the next time they came together in this desperate-tender-rough-everything way they seemed to have.

She left the corset and collar on. They gave her the confidence to make a frightening choice, to say the word aloud.

"Peter." She knew she'd whispered, because she couldn't hear it, but the name echoed in her heart.

"I'm here, sweetheart." He was, right in front of her, and she reached up, cupped his face. Not as Master and slave in this moment, though it was there, a deep bond between them.

"You said, if I decided to stay, accepted that I was yours . . . you would make love to me in your bed."

His hand was over hers, gripping hard. "I meant it."

"So do I." She hesitated as he pressed a kiss to her palm, her body already shuddering, anticipating the pleasure they'd bring each other. "I'm scared. I'll probably stay scared and mad for a while. I want to trust you, but it will all take time, won't it?"

"Yeah." He slid his arms around her, hitched her up so her legs could curl around his hips, feel the arousal he pressed between her thighs. "A really, really long time."

Her lips curved. "I don't think we're talking about the same thing, Captain."

"Yeah, we are, Sergeant. It all means the same. And I know how much you love wearing these"—his hand swept down the corset, came back to rest on the collar—"but for this, I want it to be skin to skin. I want you to know if it's all stripped away, nothing but us, that I'll be there for you, with you."

She swallowed. Nodded. Then halted him by holding his hands for a minute. "Skin to skin, Peter. Please give me everything. Don't be afraid I can't take it. Stop holding back your emotions from me. I need to know I'm not made of glass. I need everything you are, too."

His fingers gripped her harder, and she held her breath.

"I'll try," he said at last. Then he was unhooking the foundation garment. The sensation of being unwrapped, unbound by him, was as arousing as being laced into it. His hands made all the difference. Releasing the collar, he let it all fall away. With his palms he soothed the lines the tight fit of the corset had left. Then he lifted her off her feet, carried her around to the side of the bed and laid her down, stroking her face before he came down and covered her lips with his.

He was such a big man. She liked that, liked the aura of heat around him, liked the fact he didn't mind when she reached up and traced where their lips joined. He kept kissing her as she explored his face, the curl of lashes, the lines across his forehead and around his eyes, his strong facial structure. Short, silken hair, just as she remembered.

Moving down to her breasts, he nursed the sore tips, aroused and soothed at once, until she was quivering, her hips rising in signal of what she needed. His palm slid along her thigh, teased her mound, but then he capitulated to the tug of her hands and lay down upon her, chest to thigh, letting her feel all of him. He'd stripped, so they were blissfully naked in each other's arms. The curve of muscle along his back, the breadth of his shoulders and network of bone and muscle were there, accessible to her touch. The different texture of skin where the tattoo of *PEACE* followed his shoulders, the *Don't Tread on Me* flag against his impressive biceps. She traced the letters. P . . . E . . . A . . . C . . . E. Her body was spinning slowly toward a climax, as strong and pleasurable as at the club, but so soft and easy at once. This was what peace was. The pleasure and time to do this, wrapped in a cocoon of darkness that was comforting, not frightening, because every chamber of her mind, her heart and her soul was filled with him.

He was hard and ready for her. When he slid in, she tilted up to meet him, an instinct as old as life itself, two coming together to be one. It brought a guttural sigh of pleasure from her lips and he made a similar noise against her ear. Fondling her neck, he followed the line of the hearing aid and stroked the shell of her ear. "Am I too heavy, sweetheart?" His voice was throaty, thick.

She shook her head, wrapping her arms around his shoulders and breathing him in, pressing her face into his corded neck. Her heels slid over his taut buttocks, the rhythmic press and release, the matching sensation in her womb as he slid in, slid out, his movements powerful, but slow, cherishing. As he'd said, a natural skin-to-skin meeting, the need to be inside each other taking over everything else.

Loosening her hold, he curved his powerful back in order to cup her breasts together again, making her arch into his mouth as he nursed on them, his tongue flicking, at first with gentle playfulness, but then a more insistent lashing. She thought about what he said about having them pierced, and thought she would like that, knowing he would adorn them as he wished, and tease her into mindless arousal like this.

He was putting more thrust into his strokes, and her body was responding, arching up like an opposing wave to meet that impact.

"Oh, God . . ." She clasped his broad shoulders, the sensations becoming too much. She loved his mouth, his beautiful cock, all of him. Everything about him. All hers, hers, hers . . .

She clutched him with her muscles, wanting him to come, wanting to feel it, and realized he hadn't put a condom on. That bareback sensation she'd wanted was there now, and while she knew the risk was minimal this time of the month, it was all right. She just knew it was.

"I needed to feel you, sweetheart," he said hoarsely against her ear. "I'm sorry."

She shook her head, tears springing to her eyes again. *When it's the right one, you hear each other's thoughts, know his mind like your own. . . .* Gram, talking about Granddad, her eyes full of distant, misty love and memory.

In answer, she held him tighter, inside and out. He increased the power of his thrusts and she met him, the sensations inundating her such that she thought she'd probably never experienced the act as deeply or intensely, physically or emotionally.

"Peter . . . Master . . . I'm so close. Please . . ."

"Come for me."

She shattered in his arms, like plunging into waves of warm tropical waters, churned in a wild direction as the surf caught her up, headed toward shore, toward home. She cried out, and that cry intensified as his joined her, his seed releasing in a hot, searing rush that drove her higher, gave her climax an extra jolt of intensity that kept her clinging to him, working her hips up against his, her legs clamped tight around him.

As he came down, she realized he was breathing hard, harder than a fit man should, even after a climax. When she reached up to his face, he caught her fingers, but she lifted the other hand, refusing to be dissuaded. "Peter, you promised. All of you, too, remember?"

He made a noise of protest, but he couldn't grab both her hands because his other arm was holding his full weight off her. When her fingers rested lightly on his cheeks, felt the dampness of something that wasn't sweat, her brow furrowed. "Peter."

"You're beautiful, Dana. You're everything I want. And I almost lost you before I found you. It's tearing me up inside, not letting you see how crazy it's made me. I love you. I'm sorry if you can't handle hearing that, or you don't believe it. But I do."

Raw, quiet words, uttered in a rough voice that tore into her worse than shrapnel. But it was the missing piece. She'd been right to ask for all of it, to find the bravery to face it. With their emotions twining around them, binding them even closer, she was finally ready to hear anything he needed to share. Closing her eyes, she held tighter to him. She'd needed to hear the voice of his soul, as raw and fragile as her own. For months he'd written her letters, without her writing back. He'd come to her, brought her here, bullied and cajoled.

Loved her. There was nothing else to call it, no matter what skeptics said, those who relied on some irrational formula between emotion and the passage of time. In truth, those letters had been her lifeline, helping her to hold on until he got to her. Which meant she very likely loved him as much, right back.

When she'd stood at his bed, and told him she wanted him to make love to her, that she would stay, she hadn't really understood *why* she would stay. She'd still feared it might be lack of options, or something else equally destructive. But that moment had been too overwhelming, his body too close behind her, his powerful need, and she'd gone forward on faith or mindless instinct. Now she knew it wasn't anything destructive. No matter what had happened in Iraq, he was right. This would have happened between them, because something stronger than sex had forged their bond that night at The Zone.

Freeing both her hands, she brought them to his face, cupped his jaw. He was so powerful, so strong. Yet the heart was both the strongest and most fragile part of any person. Her gram had told her that, too. She'd said, "If you find someone strong enough to love you through thick and thin, you don't never take that for granted, girl. Because if he loves you that much, that means you're the person who can break his heart."

"I'm so, so sorry, Peter," she said. More tears slid along her cheeks, found his fingers. "I'm sorry I didn't write you back. I'm sorry I made you be so strong, while I've been so lost. I want to be the type of person deserving of your love."

"Damn it, you already are."

"We both know there's a ways to go. I'm going to trust you to help me get there." She swallowed, took a deep breath and gave him a ghost of a smile. "But when I do, I'm going to learn to take care of you right back, Captain Winston. So you'd better watch out."

He pressed his forehead to hers. She heard the expulsion of his breath, and ran her hands up and down the broad back, slow, kneading, the strength of a river, the constancy of a woman's love, the promise of it in a touch. In some ways, it was the most intimate moment they'd yet shared.

"My mother warned me about short, determined women," he said at last, clearing his throat. "Said they're meaner than any other kind."

"Boy, you haven't seen anything," she whispered, catching the corner of his mouth with her own. When she tightened her arms around him, he did the same, nearly squeezing the breath out of her, his intense emotions washing through her, making her ache, happy, scared and anxious all at once. "You think I'm fragile, but I'm not."

"Yeah. You are in some ways." His hands gentled on her face. "I'm going to protect you, Dana. Love you. Always."

"Same as I'm going to do for you, Master."

Eventually, he lay next to her, making her smile anew since she knew he did it because he was worrying about his weight upon her, her considerate, loving Master. She was stronger than he believed. For the first time in a year, *she* believed it.

And instead of wishing this moment could stay the same, now she was thinking ahead, to other moments. Thinking of the next time he'd roll over and they'd do this all over again. What she'd do tomorrow. Where she'd go shopping with Cassandra and Savannah. What she'd do with her life. Peter would have her six. She could do anything she wanted, including care for him as well.

Her fingers drifted down his biceps, over that tattoo, bringing another thought. She didn't know how she felt about it, and she was afraid he would think she was asking because of her situation. No, she wouldn't bring it up now.

However, he had overly fine-tuned senses himself. He turned on his side, gathering her in to him, putting a thigh over hers, her breasts against the coarse hair of his chest. "What is it, sweetheart?"

She bit her lip. "Will you go overseas again?"

His arms constricted around her, his strength such that he was able to roll her halfway onto his body with the embrace. She snuggled into him, waiting for his answer.

"No. I'm going to resign my commission."

"What? Why?" She lifted her head. "Peter, I don't want you to make that decision because of me. I'll learn to take care of myself, and you shouldn't change your life. . . ."

"You *have* changed my life, Dana." He put his lips to her temple, held them there. Tentatively she found his face, felt his closed eyes, the taut line of his jaw. "By taking care of you, I'm serving my country as well, in just as important a way."

"I'm not helpless."

"I know that. Tonight I took you into the most frightening thing a blind and deaf person can face. An entirely unfamiliar environment, lots of noise and challenges. You let it break you once, but then you put it together again. *You* did. In fact, you got pretty disobedient, playing with another slave for your own pleasure, taunting your Master and his friends. Rubbing yourself against Ben's monster dick."

He bent, nipped her throat, sharply enough she gasped, particularly when he slid his hand between her legs, reminding her of his right to touch her however, whenever he wished. Propping himself on an elbow, he touched her nose with a broad finger.

"Growing up, I had an old hound dog that was blind, deaf, and couldn't smell so well. He was fearless. Would run into things all the time, frustrating the hell out of him, but purely on an external level. He never let it get inside of him, make him stop being and doing what he wanted to be. He'd just get up and keep on going. You lost your confidence for a little bit, sweetheart, never your courage."

"Are you calling me a bitch?" she demanded.

He brought her fingers to his mouth, let her feel his smile. "If the collar fits."

After a long pause, she spoke, a near whisper. "It does."

Looking down into her face, Peter saw her staring inward, as if she'd gone deep into herself, only this time maybe she'd found something worth seeing in the place where she still had her sight. Being here with her in this bed, making love to her, sharing his feelings with her, feeling her respond to him . . . There was nothing better. He didn't want her to be blind, but life could be everything they wanted it to be. This bond between them would make up for the lack of anything else. He was surer of it than ever before.

He couldn't wait for tomorrow, the next day. Hell, the next minute and hour, to watch their relationship grow, strengthen. Learn what irritated and pissed her off, get mad and make up, deal with the millions of big and little decisions that binding two lives together would bring. Hear her say "I love you" for the first time, without any worries. But for now, she gave him the next best thing.

She touched his face again, coming back to him, her smile soft, nervous. "I think . . . I think I love you, Peter Winston."

His heart flat broke open. His throat thickened in a way he was glad the other guys weren't around to see. Unable to speak, he found her other hand, guided it to her heart so she could feel what his fingers were doing beneath her own. He made that symbol, the one she'd pressed into his chest more than a year ago.

She'd given her heart to him then, and she'd surrendered it to him now. He was a soldier. Honor bound to take care of it, now and forever, he planned to do just that, with every beat of his own.

Joey W. Hill is a bestselling Ellora's Cave and Berkley Heat author. She lives in Southport, North Carolina, near Wilmington and Myrtle Beach. Visit her website at www.storywitch.com. Don't miss her exciting new novel, *Vampire Mistress*, coming in May 2010 from Berkley Heat. Turn to the back of this book for a sneak preview.

Rhio's Dancer

DENISE ROSSETTI

One

CARACOLE OF THE LEAVES, PALIMPSEST

When the hypnotic rhythm of a single drumbeat snaked out of the shadows, Rhio was thinking about his aching feet.

Godsdammit, he detested royal receptions, even a small, private soiree like this one for the Trinitarian ambassador. He'd tried every trick he knew to stay alert—and in twenty years as a career soldier, he'd learned a few of them—wiggling his toes in his boots, flexing the long muscles in his thighs and calves, calculating his finances. Another couple of weeks and he'd have enough creds for his annual visit to the Garden of Nocturnal Delights. Despite himself, his thoughts drifted.

A slim form moved into the pool of light beyond the door, hesitated, and faded back into the darkness. He caught the impression of a voluminous hooded cloak, skimming the tops of bare feet, fine boned and high arched, a gold chain winking around one slender ankle. The evening's entertainment, right on schedule.

Rhio's breath came a little faster.

Who should he ask for at the Garden? Plump Bertha or delicate Chuoko? Bertha's breasts were full and broad, spilling into his hands like heavy fruit, her nipples dark as fine wine. Chuoko had slender, clever fingers and a way of wrapping a man in her hair. . . .

His pulse marched in time with the drum.

A mysterious shadowed figure, the drummer sat cross-legged near the arched doorway that opened from the elegant reception chamber onto a dimly lit colonnade. Beyond lay the Palace gardens. His face expressionless, his back ramrod straight, Rhio stood the prescribed two paces behind Her Majesty's thronelike chair, sweating lightly beneath his dress uniform.

He'd stationed half a dozen of his Guards out there, and all around the building. By the seven hells, he hated diplomatic duty at the Palace. The place was a security nightmare. The gardens were bad enough, providing enough cover for an entire phalanx of Trinitarian pike men. But the velvet lawns were worse, meandering down to the canals of Caracole, which in turn led to the open sea. Rhio had fought too many battles against the old enemy to trust the bastards now, peace or no peace. The Queen's Navy had increased patrols up and down the coast, but nonetheless, he'd taken no chances, selecting only his best people for tonight's duty.

They'd better be scrutinizing every dark shape that shifted in the night breeze, he thought grimly. Or he'd take it out of their hides on the practice floor.

With a grin, the drummer turned his head toward the cloaked figure and spoke a soft phrase. The light of the double moons, the Brother and the Sister, gleamed on the man's shaven scalp, the graceful calligraphy of a slave tattoo showing dark along one cheekbone. Rhio didn't approve of slavery, the whole concept being beyond him. You might be able to command a man's actions, but you couldn't get into his head and make his thoughts your personal property. So how could you truly *own* him? It was plain common sense.

The cloak swirled, parting to reveal an astonishing length of bare, slender leg, the skin tinted to a smooth honey copper by the moonslight. A fleeting glimpse and he was left staring at the spot where the woman had stood, willing her to return.

He couldn't afford a distraction, not now. Careful to keep his face impassive, Rhio shifted his gaze to the spare, elegant person of the guest of honor, Ambassador-Pasha Ghuis Gremani Giral of the Trinitarian Republic. Smooth little shit, with his pointed goatee and his retinue of bustling attendants and scantily clad slaves. The courtesans at the Garden might sell their time, their delightful company and their beautiful bodies, but they were no one's property save their own. Woe betide the man who assumed otherwise.

Soon, soon he'd be with them. He stifled a sigh. For one night in his life, there'd be beautiful music and exquisite food, cultured conversation a world away from duty and discipline. And, oh, gods, silk sheets and silken limbs, sweet, hot mouths and sweet, hot flesh, urging him inside where it was wet and strong and clasping, and he could rut and slide and thrust until he spilled. After it was over, he'd sleep with his head pillowed between soft breasts while gentle fingers petted whatever part of him they could reach.

And he could pretend someone cared.

Beneath the polished leather of his formal battle kilt, Rhio thickened. No matter, he was a man of discipline, known for his iron will. He regulated his breathing until the pressure eased.

He was well aware of his reputation in the Guards—phlegmatic to the point of being unfeeling, brutally efficient, tough but fair. New recruits were terrified of him, but those under his command knew the score. A gruff bastard he might be, and godsdammit, he drove them unmercifully, but Captain Rhiomard's Company had the best success rate in the Queen's Guards. Rhio not only completed his missions with distinction, he kept most of his people alive in the process. Which was why he'd been given this security detail.

Smiling, the Ambassador leaned toward Queen Sikara. "More wine, Your Majesty?" Rhio heard him murmur. "It's a rare vintage from our vineyards in the South." Hooking a finger through the handle of the elaborately chased silver wine jug, he raised a perfectly arched brow.

Rhio tensed, his first instinct being to rip the vessel out of the man's hand and shove it down his throat.

Which was ridiculous. He knew—who better?—that every morsel of food, every drop of wine, had been tasted before it reached the table. He'd made the arrangements himself.

"No, thank you, Ambassador Giral." The Queen gave the little man back his empty smile, her faded blue eyes shrewd and tranquil. "At my age, I find alcohol disagrees with me." A delicate pause. "I congratulate you on your excellent constitution."

Farther down the table, a high-ranking minister of state chuckled, then masked the sound with a polite cough. Rhio bit the inside of his cheek. The old girl could probably drink the Ambassador under the table. She was no fool, Sikara. He liked her, which was more than he could say for any general he'd served under.

Giral leaned back in his chair, smiling, the very image of relaxed elegance. Even in middle age, his body was trim and hard beneath the flowing robes. He'd had a reputation as a duelist since his youth, deadly with any kind of sword. Rhio yearned to pick the man up and break him over his knee. A little puzzled at the strength of his reaction, he watched the Ambassador from under his lashes.

He didn't consider himself an imaginative man, but like all soldiers who survived their first few tours of duty, Rhio had learned early on to trust his gut. His uncanny instincts had saved his life more times than he could count—and those of his squad. "Lucky Rhio" some of them called him, but he knew better. Luck had nothing to do with it.

It was all about *paying attention*. The soldier wasn't born who could lie to Captain Rhiomard and escape unscathed.

Casually, he laid a hand on the hilt of his sword. Everything about Giral was a falsehood. Brother's balls, *of course* it was. The slimy little shit professed to be negotiating a peace treaty. But the Queen and her Cabal had fenced with the Trinitarian Republic for years. They'd expect to be played. Hence this exclusive party, no more than a dozen diplomats and ministers, part of some plan, he was sure.

So why couldn't Rhio dismiss the unease raising the short hairs on the back of his neck? Fretting made him downright testy.

As the Ambassador pushed his chair back and rose, the drumming sank to the merest breath of sound. After a deep obeisance in the general direction of the Queen, he straightened, the fine cream silk of his loose, flowing trousers and embroidered tunic glistening in the light of the glowglobes.

Beautifully modulated, his voice carried to every corner of the octagonal chamber. "Your Majesty, as you are aware, the most earnest wish of the Grand Pasha, exalted be his name, is for peace and goodwill between our two great nations. As a token of his esteem and affection, I bring you a gift."

Theatrically, he paused, and with impeccable timing, the cloaked woman glided into the room and sank gracefully to her knees, her head lowered.

"This woman is unique, the last of her kind. The Grand Pasha, exalted be his name, gave me the privilege of command, and I placed my foot upon the neck of her upstart tribe. They are no more."

The woman's shoulders stiffened, the movement ceasing almost before it had begun. If Rhio hadn't been studying her so intently, he would have missed it.

Framed by the neat beard, Giral's lips curved. "Dear lady, forgive a personal observation, but it is common knowledge you suffer from the jointache." A short bow. "As do we all at a certain age. This slave has magic fingers, trained to provide ease and comfort. For the period of our visit, she is yours alone. But first"—another obeisance, his hands fluttering—"she will dance for you. My slaves have many talents. She may look dangerous, but she has been well disciplined. No need for alarm, dear lady."

Sikara's mouth opened, but before she could speak, the dancer uncoiled in a lithe, unhurried movement—a tygre rising from deep cover. The drummer added a more complicated rhythm, his hands flying, the hasty beat thudding like the heart of an angry god.

Loosening his sword in the scabbard, Rhio took a silent step forward, until he stood directly behind his Queen.

Catching the movement, the dancer's head turned toward him.

With a sweep of one arm, she threw off the cloak in a dramatic swirl of black fabric. Poised on her toes, she stood straight and tall, staring him down.

Rhio clamped his jaw shut, breathing hard through his nose. He'd never— Fuck, not in all his years as a Guard, and as a mercenary before that. Not in the markets, the brothels, the bazaars, the villages, the fairs. He'd never seen a woman like this.

Quietly, he eased his sword back into the sheath and clasped his hands behind his back. Parade rest. The dancer gave him an infinitesimal nod, as if he'd done as she bade him.

The thin, bright sound of a flute joined the drum, a Trinitarian double flute, breathy yet pure. If he glanced to his left, he knew he'd see the player standing in the colonnade, but he didn't look. He couldn't.

He had the impression of a long, lean body, of shapely, supple muscles shifting beneath flowing drapery, but there was no way he could drag his gaze from her face, too thin for beauty, with an imperious, high-bridged nose and dark, slashing brows. All he could think of was a great fierce bird, tethered to the earth, its pride in the dust. It was there in her raptor's eyes, large and dark and burning with banked fury. But her mouth was wide and soft, all woman.

Rhio blinked, resisting the impulse to shake himself like a dog just out of the water. His mouth was dry, his heart thundering in his ears.

Fine. So the dancer was unusual—what of it? With calm deliberation, he took stock. She was swaying now, her arms weaving in boneless, graceful shapes to the liquid notes of the flute, long fingers moving in complex patterns. Gods, there wasn't an ounce of fat on her. Her bones were long, her flesh taut. In fact, she could have passed for a beautiful youth, if not for that sweet, sinful mouth and the braid of shining black hair that hung down her back to brush the rise of her buttocks.

She spun around, her hips rotating as the pace quickened.

No, not a boy. The womanly dip of her waist flowed like music down to a superlative ass, the cheeks high and round and biteable.

Rhio frowned. What, in the Brother's name, was she wearing? Filmy draperies fluttered around her knees in a range of warm sunset colors from vermilion to yellow to a golden pink. But from neck to hip she was encased in glittering mesh.

A *corset*, godsdammit. A corset of the finest, most supple chain mail he'd ever seen, a feminine parody of a warrior's garb.

His balls hummed with interest, even as his disquiet grew.

The dancer's feet slapped the floor of polished seastone as she whirled and spun. The flute wailed in the strange minor harmonies so beloved of Trinitarians. The woman's movements weren't overtly erotic. Although they were fluid and graceful, they were stylized, even martial in character. But it didn't matter. He was half-hard, and only the weight of his duty and that nagging sense of something off-kilter kept him from complete embarrassment. Hell, no better than a randy lad. Rhio gritted his teeth, grateful for the hard leather of his kilt.

Gods, she was intense, wholly engaged in her artistry, lost in the music. The faintest of lines between her brows revealed her concentration. A drop of sweat trickled from her hairline and down the side of her face. His feet planted solidly apart, his face a careful blank, Rhio could almost taste the salt of that liquid on his tongue, feel the heat radiating from the dark honey of her skin.

The music built to a crescendo, dropped, and built again. No one in the chamber moved, save the dancer. When her dark gaze flicked past him, and returned, Rhio felt the touch of it like a branding iron. Clenching his fists behind his back, he fought for breath.

The drummer's palms beat out a rapid tattoo; the flute keened, high and wild. Her head thrown back, the dancer spun, too fast for the eye to follow. Abruptly, she gave a high, ululating cry, her voice echoing eerily off the walls. As if her bones had turned to water, she folded her long body to the floor, directly before the Queen, both arms outstretched before her, the long braid tumbling forward over one shoulder.

No one breathed, or spoke. Slowly, every face turned toward Sikara. The dancer's shoulders rose and fell, her forehead still pressed to the floor. The Queen blinked. "Well," she said. "That was amazing, Ambassador. I've—"

Ignoring both courtesy and protocol, Giral raised a hand, overriding the monarch. An extraordinary misstep for a man so urbane. "Dear lady, that was but the beginning." His words dropped into the shocked silence like pebbles in a pool.

Rhio returned his hand to the hilt of his sword, noting that Yachi, standing opposite, had done likewise. Her eyes moved constantly, watching hands and faces, the door and windows. He sent his Sergeant an approving nod. She'd deserved that promotion, Yachi. A good soldier.

A small, plump woman in purple velvet, a scholar specializing in treaty law, flicked an enquiring glance at the Queen. Receiving a nod in return, she leaned forward. "How so, Ambassador?" she asked. "The girl is clearly exhausted."

Giral sent her a thin smile. "Allow me to know the capacities of my own slaves, madam." Without shifting his gaze, he snapped his fingers. "Dancer."

Immediately, the woman rose to her feet in a single, unhurried movement. She didn't drop her eyes, the way most slaves did. Instead, her gaze rested on the Ambassador, cool and somehow . . . considering. A shiver crawled down Rhio's spine. Couldn't the man see it?

"That was the dance of the Battle Maiden." Distaste distorted the little man's mouth. "In primitive tribes, it is the unnatural and barbarous custom for women to fight alongside men."

Rhio glanced at Yachi. Red spots flew to her broad cheekbones, her knuckles white on her sword hilt. With an inward grin, he made a mental note to ensure the honor guard provided for the Ambassador was all male. Wouldn't want the man to trip and fall.

"The night before their first battle, any female who is, ah, untouched, selects a warrior for a test of manhood. If his courage is sufficient to pass, he is deemed worthy to relieve the woman of her virginity."

"Fascinating." The treaty scholar licked her lips. "So what is this test? Exactly?"

"She will show you." Giral's smile widened. "Remembering, of course, that she is far from virgin. Such is the fate of slaves." He settled back in his seat, with the air of a man about to enjoy a spectacle. Wrapping bejeweled fingers around his wine cup, he said, "Who do you choose, girl?"

The dancer turned a leisurely full circle, scanning the room. She had an impeccable sense of theater, Rhio had to give her that. Every man in the chamber held his breath. Oh, this was going to be entertaining. He rocked on the balls of his feet, feeling some of the tension leave his shoulders.

The woman raised an arm and pointed, directly at the Queen. What the—?

"That one." Her voice was low and husky, lightly accented.

A waterfall of hot chills cascaded down Rhio's spine and landed in the pit of his belly. Every muscle in his body locked.

Sikara gave a bark of laughter. "Well, I grant you he's a warrior." Her gaze narrowed. "Damage my favorite Captain and I will be very annoyed. Understand?"

The dancer nodded, her teeth flashing in a wild grin that froze Rhio's blood.

"Majesty." As he bowed his acquiescence, he bent to whisper. "It could be some kind of diversion, a ploy."

The Queen twisted in her seat to pat his forearm. "Possibly. But do me proud anyway," she said. One eyelid fluttered down in an unmistakable wink.

Right. Godsdammit all to hell.

Rhio straightened, meeting the dancer's gaze full on for the first time. He didn't speak, just arched a brow.

Two

A slim arm gestured. "Over there."

"Yachi." With a jerk of his head, Rhio summoned the Sergeant to take his place. He'd be damned if he left his liege lady unprotected.

The back of his neck prickling, he strode to the spot the dancer had indicated, his boots creaking in the silence. His back to the wall, he faced her. "Now what?"

Again that wicked glimmer. "Do not move, yes?"

The drummer started up again, the throbbing beat cranking up the tension, echoing in his head, making it difficult to think.

Her eyes fixed on his, the dancer drew her braid over her shoulder. Her hips swaying to the beat of the drum, she loosed the golden ribbon that bound it. Then she combed her fingers through the silky mass, bent from the waist and flung it back in a stunning, rippling curtain, a black so deep it gleamed with blue highlights.

Godsdammit, she was amazing. For a moment, Rhio lost himself in the sensual gyration of her hips, the flash of a bare leg.

The dancer's slender fingers flickered over the front of the chain-mail corset. Something glittered in her hand, razor sharp and evil.

All hell broke loose.

Rhio took a step forward, his sword half-drawn, knowing already he was too fucking late. Yachi threw herself full length over the Queen, bearing the older woman down to the floor in a tangle of thrashing limbs and embroidered skirts. Diplomats ducked for cover beneath the table.

Ambassador-Pasha Ghuis Gremani Giral sat placidly amid the chaos, sipping his wine. The members of the Trinitarian delegation followed his example.

Above the hubbub, the dancer's voice rose clearly. *"Be still!"*

Rhio froze.

Death whizzed past his ear like a sliver of furious lightning, the blade sinking point-first into the highly polished timbers of the wall behind him with a solid *thunk!*

"Again!" she called.

Noise faded away and time slowed, so he could appreciate her extraordinary economy of line. He sucked in a breath and held it. Gods, oh, gods—

A cold breeze brushed past his other ear. *Thunk!*

The dancer stepped back, her hands dropping to her sides.

"Sergeant," called Rhio, his gaze still tangled with the dancer's. "Report."

Yachi cleared her throat. "No damage."

"You were on top," said the Queen dryly. "Speak for yourself." A chair scraped, fabric rustled. "Captain Rhiomard, are you still in one piece?"

Rhio checked both ears with cautious fingers. No blood. "Aye, Majesty." Moving his eyes from right to left, he stared at the slim knives quivering in the wall. Two of them. Two *weapons*, for the Brother's sake. In the presence of the Queen. How the fuck had she smuggled them past his Guards? Heads were going to roll.

He curled his lip at the dancer. "Is this the test? I stand here while you throw toothpicks at me?"

Unsmiling, she prowled closer, until she stood well within a sword's length. Rhio understood the unspoken message. At this range, they were equal, one threat canceling the other. Although he wore boots, the dancer's eyes were barely an inch below his.

"But yes," she murmured, so softly only he could hear. Her voice was a husky contralto, deep enough to be disconcerting. "This is the test. Are you man enough?"

The chamber and everyone in it slipped away to the periphery of Rhio's consciousness. Her eyes were such a dark brown they appeared black, the effect intensified by her dilated pupils and a thick forest of sooty lashes. A man could drown in those magnificent eyes.

With some difficulty, he wrenched his gaze away. "Majesty?"

Sikara's expression was wry. "I am well protected, Captain. Your choice."

Rhio arranged his features in a skeptical expression. "Are you good enough?" he asked the dancer.

Her face lit with challenge, her shoulders stiffening. Some mercenaries became addicted to the battle fever, only truly alive when they danced on the razor edge of death. Rhio had never been one of them, but now—his blood tumbled through his veins in a singing rush, every cell in his body vibrating with half-appalled anticipation.

"Pray to your gods that I am," she said, eyes flashing, breasts rising with every inhalation.

Rhio liked big tits, the sort he could heft in his palms. The dancer's were small and high, like pretty rounded fruits, topped with pointed nipples. He could see the shadowed, enticing peaks through her filmy garments. A scant handful at the best, but nonetheless his mouth watered.

He frowned, chasing a fugitive thought. Wait a—

She'd walked away. Reaching out, he snagged her elbow, spinning her around so he could rake the front of the corset with a furious gaze. What he'd assumed were decorative toggles were thin, cunningly wrought blades, each pair a fastening that kept the edges of the corset together. She'd used the top two to damn near pin his ears to the wall. Which was why he'd been able to ogle her breasts.

There were four more of the bloody things. Eight thin, deadly stilettos. Fuck.

His face must have betrayed him, though he could have sworn he had himself under complete control.

The dancer unpeeled his fingers from her arm, her touch light and firm. "Think of the reward, yes?"

How could she be so composed? Abruptly, he wanted to throw her off balance, watch her fumble, no matter the cost.

"Your maidenhead?" he snarled.

Her face went tight, her lashes sweeping down, then up again. "That I cannot offer," she said, holding his eye. "But my final dance tonight will be for you, and you alone." Her lips curved without humor. "If you are man enough to earn it."

"Try me," he grated.

Again, he got that short nod of acknowledgment. Her air of self-possession would drive a man like Giral mad. Rhio shot a glance at the Ambassador. His posture was relaxed, urbane, but he was so tense it was a wonder the wine cup didn't shatter under the pressure of his grip. Yachi hovered at the Queen's elbow, poised to shield the monarch once again with her own body.

No flute, just the drum, timed to match the painful thud of his racing heart. Steady, Rhio, steady. Shit, why wouldn't the bloody woman stand still? Her aim would be off. He could barely concentrate on the fluid beauty of her movements because he had to fight the instinctive urge to cover his groin with his hands. He curled his lip. Like a frightened toddler, reaching for the comfort of his dick.

The dancer uncoiled faster than a snake striking. Her hands blurred. *Thunk! Thunk!* Godsdammit, *both* hands!

Rhio glanced down. His boots appeared to have sprouted slim, silver wings, the blades vibrating in the wall at ankle level.

As one, the company exhaled, but the dancer didn't pause. Going into a long spin, she called over her shoulder, "Hands down and against the wall."

Rhio pressed his palms into the timber by his hips. Brother's balls, she was good! He still felt agonizingly exposed, passive in a way totally foreign to his take-charge, soldier's nature. But he might survive unscathed yet—and with some degree of credit, if he could keep his nerve. A couple of deep breaths and he reached the still, calm center that was his battle-self.

Was that the undercurve of her breasts he could see, revealed beneath thin sunset-colored fabric as the corset fell farther op—

Thunk!

A hideous pause while he processed the evil, chilly feel of the knife at his right knee. No pain, but he knew—full well—what the body did with a clean slice. First the icy burn and the disbelief, then the flare of nerves shrieking. But he dared not look down, not yet.

Thunk!

The same sensation at the left knee.

A woman's scream echoed, then choked off into silence as if she'd clapped her hands over her mouth.

The dancer shot him a triumphant grin, her eyes flashing, and Rhio let out the breath he'd been holding. All right. He needn't embarrass himself with a downward glance.

The corset was open almost the whole way down the front, offering tantalizing glimpses of drapery and firm, honey-toned flesh. What in the gods' names did she have on under there? He'd bet his pension they were veils. Yes, a broad band of supple, silvery links lay against her collarbone, lengths of diaphanous fabric suspended from it.

"Do not move a muscle. Not a single one, yes?"

Rhio lifted his eyes from the delicious indentation of her waist. "I don't believe I have, so far," he said.

The dancer paused. Then she took two steps closer and reached out to touch a fingertip to his cheek. Rhio gave thanks he'd shaved in honor of the occasion. The spot tingled. He bared his teeth, beyond caring if his hunger showed.

"Trust me?" Her husky voice was so quiet only he could have heard it.

"In this, yes," he said, surprised that he meant it. "You won't miss by accident."

"No." For a heartbeat, it seemed she stared into his soul. "This time, I will be very quick." A gesture to the drummer and the rhythm accelerated.

Rhio allowed his insolent stare to wander over her rangy body, lingering on the remaining fastenings of the corset. "Excellent."

Two pairs of knives to go and she'd slither out of the chain mail and dance for him, clad only in those pretty, semitransparent veils. His breath quickened. Four blades. *Four.* Where the hell did she intend to put them?

Her feet pattered across the floor, quick and precise, in patterns only she—or one of her lost tribe—could discern. How old had she been when the Trinitarians came? Even as a child, she would have fought to the death, he was certain of it. She didn't lack for courage. In fact, if the dancer's people had been fierce enough, the commander would have used a diabloman to ensure his victory. A demon master. Black Magick. Rhio loathed the uncleanness of it, the stench of wrongness.

Thunk!

Lucky he'd been disciplined enough to stop his hands from curling into fists. That one had been in the narrow space between upper arm and rib cage. If he'd so much as flexed his biceps . . .

Thunk!

Shit, she'd just about shaved off the hairs in his armpit.

The dancer drew the last two blades and raised her hands over her head, spinning, her head thrown back and her hair flying. Her balance would be shot to hell. How the hell could she even see straight?

Fuck. Here it came. Fuck, oh, fuck—

Thunk!

Rhio clamped his lips shut on an unmanly yelp. Equidistant between his brawny thighs, the knife thrummed like a pinned and frantic insect. Under the stiff leather of the battle kilt, his terrified balls tried to climb right inside his body. But he didn't move, not even a fraction of an inch.

The dancer took a pace forward, exposing a length of sleekly muscled thigh. Flashing him a wicked grin, she tilted her chin and closed her eyes, as ostentatiously as possible.

Rhio's mouth fell open. A chair clattered as someone shot to their feet. Still smiling, her lashes brushing her high cheekbones, the dancer drew her arm back.

Time passed in infinitesimal increments. The thin, silver flicker of the blade, traveling through the perfumed air, the humming note of its passage. He knew his eyes were stretched as wide as they would go, the wall unyielding against his shoulder blades. In Rhio's head, a soldier's instinct bellowed like the voice of his first drill sergeant. *"Freeze!"*

Like the recruit he'd been so many years ago, Captain Rhiomard obeyed the order without hesitation.

Whoosh! Thunk!

His loins drew tight—really tight, uncomfortably tight. Helpless to prevent the immediate glance downward, Rhio stared in disbelief.

The dancer had put the blade right *through* the leather of his kilt and into the wall. Fuck, she'd come within a hairsbreadth of emasculating him. The impact still hummed through his shrinking scrotum.

And she'd done it with her eyes closed. By the Brother, was she even human?

Gingerly, he reached down, only partly conscious of the room erupting all around them. Elderly statesmen were standing, applauding, dignity forgotten. The treaty scholar had climbed up onto her chair, where she teetered, one hand on the shoulder of an embarrassed junior diplomat.

A slim strong hand closed over his. "Let me," purred the dancer, her eyes twinkling with suppressed amusement. "It is my knife, yes?" A light sheen of sweat gleamed on her skin. She smelled of healthy female and something green and fresh and wild.

No woman made a fool of Rhiomard of the Queen's Guard.

"Not anymore." Rhio wrenched the blade free. Stepping forward, he gripped her wrist with his other hand. She stood docilely enough, tall and limber beside him, the corset hanging open. "Sergeant."

Yachi's brisk tread. "Aye, Cap'n?"

"Take this knife and remove the other weapons from Her Majesty's wall."

"Aye, Cap'n."

They'd soldiered together for nigh on twenty years, he and Yachi. Rhio knew every inflection of her voice. He'd come as near as dammit to singing soprano, and she thought it was funny.

But as she brushed by him, she muttered, "Always said you had balls, Rhio." She tugged a knife free. "And what do you know? I was right."

The dancer chuckled, deep in her throat, the sound like that of a woman well pleasured. The timbre of it spread warm fingers over his belly, stroked his cock, caressed the very balls Yachi apparently admired.

Aggravated almost beyond endurance, Rhio glared into the proud face so near to his. Tightening his grip, he gave the dancer a little shake, her wrist bones shifting under the pressure.

Because her smile didn't falter, he nearly missed the flash of pain that darkened her eyes. Feeling his cheeks heat, he released her as if her skin had ignited beneath his fingers.

Turning to the Queen, Rhio bowed. "If I may return to my duty, Majesty?"

Sikara favored him with a smile and a gracious nod. "Of course, Captain. My compliments. You have proven yourself a true son of the Queendom." She shot a bland glance at the Ambassador.

Words beyond him, Rhio gave a stiff salute. With a jerk of his head, he ordered Yachi back to her station behind the Queen's chair and took up a spot near the doorway that allowed him a view of both the chamber and the colonnade outside.

It was over. He should be relieved, but instead he felt . . . heavy. Old.

The dancer sauntered closer, swinging her hips. "Captain . . . ?" The lightest brush of fingers on his arm. "R-Rhio?" The deep sibilance of her accent turned his unexciting name into something exotic, a throaty growl that filled his head with images he could not afford to entertain.

Every eye in the room was upon them. He glared, hating the sensation of exposure. *"What?"*

A waterfall of silvery mesh spilled from her grasp. "Guard this for me, yes?" A direct look from those dark raptor's eyes. "While I dance for you."

Before he could refuse, she'd shoved the corset into his arms and spun away, the veils fluttering. His spine rigid, his hands full of supple chain mail still warm from her flesh, Rhio stalked back to his post near the door. Once there, he couldn't decide what to do with the godsbedamned thing, but it was imperative he have his hands free. In the end, he threw it over one shoulder, where it hung like the heavy pelt of some strange, beautiful animal. Beneath the hard scent of heated metal, he could smell her wild, green perfume.

Stolidly, he settled, his hands gripped behind his back. Across the chamber, he caught Yachi's gaze. Her expression didn't change, though one eyelid drooped in a slow wink. Rhio cast her a glare so vicious that she stiffened into a perfect mirror image of his formal posture. But her lips still twitched.

Rhio ground his teeth.

The damn flute was wailing, a slow, sensuous thread of sound, underpinned by the soft throb of the drum. The lights dimmed, until only the center of the floor was illuminated.

The dancer undulated, boneless again. Her hips swaying, she gripped a rosy pink veil and gave it a brisk tug. It parted easily from the collar around her neck, floating softly to the floor like a small sunset cloud. Under it was another diaphanous layer, but now he could see the shadow of her navel, the dark crescents of her nipples.

So could everyone else in the chamber. Rhio's belly clenched with tension and lust. Didn't she have any shame?

Of course she didn't. She wasn't permitted to. She was a slave. Property.

The dancer circled her hips, the music slow and languorous. Closer and closer she came to the doorway, her eyes fixed on Rhio's where he stood in the shadows.

Three

She didn't speak to him again. She didn't need to. *My final dance will be for you, and you alone.*

Raising her arms over her head, the dancer turned to display the smooth sweep of her spine, the enticing cleft between those proud cheeks.

An orange veil this time, revealing a slim, sleek thigh, a long, smooth sweep of skin all the way to the curve of her hip bone. Helplessly, he stared at the remaining veils, searching for the dark curls between her thighs. Where . . . ?

Rhio swallowed. Oh, gods. If she was bare . . .

Somewhere in the back of his mind, he was grateful for the brutal training program he'd put Yachi through. His Sergeant had better be alert, because he feared he himself was drowning in the bottomless depths of the dancer's eyes, snared by the sheer eroticism of her body, of her movements. An entire troop of diablomen could have rolled in on a green cloud and had their demons devour every lord and lady present and he wouldn't have cared.

For you, R-Rhio. You alone.

This was his reward for courage, this offering before a crowd of breathless, prurient witnesses. Because the dancer had nothing else to give. Not even her body was her own.

But her beautiful eyes, the exquisite sensation of her complete focus, dreams of endless lust and love—these she created as a gift for him to keep. How did she know about the long, lonely nights, the way he ached for something he couldn't envisage or even describe? All he knew was that it was more than his own right hand.

Smiling into his eyes, the dancer cast aside a length of pale gold gauze. Her breasts . . . Oh, gods. Rhio resisted the urge to lick his lips. Small and firm and pointed, but her nipples were broader than he'd expected and stiff.

Sweat trickling down the back of his neck, he managed to sever the connection between them, checking the placement of his Guards, the doors, the windows. Yachi's face, the cold, watchful eyes of the Ambassador. Again and again, he did it, but each time it grew harder to snap the tether of her gaze.

A cold whisper insinuated itself in the back of his brain, like a worm spoiling the sweet flesh of a summer fruit.

Why me? it said. Why a mere Guard, a grizzled veteran who dreamed of taking his twenty-year bonus and buying a country tavern? Hell, she could set her sights on a minister of state. It was a charade, all of it, a complex game of feint and parry.

He was playing blind.

The veils floated away, one by one, until the dancer's long, supple body was bare save for a veil of shimmering silk over her loins. Rhio had pretty well grown accustomed to the discomfort of a spike-hard erection and blue balls, but he was so acutely aware of the dancer's spare beauty that looking away made everything hurt worse. If he missed a second of her, he knew he'd regret it 'til the end of his days.

The flute played two notes, over and over, the drum ruffling along beneath. Swaying before him, sweat gleaming on her skin, the dancer extended her palms toward his body, but stopped an inch short of contact. Rhio's tension ratcheted up another excruciating notch. If she touched him, he'd explode.

He half expected some sort of flirtatious gesture—a smile, a toss of the head. Instead, the woman's dark gaze intensified and her lips formed words he had no difficulty reading. *For you.*

The drum reached a savage crescendo. In a single, smooth movement, the dancer slipped to her knees, her shoulders arching back to touch the floor behind her. The black curtain of her hair slipped down over her shoulder to brush the tiles. Ripping the last veil away, she threw her hands over her head.

Rhio couldn't have looked away if there'd been a blade at his throat. Her mons was so lightly furred as to be almost bare. Between her sweat-slicked thighs, the plump lips of her sex beckoned, the merest hint of a darker pink within. He grunted as if he'd been gut-punched.

No more than a split second and the dancer curled herself forward into a compact ball, her head between her knees and her hair fanning out over the toes of his boots. The flute player stepped forward to throw a cloak over her. As he did so, the chamber went dark.

"Lights!" roared Rhio, swooping to grab the woman and haul her against his body, a muscular forearm pressed into her throat. The dancer stood quietly, only the faint rasp of her breath audible, her lean form a distracting presence all along his front.

The glowglobes flickered and then strengthened, the drummer smirking as a hapless Guard lowered his hand from the bank of toggle switches on the other side of the doorway. At first as pale as the snowy cloth on the table, the soldier flushed brick red when he met his commander's furious gaze. As well he might. Latrine duty was always a bitch, let alone for a solid month.

The Queen was obscured by Yachi and two burly Guards, swords drawn. Despite the uproar, the screams and shouts, Rhio relaxed a trifle.

Almost lovingly, he drew the dancer closer, ground his body into hers. "What game are you playing?" As he lowered his head, a strand of her hair blew soft against his lips and clung.

"Not me," she murmured with perfect composure, though she had to go to tiptoe to keep her balance.

Without a word, Rhio shoved her away so hard she nearly stumbled, but he kept hold of her wrist. The dancer in tow, he strode to the middle of the floor.

"*Quiet!*" His parade-ground bellow had the desired effect. "Be seated, noblelords." He glared at the babbling diplomats. "*Now!*" They sat.

"Majesty?"

A sigh. "I'm fine, Captain." The Queen waved the hovering Guards aside and shot the Ambassador-Pasha a narrow glance. "However, I am no longer amused. Ambassador Giral, it was ill-advised to alarm my Guards."

Color rose in the Trinitarian's cheeks; his mouth thinned. When he turned to the dancer, Rhio felt the tremor she couldn't prevent, though she masked it well. "You exceeded your instructions, slave. Made an embarrassment of my gift."

The dancer dipped her head, sooty lashes veiling her eyes. "It is part of the dance, Pasha."

"You frightened Her Majesty."

The dark eyes considered Sikara. Gracefully, the woman dropped to her knees. "My sorrow to you, Great Lady. I regret." Rising to her feet, she flicked a bland glance at the Ambassador. "I have always performed it thus, Pasha."

Rhio's lips twitched. He might be a career soldier, plain and simple, but that didn't mean he couldn't appreciate subtle insolence when he heard it. With grim relish, he watched rage swell the Ambassador's narrow chest.

"You are not fit to be my gift. Report to the Slave Master immediately."

The lithe body next to his went rigid. "Yes, Pasha."

But before the dancer could take a step, Rhio growled, his grip tightening. Over her head, he stared at the Queen, hoping like hell. Praying.

Disconnected thoughts ratcheted around his skull. The marks of the lash striping the smooth honey of her flanks, those fierce eyes gone dull with despair. Worse, rape, her tight flesh violated, the proud spirit broken.

By the Brother, no!

He could give Yachi the command with a single hand signal. No, wait. Gods, the diplomatic repercussions! Besides, he couldn't order a subordinate, no matter how loyal, to risk her career, not for him and his foolish whims. His mind raced, creating and discarding plans, while he drew the dancer close in the circle of his arm, his sword naked in the other hand.

Slowly, the Queen rose, shaking out her skirts. She arched a cool brow, her eyes glinting a frosty blue. "I do not care to have decisions made for me, Ambassador. If she can ease my pain, your gift is more than acceptable."

As she made her stately way toward the colonnade, Giral leaped to his feet, the ready protests continuing to spill from his lips. Sikara ignored him. "I believe I will have an early night. Come, girl," she said over her shoulder.

When Rhio nudged the dancer with his shoulder, she jumped. "Yes, Great Lady." Pulling the cloak tighter around her body, she followed the Queen without a backward glance. The royal escort closed in behind her.

Feeling vaguely piqued, Rhio snapped out orders. "Yachi, you're in command out there. Check every shadow, every bush, every doorway. The roof too. Go."

"Aye, Cap'n." Yachi sped away.

With the departure of the Queen, the gathering had relaxed, splitting into smaller groups. To one side sat a trio of gray-haired ministers engaged in serious, low-voiced discussion, while the little treaty scholar stood in the colonnade, chatting with her juniors, her face flushed with excitement and the release of tension.

Rhio leaned casually against the wall, his arms folded. With any luck, the Trinitarians would dismiss him as a piece of the furniture, the way they treated all servants. The Ambassador-Pasha and his delegation gathered their robes about them and made for the door, their soft slippers scuffing across the tiles.

"Well?" said a tall man with military bearing, bending to murmur in Giral's ear.

The Ambassador's shoulders moved in a fluid shrug. "All is in the hands of the Trimagistos." Automatically, he made the sign of the Three, touching his fingers to forehead, heart and groin.

Rhio's eyes narrowed as the others caught up. Two long strides and he gripped the last of the party by the shoulder, spinning him around. "Where do you think you're going with that, sonny?"

The youth glared up at him, big eyes outlined in black, his pink lips compressed to a thin line. A silvery fall of chain mail spilled over his arms. "It belongs to the Ambassador-Pasha."

The damn thing must have slipped to the floor in the confusion. He hadn't even noticed. "It's the dancer's."

"Yes, and the dancer also belongs to the Ambassador-Pasha." The young man sauntered off down the colonnade, hips swinging.

Rhio caught up with him. "But she's responsible for it?"

The other man's gaze flickered up and down his body with frank interest. Rhio knew what he was thinking. Big, slow—*stupid*. A vicious smile revealed small even teeth. "Indeed, she is."

Shit. They'd punish her for a fault that was his. "She gave it to me to hold."

When Rhio reached out, the youth skipped backward. "Oh, no, I couldn't." He shook his head in apparent sorrow, lips pursed.

Like most big men, Rhio couldn't claim to be lightning fast but he was extraordinarily efficient. A single step, a practiced, economical move, and he spun the youth deep into the shadow where the colonnade curved, fingers pinching a nerve in his neck and a slim wrist twisted up behind his back. The corset slithered to the flagged floor with a musical hiss.

The smaller man spat curses, writhing hard in Rhio's grip. Rhio's brows rose. Interesting. Any normal courtier would be terrified. Therefore . . .

Abruptly, he removed his fingers from the man's neck and shoved him face-first toward the building, helping him along with a knee in the small of the back. "Place your hands on the wall and do not move," he whispered, all gravelly menace.

"Or what?" With some difficulty, the youth turned his head. His lip curled. "You'll damage Giral's favorite? Good career move, clod."

"Favorite what?" Though he was pretty sure he knew. As Rhio patted the other man down, gusts of musky perfume rose off his skin and robes. Ah . . .

With infinite caution, he slid his fingers under silken fabric and withdrew a thin blade from a flat, flexible scabbard taped to the man's ribs. An assassin's trick. He held it up in the moonslight. More like a meat skewer than a dagger.

Brother's balls!

Slamming his full weight against the slender body, he gripped the man's fingers as they inched toward the intricate coil of his hair. The bastard would keep a garrote there, or a second blade. He waved his prize under that pert nose so the assassin could see the dark-colored tip. "Just a scratch," he growled. "Want to risk it?"

Silence.

"What have you used?"

Silence.

"Tell me or I'll find out for myself." He moved the evil thing a hairsbreadth closer, watching the other man's eyes cross.

Another heartbeat. "Prettydeath. Let me up, damn you! It's prettydeath."

A pool of ice grew in Rhio's guts, froze the blood in his veins. His memory supplied a searing vision—a body arched in a bow of muscle-wrenching agony on a tavern floor, hideous clotted screams, the stink of purple-flecked vomit.

With an inward shudder, he stepped back, poisoned blade at the ready.

The assassin turned, settling his clothing like a huffy cat. But he took care to keep his hands in plain view. "You are at an impasse, my friend." His lips twisted in a parody of a smile. "Kill me and the repercussions will ruin the talks."

Rhio arched his brows. "You're that important?" The man made his skin crawl, but he let his insolent gaze rove over the lithe body. Not so young, after all. There were cruel lines of dissipation graven around that pouty mouth, and in the moonlight, his eyes showed as pits, dark and empty.

"I am Simoener Selidan Sethril. The Grand Pasha, exalted be his name, is my esteemed uncle." Pushing away from the wall, he took a step forward, until the tip of the prettydeath blade brushed his outer robe. He didn't lack for nerve.

"Do not forget my name, Captain Rhiomard." Slowly, he backed away.

Rhio bared his teeth. "I'll be watching you."

Sethril glared. "The old bitch has your balls beneath her heel." His lip curled. "Eunuch." Turning on his heel, he disappeared toward the guest wing.

Amae stood quietly in the shadows of the Queen's antechamber. Her heart beat hard and heavy with the aftermath of gut-churning fear, but she willed herself to breathe deeply, to ignore the cold air whispering under the cloak and around her bare legs. Once a warrior of the Shar'd'iloned't'Hywil, always a warrior. She'd survived another day. Let that be enough.

From under her lashes, she observed the half a dozen women milling about the luxuriously appointed room, taking each in turn. A simple matter of self-preservation. When your continued existence depended on a master's caprice, you learned to read faces.

Slowly, she relaxed, leaning back against the wall. The court ladies were lightweights not worth her concern, save for a tall woman in red trimmed with seed pearls, standing with her arms folded, a faint frown creasing her brow. She had the Queen's hairline and the same long jaw. But this one was eaten up with jealousy and resent-ment. Sikara—bah, what hard, ugly names these people had!—would do well to watch her back. Still, the Queen was lucky. Amae had the feeling not much slipped past her Guard Captain. Rhio would protect his royal charge with swift and brutal efficiency.

Rhio. *Rhi-o-marr-d*. She sounded it out under her breath, curling her tongue around each syllable, inflecting the word in the way of her people.

Name the child, shape the life, went the Ancestors' proverb. Long, descriptive names were an integral part of Shar'd'iloned't'Hywil culture. Or they had been. The Captain's name was too short for true beauty, but nowhere near so . . . so *angular* as those she'd heard so far in Caracole of the Leaves.

Rhiomard. A growl with a purr at the end. It suited him well enough, a four-square soldier, dedicated to his duty. At first glance, he'd struck her as stolid, possibly dull. She'd selected him for the Test of the Battle Maiden out of pure devilment, because he alone had remained perfectly expressionless through her performance. Not many men managed that. To her delight, he'd taken her choice very personally indeed. Temper had sparked in that steady gaze and he'd risen to her challenge—Amae bit the inside of her cheek to stop the reminiscent grin—in every possible way.

She'd seen men lose bladder control during the Test. Not this one. He'd honored his Ancestors, holding his nerve as well as any Shar warrior. And it seemed he was a decent man. By the First Mother, she'd almost forgotten they existed. Those cool gray eyes had darkened with genuine concern when Giral ordered her to re-port to the diabloman he employed as his Slave Master.

Don't think of it, of slashing claws, and glutinous sniggers.

Suppressing a shudder, she pulled the cloak tighter around her shoulders. Someday soon a chance must come! She'd have only the one. But then, oh, then . . . Giral would pay until his bones cracked, his screams never-ending. Music to her ears.

This Rhio, he might be useful. Curling her bare toes into the deep pile of the rug, Amae considered.

The Captain was by no means a youth—there'd been a sprinkle of gray at his temples—but he had good muscle tone and excellent reflexes. The nearest thing to a real warrior she'd seen since her last sight of her eldest brother, the iron-shod quarterstaff a blur in his hands. Young and strong and brave, standing his ground. But step by step, an evil green cloud forced him back, roiling with armored, segmented limbs and pincers and snapping mandibles.

"Run, Amae, *run!*" he'd yelled, the quarterstaff ringing as it cracked a chitinous elbow joint. An eldritch howl issued from the cloud, echoed by the scream of the diabloman linked to the foul thing.

Whirling around, Amae had ducked under the thrust of a six-foot pike and shoved her blade into the belly of the Trinitarian soldier blocking her path. Jerking it across and up, she registered his grunt of pained surprise and felt the warm, slippery rush of his blood across her knuckles. But before she could yank the dagger free, something atrociously hard slammed into her temple.

"Amae!" Her brother's anguished bellow echoed across the parched landscape, fading away as oblivion rolled her under and into the dark. She'd been fifteen.

Now she sucked in a breath, folding her arms across her chest so she could hold herself together unnoticed. Alone. The last warrior of the Shar'd'iloned't'Hywil. Vengeance was hers, her sacred duty to the Ancestors, her personal pleasure. It mattered not how long she had to wait. If nothing else, slavery had taught her patience.

Amae'd'haraleen't'Lenquisquilirian.

Every day of her captivity, she found a mirror, even if it was only a reflection in a pond, or the dregs in the bottom of a cup. Over and over, she murmured her name, so that it at least would not disappear into the empty dark. If there was time, she repeated the roll call of those she had lost, but as the years went by, one name after another slipped from her memory and she grieved for that bitter death as well.

There wasn't a literal translation of her name, though "Green Sapling Growing" was near enough. Like all the names of her people, it included a subtext covering every possible connotation and nuance. Encoded in the flowing syllables was the blind determination of new life to fulfill its purpose, to grow and bloom, the joy of unfurling in the light, of twig and blossom and green tendril.

She gave herself a mental shake. Where had this foolish spurt of memory and grief come from? It was of no use whatsoever, a weakness she could not afford.

Boots rang on the tiled floor of the vestibule. Rhiomard and his Sergeant strode into the chamber. Amae's heart skipped a beat.

Ah, of course. The stern-faced Captain had set her off. A warrior who respected a woman enough to serve her—a man with nothing left to prove, a *real* man! Taking her wayward thoughts in a firm grip, she steered them away from everything she could never have.

Four

Could she turn this Rhio into an ally? No, that would mean trust. Too dangerous by far. A tool perhaps. Amae bit her lip. A pity to use him thus, because it would not go well with him if he failed in his duty, but there it was. She might not have a choice.

Deliberately, she shifted her gaze to the homely face of the female Sergeant. What had he called her? Yachi, that was it. By the bones of Those Before, just the sound of the name set her teeth on edge! Like a cat hawking up a fur ball.

The woman could hardly have missed the reaction of the Trinitarian delegation. They hadn't been able to stop shooting her sideways glances, appalled, fascinated and insulted all at once. Not only a plain-faced female out in public without a veil, but even more unthinkable, aping a soldier. A woman in a position of authority, giving orders and bearing weapons with casual confidence. Anathema!

The members of the delegation had prepared themselves for the barbarism of Caracole, for a *queen*, for the Trimagistos' sake! They'd had innumerable serious discussions, studied the culture of the

Queendom, readied themselves for the shock. Giral was clever; he'd selected men with flexible minds, no one too hidebound or conservative.

But a female Guard was something way beyond their experience. For a wonderful moment, Amae had thought Sethril might vomit on the Queen's fine gilt dinnerware. His mouth had worked, but the vicious little shit had managed not to disgrace himself. Pity. Giral's pet was a complication she could do without.

Her belly tightened with apprehension. The slippery bastard had her corset. She'd seen him scoop it from the floor, forgotten in the confusion. How he'd relish having a hold on her. To survive in the service of a high-ranking pasha meant navigating a murky world of intrigue and treachery, where the ground shifted beneath your feet without warning. What would Sethril do? Force her to play a part in his schemes? Have her whipped for carelessness? Or—a shudder ran down her spine, icing the blood in her veins—send her to the Slave Master and his demon?

One thing at a time, one day at a time. The wisdom of the Ancestors. Amae regulated her breathing, distracting herself by dwelling on the Captain's powerful legs, nicely displayed beneath the leather kilt of his uniform.

Rhio gave a respectful nod. "You sent for us, Majesty?"

The Queen set aside the elderly maid fussing with her outer robes. "Indeed, I did. Our guests are settled for the night?"

Rhio glanced at his companion. "Report."

Yachi's broad face creased in a grim smile. "Yes, Majesty. All present and accounted for. I double-checked."

"Good," said the Queen. "I want you to take"—glancing around, she broke off. A long forefinger beckoned Amae closer—"this one for a security check. And find her accommodation. What's your name, girl?"

Amae sank to her knees, keeping a decorous clutch on the cloak. "Dancer, Great Lady."

The royal brows drew together. "I know what you do. I asked your name."

"It is also how I am called, Great Lady. Dancer." Amae risked an upward glance. "Trinitarian slaves are named for their principal duty."

The Queen arched a brow. "Really? For example?"

"Drummer, Groom, Cook." Amae shrugged. "Dancer."

A pause. "I see. What's your real name? And for the Sister's sake, stand up."

Amae rose. "I am Dancer, Great Lady," she lied.

"Hmpf." Amae was aware of an uncomfortably shrewd gaze. "I thought Giral said you were some kind of healer."

"I have been trained in healing massage, yes, but I am no physician."

Yachi stepped forward to poke Amae's shoulder with a hard forefinger. *"Majesty,"* she hissed.

"Majesty," added Amae obediently.

"Hmm. Look at me, girl."

Amae raised her eyes.

Sikara displayed her hands, every knuckle knobby, distorted by the jointache. "He promised you could help me with the pain. Do you think you can?"

'Cestors' bones, it must hurt like a bitch in the cold weather. Automatically, Amae reached out to take the Queen's hands in hers.

Iron fingers clamped over her wrist. "Not so fast," growled Rhio. "No one touches the Queen without my permission."

Amae turned her head to snag his gaze with hers. "Really?" she murmured and watched his gray eyes turn storm dark.

Rhio released her and stepped back. "Majesty, I'll process this woman immediately. If she's safe, I'll send word tomorrow."

Sikara sighed. "Very well." She waved a hand in dismissal, already turning to speak with a small woman in purple velvet.

⬗⬗⬗⬗

The dancer had lied.

Rhio glanced at her unresponsive profile as they walked with

Yachi through the shadowed colonnade. She was a cool one, but she'd lied just the same.

"Dancer?"

"Yes?" She drew the cloak close.

If she'd played fast and loose with something as straightforward as her name, it was up to him to discover what else she concealed. "Are you cold?"

"No."

She must make a habit of falsehood. He had every reason to know she was naked under the cloak. The image still seared—her lithe body bowed back, spread for him, offered like a pagan sacrifice. *Only to him.* All that sleek, hot skin, the sweet little furrow between her thighs. Gods! Rhio gritted his teeth.

"Where are your . . ." Hell, he had no idea what a slave was permitted to own, if anything. He started over. "You must have other clothes, uh, possessions."

He caught the flash of teeth in the moonslight. "Of course." A sideways glance. "I do not go naked all the time."

Yachi snorted. "You'd frighten the children."

Dancer stopped dead. "But no," she said seriously. "That I would not wish. I like children."

Rhio's heart gave the strangest twist. "It was a joke." Lightly, he touched her arm. "Dancer, you come with me. Yachi, see what food you can scrounge from the mess. Then collect her things from the guest wing and meet us in my quarters."

But the dancer blocked Yachi's path. Rhio's brows rose. This should be good.

"You will have to go to the Slave Master." Dancer hesitated for a moment, her knuckles shining white where she gripped the cloak. "Do you know what a diabloman is?"

The Sergeant cursed. Metal rang in the quiet garden as she loosened her sword in the scabbard. "Aye."

"Good." Releasing a breath, Dancer stepped back. "Be careful, yes? Very careful."

Rhio met Yachi's eyes. "Take Kano with you and tell him to look menacing."

"But Cap'n——"

"That's an order, Yachi."

A grunt. "Aye, Cap'n." She strode away.

Dancer said, "Who's Kano?"

"This way." Rhio allowed himself a grim smile. "He's the nearest thing to a mountain I have under my command. Huge."

Another of those sidelong, flirtatious glances. "Bigger than you, Captain?"

"Much," he said repressively.

The rest of the short walk was accomplished in silence.

"In here." Rhio unlocked the door to his quarters, a small free-standing building at the Palace end of the Guards' barracks. It wasn't much, an office with a desk, a fireplace and a battered couch. Another door led to a bedchamber and a utilitarian bathing area. But after years spent in crowded barracks, he found he relished the privacy, the solitude a gift he hadn't known he craved. Twenty years on, and now he was dreaming of a place of his own. He averted his eyes from the drawer where John's letter lay. On his next leave, he'd take up his old friend on that invitation.

Once he had the lamp lit, he gestured at the upright wooden chair in front of the desk. "Sit."

Every cell in his body vibrating with awareness, he put the desk between them. Safely seated, he busied himself with the ink block and a new brush. "Name?" He didn't look up.

A delicate snort. "You already know it, Captain R-rhio-marrd."

That familiar flicker of delight in his groin, as if she'd placed her lips against his balls to speak. Deliberately, Rhio set the brush down on the block. "You are a major security risk. Either we work through this process or I return you to the Ambassador." Hoping for magisterial, he clasped his fingers together on the blotter, but he had the uneasy feeling he just looked stuffy. "Up to you."

Dancer's spine stiffened, but she lost color. "No. I'd prefer not."

As he'd thought, she didn't lack for guts, this one. "Then it's simple. Answer the questions."

Dancer inclined her head, regal as any queen. "Ask."

"Where were you born?"

"What has that—?" Catching his eye, she broke off. "In the southern desert beyond the Trinitarian border."

"How long have you been a slave?"

"Fifteen years, four months and twenty days."

"How old are you now?"

"Thirty."

Rhio glanced up from his notes in time to catch the shiver she couldn't prevent. "I ask you again, Dancer. Are you cold?"

She hesitated. "A little."

Without a word, he rose and went to light the fire. Hell, she'd walked all the way from the royal chambers barefoot without a word of complaint. He should have done it the moment they entered the building.

"So you were fifteen when they took you?" he said, crouching to arrange the kindling. Flames sparked and spread in orange tongues.

"Yes."

Rising, he turned to face her. "Come here."

In silence, she rose and walked steadily toward him. He thought she'd stop, but she didn't—not until they were breast to breast, the folds of her cloak brushing his kilt, their faces inches apart.

Rhio fought the urge to swallow. Brother's balls, she thought he wanted— Unfortunately, she was right. He did; any man would.

If he stepped back, he'd lose face. If he stepped forward, he'd lose everything else. He held her eye, trying to ignore the wonderful scent that rose from her skin. "Sit down on the couch. I'll find you something warmer to wear."

Dancer's lashes swept down, effective as a courtesan's fan. Gracefully, she sank down onto the couch.

"Don't move, you hear me?"

Her eyes glinted with amusement. "But yes, Captain."

Rhio stalked into his bedchamber and rifled through his clothes chest, swearing under his breath. He wasn't sure what he'd expected, but Dancer was still there when he returned, her long body stretched out, feet toward the fire and a couple of tattered cushions under her head. Her eyes were half-closed, her cheeks delicately flushed. That was better.

"Here." Rhio tossed the bundle of clothing onto her chest. "And take this too." He produced the chain-mail corset.

Dancer shot upright with a cry. The clothes fell to the floor, but she buried her fingers in the silver mesh. When she raised her eyes to Rhio's, they were shining. "I saw Sethril take it and I thought— How did you get it back?"

Rhio shrugged, feeling his chest expand like a boy showing off for his first girl. "Took it away from him."

Dancer's gaze flicked up and down his body as if scanning for visible signs of injury. Finally, she said, "He's a dangerous enemy."

"I know. Now get dressed. I haven't finished with you."

"What is it your Sergeant says?" In Dancer's grin, he caught a glimpse of the girl she must once have been. " 'Aye, Cap'n.' " Her pretty accent slurred the words.

In a single smooth movement, she came to her feet, ripped off the cloak and threw it aside.

Rhio nearly swallowed his tongue. "Wha—?" he got out. "What the fuck are you doing?"

Dancer stood naked before the fire like a temple statue fashioned of pure gold, the flames caressing her lean, magnificent body with a warm glow. The dark curtain of her hair flowed over her shoulders, a fall of midnight.

She met his eyes, her level brows drawn together in puzzlement. "What you ordered. Have you changed your mind?"

Had he changed his mind? Gods, did she think he was made of stone?

Rhio spun around, giving her his back. "No." He gripped the mantelpiece with both hands. He'd been right. She was playing him after all, the bitch.

Rustling noises came from behind him. "These are a man's clothes. Yours."

"They'll do to keep you warm. Put them on." Rhio stared at the pennant of his first mercenary company. In a sentimental gesture, he'd had it framed when he left Torza's Band to join the Queen's Guard. It needed dusting. "Trying to seduce me won't work," he said to the pennant.

The rustling stopped. Dancer gave a quiet chuckle, a completely female sound. "Believe me, R-Rhio," she said. "It would. But you are safe, my friend. I will warn you first."

"But . . ." Rhio ran a hand through his hair. "You stripped. Right in front of me, godsdammit."

"*Oh,*" she said. "I see."

He sure as hell didn't.

Her fingers brushed his arm. "Turn around, Rhio."

Almost reluctantly, he faced her. Dancer stood quietly, so swamped by his old shirt and trews she looked like an urchin child. A pair of army socks flapped around her narrow feet. "In Trinitaria, slaves are allowed no modesty," she said gently. "My sorrow for the embarrassment. I forgot it is different here.

"For example"—she gestured at the enveloping garments—"a Trinitarian master would order me to remain naked rather than wear such unbecoming coverings, even if I froze. Now do you see?"

Rhio shook his head, a slow burn starting in his gut. "Tell me more." He pointed to the couch and Dancer sat back with a sigh.

"The only reason I go unveiled is because I am a slave." Her pretty mouth twisted. "Whores are also forbidden the veil."

"I've been to the Trinitarian Republic. I know how respectable women dress."

"The covering is protection, and real enough." Dancer shot him an unreadable glance. "But did you know that older slaves and whores, or those of them considered ugly, are also required to wear the veil?" She smiled without humor. "I do not think your Sergeant would fare well with a Trinitarian master."

Rhio laughed aloud. "She'd cut off his balls and shove them down his throat."

"As punishment, they'd give her to a diabloman with a hungry demon. Her death would be one long violation. Not only body, but mind and spirit. Hideous."

Rhio's mouth went dry. Hadn't she said Giral's Slave Master was a diabloman?

"You," he said. "Have you——?"

Someone knocked on the door, three brisk raps. "It's me, Cap'n."

"Enter." Relief and frustration warred for his attention. Fuck, did he really want to know?

Yachi clumped in, a small battered pack slung over one arm and a greasy paper-wrapped bundle in the other hand. She hefted the pack. "This it, Dancer?"

Dancer smiled. "My thanks to you, Yachi. Are you all right?"

Rhio clamped a hand on Dancer's shoulder to prevent her from rising. "Give it here, Sergeant. Report."

Yachi scowled. "He spat at me, the filthy bastard. Would only look at Kano, though I'm the senior officer."

"You mean the Slave Master?" Rhio spread the meager contents of the pack on his desk. "So what did you do?"

Yachi shrugged, a shadow crossing her face. "I had your orders. I told Kano to keep his trap shut and let me do the talking. The Slave Master tried to act like he was deaf, but I kept insisting. Once he realized Dancer's pack was the only way to be rid of me, he found it soon enough."

"You insulted him," murmured Dancer from the depths of the couch. "Be careful from now on, yes?"

"Was he alone?" asked Rhio.

"Yes, but you know . . ." Yachi's brow knotted.

"What?"

Her wide brown eyes were thoughtful. "He's a scrawny little runt, but he wasn't scared, not at all. Even if I was beneath his notice, you'd think he'd worry about Kano. You should look at that promotion, Cap'n. He did us proud, what with all the growling and glaring like he'd break the little bastard in half with his bare hands."

"Did you hear noises?" asked Dancer suddenly. "Anything . . . unusual?"

"Nothing that sounded like a demon, if that's what you're asking. Someone singing in the next room, high and thin, like a little girl."

Dancer turned her head away and gazed into the heart of the fire.

Yachi tossed the greasy bundle to Rhio. "Here's your supper. I did the best I could. Cap'n. May I go now?"

Rhio smiled. "Enjoy your leave."

Dancer shifted to brace her arms on the back of the couch. "What are you going to do?" she asked, her eyes bright.

Yachi stretched 'til her shoulders creaked. "The taverns in the Melting Pot will be hoppin'. I've got me a two-day pass. Going to find me a pretty man." Her unabashed grin made her look almost handsome. "Or two."

Dancer blinked. "Good luck."

Another grin and a wink. "Don't need it. Bye, Rhio." A casual wave and she was gone.

The fire crackled. Dancer combed her fingers through her hair, gathered up the silken mass of it and began to plait.

"Have you eaten?" asked Rhio.

"No."

Opening the paper parcel, he found a small loaf that he tore in two. Then he used his long dagger to divide the chunks of cheese and cold roast meat. Grabbing a sheet of clean paper, he shoveled half of the food onto it and laid it on the arm of the sofa. "Here."

Dancer's eyes widened, but she thanked him calmly enough, continuing to braid.

Rhio picked up his ink brush and cleared his throat. "I have more questions."

"But of course." Had she smiled?

In his mind's eye, he saw the hard handsome face of his old friend John Lammas, the dark calligraphy of ownership sprawled across one cheekbone, a slave tattoo. But John was lucky: He'd been one of the very few to escape the brutal servitude of a Trinitarian galley. He and his Meg had bought a country tavern in Holdercroft, way out in the Cressy Plains. Nonetheless, what must it be like to look at that desecration, that offense against his manhood, every day in the mirror? To see it reflected in Meg's soft blue eyes when he kissed her?

"Every Trinitarian slave I've ever seen has a tattoo. Why don't you?"

Her busy fingers stilled. "I do."

Rhio frowned, remembering a feast of honey-toned skin, topped with the burgundy rose of her nipples. Against his will, he thickened. He'd seen every gorgeous inch of her. How could he have missed it?

Dancer's dark brows winged up. Her lips curved, very slightly. "Let me show you, yes?"

Releasing the plait, she rose in a single sinuous motion and sauntered over to his desk. A drop of ink gathered on the end of Rhio's brush and plopped onto the paper, but he didn't notice.

Five

Silently, Dancer padded around the desk. "Where do you think it is, Captain R-Rhio-marrd?"

"No idea." Her eyes reminded him of Concordian chocolat, dark, bittersweet and incredibly expensive. Rhio had a weakness for Concordian chocolat.

When she dropped gracefully to her knees beside him, the brush in his fingers snapped clean in two. What the—?

Dancer dropped her head, shifting the mass of her hair off her neck with one hand. "See?" she said, her voice muffled, her breath warm and moist against his bare knee.

Rhio stared down at the vulnerable nape of her neck, appalled on so many levels he didn't know which to deal with first. Unable to prevent himself, he reached down to trace the small, looping characters tattooed across the narrow span at the base of her skull. Fine downy hairs caught on his callused fingers, the skin beneath like heated silk.

"How?" he rasped. "How did—?"

"It's what they do to avoid an obvious mark. Don't want to spoil luxury goods. They shaved my head first." The fall of her hair spilled over his kilt and down his leg, the plait unraveling one lock at a time, a tickling, maddening caress along the swell of his calf.

"When you were fifteen." He took great care to expunge any hint of pity from his voice, though his heart squeezed. The fact that she'd been little more than a child then made no difference to the danger she posed in the here and now. With or without her knowledge, Dancer might yet be a weapon in a subtle game of political intrigue.

Rhio slid his hand around to cradle her cheek, preventing her from turning her head toward his body. Because if she did, she'd know at once he was harder than a pike. He felt the sweat pop on the back of his neck and trickle underneath his collar. Brother's balls, his nose was full of the fresh green of her perfume. How could she miss the scent of lust pouring off him?

"Sit up," he said gruffly, tugging at her shoulder.

To his relief, Dancer raised her head and sat back on her heels, folding her hands in her lap. She shot him a smoldering glance, but he could have sworn it was automatic and that underneath, she was amused. "Now what, Captain?"

Rhio gritted his teeth. "What does it say, the tattoo?"

Every trace of expression left her face. "Literally? 'Property of Ghuis Gremani Giral.' "

"What happens if . . . if you're sold?"

"The first tattoo will be removed and the new master's name applied." Her gaze was bleak. "The healers have the art, but it's very painful." She shrugged. "Clever slaves take care to please their masters."

He hated having to ask, but he had to know—for any number of reasons, and the Queen's safety was but one of them. "Is giving sexual service part of your duties?"

"Of course," she said matter-of-factly.

"Giral uses you as a whore?" It came out more harshly than he'd intended.

"He has a number of expert bedslaves, but yes, even me if he wishes." An angry wash of color bloomed on Dancer's high cheekbones. "He *owns* me, Rhio."

"Do you enjoy it?" What the fuck was the matter with him? "Wait." He raised a hand before she could reply. "I withdraw the question. It's not relevant."

"I agree." Rising, she glared down her nose, reminding him of his first vivid impression of her, fierce as a raptor. "You're an intelligent man, Captain. You can work it out for yourself, yes?"

"Aye." On impulse, he said, "Here with me, you're not a slave, Dancer. Do you understand?"

A level look. "What am I, then?"

"A woman." He tilted his head back against the chair, gazing at her from under his lashes. "A mind and a heart and a soul. Perhaps even an enemy." Her dark eyes met his and held. "You're a fighter, aren't you? To the bone."

For the first time, he saw surprise cross her face. She folded her arms. "If I am not a slave, then I refuse to answer."

"You don't need to." He gave her a wolfish grin. "You're from a warrior tribe and the Brother knows you have cause to hate. Are knives your favorite weapon?"

"They are now," Dancer said after a pause.

"And before?"

Another silence, then, "I used to be good with a quarterstaff."

"What's your name?"

"Am—" She shut her mouth with a snap. "You're very good."

"True. A little while ago you said you'd give me fair warning. Let me return the favor." Rhio reached for bread and cheese. "If a plot exists to harm Her Majesty, I'll find it. If you're involved"—he stabbed his dagger into the meat, razor sharp—"I will have no mercy. Got it?" He took a savage bite.

Dancer gave a curt nod. "I have it."

Her stare flickered down to his mouth. Spinning on her heel, she took two steps to the couch and seized her portion of the food. She didn't quite gobble—she was tidy enough—but every morsel disappeared long before Rhio had finished. Watching her lick her fingers, fastidious as a cat, he had that same strange twisting feeling in his chest.

Invisible chains and she had no idea she wore them. Godsdammit, a slave couldn't eat until her master did, and she'd been hungry. Shit, all her adult life. It was a miracle the spirit hadn't been beaten out of her.

Some soldiers had extraordinary physical courage. Others didn't. Rhio had known them all. When the blood ran hot, a man might do something so brave it was downright reckless, but to go on living, bending but refusing to break, day after day, year after interminable year . . . Not only guts, but stubborn pride and clear-eyed intelligence.

Ah, she was something! He didn't give a shit what her name was.

The tide of wanting that swept over him made his earlier lust seem feeble in comparison. Heat flashed up and down his spine, gathering in his aching balls, the small of his back, his skull. Abruptly, his skin became too small for his body. His imagination supplied a searing vision of his fingers gripping her taut buttocks, while he shoved his throbbing length deep—gods, so *deep*—into satin-slick flesh. Fuck, she'd be narrow and tight and strong, her dancer's legs wrapped around his waist. And afterward, she'd lie with her head pillowed on his shoulder, her hair spread across his bare chest, and she'd whisper, all throaty and sated, *R-Rhio, oh R-Rhio* . . .

She'd dance too, but for him alone. No one would ever hurt her again. He'd hear her laugh, make her happy. The pain and fury would vanish from those magnificent eyes and—

Fuck!

What in the seven hells? He must be losing his mind. For the first time in longer than he could remember, Rhio felt a leaden chill in the pit of his stomach. Brother's balls, he was actually contemplating a . . . a *rescue*. Only for a split second of insanity, true, but—Gods, the theft of a foreign slave! Even a whisper on the breeze would get them both killed.

He could barely breathe. Blankly, he gazed at the collection of items he'd taken from Dancer's pack. A few simple cosmetics, a small bundle of clothing, two packets of mothermeknot, the contraceptive herb all women of child-bearing age on Palimpsest brewed and drank as a matter of course, and a polished wooden box with a complicated latch.

His eyes narrowed. *"What's this?"*

A full stomach, a warm fire—and a man who treated her as though she had a brain, as though she *mattered*. Amae gazed into the flames, enjoying the good things while she had them. Rhio's snarl snapped her out of her reverie. Ah, well, it had been lovely while it lasted.

Reluctantly, she turned her head. "My box of oils."

"Your what?"

"For massage. Remember? Giral offered me to the Queen." When his brow creased, she added, "For her jointache."

The Captain's lips thinned. Placing the tip of his knife under the latch, he flipped it open. One by one, he extracted the small vials from their padded slots and set them in a neat row on the desk. "Come here."

So much for having a mind and a heart and a soul. With an inward curse, Amae abandoned the fire and did as she was bid.

"Tell me what's in them," he demanded. "One at a time."

Amae folded her arms. "They're labeled."

A rumble of displeasure. "I don't read Trinitarian."

"Very well." She laid a finger on the lid of the first vial. "This is healall. You know it, yes?"

He grunted. "I'm a soldier. What do you think? Go on."

"Scaldcream, essential oil of mothermeknot, boneknit, coolbalm, hotbalm, essential oil of Lady's lace . . ." She worked her way from one end of the row to the other, while Rhio watched, his eyes flickering from her face to the bottles and back again, suspicion in every line of him.

Pity. For a moment there, there'd been companionship between them, something like the beginnings of friendship.

Gods, she was getting soft. Friendship—*trust*—was stupid. And stupid meant dead. Unavenged.

Without waiting for the Captain's permission, she pulled out a chair and sat. The too-big shirt slipped off her shoulder and she hitched it up again.

He said, "It appears you have many uses." The moment the words were out, dark color bloomed on his stubbled cheek.

A decent man, probably faced by the reality of slavery for the first time and troubled by it. 'Cestors' bones, he was even more dangerous than he knew. Bitterly amused by her own train of thought, Amae fought to prevent her lip from curling. "Yes," she agreed. "I do." She couldn't stop herself from adding, "Giral gets his money's worth from all his property."

"How were you trained? Who did it?"

"Giral sent me to a Master Physician to be tested. When I showed promise, I had lessons for three years."

"Hmm." Rhio rubbed his jaw. "Why did the Ambassador have you tested in the first place?"

Amae shrugged. She had no intention of revealing any real information about the medical arts of her people. Healing was the gift of her Ancestors, sacred and private, handed down through all the generations from the First Mother.

"It amused him. He's an intelligent man, something of a dilettante. About a year after . . . after my people were . . . gone, he found a line in an old history describing the desert tribes and their primitive healing Magick. I was all that was left, but he was curious enough to try."

"Can you? Heal the sick, I mean." His gaze was level, assessing. Why were some men blessed with extravagant eyelashes? It wasn't fair.

She refused to look away. "Not disease, or anything truly serious. I'm best with strains and sprains."

A skeptical grunt. "How would you help me, for instance?"

Amae smiled without amusement. Yet another test. By the bones of Those Before, she was tired of it. "You've been wounded many times, I think? Your right shoulder is stiff. It hurts you in the winter. I'm guessing you've dislocated it two or three times. There is some issue with the muscles in your lower back, probably related to the shoulder. They go into spasm when you're overtired. You have a problem with the ankle you broke and the wound in the big muscle of your thigh. Now that you're getting older, you worry about your eyesight and your stamina and your—"

"Enough!"

"You asked." Amae showed her teeth. "I answered, yes?"

Rhio appeared to be breathing hard through his nose. "All right. What about my shoulder, then?"

Coming to her feet, she moved to stand at his side and folded back her sleeves. "Give me your right hand."

Warily, he did so. His flesh was firm and warm, his fingers square-tipped and capable. There were sword calluses on his palms, old scars and nicks marring the olive skin. Enjoying the contact, Amae closed her eyes, allowing herself to sink into a state of concentration almost intense enough to be a light trance. Under her fingertips, his energy flowed and pulsed. By the First Mother, he was strong, not only physically, but mentally. Like a great tree, firmly rooted in his world, knowing his place and what he stood for.

Carefully, she worked her way over the flesh at the base of his thumb. What would he do if she bent her head and nipped him there? Would he slap her away? Giral would, with casual brutality. Her breath hitched. No, the Captain would never be casual; she knew it in her bones. He might spread her across on the desk, crush her under the weight of his hard warrior's body, breast to breast, hip to hip—but gods, she'd have his absolute attention. She'd fight back, a lover and an equal, knowing she was safe—that they both were.

A hot pulse pattering between her thighs, Amae breathed deep, trying to ground herself. This was ridiculous. Desire was a tool to be used, a luxury she could not afford. *Get on with it.*

Biting her lip, she followed the stream of his life force to the *ch'qui* nexus point in the webbing between his thumb and forefinger. Rhiomard had shown her a certain rough kindness—the least she could do was give him ease in return.

"This may feel strange, but it won't hurt," she murmured, putting pressure on the point with her finger and thumb, smoothing the blockages, stroking, persuading the flows to relax.

Vaguely, she heard the rumble of his deep voice, but all her attention was focused on tracing the *ch'qui* up the inside of his arm, left bare by the formal battle vest he wore. A tremor ran through the smooth muscular flesh under her hands, his skin pebbling with gooseflesh. She'd be willing to bet he was rock hard beneath the kilt—and furious with himself.

"Take the vest off," she murmured. "I can't reach the bad spot."

A muttered curse and he flung it aside. Amae allowed herself a single swift glance. Thanks to their Ancestors, the Shar'd'iloned't' Hywil were perfectly suited to life as nomadic hunters. They were a lean, wiry people, fleet of foot and bronze of skin, with little body hair. Rhio was nothing like a Shar. Only his height saved him from looking blocky. His chest was deep and broad, a set of strong, muscled planes, furred with a light mat of dark hair that arrowed down toward a cobbled belly. His nipples showed as small brown disks, tightly peaked.

Her lips quirked as she palpated his shoulder, feeling for the knot in the muscle. That inconvenient arousal wasn't going to trouble him much longer. Amae uncorked the hotbalm and worked a generous amount well into his skin, watching his lashes flutter with the spreading heat, the comfort of her firm touch.

Now!

Ruthlessly, she dug into the sore spot with both thumbs, using all her strength.

The only warning was the sharp inhalation of Rhio's breath. Merciless fingers clamped over her wrist, but she refused to let up.

His eyes blazed into hers. Stormy, furious. Magnificent. "Fuck! What—?"

If he exerted the merest ounce of extra pressure, her bones would crumble to dust. Through her teeth, she said, "Wait."

Another instant of strained silence, then, "It's releasing. Feel it?"

His face was only an inch from hers, so close she could count the crinkles at the corners of his eyes.

Those sinful lashes flickered. "Aye." His jaw relaxed. "Gods, that I can." One finger at a time, he released her wrist.

Amae used her palms to cup and rub his shoulder. Then she stepped back. "There, that's the best I can do." Unobtrusively, she cradled her wrist. "It's more painful if you're tense, which is why I didn't warn you. Do you see?"

"Hmm." As Rhio stood, rotating the shoulder, she busied herself packing the oils back in the box, refusing to look at the muscles flexing fluidly beneath his skin, the fine warrior solidity of him.

He cleared his throat. "Dancer, I—" He touched her hair. "You really should have warned me. Did I hurt you?"

"Of course not."

"Is that what you'd do for the Queen?"

"No." Two scars marred the skin over his ribs, one a long curving slash, the other a ragged pucker. Either could have cost him his life. Amae kept her gaze fixed firmly on his face. "Massage is no great help for jointache, but Giral didn't bother to ask before he decided to loan me out to the Queen. I'd use hot and cold compresses, work oil of Lady's lace into her fingers. It has a slightly numbing effect in the right concentration." She smiled a little. "Besides, it smells nice."

Rhio frowned, tapping his fingers on the desk. Amae did up the last buckle on her pack and folded her cloak over her arm. Idly, she wondered what he'd decide to do. Would he march her straight off to some cold, narrow bed in the servants' quarters or would he want her to service him first? Ah, well, it wouldn't be any particular hardship; in fact, it might even be a pleasure—he was really quite attractive in a rough, soldierly way. In any case, it wouldn't take long and if she paid attention during the process, she could pay him back for his fairness in the only coin she had to offer. Stifling a yawn, she wished he'd make up his mind.

The Captain threw himself down on the couch, the firelight gleaming on the smooth swell of nicely shaped biceps, highlighting the fur on his chest. Here it came, the first move.

"Bring the Lady's lace over here and show me exactly what you intend to do to Her Majesty."

Amae blinked. Oh. Well, fine, if that was what he wanted. Digging through her pack, she extracted the oil box and removed the vial. There was nowhere left to sit on the couch save by his hip, so she perched herself there, picked up his hand and laid it on her knee. For some strange reason, it felt remarkably heavy.

Rhio relaxed against the shabby cushions, looking every inch a bare-chested pasha. His lips curved, very slightly. He was enjoying this, damn him. But in an odd way, so was she.

Fixing her gaze on his face rather than an indolent length of a brawny, hair-dusted thigh, she gave the vial a brisk shake, holding it high so the firelight struck gleams off the translucent oil.

"Dancer." He'd gone still, every muscle. "Exactly how, uh, nice does this stuff smell?"

She chuckled. "Very floral and feminine. It's called Lady's lace, after all. You'll have to wash it off before you return to duty. Here, try it."

But he waved the small vessel aside. Smiling into her eyes, he said, "No, no, you do it."

Something was very wrong, but what? Warily, Amae glanced around the room, tasting the tension in the air. Whatever it was, she'd best be ready. With an inward shrug, she uncorked the vial and tilted it over her palm.

In a single abrupt movement, Rhio surged up, knocking it out of her hand so that it tumbled to the rug, the oil trickling out in a thin stream as it rolled back and forth.

Six

"What are you *doing*?" Amae shot to her feet. "Do you know how much that stuff costs? Slave Master will kill me!"

Rhio gripped her shoulder. "Not likely. Look."

The oil stains on the rug were turning a purplish brown. Another odor, metallic and evil, lurked beneath the flowery sweetness of the Lady's lace. 'Cestors bones, was that—? Amae dropped to her knees, a hand outstretched.

"*Don't touch!*" Rhio jerked her back to her feet and tucked her under his arm. "You recognize it?"

Amae gripped his hand with both of hers. "Prettydeath." Her mouth was so dry she had to wet her lips before she could go on. "I didn't know it was there. Rhio, I swear on the bones of my Ancestors."

"I believe you," said Rhio.

And he did. Shudders ran bone-deep through the slim body pressed against his. In fact, when he thought of how close he'd let her come to an agonizing, hideously protracted death, Rhio felt his guts heave. But he'd had to know.

"If you hadn't—" Her eyes dark with horror, she swallowed hard and tried again. "I would have, have . . . By the First Mother!"

"The color changed when you shook it. I'd say someone painted the underside of the cork. When it's prettydeath, you don't need much. Dancer . . . it was meant for the Queen. You were just expendable. No loose ends."

Dancer growled, deep in her throat, like the tygre he'd once thought her. "I swear," she said. "I swear I will kill him. No more waiting." The rest was in a language he'd never heard, liquid and sibilant, every word suffused with rage and pain.

Pulling away from him, she would have stepped in the oil if he hadn't swooped and swung her up in his arms, the worn linen of the old shirt soft against his bare chest. "Not here," he said. "It stinks."

Striding into the bedchamber, Rhio deposited Dancer on the mattress and lit the lamp. "Stay there." He grabbed a dusty bottle of spirits and a cup from the bottom drawer of his desk and poured a healthy measure.

"Here." Tears glittered in her eyes and her honey-toned skin had a gray tinge he didn't like, but when he proffered the cup, she shook her head.

"Drink," he said more gently, wrapping her fingers around the cup and guiding it to her mouth.

Dancer sipped, coughed and sipped again. The color returned to her cheeks.

Thank the Brother, the bedchamber had its own fireplace. Rhio built up the fire and closed the door to keep the heat in. That was better.

When she offered him the cup, he drained it in a single swallow and leaned back against the pillows, Dancer in the crook of his arm. She didn't object, curling up against him, one hand coming to rest over his pounding heart.

"Now," he said. "I will have the truth. Who is it you wish to kill?"

Dancer shot him a narrow glance. "Who do you think? Giral, the bastard, the—" She went on for some time in her own language.

Absently, Rhio rubbed his palm up and down her spine. "It doesn't make sense. Using you to poison Sikara implicates him directly. He's a subtle man, Giral. Devious."

"Yes." Dancer allowed her cheek to settle against his shoulder. "The Grand Pasha would have his head. For being clumsy, you see?"

Rhio snorted. "Not to mention the Queen. She'd take it as a declaration of war and damn the treaty talks." Thoughtfully, he went on. "I've encountered prettydeath twice tonight. An interesting coincidence, don't you think?"

Dancer reared up to stare into his face.

Rhio curled a lock of her hair around his finger. "Simoener Selidan Sethril carries a poisoned blade. Did you know that?"

Slim fingers dug into his shoulders. "What happened?"

"I took it away from him, like the corset."

A short pause and she shrugged in the fluid way she had. "You must be good. Sethril's a trained assassin, lower than a sewer snake. He hates me."

Rhio gave a grim smile. "He's not exactly in love with me either. He told me not to forget his name. Also that the Grand Pasha is his uncle."

Dancer sat up, her face alight with a warrior's purpose. Immediately, he wanted to pull her close again. "Yes, but Giral has a new favorite, a boy slave with pretty eyes and soft hands. He no longer sends for Sethril in the night." She huffed with amusement. "Ah, R-Rhio, you should see your face. It's impossible for a master to keep secrets from his slave."

He shook his head, smiling. "By the Brother, you're a dangerous woman."

Dancer laughed outright, enchantingly throaty. On impulse, Rhio slung an arm around her neck, raised his head and pressed his mouth to her smiling lips.

The laugh ended in a strangled gasp.

Rhio flicked his tongue across her lower lip, stroked a fingertip over her cheekbone and withdrew, more than a little puzzled. He'd expected more of a welcome. "What?" he said.

Dancer pressed her fingers to her mouth, her cheeks flushed a delightful pink. "Uh, n-nothing." Then she shook her head as if to clear it.

He hadn't meant to do that—or at least, not quite so soon—but everything in him that was male urged to go back for more, to sink deep and demand the response he craved. Her lips had been satin beneath his, and so very warm. "Now that was definitely a lie." Gently, but firmly, he spread his whole hand over the side of her face, compelling her to look at him. But her lashes fluttered down, concealing her thoughts, and everywhere their flesh touched he could feel her shaking, deep tremors she was trying valiantly to suppress.

"Dancer—" he said and broke off, more confused than before, but so hyperaware of her, every cell in his body hummed with it.

After a tingling silence, he removed his hand and cleared his throat. "Tell me more about Sethril."

Dancer cast him a fleeting glance, relaxing into his embrace. "It's said the Grand Pasha uses Sethril for his—what is it called?—dirty work, but that he doesn't trust him." She snorted. "Who would?"

"If the Queen is murdered, Giral is discredited and Sethril has much to gain."

Eyes dark with trouble met his. "So does the Grand Pasha. Giral is a powerful rival. He has many friends at court, merchants and pashas with money and influence. They've been urging a peace, trade talks."

"I thought the Grand Pasha wanted the treaty?"

A shake of the head, her hair a silky whip on his skin. "It's all Giral's idea. The Grand Pasha bowed to the pressure, but reluctantly. He's an old man, conservative, and he was a priest before he ascended the throne. To him, your Queen is an abomination, an offense in the face of the Trimagistos."

"Gods, what a tangle."

"You said I was . . . expendable. Of no importance." Her face shuttered, all the vivid life draining from it, leaving only a resolve as bleak as winter. "I am already dead." A long sentence followed in the liquid tongue he'd heard before.

"What was that?"

"An oath. To my Ancestors, to those I lost. I will avenge them before I die."

Rhio's heart did that strange twisting thing again. "No," he whispered, cupping her cool cheek, feeling her jawbone hard beneath his fingers, so strong and yet so easy to break, to smash, to splinter, to—

Gripping her shoulders, he stared into those raptor's eyes. "Don't you see?" He gave her a little shake. "You can *die* anytime you want. We'll fake it. And once you're dead . . ."

Her eyes widened. "I'm free." Dancer's lips framed the words, but no sound emerged.

"Welcome to my world, sweetheart." His blood singing, Rhio wrapped both arms around her and tugged her down, the lean body sealed against his, all the way from chest to thigh. She didn't tense, but she went very still, like a wary animal.

Gods, what had the bastards done to her? What had they made her do?

"Shhh." He rubbed her shoulder blades in soothing circles, murmuring nonsense. He wanted her so badly he ached, but more than anything else, he wanted her coming to him free and light, the joy of desire shining her beautiful eyes.

Turning his face into her hair, he breathed deep of her wild green scent, acutely conscious of the firm cushion of her breasts pressed against his ribs. "I'll get us a private audience with Her Majesty, first thing tomorrow."

"But—"

"It's her life too—and her Queendom. She has to know." His tone brooked no argument. "She's my commanding officer. Brother's balls, she's nothing like those bastards. We can trust her."

Every muscle in her back went rigid. "I am a Shar warrior—the last of my people. I will not give up my vengeance."

Rhio gave a dark chuckle. "No problem. We'll work out a way."

"This is my duty, you understand?" she said into his neck. "Mine and mine alone."

"Of course, but I'll help." *Make sure you live to savor it—and me.*

He thought she relaxed a trifle, but she said no more. Rhio went back to stroking her long spine, up and down, up and down. "Will Giral be angry if I keep you here tonight? It would be best," he said softly.

She seemed to have regained her composure. "He'd be surprised if you didn't." A small smile playing around her mouth, she moved a thigh far enough to nudge his semi-erection. "I'm grateful."

Between one blink and the next, he swelled to full, throbbing life. "That's not enough," he rasped.

Dancer undulated against him, a mind-spinning combination of supple muscularity and feminine delicacy. "You still want me though?" she murmured.

"Can you doubt it?"

"Not from the first moment." The ghost of a chuckle.

Rhio nibbled the tip of her earlobe and for a moment, she went still. "Was I that obvious?" he said.

"Men usually are." Skimming a palm up under his kilt, she stroked his length through the regulation linen drawers he wore beneath. Expertly, she strummed him with wicked, knowing fingers, not too hard, not too soft—*perfect*—while Rhio fought for breath, his hips arching, thrusting himself into the magick of her touch. His mind recognized the way she'd been trained, but his cock didn't care.

Just as he regained enough control to speak, to stop her before it was too late, she rasped her thumb gently over the head and withdrew. Making a production out of licking each of her fingers in turn, Dancer sat up, watching him through a sweep of sooty lashes. "Mmm." Her thumb slid between sweet lips, all the way to the first joint.

"Why, you little—"

With a breathless chuckle, Dancer evaded his grab. Gripping her shirt by the hem, she reefed it off. She tossed her head, so that her hair flew about her in a shining curtain. "Take," she said, spreading her arms, her breasts mouthwateringly pert, honey copper and high. "I'm yours, yes?"

Too much, she was too much. He was only flesh and blood. To the seven hells with scruples. "Gods, yes!"

When Rhio lunged, she gave before him like water, like a dream of consummate grace. Her thighs fell open, her hips cradling his desperate cock. The too-big socks flopped against him as she braced her feet on his calves.

"Wait," she panted. "A minute only, I promise. Just . . ." A fumble at waist level and she was wriggling out of the trews he'd given her.

Yes, yes, *yes*! Rhio's entire being narrowed down to his genitals, pulsing with the hot swell of his seed. Splayed beneath him was the relief he craved, a receptacle for the bursting, agonizing weight that was his cock. With one hand, he pushed up his kilt and freed himself from the drawers. His shaft brushed smooth, soft flesh, deliciously hot. A groan ripped out of his chest.

"Dancer?"

"I'm fine. Go ahead."

He dipped his head to nuzzle her neck, licking across the hard strut of one collarbone, enjoying the taste of her. "You're more than fine; you're fucking gorgeous."

He didn't give her the chance to speak again. Bracketing her head with both arms, he leaned down and took her mouth. Insinuating his tongue between her lips, he explored the moist, velvety interior, tasting, licking, twining. Shit, he couldn't wait another second to get his cock inside her, not one! He flexed his hips, probing, his head swimming with greedy anticipation.

Dancer raised one leg and wrapped it around his upper thigh, tilting her pelvis and opening herself more fully. In direct contrast, her mouth was soft and pliant, hardly responsive at all.

Rhio's eyes snapped open. She was watching him, her wide dark gaze calm and a little wary.

What the fuck——? Not again!

He rubbed her cheeks with his thumbs. "What's wrong?"

"Nothing. I'm ready."

Growling a heartfelt oath, Rhio pulled back. Without preamble, he reached down to brush his fingertips over the folds of her sex. Warm, soft and relaxed, moist enough that he probably wouldn't hurt her, but no more.

Now he came to think of it, she hadn't kissed him back.

The suspicion that entered his mind was so startling as to be impossible. Until he thought about it some more.

His blood drumming an insistent demand, he rolled away from temptation and sat on the edge of the bed, swearing.

"Rhio? What's wrong?"

He still had his bloody boots on. He wrenched them off. "You might be ready, but I'm not." Coming to his feet, he unbuckled the kilt and let it drop, peeled off the drawers.

A sparkling glance burned from his head to his heels, with a significant pause at groin level. "Doesn't look that way to me."

Was there admiration mixed in with the amusement? Cursing himself for a vain fool, Rhio glanced downward, but his erection did him proud, thick and flushed rose-red—so full and eager it was damn near vertical.

"You're one fine man, Captain R-Rhio-marrd," whispered Dancer, the accent much in evidence. "Come back here." She reached for him.

Rhio set a knee on the bed, heart thundering like a battle-drum. "Slow," he said. "Slow and sweet."

A slender fingertip skimmed up the inside of his thigh. "How about hard and fast?"

"Lie still," he growled. Deliberately, he trailed his fingers down the center of her body, from the pit of her throat to her mons, and watched her tremble.

Drawing her into his arms, he dusted kisses at random over her face, never giving her time to settle—forehead, eyebrows, eyelids, those glorious cheekbones, the tip of that imperious nose. When she tried to speak, he silenced her by the simple expedient of nibbling on her lower lip, tracing it with his tongue, seducing, coaxing. Loving.

Dancer's lips parted on a soundless—*oh!*—and Rhio slipped inside.

An effective commander paid attention to every detail and Captain Rhiomard of the Queen's Guard had a box full of medals attesting to his skill, not that he could remember where he'd put it. He missed nothing—not the hitch of her breath, nor the hand that crept into his hair, or the instinctive arch of her hips. But best of all were the tentative forays of a sweet little tongue, the mewling sounds she made deep in her throat.

When he stole a glance, her eyes were firmly closed, a pulse fluttering in her throat.

"Mmm." Rhio hummed his pleasure into her mouth, cupped a breast and rasped the nipple gently with his thumb.

The grip in his hair tightened to the point of pain. With a final regretful lick, he freed her lips.

"Dancer." When he stroked the other breast in the same rhythm, she fucking *purred*, her shoulder blades rising clean off the mattress. "Look at me."

She blinked, her obsidian gaze clouded and her lips delightfully swollen.

By the Brother, the restraint was going to kill him, but first times were special. And somewhere during her heartbreakingly inept kiss, Rhio had decided this was indeed a first—of many.

He tucked a lock of hair behind her ear. "Sweetheart, do you remember I asked if you enjoyed sex?"

She stiffened under his hands, her jaw setting hard. "Yes."

"I'm asking again, but for a different reason, I swear. Does fucking give you pleasure?"

When her lashes swept down, he tugged a nipple. "Look me in the eye. I'll know if you lie."

She bit her lip and glared. "Sometimes."

"How often?"

"All right! Not often."

Rhio changed tack. "You don't know how to kiss."

Her lips twisted into an ugly line. "My sorrow if I failed to provide satisfaction, *Master*."

Shit! Rhio ran a hand through his hair. "Dancer." He grasped her chin in his strong fingers. "There are two of us in this bed. Your satisfaction is as important as mine. I want to give *you* pleasure. Do you understand?"

She blinked, her head moving from side to side on the pillow. No.

"The men you've had, they didn't kiss you, did they?"

Her brow creased. "Why would—?"

He overrode her. "Did any of them go to the trouble of taking care of you? Even once?"

"Taking care—? I don't know what you mean."

"Doesn't matter. You've answered the question." Thoughts and emotions tumbled by so quickly he didn't know whether to laugh or cry, to yell hallelujahs or fuck her 'til she fainted. Brother's balls, he'd kill the first Trinitarian he saw. With his bare hands.

"So," he said. "Do you take care of yourself?"

"I still don't know what you mean."

"Don't give me that." Dipping his head, Rhio sucked in a velvety, burgundy-colored nipple.

Ignoring her startled hiss, he lashed it with his tongue, loving the way it plumped, rising against the roof of his mouth. He could swear she tasted spicy and sweet together, like a chocolate liqueur. Delicious.

He lifted his head. "Do you masturbate, Dancer? Make yourself come? Orgasm?"

Her cheeks had gone pink, quick breaths rasping in her throat. "I—ah—"

Rhio grinned. Thank the Brother, it was going to be all right. The tension of the last few minutes had taken the edge off his arousal, but now it returned in full force. Combined with the relief, it made him as light-headed and nearly as stupid as the randy lad he'd once been.

"Good girl," he said, dropping a consoling kiss on the nipple he'd neglected. "You'll have to show me one day."

He hadn't thought someone with that particular shade of honey copper skin could get so red. Dancer heaved beneath him, all lithe muscle and baffled fury. If he hadn't been ready, she might actually have thrown him off.

"Listen to me." He trapped her head between his hands. "I don't want to fuck you because you think you owe me. Or because you think it'll make me help you. I'll be doing that regardless." His voice had gone so gravelly, he had to pause to clear his throat. "I want you to want me back. I've wanted it from the first moment I saw you."

She stared, the flush fading slowly from her cheeks. After an eon, she said, "You give the choice to . . . me? Truly?"

Rhio willed the trepidation, the vulnerability, not to show on his face. Women he'd had in plenty, but he'd always known they were with him of their own free will. "Truly. But I reserve the right to show you pleasure." He gritted his teeth, knowing the risk had to be taken, that what happened in the next few moments would change his life in some fundamental way. "Please."

"I've heard there are men—" She broke off, her teeth sunk into her lower lip. "But you are a real man, Rhio, worthy to be a Shar. You are not weak."

"There's nothing weak about caring for your woman, about giving her joy, keeping her safe."

He ploughed on before she could ask the question swimming in the sudden softness of her gaze. "Did you like kissing me, Dancer? I know it felt good when I sucked your pretty tits."

The rosy flush returned. "But yes," she whispered. "Did you like it?"

His chuckle came out more like a groan. "Fuck, yes! Here." Taking each wrist in turn, he arranged her arms over her head. "Stay like that, all right?"

"What are you going to do?"

Rhio bared his teeth. "If my heart doesn't give out, I'm going to pleasure you 'til you scream for me to fuck you. Close your eyes, love."

For an endless moment, she stared into his face. Then, with a little sigh, she relaxed into the pillows, her lashes fluttering down.

Rhio reached down and grabbed his balls. Without giving himself time to reconsider, he pulled. Hard.

Even as he winced and shuddered, he couldn't take his eyes off Dancer, spread out beneath him for their mutual pleasure. There wasn't any doubt she didn't really trust him, a man she barely knew. Why should she, after the life she'd led? But here she was, all courage and beauty, risking her pride as well as her life.

He'd never met a woman to match her. He hadn't thought it possible.

Seven

Amae could hear his harsh breathing, smell the perfume of masculinity coming off his skin, something unique to Rhio—a combination of leather, cold metal and heated male. She had no doubt she'd recognize it, anywhere, anytime, until the very end of her days.

When would that be? How soon?

"Stop thinking," a voice rumbled in her ear.

Fingertips skated down the inside of her arm, traced the vulnerable arch of her armpit. On the sensitive skin, the sensation threatened to become an outright tickle. Amae squirmed. Goose bumps sprang up in a rush behind that teasing touch.

Rhio chuckled, deep and raspy. Gods, if she wasn't careful, she'd finish up addicted to the sound of his amusement, tempted to provoke it again and again so she could watch the dawn of that slow, beguiling smile. Such a serious man, Captain Rhiomard.

"Your skin's so smooth. You don't have body hair, even here." Lips followed the finger, stubble prickling her skin. When he licked, she yelped, her eyes flying open to meet a purposeful slate gray gaze. "Keep them shut, Dancer, or I'll use a blindfold."

From behind the darkness of her eyelids, she murmured, "Is that an order, *Cap'n?*"

"Aye, that it is."

A giggle bubbled in her throat. Amae'd'haraleen't'Lenquisquilirian, the last of the Shar, *never* giggled. More than a little shocked, she spoke before she thought. "You're the most fun I've ever had, Rhio."

Silence. Then, "Ah, sweetheart." Strange, he sounded so gruff.

The mattress dipped as his big body shifted over hers, overwhelming her, making her feel small and feminine. By the First Mother, what an astonishing sensation. Secure in her warrior heritage, she'd never feared any man physically. A diabloman like the Slave Master filled her with primitive, gut-wrenching terror, but that was Black Magick, evil and unknowable, something for which she had no defense.

Rhio nibbled up the side of her throat and she sighed. But when he kissed one corner of her mouth, then the other, she tensed. He'd said she didn't know how to do this and it was true, damn him, she didn't. The men Giral sent her to service weren't interested in using her mouth for kissing.

"Do what I do," he whispered into her mouth.

He kept it remorselessly tender, seducing her lick by lick, nibble by nibble. Oh, *oh*. Floating in a warm sea of the senses, Amae did the only thing she could think of to anchor herself—she speared the fingers of one hand into his hair, grabbed the back of his neck with the other and hung on.

In self-defense, she followed his lead, sucking on his tongue, at first tentatively, then with growing confidence. Her whole body tingled, coils of heat growing at the base of her spine, spreading deep into her pelvis, her sex, so she was compelled to arch, to rub against his unyielding strength.

Rhio slid a caressing palm up and down her flanks and she purred into his mouth. This was what it must be like to be pampered. Gods, it was good!

His fingers reached her nipple. Tweaked. Arrows of liquid fire streaked from her breast to her sex. The soft folds were swollen, slicker than she'd ever been. Her clit pulsed with desire. There wasn't a word for that part of the female anatomy in Trinitarian, but she knew what the foreign slave women called it. At least other cultures acknowledged its existence. Hardly daring to hope, she wondered if Rhio would too.

A final lick, a regretful grunt and he pulled his lips away. Her eyes fluttered open. Rhio's face hung over hers, his cheekbones painted with a ruddy flush, his beautiful eyes blazing with lust. 'Cestors' bones, she was amazed at herself, but she wanted that huge, scarred body, wanted to climb inside his skin, make them one.

For the first time in her life, Amae took the initiative, rearing up to nip at his mouth. "Roll over," she panted. "Let me—"

"No." He pushed her back into the pillows. "But you can watch now." A feral grin. "I want you to. I'm a real man, Dancer. This is what a real man does for the woman he—"

Abruptly, he shifted, clamping his mouth around one nipple, strong fingers tugging and rolling the other. Amae's head fell back as all the breath gusted out of her.

When he swapped sides, she sank her fingers into his shoulder, riding the swell of heat, the wet lightning between her thighs. "Please." What she wanted him to do, she didn't know, only that she had to have it—now!

Rhio released her nipple, licked all around the underside of her breast and nuzzled her meager cleavage. "You can scream, love. No one will hear you."

The mists cleared enough for a glare. "Scream? A warrior of the Shar does not— Aaargh! *Rhio!*"

Her thighs fell open to accommodate the finger he'd slid deep inside her. His eyes fixed on hers, Rhio gave her that slow, serious smile and caressed her clit with his thumb. Amae saw stars. When he twisted his finger gently, it flexed against a delicious spot she didn't know she had.

"Ah," said Rhio. "There you are." A lock of hair fell over his forehead, but he didn't notice.

He set up a slow in-out rhythm designed to drive her mad, increasing the pace only when she lost control and swore at him in Shar. Inexorably, he drove her up and up, while she shivered and shook and cursed, her hips lifting into his touch. Begging.

Amae knew what was coming; of course she did. But this was nothing like what she did for herself on her pallet in the dark, furtive, fast and frantic. This was a grand parade with drums and trumpets, a swelling chorus of erotic delight that drove her insane. She wanted the culmination with a desire beyond desperation, yet she couldn't bear for it to end. Because she'd never experience this again, never, ever.

Without missing a beat, Rhio licked around her areola. "Now," he said with decision. On the word, he opened his mouth and engulfed as much of her small breast as he could, compressing the nerve-rich flesh between his tongue and hard palate.

Amae shrieked, every muscle in her body going rigid with the vicious snap and recoil of tension released. The world imploded, swinging from the heights to the depths and back again, at first so rapidly she couldn't keep up, couldn't predict, then more slowly as the aftershocks took her and she became aware of Rhio, swearing softly and continuously. His pupils were so widely dilated as to make his eyes charcoal, almost black.

"Good?" he asked, his voice husky.

"Uh." Amae stared, speechless.

The corners of his mouth tucked up. "I see it was."

He leaned over to drop a kiss on her navel.

"Rhio, I—"

"Shhh." A fraction at a time, he slid his fingers free, giving her the smallest, sweetest aftershock of all.

"Gorgeous," he said. Lifting his glistening fingers to his mouth— how had she not noticed he'd added the second?—he licked them clean, as avidly as a hungry cat. "Delicious."

The eyes must be falling out of her head, her cheeks incandescent with embarrassment and shock. "D-don't," she stammered. "Gods, no one does—"

He shot her a stern glance. "I do."

Amae came up on her elbows. She studied his face, the flesh drawn tightly over the strong bones, the lines around his mouth. The smooth head of his cock was so suffused with blood it was very nearly purple, glistening with the evidence of his desire. Beneath, the pouch of his scrotum swung heavy and high, painfully swollen.

"You're hurting," she said softly. She smiled. "My turn."

He fixed her with the type of frown calculated to terrify a raw recruit. "Not all men are like the bloody Trinitarians. You're going to know that, believe it with every fiber of your being." Without ceremony, he pulled a pillow out from under her head and tapped one hip bone. "Lift up."

Oh, he wanted a better angle. Obligingly, Amae lifted and he shoved it under her.

Rhio pecked a kiss on her lips. "I enjoy this, Dancer. Do not think otherwise. In fact, I love it."

"You'd be a strange man if you . . ."

He was kissing his way down her body—a quick, pulling suck for each nipple, a skim over her sternum, flutterbye kisses over her belly that made every nerve quiver, a nibble along her hip bone.

'Cestors, surely not? A Trinitarian would be appalled, disgusted. No longer worthy to be called a man, lower than a sewer snake— slave to a woman's filthy desires. No, no there wasn't a man born who'd—

Over the slight curve of her belly, their eyes met. Holding her gaze, Rhio pursed his lips and blew a stream of warm air over her clit. Every nerve in her pelvis convulsed with delight.

"Are you mad?" she gasped. "You *can't.* I'm too, too—" She broke off, struggling to find the words.

"Mmm. You surely are." Taking her knees in his big warm hands, he spread her wide. He gave the tender skin on the inside of her thigh a reproving nip. "Don't wriggle. Fuck, you're beautiful. Look at you, all bare. Showing me everything. *Gods!*"

He ran his tongue in a broad, flat sweep from her clit to her perineum and back again. Once, twice.

Amae choked, her head thrashing on the pillow. As the world slid sideways, she speared her fingers into his hair and gripped, double-fisted.

"Sweetheart, let go." A pause. *"Dancer!"*

She cranked her eyes open to see his pained expression. Oh. She uncramped her fingers.

Another leisurely lick. "So I'm your first." His eyes sparkled like a boy's, the curve of his lips positively smug. "You've never had this, have you?"

She shook her head.

"Good."

On the word, he bent his head and started all over again, tracing every ruffle and fold with the tip of his tongue, humming deep in his throat. She'd had no idea a man could have so much tenderness in him, or how much he might truly enjoy this. Rhio was wet and noisy, more uninhibited than she could ever have imagined. He gave her no mercy, drowning her in sumptuous pleasure, laving, licking, suckling, nuzzling.

Believe it, he'd said. By the First Mother!

As it went on and on, her bones turned to butter, her neck going loose on the pillow, the muscles in her thighs lolling open for him. Rhio slid a finger back into her sheath, crooking it to massage the spot that drove her crazy, right behind her clit. Grabbing one of her hands, he placed it on a tingling breast. "Play with yourself, love."

Then he settled in to drive her insane, spreading her thighs with his shoulders, swooping on her swollen clit, pushing back the little hood with his tongue, tapping and suckling—all of it in time with the busy finger stroking that fluttering patch of sensitive tissue inside.

He was building it for her again, that overwhelming conviction the rapture would break her apart, with only his strength to anchor her shattered soul as she spun out into the exquisite dark. The tension wound up another excruciating notch, an all-encompassing clamp in her loins, so cruel and beautiful she couldn't bear it, not another moment.

Shuddering, she forced out a single word. "Rhio."

A lingering, spiraling lick that nearly brought her undone. "Mmm?"

"Not . . . without you." Amae squeezed her breasts, raised her hips in shameless invitation. "Now . . . fuck me now."

An instant's silence and he was surging over her, taking her thighs in his strong hands to splay her wide. Smooth and hot, his broad head notched at the narrow opening to her body and she gasped. Rhio thrust, seating himself to the halfway point in a single luxurious plunge. *"Fuck!"* His lashes fluttered.

She clenched around his girth in delighted apprehension.

Rhio pulled in a huge breath. "All . . . right?"

Almost sobbing, she locked her ankles in the small of his back, urging him forward. "Yes, yes!"

He slid balls-deep, a bar of thick hot flesh furrowing through slick tissues, cramming her full. The mat of hair on his chest rasped her burning nipples; his big body wrapped her up. He clasped her head between his hands, hips already flexing. "Won't . . . last long."

For answer, she pulled him down, plastering her mouth against his. Rhio opened to let her in, his taste strange, different—sweet, salty and musky. The essence of her femininity covered his tongue, his lips. He'd loved her as no Trinitarian male would stoop to do, this consummate warrior—gods, this *man*!

The thought tripped a switch in the most primitive part of her brain. Moaning into his mouth, Amae rode the exploding wave of her climax as if it were a sandstorm whirling across the desert. Helplessly, she shuddered, the spasms grinding her down on Rhio's long bulk, her strong internal muscles clenching hard, harder.

Cursing, Rhio pulled back and thrust. By the fourth stroke, he was thundering into her, the head of the bed rattling and banging into the wall, prolonging Amae's orgasm almost beyond her endurance. By the eighth, his rhythm had degenerated to a rub and grind, desperately deep, and she was savoring the last lingering ripples of her climax, coming down. Slipping over the peak into a warm sea of bone-melting contentment, she held him tight, watching in awe as he lost the battle to hold back the inevitable. He threw his head back, every tendon on his neck standing out in high relief.

"Gods! Ah, fuck! Fuck!"

As Rhio jammed himself inside her, groaning, Amae reached down to grip his taut buttocks, digging in, feeling the strong muscles flex with the power of his release. Again and again. It seemed to last a long time, but at last, he collapsed, burying his face in her neck, his breath hot and rapid, stirring her hair.

Strangely content despite the not inconsiderable weight of him, she relaxed, hooking her feet over his calves and drawing her fingertips along his sides, caressing a shoulder blade in small wobbly circles. Her mind had gone foggy, a soft, dark mist, and she was happy for it to be so, to have this moment.

Rhio let out a long breath. He braced himself on an elbow and stroked the hair out of her eyes. "Sorry. Got away from me at the end. I didn't hurt you?"

When she smiled, her lips trembled. How odd. "No."

He eased himself away, the wash of his seed trickling over her thighs. Rolling onto his back, he scooped up the shirt she'd discarded from the floor and spread it beneath her hips, shielding her from the wet spot. "Come here." He tucked her against his body, radiating as much heat as the fire at her back. "Warm enough?"

The tears came out of nowhere. To her horror, she couldn't hold them back. The sobs were worse, wave after wave of them, gathering in her chest, so big and hard-edged they bruised her throat on the way out. Rhio froze. When she tried to wrench herself away, hide her face, he held her firmly, secure in his embrace.

He rubbed a bristly cheek against the top of her head. "Shhh, love, shhh."

Amae had grieved for her parents, her brother, her people, but now the storm burst for *her*—for the child-woman she'd been, for the brutal theft of possibility from her life. For the first time, she comprehended the full measure of what she'd missed, what had been ripped from her—arms to hold her in the night, a man, a *good* man, who thought she was a friend worth the having, a woman worth the loving. Like the man who cradled her against his chest, rocking her back and forth. When Rhio looked at her, he didn't see a receptacle for his lust, a dancer or a pair of hands to ease his hurts. He saw the woman she was—mind, body and warrior's soul.

"What's wrong?" He stroked her back. "Dancer, tell me."

"Call me by my name." She ripped herself out of his arms and sat up, tears pouring down her face, her head held high. "I am not Dancer. I am Amae'd'haraleen't'Lenquisquilirian, last warrior of the Shar'd'iloned't'Hywil."

Eight

Amae had never imagined the capable Captain Rhiomard could look so completely nonplussed. "Uh, say it again, slowly."

She wiped her cheeks with her fingers. "Amae'd'haraleen't'Lenquisquilirian," she said, slowly and distinctly. "It means 'Green Sapling Growing.' I would have you know it." She swallowed. "And remember."

Clear gray eyes searched her face. "Suits you. It's a beautiful language." The hint of a smile. "Even when you're screaming and cursing. I am honored to know your name." He took her hand and tugged her down. "Teach it to me, bit by bit. It's quite a mouthful. What did your parents call you?"

The tears threatened again. Defiantly, she sniffed them back. "Amae. You're a surprising man, Rhio."

He drew the bed coverings up over their shoulders. "How so?"

She hesitated, uncertain with this new intimacy.

"Go on . . . Amae."

"I've never known a warrior to be so . . . so . . . soft."

A dark brow winged up. "I think I've been insulted. *Soft?*"

She drifted her fingers across his chest, silky-rough hair and solid muscle. "My sorrow, Rhio. I cannot think of the right word. I am a slave, a stranger. You could not know I am not an enemy. I think you thought I was. Yet you fed me, gave me clothing. You *listened* to me."

"A good soldier, a good *commander*, pays attention always. Faulty assumptions tend to get you killed."

"True, but you, you—" She pressed her palms to her hot cheeks. "You're *snuggling* with me."

Rhio chuckled. "Do you want to stop?" One hand cupped her breast, caressing the smooth skin.

"You gave me my pleasure before you took your own." There, she'd said it.

Using two fingers, he tipped up her chin. "Next time, you can pleasure me first. I'd like that. Would you?"

Unable to help herself, Amae rubbed her cheek against his thick wrist. "Oh, yes." How she'd love to explore that magnificent body, take him in her mouth, use the bed skills she'd been taught for the sole reason that she wished to. How he'd swell against her tongue!

"Mmm. You can ride me," he said.

On top? Her breath hitched. 'Cestors' bones, another first. He was going to kill her, though she wasn't sure whether she'd die of sheer happiness or pure physical pleasure. "My name," she demanded. "Listen carefully now."

His accent needed work, but he almost had it right when she fell asleep on his shoulder.

Rhio woke spooned around a lithe, warm body, his cock pressed happily against silky buttocks. His eyes snapped open, battle-ready, as always.

Dancer—no, *Amae*—was awake, her breath too light and too regular for sleep.

Luxuriously, he ran a hand over the dip of her waist, traced the steps of her narrow rib cage and cradled one breast. He'd been right, a perfect handful, the nipple furling up tight to nudge his palm. Gods, a man could get used to this.

He judged it was about an hour past dawn. Outside the warm nest of their bed, the air was chilly, the ashes cold in the grate.

"Good morning, Amae'd'haraleen't'Lenquisquilirian," he said, stumbling only twice.

Slowly, she rolled over, her obsidian gaze watchful. "Good morning, Captain Rhiomard. Did you sleep well?"

So polite. Inwardly, Rhio grinned. "Indeed, I did." He pulled her over on top of him. "Kiss me."

Hesitantly, she leaned forward, her hands braced on his chest. Rhio held himself perfectly still, not helping. If he as much as moved a muscle, he'd end up shoving her beneath him and ramming himself inside where it was slick and hot and tight. No, not the best way to establish trust. Instead, aching, he parted his lips and let her play.

When she finally drew back, she looked dazed, but still wary. Ah, well. Rhio exhaled carefully. "The bath chamber's yours, but be quick," he said, enjoying the yelp when her bare feet hit the cold floor. Idly cradling his cock, he admired her slender, well-muscled back as she made a dash for the other room. He had plans for that mouthwatering ass.

A few moments later, she was back, leaping beneath the covers and burrowing into his body, shivering, all caution forgotten. She was such a strange mixture, part courtesan, part little girl, part warrior. He found it hard to decide which was the most dangerous.

He took his turn in the bath chamber with more than his usual dispatch, returning to bed to take her in his arms and sink into another long, luxurious kiss. "You're getting to be good at that," he murmured.

Amae sighed with pleasure, her cheeks pink, but when he drifted questing fingers down to pet the plump furrow of her sex, she grasped his wrist. "No."

Rhio dusted kisses over her collarbone, the upper swell of a pert breast, while he used his fingertips to circle the fascinating separation where her cleft began, the skin so silky to the touch, so bare. "Let me persuade you."

"No." Her dark brows drew together, even as her moisture spilled over his fingers. She'd stopped breathing.

Shit, he was so needy, he could rub himself against her thigh and spurt like a boy. With a curse, Rhio flopped onto his back and stared up at the ceiling. He wasn't seventeen any longer; he could do this. But for the sake of his aching balls he wished she'd chosen a different way to test him. Except from Dan—*Amae's* point of view, there wasn't any other. Bed was the only place she had power over him, and that only because he permitted it. He'd be a bastard to take it from her.

"Fine." He rose, grabbed a pair of regulation trews, stuffed himself inside. "I'll take you to the mess for breakfast. Then we'll ask for an audience with Her Majesty."

"Are you angry?" Her voice was low and even, her face expressionless.

"No." And he wasn't. "I think I know how your mind works." He shot her a predatory grin. "You'll keep, sweetheart. Shall I tell you exactly what I'm going to do to you tonight? What you're going to do to me?"

Amae's mouth fell open, but the tension left her shoulders. She shook her head. "No need. I can im—"

Casting him a filthy look, she hopped out of bed. His equilibrium restored, Rhio gave her delicious bottom a lingering pat and left her to dress. A litany of Shar curses followed him out of the room.

※

In the Queen's antechamber, Amae sat next to the giant Guard Rhio had introduced as Corporal Kano. The Captain hadn't given her a choice. If he couldn't be with her, she must be accompanied by Kano or Sergeant Yachi.

Kano appeared to be a sunny soul, but he was a man of few words, watching placidly enough when Amae sprang up to pace back and forth. "What's taking so long?" Rhio had been closeted with Sikara more than half an hour.

Kano shrugged, his pleasantly ugly face expressionless.

The tall, carved doors clicked open. "Dancer."

Rhio was wearing what she'd come to think of as his Captain's face, giving nothing away. Silently, he ushered her into what was clearly a working office, if a large and luxuriously appointed one.

Her lips a hard line, Queen Sikara was gazing at the row of oil vials lined up on her vast desk of polished wood. Their contents glittered in the light pouring in through the arched windows. The one on the end swirled with the faintest trace of evil, iridescent purple. Amae suppressed a shudder and stiffened her spine.

"Rhio says you knew nothing of this."

"No, Great Lady. I would have died also."

A sharp glance. "Dying for a cause is not unknown, even for a slave."

Amae made a face. "But not with prettydeath."

"Unlikely, I agree." The Queen seated herself behind the desk, her stiff skirts rustling. She drew a bundle of papers toward her and scanned the topmost. "Is Giral behind it?" she asked, not looking up.

Amae couldn't help glancing at Rhio. Hands clasped behind his back, he gave her a slight nod. "I don't believe so."

"Why not?"

"Too obvious. Besides, he owns many caravans. He has money riding on the peace."

"You're no fool, Dancer." Shrewd blue eyes scanned her face. With one finger, the Queen flicked the paper in her hand. "Your assessment is the same as that of my head of spies. Who, then?"

Amae shrugged. "I think . . . Sethril."

"Is there proof?"

Rhio's deep voice said, "Majesty, you told me he is a known

assassin. Also that he works for the Grand Pasha, who is opposed to the treaty talks."

"Indeed, he does." Thoughtfully, the Queen rubbed her distorted knuckles. Slowly, she smiled and Amae remembered her grandmother was rumored to have murdered two rivals on her way to the throne. "The Trinitarian system of justice requires torture before the execution. I think Giral should take care of his own traitor, don't you? I look forward to informing him of this, ah, plot."

She stretched her hand toward a bellpull. Clearly, the audience was over.

Her heart hammering, Amae took a step forward. "Great Lady—I mean, Your Majesty, you won't give me back, will you? To Giral?"

Sikara looked amused. She shot a glance at Rhio, standing impassively by the door. "Not until the delegation leaves. Captain Rhiomard is responsible for you in the interim."

Amae blew out a relieved breath. She opened her mouth to ask the other question at the forefront of her mind, caught Rhio's eye and shut it again. Giral? By the Ancestors, *what about Giral?* It took every ounce of willpower she possessed to murmur the appropriate farewells and courtesies.

As Rhio ushered Amae out, the Queen called, "Oh, Captain?"

He turned. "Yes, Majesty?"

"About that other matter. I will approve the paperwork, though I still think you're mad. Are you sure?"

"Yes, Majesty. Yachi is more than ready."

"Very well." She waved him away. "Go, go. I'll take care of the Ambassador-Pasha."

Amae followed Rhio out into the Palace colonnade, her blood seething with frustration. "Rhio," she hissed, grabbing his arm and setting her feet. *"Rhio!"*

He towed her into the shade of a touchme bush. "What?"

"What's going to happen to Giral?"

He glanced around, lowered his voice. "Nothing beyond an embarrassing diplomatic incident, I imagine."

"He's a monster! He murdered my people, Rhio! Everyone I knew, everyone I loved, right down to the smallest child!" The fronds of the touchme bush curled away, its silvery blossoms chiming in distress.

Rhio frowned down at her, his eyes like flint. "We can't talk here. Come on."

The moment the door of his quarters closed behind her, she turned on him, her fingers buried like claws in his shirt. "I'll never have a better chance. He'll be concentrating on Sethril. He's far away from home and I— I have you." Pink stained her cheeks. "You have to see it."

"I agree. Amae . . ." He brushed the hair out of her eyes, stroked a palm the length of her braid. "In the long run, vengeance is more poisonous than prettydeath, a stain on the soul. Think again."

Her lips lifted in a snarl. "I have sworn."

"I have an idea. Tell me, what will Giral do when he realizes how Sethril set him up?"

"Do?" She barked out a laugh. "That's easy. He'll challenge him to a duel. Sethril's an assassin, but he works in the dark; he's no swordsman. Giral will play with him, cut him to pieces one bloody slice at a time, and he'll laugh while he does it. But he won't kill him because then he can have Sethril tortured for as long as the diablomen can make it last. He'll enjoy that even more."

She shivered, her stomach roiling with remembered dread.

"Suppose . . ." Rhio hesitated, his palm warm and firm in the small of her back. "Suppose I gave Sethril back his prettydeath blade. Would that even out the odds?"

Amae stared, all the hair rising on the back of her neck, down her spine, her arms. A single scratch and Giral's death would be as far from pretty as it was possible to imagine. Hours of it.

Rhio read her expression easily enough. His lips thinned. "A fitting vengeance, but not by your hand. Evil destroys evil. You'll sleep better, I guarantee."

She had to moisten her lips. "It could . . . work. But your Queen will be angry if the talks fail."

He shrugged. "There are other capable men in the delegation. She'll make do. This is more important."

Amae uncurled her fingers, smoothed the crumpled shirt. His heart beat steadily under her touch, a reassuring *thump-thump*. "You take a great risk for me."

"Not really," he said matter-of-factly. "There are greater ones than this."

She was still puzzling over that when he asked, "Are we agreed, then?"

There was no way she could kill Giral face-to-face and survive. She'd always known that; it had simply been a question of waiting for the opportunity and accepting the consequences. All these years, he'd treated her like an exotic but dangerous pet, a performing tygre. But a tygre was never truly tame, and Giral had known. He was never alone with her, never turned his back.

She met those clear gray eyes, knowing it would destroy her to see them shadowed by disappointment. How had Rhio's opinion become so important so quickly? Because he listened? Because when he looked, he saw her mind as well as her body?

All that, yes, but he'd given her something precious. Hope, the possibility of a future. She hadn't realized how dark her existence had been without it.

But to abandon her vengeance, so much a part of her for so long . . . Her head whirling, she sank down into the squashy embrace of the sofa, gazing blankly at the cold embers in the grate. Her life had been like that, gray and cold, the ashy remnant of something real and warm. Giral must pay, it was a given, set in stone. But, oh, if she could live! Knowing she was doomed, she'd never considered it before. By the Ancestors, surviving to spit on the bastard's grave would be the best, most perfect, revenge. The dream, so long denied, was almost unbearable in its intensity.

Gripping her hands together in her lap, she said, "You are right. It will be fitting—if it works. If it doesn't . . ." She shrugged. "I'll do it myself."

"Good enough." He dropped a kiss on her lips, closemouthed,

almost chaste. It felt strangely like a promise. "Come on down to the practice floor and show me what you remember of the quarterstaff."

Amae bared her teeth. "Ah, Captain, I shall teach you to dance, yes?"

Rhio gave the quiet chuckle she'd come to love. "You can try, my Shar warrior. You can try."

⁂

Swathed in her dark cloak, Amae sat where Rhio had put her, in a dusty cupboard on an upper floor, her eye pressed to a discreet spy hole in the wall. She had a surprisingly wide field of vision, the Queen's reception room and its occupants spread out beneath her. Unfortunately, she couldn't hear very well, so the whole thing had the flavor of a mime show.

Giral sat quietly enough, though his plate was untouched and a muscle jumped in his cheek. Amae smiled. She knew that expression. The Ambassador-Pasha was beyond furious.

Sethril, on the other hand, was leaning across the table, his mouth hanging slightly open, mesmerized by the half-naked dancers. Rhio had laughed aloud when he heard Sikara had hired a male troupe from a local courtesan house called the Garden.

In the cupboard, Amae clapped a hand over her mouth, just to be on the safe side. The Queen certainly had a strange sense of humor. The entire Trinitarian delegation, save for Sethril, was rigid with offense. She couldn't fault the grace of the performers—or their beauty. Acres of gorgeous male muscle, shamelessly displayed. 'Cestors' bones, the Trinitarians' faces were so funny!

But after that, the evening wore on and on. Amae entertained herself by staring at Rhio, standing behind the Queen at parade rest. His face was a studious blank, but it gave her ridiculous pleasure to realize she could read the subtle changes in his eyes, the way he held that magnificent body. By the First Mother, he was fine! She couldn't ask for better.

If his plan worked . . . Her heart turned a somersault and tried to climb out of her throat. Ruthlessly, Amae forced it back down. There'd never be a better time to run. Caracole was a big city. She could lose herself in the streets and the bastards would never find her. She'd find a way to live. But—oh, gods, Rhio! How she'd miss him. But if she stayed, she'd put him in an impossible position. What was the penalty for harboring a fugitive slave in the Queendom? Let alone treason. She shivered.

Below, Giral bowed over the Queen's hand, following her out into the dark of the colonnade, trailed by a gaggle of courtiers and diplomats. Over his shoulder, he cast a look of grim relish at Sethril. At last! Amae gripped her hands together to stop them shaking.

The assassin was working his way through a crowd of junior officials toward the dancers. When Rhio stepped forward to tap him on the shoulder, he spun around, looking none too pleased. Rhio bowed, said something, and produced the prettydeath blade with the air of a conjurer. Immediately, a space opened around them. Heads turned; conversation ceased.

As Sethril took the blade, Rhio spoke again. Even from a distance, Amae could see the blood drain from the assassin's face. A jerky nod, and Sethril pushed his way through the crowd to vanish into the dark.

Feeling a little ill, Amae extricated herself from her hiding place. Gods, she was getting soft. Where was her warrior's soul? Stealing downstairs, she flitted through the Palace gardens like a wraith. By the time Rhio returned, she was sitting up in his bed, freshly bathed, the fire lit.

"What did you say to Sethril?"

Rhio set aside his weapons, sat on the bed and slung a heavy arm around her shoulders. "I told him I found the body of the slave called Dancer in the Queen's quarters." At her strangled gasp, he hugged her into his side, kissed her hair. "Steady, there. Dancer's dead; Amae lives. Right?"

Gulping, she nodded.

The deep voice went on. "Dancer was poisoned by prettydeath

in the massage oil intended for use on the Queen. Given that a slave is of no importance, we disposed of the body immediately, as a courtesy. Naturally, Her Majesty has informed the Ambassador-Pasha of this shocking and unfortunate turn of events." A short pause. "Sethril understood."

"Oh."

Rhio stripped and slid into bed beside her, warm and solid.

"Rhio, do you think . . . ? I mean, right now, this very minute, they're— Oh, gods."

He rose on one elbow to lean over her, his face very stern. "Apart from the matter of your death, I told no untruth. It's in their hands now, Amae, not yours. They committed the crimes. This is the gods' justice."

Hot chills danced up and down her spine, lightly as a breeze across the desert sand. "I feel the spirits of my Ancestors, watching." She'd always known hers would be a brutal, bloody death, made bearable only by the accomplishment of her vengeance. She'd never realized justice would be so different, much colder, more impersonal—infinitely more shocking.

"I don't want to think about it." Amae ran her hands over his shoulders. "Make me forget, Rhio. Please?"

They came together slowly, quietly, learning tastes and textures. Amae luxuriated in the leisurely exploration, all that toned and muscled flesh at her disposal. Slithering down his body, she licked and nuzzled, conscious she was showing off, but wanting so badly to make it good for him, the best he'd ever have. In the process, she discovered fascinating things about Captain Rhiomard. His nipples were sensitive, drawing up into small hard peaks under her avid tongue. He was ticklish around the ribs, but he wouldn't admit it, no matter what she tried. Kisses across the belly, hot breath in the notch between hip and thigh—all these increased his arousal, thickening that beautiful cock.

Amae lavished it with kisses, loving the smoothness of the domed head with its weeping slit like a little mouth. Heated velvet against her eager lips. She trailed kitten licks down to the base, dragged the flat of her tongue back up. Rhio lay tense beneath her, his hands fisted in the bedclothes.

No more teasing. Amae drew him into the warm wet cavern of her mouth, loving the tremors he wasn't able to suppress. He was so hot, so musky. *Alive.* She set up a strong suction, lashing the sweet spot under the head on every pass, stroking his balls with her fingertips.

Rhio grasped her shoulder. "Close," he grunted. "Fuck, if you don't want—"

Smiling to herself, Amae drew a breath and relaxed her throat. On the next suck, she swallowed him to the root.

Rhio's hips rose, his shaft swelling against the roof of her mouth, pulsing with intimations of the spasms to come. When he hauled her away to spurt on his belly, she discovered to her surprise she was disappointed. She'd wanted to do that for him as well.

He stared up at the ceiling, his chest heaving. "Godsdammit, woman, you're going to kill me."

Delighted, she chuckled deep in her throat.

"Back in a minute." He padded off to the bath chamber, satisfaction in every line of him.

On his return, he drew her into his arms and proceeded to kiss her into a drugged stupor. Once she was suitably boneless, he compounded the crime by teasing her breasts with his mouth while he danced his fingers up and down her vulva, soothing and stroking over the slick folds, never quite providing the pressure she craved.

She was reduced to pulling his hair and swearing, which made him chuckle. Mercifully, he slid his thumb inside her, while he bracketed her tingling clitoris between two fingers. The gentle pincer movement drove her insane. Coupled with the divine suckling sensation on her nipple, it coalesced into a starburst of a climax, white lights flashing behind her eyes and ending with a long sweet shudder of completion.

By the Ancestors, it was good!

Amae yawned, curling into his body, hooking one slender leg over his muscled calf.

She was sinking toward sleep, her body still humming, when a remarkable thought occurred to her. This must be what happiness was, this bone-deep content.

How extraordinary.

Nine

The screams began in the early hours before dawn. Not a man's voice, but a woman's. Then a babble of voices, running feet.

Rhio stamped into his boots, buckled his sword belt. "Stay here. I'll be back as soon as I can."

Half an hour later, he appeared at the door, his expression unreadable. "The Shar are avenged." His jaw clenched. "Do you want to see the bodies?"

"Yes." Amae tugged at her hair. "No. 'Cestors' bones, just tell me."

"A slave girl found them when she went to light the fire in the Ambassador's sitting room. The place was a shambles, every stick of furniture broken. Giral must have thrashed around for hours. I could only find one scratch, on his forearm. Sethril was in the corner, in a pool of blood. I counted more than a dozen wounds, but in the end, he slashed his own wrists."

Amae choked on the sour bile rising in her throat. "He escaped the diabloman."

He touched her hair. "Do you feel better now?"

"No. It's strange, I thought I would. Neither of them deserved a warrior's death, but it's still . . . horrible."

Rhio searched her face. The hard line of his mouth relaxed. "Pack up everything you need. And don't forget this." He tossed her the chain-mail corset. "We're riding out this afternoon, as soon as I've cleaned up this mess and briefed Yachi."

"Riding out? Where?"

His eyes twinkled. "I'm taking a small troop out to the Cressy Plains. Her Majesty has a mission for me there."

❦

A few hours later, Captain Rhiomard signed the last of his orders, leaving a disgruntled and hungover Sergeant Yachi in command at the Palace. He and his small compliment of half a dozen Guards clattered over the canal bridge in a tight bunch. At the far side, Rhiomard gave a crisp command and they wheeled about.

The Captain stood on the stirrups and snapped off a perfect salute in the direction of the Palace. A tall indistinct figure in blue waved a farewell from behind a window in the royal apartments. All the way out of the city, the Guards argued in muttered asides.

It was Her Majesty.

No, it wasn't. It's a routine patrol. Why would she do that?

His usual gruff self, Rhio refused to be drawn.

It was all very odd.

There was a new recruit, a slim lad who sat his horse awkwardly and in silence, but no one had the balls to remark upon it. Not only did the young man stick close to Rhiomard, but he handled a quarterstaff as if to the manner born and carried two knives in forearm sheaths. His dark eyes never left the Captain, but Rhio accepted the hero worship with his usual calm.

Three days out of Caracole, the youth removed his helmet to shake out a waterfall of coal black hair. When he belted his loose tunic to reveal tight high breasts and a slim waist, it became apparent that Lucky Rhio's fortune still ran true. Only Corporal Kano appeared unsurprised.

By the fifth day, everyone knew the woman was sharing the Captain's tent. Fraternization was an abuse of rank. A couple of the veterans became profoundly uneasy until the youngest Guard, who happened to be female, pointed out that Rhio's woman wasn't a Guard and never would be. There was something wild and fierce about her, too free for discipline. No one knew her name, or where she'd come from, and the information was not volunteered.

By the time the dark bulk of the mountains reared out of the plains in the far distance, the troop had grown accustomed to the woman's unobtrusive presence. She rarely spoke, but she pulled her weight with the camp chores, rode long hours without complaint. Even more to the point, their imperturbable Captain was crazy about her. It was pretty funny, but as far as the Guards were concerned, what Lucky Rhio wanted, he got. Without precisely intending to, they fell every day into a tight formation, the Captain's woman riding in the middle, protected on all sides.

Amae had never seen a village, only the desert and the big cities. She looked around with interest. Holdercroft on the Cressy Plains had a market square and a single rutted main street, with a wooden boardwalk. But the buildings were well kept and several had small gardens or flower baskets hanging from the eaves.

Rhio brought them to a rattling halt at a sprawling structure that appeared to be a tavern. A tall shadow loomed in the doorway, the man ducking his head to avoid the lintel as he came out onto the boardwalk.

"Well, well," he said. A slow grin. "By the Brother, Rhio, it's good to see you."

"I got your letter, John." Rhio dismounted and met him halfway so they could indulge in the required hand shaking and back slapping.

John turned his head and Amae froze in the saddle.

Rhio touched her knee. "You'll be safe here," he said.

"Property of Pasha Imaran Indivar Imalani," she whispered, her voice a thread. She slid to the ground. "How did you—?"

"A long story," said John calmly. He arched an enquiring brow. "So you can read a slave tattoo?" He glanced at Rhio. "Not many in these parts who can do that."

"Later." Rhio slipped an arm around Amae's waist. "Where's Meg? Is she well?" His voice was warm with affection and concern.

Amae stiffened. Meg? Who was Meg?

John's dark eyes softened. "Only a couple of months to go. She can barely waddle. Come on in, all of you."

⚬⚬⚬⚬⚬

Go or stay.

He couldn't put it off any longer.

In the private bathhouse attached to the tavern, Rhio lowered himself into the deep, steaming tub, watching as Amae bent to unfasten her sandals. So innately graceful, so proud and strong. She'd only just tasted true freedom. Who was he to fetter such a spirit?

But he was a soldier, a professional taker of calculated risks. He'd put his life on the line times without number. What was this but one more roll of the dice? He'd survive.

Right. Of course. No problem.

Amae turned, a bottle of something in one hand and all over again, the totality of her hit him like a fist in the guts, stealing his breath.

She sauntered closer, smiling at him through lowered lashes, enjoying her power over him, the little witch. Unable to help himself, his gaze zeroed in on the pouty lips of her sex, silky-soft and bare. Fuck, he was so lost.

"Your shoulder hurts, yes?"

She climbed in behind him and slapped a handful of something perfumed like distilled flowers on his skin.

"I'll smell like a girl," he rumbled, wrinkling his nose.

Her strong fingers probed the sore spot on his back, pressing unmercifully. Rhio gritted his teeth, waiting.

"Yes," she teased. Sharp teeth nipped his earlobe. "A great big girl."

Blessed relief flowed through aching muscles as the knot released. He dropped his head back to rest on her shoulder. "Gods, that's better."

One last time before he gambled the rest of his life.

"Come here, sweetheart."

He arranged her on his lap, kissing her deep and slow, an endless melding of mouths that made his brain melt and his balls contract with longing.

"Rhio?"

"Mmm?" Which breast tasted sweeter? It would take him a lifetime to decide.

"What is Meg to you?"

Rhio froze, his heart skipping a beat. "Why do you care?"

A feminine growl. "Answer the question."

"She is the wife of my friend John, soon to be the mother of his child. A beautiful woman, good and true. My friend also."

Eyes darker than a desert night burned into his soul. "And?"

How did women do it? Rhio capitulated. "I thought I loved her once. Now I know I didn't."

A long silence. Then, "I wish to ride."

"What?"

Her face was a study in challenge. "You said I could go on top. Did you mean it?"

"Fuck, yes!'

Rhio stood so abruptly, water slopped over the rim of the bath. Handing Amae out, he wrapped her in a big towel, drying her with brisk swipes until she begged for mercy between throaty chuckles.

Godsdammit, *where?*

On the other side of the room was a thick rug, laid before an unlit fireplace. It would do.

Grabbing more towels, he spread them out, pulling her down

with him. Lying on his back, he hauled her supple body on top of his and spread out his arms. "All yours."

In the small chamber, the words echoed with the ring of truth.

Amae gazed down at him for an endless moment, spots of color flying in her cheeks. "You're still wet," she said.

Rhio grinned. "Not as wet as you, love." He rolled his hips as a hint.

"You have a high opinion of yourself, Captain R-Rhio-marrd." She leaned forward to lap a rill of water from his collarbone, to lick a nipple.

He choked on a laugh. "Perfectly justified."

Amae breathed a sigh against his skin, stirring the hairs on his chest. "That is true." His belly fluttered in the strangest way.

Slowly, she sat up, his cock splitting the lips of her sex, all warm, welcoming satin. Slender fingers traced the line of hair from his chest over his belly, down to the bush around his shaft.

When she hesitated, he thought he might die. "There's no wrong way to do this, Dancer."

Grasping him firmly, she hauled in a breath and sank down the first delightful, excruciating inch. Then she stopped, tossing her head. "I am no longer Dancer. My name, say it."

"Gods, you're hot inside. Amae, you're killing me."

A purring murmur and she took another inch. "Very good. What comes after that?"

"Shit!" Rhio resisted the urge to punch up into all that gorgeous, gloving heat. "d'hara . . . d'haraleen."

"Yes!" She took him to the halfway point. His eyes rolled back in his head. "Come on, Rhio, the rest, say the rest!"

He licked his lips. "In a hurry, are you?"

Instead of answering, she whimpered and squirmed. Rhio lost his mind. "Fuck it! t'Lenquisquilirian!" He got it out in a single breath. Gripping her hips, he thrust himself inside, all the way to the hilt.

Amae shrieked, her hair whipping about her shoulders.

She rode him as if she were riding to battle, pennants flying, drums beating. With each downward plunge, she tightened her internal muscles, milking his cock, just as knowing, just as uncompromising as his own strong fist. The pleasure was so intense, Rhio's vision grayed out at the edges. All he could see was Dancer, giving him everything she had to give, her nipples stiff, her skin gleaming with drops of perfumed water and sweat.

Fumbling, he stretched out a hand, rubbing a finger over the glistening prow of her clit. With a cry of triumph, she redoubled her efforts, milking, squeezing, compressing.

Rhio came so hard his vision blanked out entirely, leaving him to jet his seed in a dark pulsing space, the excruciating rush of release from balls to cock almost more than he could bear. Vaguely, he was aware of Amae's high, formless whimpers, ending with a near-masculine grunt of satisfaction as she collapsed on his chest, breathing like a runner. Thank the Brother for that.

Too stunned for speech, Rhio wrapped both arms around her and concentrated on putting himself back together.

But when she began to shiver, he knew the time had come. With a sigh, he rolled them over, found a dry towel and tucked her underneath it.

Kissing her forehead, he said, "You need to know John will keep you safe for as long as you want to stay in Holdercroft. Your future is your own."

"I know."

Fuck, this was impossible!

He cleared his throat. "John wrote to me a few months ago. When he heard my twenty years was nearly up."

Amae traced a scar with one fingertip. "What does that mean?"

"I can choose to sign on again, or I can leave and take my pension. Either way, I get a twenty-year bonus. The Queen signed all the papers for me before we left."

He didn't think it would be tactful to mention that the slave Dancer had cost him exactly half his bonus, to be paid into the Royal Treasury of Sikara IV. Godsdammit, lucky he had savings. She owed Dancer her life, Her Majesty had pointed out with a twinkle. What was more, the poor child had no relatives to look out for her. Rhio could regard the money as a form of dowry.

Amae would be vastly amused when he told her, he thought wryly.

She made an indeterminate noise. The finger tracing patterns on his skin stopped moving.

He plowed on. "I grew up in the country. Not around here, but nonetheless . . ." *Get on with it, coward!* "I know it's not very . . . exciting, but for years I've dreamed of returning to the life I knew as a boy. Of having my own family—sons, daughters, it doesn't matter."

Amae had gone completely still, her head pressed to his chest.

"John wants to go back to his family's farm. He's asked me to take over the tavern, maybe buy it from him one day. I could do that, Amae. I'd enjoy it."

"Then why don't you?"

This was it.

Gently, he cupped his hand under her chin, raising her face. "That depends on you. I can't stay here unless you want me to."

She blinked. "Me?"

He grunted an affirmative, unable to do more.

Amae braced her elbows on his chest and took his stubbled cheeks between her hands. "R-Rhio, do you want to stay in Holdercroft or do you want to stay *with me*?"

It took all the courage he possessed to meet her gaze, to expose the depth of his need. "You," he said baldly. "Forever. Please."

"Ah," said Amae thoughtfully. "There is a price, yes?"

His heart flopped like a landed fish. "What?"

"Do you love me?"

"Of course."

Her eyes flashed. "You will tell me you love me every day, yes? And also . . ." She paused, her face alight with wicked amusement. "You will teach me how to fight bare-handed. In return . . ."

Rhio didn't know whether to laugh or cry. His fingers tightened on hers.

"I will teach you how to dance," she said with decision. "You will be *my* dancer, yes?"

"I most certainly will not." When she would have protested, he tapped the end of her nose with a stern forefinger. "I mean it, Amae. Teach me to swear in Shar instead."

She smiled, shining so bright his breath caught. "As you wish, carazadi."

Rhio regarded her warily. "Carazadi? Is that a curse? What does it mean?"

Amae shook her head, her magnificent eyes glistening with unshed tears.

"It means so many things—everything. Beloved," she whispered against his lips. "Heart of my heart. *Carazadi.*"

Denise Rossetti lives in Australia. Visit her website at www
.deniserossetti.com. Don't miss her exciting novel, *The Flame
and the Shadow*, now available from Ace Books. Turn to the
back of this book for a preview.

Bound, Branded, & Brazen

BY JACI BURTON

Available March 2010
from Berkley Heat

In the wilds of Oklahoma, three sisters have a hot date with destiny.
Valerie, Brea, and Jolene McMasters reunite on the family ranch that
should have been called Bar Nothing . . .

Bound . . .

When Valerie left for the big city, she kissed her foreman husband,
Mason, good-bye—and also experienced the best sex she'd ever
had. Now, seeing him brings back sizzling memories. But their
rekindled fire threatens to burn them both.

Branded . . .

Watching Gage wrangle untamed horses with a gentle but firm
touch leaves Brea hot and bothered. But can she live out her fantasy
with a man who might ask for more than she's willing to give?

Brazen . . .

Ranch hand Walker Morgan can't afford to lose his job by getting
too close to his new boss, Jolene—no matter how much she tempts
him. But Jolene's prepared to make the first move, because what
Jolene wants, Jolene gets. And she wants Walker.

Hers for the Evening

BY JASMINE HAYNES

Available May 2010
from Berkley Heat

Jasmine Haynes jacks up the sexual tension with the Courtesans who help men and women devise steamy plans to seduce and ravage the loves of their lives . . .

In *"Three's a Crowd,"* a couple's steamy ménage à trois fantasy seems destined to tear their marriage apart. So husband Seth plans to fulfill Courtney's every desire—by giving her his undivided attention. Now all he needs is a little bedroom help from the ever-inventive Courtesans.

She knows it's unethical, but CEO Devon Parker's whole body burns for CFO Hunter Nash. So she consults the Courtesans, who figure that sleeping with a *"Stand-in"* should suffice. A perfect plan, except for one thing: the real Hunter's watching.

In *"Surrender to Me,"* when Haley's husband dies in the arms of another woman, she can hardly forgive his business partner, Simon, for keeping the infidelity a secret. For Simon, there is no forgiveness to be had . . . until he forms a plan with the Courtesans. And, as a result, Haley might just lose her inhibitions—and her heart.

Vampire Mistress

by Joey W. Hill

*Available May 2010
from Berkley Heat*

*Joey W. Hill returns to the dark and seductive landscape of her Vampire
Queen novels as a desperate woman finds herself trapped between the
desires of two men, each with his own mission of the night . . .*

Gideon Green is a hard-core vampire hunter. But in the past year
Gideon's only family—his little brother—became a vampire
queen's servant . . . and then a vampire himself, giving Gideon a
different view of the vampire world. Since Gideon's sole purpose
for over a decade has been killing vampires, the violence that has
scarred his soul now haunts his conscience.

Then he crosses paths with sexy nightclub owner Anwyn. Their
connection is immediate and intense, but she has a silent partner—
the vampire Daegan Rei. When Anwyn is viciously attacked and
turned by a rogue vampire, Gideon and Daegan join to protect
her through a dangerous transition. As the bonds between the
three of them draw tighter, Gideon faces an unbelievable truth:
that the path to meaning in his life may be found in surrender-
ing to the desires and needs of two vampires.

The Flame and the Shadow

by Denise Rossetti

Now available
from Ace Books

Grayson of Concordia, known on countless worlds as the Duke of
Ombra, is a mercenary, a sorcerer of shadows—a man whose soul
is consumed by darkness. For Gray, the bleak savagery in his heart
is manifest in an entity he calls Shad. He has long resisted Shad's
enticements, but when he is hired to kidnap a fire witch, he seizes
the chance to restore his soul—no matter the cost.

Cenda's heart is ash. Since the death of her precious baby daughter,
life has lost all meaning for the fire witch. Slowly she has worked
to master her powers and go on living. But when she encounters
Gray, her will is no match for her desire. But her love may not
survive the terrible discovery of Gray's betrayal . . .